The Shadow Legions

CRIMSON WORLDS VII

Jay Allan

Crimson Worlds Series

Marines (Crimson Worlds I)

The Cost of Victory (Crimson Worlds II)

A Little Rebellion (Crimson Worlds III)

The First Imperium (Crimson Worlds IV)

The Line Must Hold (Crimson Worlds V)

To Hell's Heart (Crimson Worlds VI)

The Shadow Legions(Crimson Worlds VII)

Even Legends Die (Crimson Worlds VIII)
(April 2014)

Also By Jay Allan

The Dragon's Banner

Gehenna Dawn (Portal Worlds I)

The Ten Thousand (Portal Worlds II)
(June 2014)

www.crimsonworlds.com

The Shadow Legions

The Shadow Legions is a work of fiction. All names, characters, incidents, and locations are fictitious. Any resemblance to actual persons, living or dead, events or places is entirely coincidental.

Copyright © 2014 Jay Allan Books

ISBN: 978-0615965765

Shall I tell you what the real evil is? To cringe to the things that are called evils, to surrender to them our freedom, in defiance of which we ought to face any suffering.

- Lucius Annaeus Seneca

Chapter 1

AS Pershing
Inbound to Sandoval
Delta Leonis System

Cain sat quietly in the officers' mess, staring at the bulkhead as he pushed the food around his still full plate. He'd been in his acceleration couch for most of the past week, and he was going to be back there again as soon as the naval crews finished their maintenance. He knew he should eat something solid while he had the chance, but he just wasn't interested.

He was lost in thought, his mind filled with images of a beautiful woman, her reddish blonde hair waving gently in the breeze…a perfect smile on her face, just for him. Sarah Linden…she was Cain's lover, but so much more too. They'd been devoted to each other for 20 years, though war and death and hardship had kept them apart most of that time. He'd spent ages away from her embrace, with lightyears between them and endless struggles prolonging their time apart. Cain was sick of it. He was fed up with the blood, the constant sacrifice, the endless separations. He was fatigued to the bone, tired of it all. But there was no end in sight. There never was.

Now they were apart again. Sarah wasn't just Erik Cain's companion, she was also the Corps' top surgeon, a Marine as dedicated to her own duty as Cain had always been to his. They'd had one day together after Garret blew the warp gate and cut the First Imperium off from human space. One day, one night. Cain felt the anger, the frustration rise up again. For one miserable night he'd held her in his arms. For those few hours they were a normal couple, in love, together. Then duty tore them apart again.

There was trouble back home. Serious trouble. Cain and his brethren had fought an impossible war against the First Imperium. They'd found a way, against all the odds, to save human space from invasion, from utter destruction. But there was no reward, no respite for the battered, devastated survivors, still too stunned even to mourn their dead. No rest…just new distress calls, mysterious pleas for help. Something was attacking worlds in Alliance space, something mysterious and unknown.

There'd been no choice for Erik and Sarah, no option but another separation. Admiral Garret had to rush back with the fleet, and Cain had to go along, ready to lead his battered ground forces into whatever new battles were ahead. But Sarah Linden couldn't come with him.

She was the senior medical officer of the entire fleet, and her flotilla of hospital ships didn't have a prayer of keeping up with the warships. Her vessels were packed to the rafters with wounded Marines and allied soldiers, shattered men and women who had no chance to survive the levels of acceleration the combat ships of the fleet would undergo as they rushed back to Core Space. Even if hospital ships had the thrust capacity to keep up with the combat craft. Which they didn't.

Erik ached for her to come with him, to turn over command of the medical ships to her exec and stay at his side. He wanted to ask her, more than anything. But how could he? They were his people she was caring for. The loyal Marines and their allies, the men and women who had followed his orders and marched into the inferno. They were mangled and suffering – and dying - because of him, because of what he had done, what he had commanded them to do. He couldn't deny his Marines the most capable and dedicated surgeon in the Corps. No, there was nothing he could do…except endure separation while he prepared to face yet another new threat. He didn't know what they were up against this time, or what battles lay ahead, but his gut told him he and his Marines were about to face their deadliest challenge.

Maybe it's better this way, he thought sadly. Perhaps being torn apart like this was a blessing of sorts. Erik Cain would do whatever was necessary to win the battles he fought…he'd proven that again and again. His successes had won him accolades and widespread admiration, but at a cost. He was the cold monolith, the warrior made of solid stone. His men followed him with fanatical loyalty, but it was awe and respect, not love that drove them. Cain was too hard, too cold to truly love, at least when he was in the field. Perhaps, he thought, it was best that she hadn't been there much of the time. Cain had led his Marines to victory after victory, but he'd also sent thousands of them to certain death, drove them past the point of human endurance…even executed them by the hundreds when he'd found it necessary. He didn't much like himself when the shadow of battle was upon him, and he wasn't sure he wanted to put Sarah to the test.

"Mind if I join you?" Isaac Merrick stood next to the table. Cain had been so lost in thought, he hadn't seen his chief of staff walk over.

Cain gestured toward one of the empty chairs, but he didn't say anything. Merrick's entry pulled him from his daydreaming, and he glanced over and offered his visitor a slow, silent nod. He was grateful for the distraction.

Merrick lowered himself slowly into the chair. "We just received another report, Erik." Cain could tell from Merrick's voice the news was bad.

"What is it?" He spoke slowly, deliberately. There was no emotion in his voice; he wasn't sure how much was even left in him.

"General Teller apparently responded to the distress call from Arcadia." James Teller was a Marine general, one of Cain's old comrades…and a friend too. He and John Marek had been placed in command of the Corps' forces left behind when Grand Fleet departed for First Imperium space. Mostly convalescents and new recruits graduated from training too late to join the fleet, the forces they commanded weren't even close to the Corps' idea of combat ready.

Merrick's expression was troubled. "Somehow he scraped up a heavy battalion – he must have raided the graduating class at the Academy to do it – and took off for Wolf 359 with Admiral Davis." Garret had left Josiah Davis in command of the ships he deemed unready to join Grand Fleet. It was a collection of barely spaceworthy rust-buckets, plus whatever repaired vessels had reported from the Wolf 359 shipyards before the system was attacked and cut off.

"That's just great." Cain's face was sour. "A regiment of raw newbs and a fleet of old junkers. How did we come to this?" Still, it made sense, Cain realized. When Teller responded, Wolf 359 was the only system reporting trouble. He probably thought it was an isolated incident. Since then, the floodgates had opened.

"It's worse." Merrick looked down at the table as he spoke. "Reports suggest he was able to land, but shortly after that, all communications were lost." He hesitated for a few seconds. "With both the ground forces and Admiral Davis' ships." He glanced up at Cain, but the Marines' number two general just sat quietly, looking back, his face expressionless, waiting for Merrick to continue.

"Apparently, Davis' ships were attacked shortly after landing Teller's forces. We've had no communication at all except a single drone launched early in the battle." Merrick paused and took a deep breath. "It appears he was putting up quite a fight at the time the drone was launched, but he had no useful information on who or what was attacking him. There were no further transmissions. We must presume his entire command was lost or captured."

Cain sat silently for a few seconds. "We can't know. Perhaps Davis' forces are cut off from the warp gate and unable to get a message through." He didn't sound like he really believed what he was saying. "And don't be too quick to give up on James Teller. He's one of the best we've got, Isaac." Another pause then: "Does Garret know?"

"I assume so." Merrick was sitting bolt upright in the chair, his tension obvious. "It was Admiral Harmon who briefed me, so she must have updated Garret. I came to fill you in right away."

Cain winced when Merrick mentioned Harmon, feeling a twinge of guilt at his earlier whining. Nothing drove away self-pity faster than the mention of someone in far deeper pain. Camille Harmon's son, Max, was Terrance Compton's tactical officer. Admiral Harmon had remained silent on her own flag bridge, coolly doing her duty as she watched Garret order the detonation of the alien antimatter bomb, trapping Compton... and her only son...in the X2 system with a massive First Imperium fleet. She couldn't be sure Max was dead...it was possible Compton had devised a way to get his forces out of the trap... but it was almost certain she'd never see him again. Even if Compton's people had survived, the warp gate leading home would be scrambled for centuries, and the trip back through normal space would take a lifetime. Cain didn't know where to begin trying to understand Harmon's pain.

"Attention all personnel." The AI on the shipwide com sounded human enough. Veteran spacers and Marines could tell the difference, but only after years of listening. "This is a modification to the navigational schedule. The Fleet will be initiating full thrust in 50 minutes. All crew are to report to acceleration couches in 35 minutes. Repeat...attention all personnel..."

"I guess that answers the question. Garret knows." Cain glanced at the chronometer as the announcement repeated twice more in the background. They'd been scheduled to remain at 1g for maintenance for at least another 12 hours. He could only imagine the groans going on all over the fleet. They'd been cooped up in the couches most of the way from Sigma 4, and now they just lost their first decent break.

"Erik?" It was Garret, calling on Cain's com.

"Yes, admiral?"

"I'd like to go over a few things with you before we blast if you can get up here right away." There was something with Garret's voice...he sounded a little off. Cain had noticed it since the final encounter with the First Imperium. There were a lot of sacrifices in war, but there weren't many as soul-scarring as abandoning your best friend and 40,000 of your people...leaving them to almost certain death while you ran for home. No one could doubt Augustus Garret had done what he had to do, and probably saved mankind doing it. But justifying something and living with it are two different things.

"Yes, admiral." Cain hopped out of his chair. "I'll be there in five." He turned toward Merrick. "Maybe he's got more info." A brief hesitation, then: "Make sure the staff is all set for the acceleration, and get yourself down there too. I'll catch up with you in a few."

"Yes, sir." And with that, Cain was gone.

"I agree, sir." Cain was nodding slowly. "But I'm still worried about charging right in when we have no idea what we're facing." He looked down at the floor for a few seconds, then back up at Garret. "Do you agree with the theory that we are dealing with rogue First Imperium forces left behind when we blew the warp gate?" Cain's tone expressed his own doubt.

"It's not the First Imperium." Garret sounded exhausted, but his voice was firm, confident. "If we were just dealing with Wolf 359, maybe. But you and I both know they don't possess the strategic capacity to plan an extensive, multi-system offensive and pull it off with hidden forces without us detecting them." He paused, taking a deep breath. "A raid on one world, maybe, but nothing on this scale. No, this is something else. Something new."

"Or something old, sir? Perhaps this is one of the Powers trying to gain an advantage now that the First Imperium threat is contained." The timing was certainly suspicious, coming as it did on the heels of Grand Fleet's success. But Cain doubted it even as he said it. None of the Powers had the military force available. Most of humanity's combat ready strength was with Grand Fleet. He shook his head. "No, forget it. That's not it either."

"I'd considered that too. It seems like the likeliest possibility, but I don't see how it's possible. They would have needed to assemble and support a large force, entirely in secret. I'd like to roast our friend Stark over a slow fire, but we both know he's good at his job. None of the Powers could have sneaked something that big by Alliance Intelligence."

Cain nodded. He agreed completely. Gavin Stark was a sociopath and an evil son of a bitch, but he was also a genius, and one of the most effective spymasters in history. He would never fail to notice a massive force buildup by one of the Powers.

"I agree about Stark, admiral. I can't see how anyone could have assembled military assets on this level without Alliance Intelligence discovering it." He paused uncomfortably, not sure he wanted to say what he was thinking. "But are we certain they would have alerted us? We've tangled with them more than once before."

Garret stared back at Cain. "You think Stark has a role in this? That he has some reason to keep us in the dark?"

"I don't know. Not an active one...at least." Cain couldn't think of any way Stark could be directly responsible. "But would he necessarily tell us if one of the Powers was making a play of some kind?" Cain's voice was getting darker, more suspicious. "Could he be cooperating with another Power? You don't doubt he'd commit treason if it served his purposes, do you?" He stared right at Garret. "Maybe he'd like to see us neck deep in liberating colonies so he can pull off some other mischief. If we go right into another fight now, we're not going to have much left by the time it's done. We're sucking wind already. Maybe he's planning on settling a score with us." He hesitated. "Or maybe he wants to provoke another war." Cain couldn't see any gain for Stark in a Fourth Frontier War, but that didn't mean there wasn't something he didn't know about.

Garret looked back thoughtfully, but he didn't say anything...not right away. Finally, he sighed and ran a hand through his coarse hair. It was long...getting a haircut hadn't been a priority for a long time. He was grayer now than when he'd set out from Sandoval, chasing Terrance Compton and the advance guard into the unknown. He still hadn't really dealt with the full emotional impact of what had happened. It was one thing to lose a friend. He and Compton had been warriors all their adult lives, and both had known that men and women die in war. But this wasn't just a friend lost in battle. Garret knew Compton's blood was on his hands…and that of the 40,000 naval crew and Marines he'd stranded in the X2 system. He had given the order. There hadn't been a choice, not one that didn't put all of humanity at grave risk. But Garret was finding that meant less and less to him. He'd done what he'd done, and all his life, Augustus Garret had taken responsibility for his actions. It was his order and no one else's that killed his friend, and that was what really mattered.

"Sir?" Cain was looking across the table, clearly reluctant to interrupt the admiral's introspection.

Garret shook himself out of his daydreaming. "Sorry, Erik."

Cain just nodded. He understood…more than anyone else could, and Garret knew it.

"There is nothing that Gavin Stark wouldn't do it he felt it was in his interest. Treason isn't even far down on that list. The man is soulless. He is a pure sociopath." Garret took a breath, pushing back the rage the mere mention of Stark caused, thinking for a few seconds before he continued. "But I still find it hard to believe any of the Powers could be behind this. The resources required to build a secret military force would bankrupt any of them now. The time required to train a truly combat-ready army would be considerable, especially with all the suitable cadres out on the Rim with us." He paused again and sighed. "However, I have no other theory." His eyes were locked on Cain's. "Nothing…not even a hunch."

Cain leaned back in his chair. "Then we agree…reluctantly." His eyes were staring back at Garret's. "Our primary theory is that one…" He paused for an instant. "…or more…of the Powers is behind this aggression?" He didn't look at all satisfied.

"Yes, I suppose. However unlikely this may seem, it is a far more reasonable assumption than anything else I can think of."

The two sat quietly for a few minutes, both deep in thought, profoundly unsatisfied with their determination. Finally, Cain rose slowly. "Well, whatever is going on, it looks like we're going to have some fighting to do." His voice was somber, thick with resignation. He'd lost a lot of his people in the combat on Sigma 4. Now it looked like his Marines weren't through. "I've got a lot of work to do if we're going to have any kind of battle-ready force." He looked down at his chronometer and then at Garret. "If you'll excuse me, sir, I need to attend to a few things before I strap in."

Garret stayed in his seat, but he looked up. "Of course, Erik." He tried to force a tiny smile, but it died on his lips. "Do what you can to get your people ready...for whatever." Neither of them mentioned that a lot of the troops Cain was commanding were ground forces from the other Powers. That was going to be a sticky problem if one or more of those nations were currently invading Alliance colonies.

Cain started to walk to the door, holding his hand in front of the security panel. The hatch slid open.

"Erik?"

Cain turned back toward Garret. "Yes, sir?"

"Be careful what you say to anyone."

Cain nodded. They both knew what Garret meant.

The cabin was silent. Cain was lying on the bed on his side, reading the reports on his 'pad. They'd practically been living in the acceleration couches as Garret pushed the fleet to the breaking point, but the admiral hadn't been able to put off heavy maintenance any longer, and the tired and sore men and women of the fleet got a 36-hour reprieve from being bruised and bloated at 35g.

Erik had been at the desk for hours, but the pain in his back finally became too much to ignore, and he retreated to the bed. Too many wounds over the years, he thought. Sarah and her people had put him back together more than once, and they'd worked wonders doing it. By all rights, Erik Cain should have been dead long ago. But even the Corps' crack medical staff couldn't undo every hurt. Cain's body wasn't 23 years old anymore and, rejuv treatments or not, men weren't built for the kind of abuse he'd taken over two and a half decades of war.

Stretching out on his side usually gave him some relief. At

least from his back pain. There was no way to make his current job any less burdensome and depressing. He couldn't escape the truth. His Marine units were shattered. Endless war had cost them most of their veterans and left them pale shadows of what they had been. If he lost the allied contingents – the Janissaries especially - he'd be lucky to put two or three decent battalions in the field. And that wasn't going to be enough. Not even close. If the Grand Pact disintegrated, he didn't know what he was going to do to liberate captured colony worlds.

Cain thought of Farooq…and the other allied contingent officers. They'd learned to respect, even like, each other during their bitter struggle against the First Imperium. Even a grim cynic like Erik Cain had begun to wonder if the mutual respect and camaraderie that had developed might open the door to a brighter future, one of cooperation and friendship rather than constant war and strife.

Now he began to wonder. Would he soon be facing his new comrades again…would they be back, staring at each other from opposite sides of a bloody battlefield? He had begun to develop a real friendship with Farooq. Despite a long history of enmity between nations and vastly different cultures, he'd been surprised to find somewhat of a kindred spirit in the Janissary commander. What would happen now? Would they become enemies again? Would his duty compel him to try to kill his new friend?

If it did, he wondered, would he do it? Or would he refuse, resist a return to the old grievances? He let out a deep, exhausted breath. He knew it was never that simple. He might want to stand on principle, but if Alliance worlds were under attack, Cain was going to defend them. Whatever he had to do.

Besides, he thought, it wasn't as if it was solely his decision to make. When the fleet got back to Core space, Farooq would receive orders from his own government. The First Imperium was contained; the Grand Pact had served its purpose. Now it would disband and the various national contingents would go their separate ways. What orders would the Caliphate high command send Ali Khaled and Farooq and the rest of the Janissary officers? And what would they do when they got those orders?

Chapter 2

Diplomatic Directorate Building
Washbalt Metroplex
Earth, Sol III

"This diplomatic doubletalk is intolerable. My government needs an immediate explanation, Ambassador Monroe." Lord Salam was the head of the Caliphate's Ministry of Diplomacy. Normally a calm and measured man, he was angry now, and it showed. "I trust you appreciate the gravity of the situation."

"Lord Salam, I can assure you that my government is as concerned as yours regarding an explanation of recent events." Gwen Monroe was trying to hide her exhaustion. Salam was the fourth ambassador today to have a shot at her. "We are as much at a loss as your government as to what is happening. We can only assume that rogue First Imperium forces remain on this side of the Barrier." The disrupted warp gate that separated human from First Imperium space had acquired a name almost immediately.

"That is a most convenient explanation, Ambassador, but not one I find terribly compelling. We had a large number of damaged warships in the repair queue at Wolf 359, and we have lost all contact with them. We demand an explanation as to their current whereabouts and condition."

Monroe almost sighed, but she caught herself. It had been a long day, and it wasn't over yet. Not by a long shot. "Lord Salam, I remind you that there were Alliance ships in the system as well. More, in fact, than Caliphate vessels."

"Wolf 359 is an Alliance system!" Salam was starting to

lose his temper. "We joined with you in good faith to confront the First Imperium invasion, and now, as soon as that threat is defeated, we are expected to believe that you do not know the status of our forces deployed with yours? And that you know nothing of those of any other power either?" He paused, reining in his temper. "Is that what I am expected to bring back to the Caliph?" Another pause, slightly longer. "So, is this how your nation treats its allies?"

Monroe gripped the armrest of the chair, trying to keep her hands from moving up and massaging her temples. The headache was the worst she'd ever had, and it didn't seem likely to get any better before this interminable day ended. Tension had been building for two weeks, but today the diplomatic floodgates had burst. It's not a good sign, she thought, that Salam's anger is so obvious. The Caliphate diplomatic chief wasn't a hothead prone to outbursts. His visible fury meant the situation was gravely serious. If things got out of hand, there was no way of knowing the possible implications...but none of them were good.

"I can assure you that we have shared all the information we have." Monroe was trying not to let her own anger flare up, but it was becoming more difficult to maintain her restraint. She was reasonably confident the Alliance wasn't involved in any of what had happened...though she'd been part of the government long enough to know she could never be sure she knew everything. "I remind you that all of the planets that have apparently been attacked have been Alliance worlds." That comment was a mistake, she thought immediately...it can only escalate this.

"And you offer no evidence that these alleged attacks have actually taken place." Salam's voice was rising again. "Nothing but your assurances." He stood up. "Perhaps these claims are nothing more than cover for whatever your government is up to. Otherwise, I challenge you to explain why only Alliance planets seem to have been targeted." His eyes tracked hers as she followed his lead and rose to her feet. "No. Such explanations are nonsense. The First Imperium threat has been contained. Now, I fear we see Alliance treachery in the aftermath." He turned and started toward the door. "I waste my time here."

"Lord Salam, please. Nothing will be served by allowing this matter to deteriorate. My government is sending an expedition to Wolf 359 to investigate. We are more than willing to allow the Caliphate to send its own representatives along with ours."

Salam looked unconvinced, but he stopped and didn't continue toward the door. "And our forces in the Grand Fleet? Will you allow us to utilize your Commnet network to communicate with them?" Each Power had its own network to facilitate system to system communication, but the path that led to the First Imperium passed mostly though Alliance space. None of the other Powers could communicate with the returning fleet, not without using the Alliance's system. They had been allowed to utilize Commnet during the campaign, but in the wake of the recent troubles, Alliance Gov panicked and revoked access.

Monroe paused. She wasn't authorized to give Salam what he was requesting. That refusal had come all the way from the top, and there was no use questioning it. It made sense...the last thing Admiral Garret needed was for his allied contingents to start getting disruptive orders from their respective governments. They'd be lucky if Grand Fleet didn't disintegrate into warring factions while it was still out on the frontier. But refusing to allow communications only reinforced the impression that the Alliance was behind whatever was going on.

"I cannot authorize that without permission from higher up, Mahmoud. You know that. However, I will forward your request to my superiors." She'd never get that permission...she was sure of that much. But playing for time looked like her best option.

Salam stared at her suspiciously. He figured she was only trying to delay, but he also knew she was probably telling the truth about not having the authority to grant access herself. "Very well, Gwen." His voice was a bit calmer, though there was a coldness still there, making it obvious he was still angry. "I suggest you request authorization at once." He turned again and started toward the door. He paused and looked back. "You will have my government's formal request within the hour." He bowed his head slightly, and walked out into the corridor without another word.

"I wish to thank you for coming to my office at this hour, Mr. Chairman. I felt that our interests would be best served by keeping as low a profile as possible on this matter. At least for now." Li An's voice was hoarse and weak. She was old, very old, and her legendary constitution was at last beginning to fail her. The current situation, she suspected, would be her last crisis. And it was shaping up to be a big one. "This is the one place I am absolutely certain is secure." C1 was the CAC's primary external intelligence agency, though that was a designation without significant meaning. It was well known that Li An and her people flagrantly disregarded their lack of a mandate to spy internally. The "Old Bitch," as she was called by rivals on the Committee, had extensive dossiers on every senior member of the government. It had proven to be the world's most effective insurance policy, saving her ass more than once.

"Indeed, Minister Li. If our history of working together has proven anything to me, it is to respect your judgment." Huang Wei was the Chairman of the Central Committee, and the official head of state of the Central Asian Combine. By all rights, Li should have gone to his office or official residence if she wanted a private audience. CAC culture was based heavily on tradition and formality. But Huang knew Li An well. He didn't trust her - no one with any sense really trusted the head of C1 – but he knew better than to ignore her concerns. "I presume this pertains to the current crisis involving our forces at Wolf 359 and with the Grand Fleet?"

"Indeed it does, Mr. Chairman." Li was sitting in one of the plush leather chairs at a small conference table next to her desk. Huang sat facing her. "I fear the matter may be far more complex than we have believed."

Huang looked across the table intently. "Indeed, Minister Li, I would be most interested in any information you may have. The situation is rapidly escalating, and I fear how far it may lead us." He paused, clearly uncertain if he wanted to tell her something. Finally, his face relaxed. Li, a master of reading people, knew immediately that the CAC's Chairman had decided to provide her information of grave importance.

"Ministers Chen and Zhao have approached me in confidence." Huang instinctively lowered his voice. It was an unnecessary precaution...there were few places on Earth as secure as Li An's office. "They have requested that I bypass the Committee and issue a secret emergency order authorizing a military mobilization..." He stared into Li's eyes as he spoke, and she could see the fear. "...of our Earth-based forces."

Li An just stared back silently. She wasn't surprised very often, but this was unexpected. Things were moving even more quickly than she'd anticipated. She felt a flush of anger too. If three Committee members were discussing something like this, she should have known. Her people had dropped the ball, and that was not something Li An tolerated. Someone's head was going to roll, that much was certain.

"Mr. Chairman, you cannot...I mean I strongly recommend that you refuse such requests." Li felt a wave of frustration and chided herself. She'd almost let her surprise get the better of her judgment. The CAC leader was a prideful man, one who would not react well to being told what he can and cannot do. "That would be a violation of the Treaty of Paris." She was using a lifetime of discipline to maintain her calm demeanor. "If it is discovered by the Alliance or the PRC, they would almost certainly respond in kind. It could very well lead to open war on Earth."

The Superpowers had adhered to the Treaty of Paris for over a century. The Unification Wars had come close...very close...to exterminating mankind, and the exhausted and terrified Powers had welcomed a chance to export their quarrels to space. The entrenched political and privileged classes that ran every Superpower much preferred to keep the fighting light-years away while they enjoyed the perquisites of their pampered lives. The very thought of risking total war on Earth once again seemed inconceivable. Clearly, though, it was not. Li had been concerned the crisis would spiral out of control, but this was even worse than she'd expected.

"I am, of course, aware of that, Minister Li."

She tensed immediately. She could tell from his tone he was actually considering issuing the mobilization order. She almost interrupted, but she held her tongue. She wasn't going to be careless twice. Huang had come as she had requested, but she was far from sure what his intentions were.

"No one appreciates the ramifications of risking open war on Earth more than I do." He looked right at Li. "We are dealing with many uncertainties right now, but if the Alliance is indeed perpetrating some subterfuge, we may very well have no alternative." He was clearly conflicted. Huang was no zealot who would launch the CAC into an insane war, but he wasn't to be trifled with either. He wasn't about to allow Washbalt to achieve dominance over Hong Kong, no matter what he had to do to prevent it. Even if that meant war on Earth.

"Of course I agree, Mr. Chairman." He's close to issuing the order, she thought...I have less time than I guessed. "However, we have very little evidence in all of this and much speculation. All we know for sure is that communications with Wolf 359 have been lost. And the Alliance claims that it is also unable to reach its people there." Her voice was becoming hoarse, and she had to struggle to speak loudly enough. She could feel the growing weakness in her body. She didn't have the stamina she once did, and protracted, emotional meetings wore her down.

"It is extremely plausible that a residual First Imperium force or a natural event of some sort is to blame." She didn't believe that, not for an instant. But she suspected the truth of what was happening was far more complicated than an Alliance bid for power. She had well-placed double agents in the Alliance governmental departments, and none of them had alerted her to anything unusual. She couldn't imagine any official operation of this scale completely escaping her notice.

Huang leaned back, an unconvinced scowl on his face. "Minister Li, you know I have the greatest respect for your insight. It is why I am here this evening." He paused, his eyes fixed on her shriveled form. My God, she is frail, he thought...age has really caught up with her. His voice softened. He knew Li An was a merciless viper, but he couldn't help but feel a wave of sympathy at her frailty. "An, perhaps your people simply didn't discover the preparations. The Alliance would have exerted every imaginable precaution…and you know Gavin Stark is highly capable."

She felt another rush of anger. The last thing she wanted from anyone was pity and reassurance. She'd lived a long time, and she knew didn't have much left. But she was as mentally sharp as ever, and she wasn't about to let anyone write her off and throw her on the junk pile. Her people hadn't missed anything. Whatever was going on, she was sure Alliance Gov wasn't behind it…at least not directly.

"Mr. Chairman, what of the forces with Grand Fleet? We have had no reports of anything out of the ordinary." She knew what his response was going to be, but she was grasping for any argument.

"Yes, that is true." His voice hardened again. "However, you know very well the fleet is still deep in Alliance Rim space and can only be contacted through the their Commnet system. And they have cut all access."

"Mr. Chairman, I understand the suspicion, but I must counsel extreme caution. It is understandable that the Alliance is reticent to allow us unfettered communication in light of what has happened." She cleared her throat, mustering all the strength she had to keep her voice strong. "Indeed, what would we do in the same situation? If they are not responsible for whatever has happened at Wolf 359, it is highly likely they suspect us or the Caliphate." She paused then added, "I submit that our response in the same situation would be similar to theirs."

Huang sat quietly for a few seconds before answering. "Certainly this is a dangerous and touchy situation. Yet we must look to our own security. If we cannot obtain facts, we must proceed on supposition. Inactivity is simply not an option." He paused again. "I sent a communique to Ambassador Monroe at Alliance Gov just before I left to come here."

She felt a pit in her stomach as he spoke, but she managed to keep the emotion from her expression.

"We have joined with the Caliphate in a formal request for direct communications access to our task forces in Grand Fleet."

She forced back the sigh before it escaped. "But Mr. Chairman, we are putting the Alliance against a wall. This is very dangerous…and it can only increase the tension level." It was pointless, she realized. She needed facts to convince Huang, not vague warnings. Her life's trade was information, but this time she didn't have any. "I find it hard to believe that Admiral Garret would betray and ambush the forces that just fought under him."

That wasn't a fact either, just an emotional analysis, but Augustus Garret was one of the few universally respected figures in all of the Superpowers. Li's perspective was hardly an unbiased one with regard to the Alliance's brilliant admiral. She'd even tried to have Garret assassinated during the Third Frontier War. But she'd come to respect him…and believe his word as much as she ever had anyone's.

"Minister Li, I have as much respect for Admiral Garret as a man as you do." It was well known that Garret had tangled with both Alliance Gov and Gavin Stark. He was no puppet of Alliance Gov's bureaucrats, and he'd proved it more than once. "But that is simply not sufficient to justify policy decisions." He sounded almost regretful. "Consider our options. If the Alliance is able to capture or destroy our forces at Wolf 359 and those attached to Grand Fleet, we will be virtually defenseless in space. And the other Powers as well. The Alliance would be able to sweep up all of our colonies. They would utterly dominate space." He paused again. "You know what that would mean to our economy and the balance of power on Earth."

Li was silent, listening. She wanted to argue…she was sure he was making a mistake. But his logic was flawless, and she had nothing to counter it.

Huang sighed. "Do you think I want to bring us to the brink of global war?" He hesitated. "But what alternative do we have? If the Alliance is able to gain hegemony in space, what option do we have other than to expand the conflict to Earth? If we mobilize early, we may be able to gain the upper hand on Earth and offset their advantage in space." He stopped again, looking into Li's eyes. "Your own reports confirm that the Alliance has taken no detectable steps toward terrestrial mobilization."

"No." She shook her head as she spoke. "They haven't." She'd tripled the assets watching Alliance military installations, and they all reported the same thing. The Alliance's army was as inactive and atrophied as all the Powers' Earth-based forces. Huang was right about one thing…any of the Powers that mobilized early would have a big advantage if it came to war on Earth.

The two sat quietly for a few minutes. Finally, Huang turned his head back toward Li. "Minister, may I suggest that if you wish to prevent what it appears is rapidly becoming inevitable, you will redouble your efforts to obtain some quantifiable facts." He paused briefly. "I'm afraid that nothing less will serve to stop what is coming."

She could tell from his voice he didn't expect anything. He's already resigned to war, she thought…and he thinks I'm a spent force, that I have nothing left. Am I? She took a deep breath. No, she thought, not yet. If anything followed her mortal existence, Li An suspected she was going to have a heavy reckoning. She'd answer for her sins, for the thousands she'd killed and tortured over the years. But she'd be damned if she'd go to her maker as a failure, a fool who failed to see what was happening around her.

She knew how the Committee members thought. They were old men, insulated and living lives of almost unimaginable luxury. A century had diminished the fear of the horrors total war could unleash, the terror that had driven their great-grand-fathers to sign the Treaty of Paris. They were all pampered and arrogant, accustomed to the privileges their power had always provided them. They and their families would be ensconced in plush underground bunkers while Hong Kong was being pul-verized to radioactive dust. Li didn't care much for the stupid, cowardly masses who would inevitably bear the heaviest brunt of war, but in her own way, she loved her country. And she didn't want to see it destroyed, even if she herself was able to hide deep enough to survive the conflagration.

"Yes, Chairman." There was a renewed strength in her voice. "I will do whatever is necessary."

Chapter 3

Foothills of the Red Mountains
Northern Territories, Far Concordia
Arcadia – Wolf 359 III

"We have to keep moving, Kara. We can't face them in the open again. If we don't retreat right now, we're not going to have any army left." Colonel Edward Calvin had been one of the heroes of the rebellion, fighting alongside the legendary William Thompson. He'd served with the rebel army from the day the first shots were fired until the victory was finally won. After the Confederation Agreement was signed and the federals left the planet, Calvin accepted Gregory Sanders' offer of a colonel's commission in the armed forces of the new Arcadian Republic. He'd spent the last six years helping to build that force into a professional army…and three weeks watching it ripped to shreds and driven deep into the wilderness, very near to where the rebel forces had sought refuge during the nadir of that war.

Kara Sanders' face was streaked with mud, her dirty blonde hair tied back in a disheveled ponytail. There wasn't the slightest hint of the spoiled rich girl she'd once been. All that was left was the tireless workhorse who had almost singlehandedly kept the rebel army supplied with weapons and ammunition. That seemed like a lifetime ago now, yet here she was again, trying to keep another battered army in the field. Her assault rifle was slung over her back, the canvas strap slowly digging a trench in her shoulder. "We've given them Arcadia City…and now Concordia. If we don't make a stand somewhere, what will we need an army for? They'll control the entire planet."

"Kara…"

"Don't worry, Ed." Her voice was hollow, lifeless. "I know the deal…and I don't do foolish things, no matter how hopeless the situation. We will continue the retreat. There's no other option." She'd been through these hills before, during the darkest days of the rebellion. Defeat had seemed certain then too, yet events had taken a course she couldn't have imagined. She tried to tell herself it could happen again, but she didn't believe it. Kara didn't believe in much anymore. She wouldn't have thought it possible, but things felt even more hopeless now than they had in those difficult days of the rebellion when defeat seemed all but certain.

She put her hand to her neck, felt a small lump of metal on a silver chain. It was a ring…Will Thompson's Marine ring. Thompson had been Kara's lover, the father of her son. He'd also been the commander of the Arcadian forces during the rebellion. He took a ragtag group of farmers, shopkeepers, and miners and turned them into a well-drilled army…one that ultimately drove the federal forces off of Arcadia, albeit with a little help from a small Marine relief expedition. William Thompson built his army into the instrument that won the victory, but it hadn't been his fate to be with them when it arrived. He fell in battle near the lowest point of the rebellion. He died broken, believing all was lost.

Kara had wondered many nights, lying alone, what thoughts had last gone through Thompson's head. She liked to believe he hadn't died in utter despair, the bitter taste of defeat thick on his lips as he drew his last breath. She wanted to believe it, but she didn't. She knew him too well. He never even knew she was carrying his son. The two of them, both headstrong and difficult, had wasted so much time, years of an on again, off again relationship that seemed like a contest to determine which of them was more stubborn. When it really mattered they had no time left. The years since had dulled the edge of Kara's pain, but the sadness was just as deep as ever. She knew it always would be.

Now she'd lost her grandfather too, her last living relative.

She'd been a few hundred meters away when he was summarily executed by the invaders. Gregory Sanders had been one of the original colonists on Arcadia and one of the wealthiest men on the planet. Already an old man when the rebellion began, Sanders took the field with the army, becoming Thompson's second-in-command until he was captured by the federal forces. Released after the end of hostilities, Sanders was at the center of the organizational efforts of the fledgling Arcadian Republic, shouldering the burdens of building a new government after the war. Since the end of the fighting, he'd been prime minister, and he'd worked tirelessly to build the republic into something to be proud of…something that could justify, at least partially, the deaths of William Thompson and the thousands of soldiers who'd given their lives to its birth.

Sanders had barely had time to figure out what was happening. Arcadia received a cryptic warning and distress call from the shipyards orbiting planet 5, and a few hours later the scanners started going wild. The landing looked like a textbook Marine operation, right down to the Gordon assault ships streaking through the atmosphere, fiery trails lighting up the pre-dawn sky.

The troops streamed out of the landers and snapped into perfect formations, setting out immediately for Arcadia City. But the invaders didn't behave like any Marines Sanders had ever seen. They moved right through the town, opening fire on anyone they encountered. Police, army patrols…even civilians who wandered into their path.

The armored soldiers broke into the government building and dragged him from his office. He argued with them, demanding to speak with a superior officer, but they ignored his entreaties. They threw him down in the street and shot him in the head, right outside the park where William Thompson's statue stood.

Kara had been nearby when it all happened. She was transfixed in horror, motionless for an instant in her shock. Then she started running toward the main square in a suicidal rage, pistol in her hand, firing wildly in the direction of her grandfather's murderers. Ed Calvin grabbed her and shoved her into a waiting transport. She clawed at him trying to get away, but he wouldn't let go. She gave him a few good bruises that day, but he saved her life. He wasn't about to allow her get herself killed for no reason…and he wasn't going to let down Greg Sanders or Will Thompson. All he could do for either of them now was save Kara, and he made damned sure he got that done.

They fled to the army's assembly point and organized a counter-attack, trying to drive the invaders from the capital. They fought two battles, one on the edge of the city and the other at their rally point about ten klicks north…and the enemy crushed them both times. The army was far below half strength now and barely holding together, its morale leaden. The invaders didn't just look like Alliance Marines…they fought like them too. The Arcadian forces hadn't had a chance.

Kara had wanted nothing more to do with politics and war. She'd spent the lonely years since the end of the rebellion at her family's home in Concordia, living quietly with her son and working to aid the citizens who'd lost everything during the fighting. But she happened to be in Arcadia when the invasion took place and the capital was occupied. When she saw what was happening, saw her grandfather murdered, she knew she had to fight. Her first thoughts had been for immediate revenge, but Calvin had saved her from that foolishness. Now she devoted herself to a higher goal…winning this war, somehow. For her grandfather…for Will. For the future of her son and every other Arcadian. She had no official military rank, but the army to a man idolized her and treated her as its commander. Calvin was the military's senior surviving officer, but all Arcadians were looking to Kara to lead them. Including Ed Calvin. William Thompson had been more than a general; he'd been worshiped by his troops…and by the entire population. And Kara had inherited Will's place in the peoples' hearts.

They were heading into rough terrain now, the undeveloped badlands north of Concordia District. It was rocky ground, crisscrossed with fast rapids and deep gorges. Kara knew she had to move her soldiers quickly and get them entrenched high up in the hills. The enemy troops were better trained and equipped with powered armor and heavy auto-cannons. The Arcadians didn't have a chance in a stand up fight. They'd tried that twice, and they had almost 6,000 dead to show for it.

Worse, they'd all seen the streaks across the sky the week before…new forces landing near Arcadia. The enemy was easily strong enough to crush them already, and now it looked like they'd been reinforced. There was no choice but to abandon the occupied areas of the planet and force the invaders to dig them out from the rocks and gullies of the wild country.

Kara knew deep down she was kidding herself. She knew her people had no chance, even in the mountains. They could prolong things, but they were too outclassed and outgunned to hold out forever. Digging in bought time…time to hope that help came from somewhere. But where, she wondered…who would come this time?

Calvin interrupted her daydreaming. He had wandered to the flank, checking on the columns to the right. Now he trotted up behind her. "Kara, I remember this country from the rebellion."

"Yes, Ed." She nodded, but didn't turn around. "I do too."

"You know that section with the jagged gorge." He sped up, moving alongside her as he spoke. "The one that zigzags back and forth half a dozen times?"

She nodded.

"That can't be more than four or five klicks from here if we turn our heading west."

"I think you're right." She turned and threw a glance his way. "You thinking of that as a defensive line?"

"Yes." He was breathing hard as he walked and spoke. He'd jogged up and down the marching columns, checking on the men, and he was tired now. "Attacking across that canyon would be brutal. We might even be able to stop them cold if we get dug in deep on the far side."

She looked straight forward, hiding the doubtful look on her face. He was right; the terrain was extremely difficult. But it wouldn't be easy getting their people across and into the position. And it would slow their movement…the enemy would catch them that much sooner. She'd been planning to continue the retreat, giving up ground in exchange for time. Still, she thought, maybe Calvin was right. It sounded like something Will would have done. She didn't think they had a prayer of holding the enemy off indefinitely, even at the gorge, but nothing else she could think of offered that option either.

"Why not, Ed?" She stopped and turned to look at him. "It's as good a place as any to make a stand." She paused. "If we can get the troops across. I'm not sure you remember just how brutal that ground is."

"Oh, I remember."

"You know our only hope is to hold out until help gets here." She didn't sound confident, but she hadn't lost all hope yet.

"And who will that be?"

"Erik Cain and the Marines came last time. You remember, Ed. You were there." She turned forward and started walking again.

Calvin made a snorting sound. "A lot of the troops think it's the Marines we're fighting now. They think the Corps made a deal with Alliance Gov and sold out the colonies."

She stopped again, dead in her tracks, turning to stare at him. "I better never hear that from anyone in this army." He voice was edged like a knife. "You understand me, Ed?"

"Sure, Kara." Calvin's voice was chastised, sheepish. "I didn't say I believed it."

Kara wasn't going to put up with anyone slandering the Marines. Will Thompson had been a Marine, and Erik Cain's forces had saved Arcadia, going against Alliance Gov orders and risking treason charges to do it. Kyle Warren was another Marine, one of Thompson's lieutenants during the rebellion, and a good friend. He'd stepped in and taken field command after Will was killed. Later, he left Arcadia to go fight the First Imperium. He never came back from that war, but there was still a fond place in her heart for him. She didn't care what it looked like…she knew Alliance Marines would never slaughter colonists.

"I don't care who. If I hear somebody accuse the Marines of this…" Her voice was thick with anger. "…I'll shoot him myself."

"Who the hell are these guys?" James Teller was frustrated. He was crouched low behind the remnants of a small masonry building, his assault rifle gripped tightly in his hands. The fire was thick all around. His people were fighting hard, but they were outnumbered and falling back.

The last few weeks were a blur. Teller had gotten the distress call, and he didn't hesitate. He loaded almost every available Marine onto Admiral Davis' fleet, and set off for Wolf 359. It was a quick trip, only two transits, with short intra-system hops between. Everything seemed quiet when they emerged into the Wolf 359 system…except for the total communications blackout.

The fleet took position around Arcadia, and Teller's Marines executed a perfect landing. That's when everything started to go to hell. Davis' ships were ambushed by a force hiding behind Arcadia's moon. Teller had a hard time following what was happening from the ground. There was too much jamming. But he hadn't been able to contact Davis for days now…and that could only be bad.

"We have no intel at all, sir." Major Barnes was Teller's second in command, one of his tiny pool of real veterans. "They're outfitted and equipped just like us, sir." He paused, then added, "If I didn't know better, I'd swear they were Marines."

Teller flinched as a section of masonry was blasted apart by an enemy SAW, showering his armor with jagged chunks of plasti-crete. "Well they know how to fight, that's for sure. Their arms, equipment, tactics…they're all copies of ours." Teller hadn't been sure what to expect when he set out for Arcadia… probably a First Imperium remnant of some sort. But he'd never imagined running into a first rate powered infantry formation, especially not one that walked, talked, and fought just like his Marines.

Teller pulled up his tactical display, scanning the entire line.

His people were starting to take heavier casualties, losses he couldn't afford. He turned to face Barnes, a pointless gesture when you were buttoned up in armor. "We better pull outta here, Mike. They've got numbers and we're starting to catch hell." He paused, staring at his display for a few seconds. "Let's get the right flank pulled back, A and C companies. Leapfrog by odd and even sections."

"Yes, general." Barnes hated to retreat, but he knew Teller was right. They didn't have a chance of winning the fight where they were. They were heavily outnumbered, and they needed to get some maneuvering room and find a stronger position.

"B company is to peel off one section and refuse the open flank when A and C pull out." He paused. "I want you to lead A and C, Mike. Pull back about a klick and find some good ground. I'll try to pin the enemy with the left and, when you're set, you'll cover our retreat."

"General…"

"Save it, major." Teller knew what was coming. "I'm staying with the rearguard, and that's the last we're going to discuss it."

"Yes, sir." Barnes voice was sullen but obedient.

"Don't worry major, I can take care of myself." Teller was mildly amused at Barnes' protectiveness. He tended to think of the top hierarchy in the Corps being officers like Erik Cain and General Holm…not jacked up ground pounders like himself. But Teller had fought through the entire Third Frontier War and led the last ditch defense of Cornwall in the first large fight against the First Imperium. In addition to a pile of medals, that last campaign had gotten him a six month stay in Sarah Linden's hospital and a small limp she was never able to completely heal. He tended to forget that the younger officers looked at him the same way he viewed Cain and Holm. It tended to make him uncomfortable, but there wasn't anything he could do about it, so he tried his best to live up to their expectations, something he'd come to realize was not an easy thing to do. He had begun to understand some of Cain's more brittle moods, the darkness that always seemed a part of his otherwise likable personality.

"Yes, sir." Barnes answered sharply and paused for an instant before crouching low and crawling from behind the shattered structure, heading for C Company's position.

Teller looked back at his tactical display. The enemy was advancing, steadily but cautiously. They were wary, showing the Marines a lot of respect, but Teller had to admit their maneuvers were as sharply executed as any his people had managed.

He switched his comlink, contacting the support units. "All mortar teams, switch to bunker-buster rounds immediately." He didn't have any heavy emplacements to bombard, but the burrowing rounds were good for chopping up the landscape too. Whatever slowed up the enemy helped him right now. His SAWs and SHWs were well-positioned, and they were holding the enemy off for the time being, but eventually mass would tell. He might be able to compensate for being outnumbered, but only if he could get out of this narrow valley and find some space to move.

The acknowledgements came in almost immediately, and a few seconds later he began to hear the distinctive sound of the heavy bombardment rounds. Hopefully, the ammunition switch would confuse the enemy, at least for a few minutes. Anything to buy time right now.

He could see on the display that Barnes already had his first groups falling back. The units in place were firing full, providing cover for those still retreating. The leapfrog was one of the most effective and frequently used maneuvers in the drill book. There were numerous variations, but the basic concept was one of the major building blocks of infantry tactics.

He glanced down at the display, pulling up the casualty figures. They were still moderate, at least so far, but they were getting heavier. The two forces had been dancing around each other for days, trying to take the measure of their respective adversaries. That had worked to Teller's favor, so he'd done nothing to escalate the intensity of the conflict. He had about 20 men down today, about 50 since the landing. It was going to get worse than that, he knew. Much, much worse.

He had his assault rifle out, but he was just holding it at his side. His job wasn't on the firing line…not unless things got really bad. He watched the right flank on the display. The forward groups were pulling back now. In another minute or two he'd direct the mortar fire to cover their retreat. Then he'd start pulling back the left.

Then, he thought, all I have to do is figure out how to defeat an enemy just as good as my force and five times as large.

Tommy Handler's face and hands were soaked with sweat, his heartbeat thundering in his ears. He was a Marine, officially at least, but he was fresh from graduation, and the closest he'd come to real combat was getting his ass chewed out by a drill instructor. The training was extensive, but there was one thing he realized it couldn't prepare you for. The fear. He was scared to death.

You feel pretty invulnerable the first time you climb into a fighting suit, but then you get on the battlefield and see what a hyper-velocity round can do, even to an armored man. Handler had seen fatalities in training…the Marine regimen was pushed to the max, and that meant there were usually casualties. But that was different…more like seeing an accident in civilian life. But here he was facing thousands of troops, armed and trained just like he was…and they were all trying to kill him.

This is crazy, he thought…how the hell did I end up in the rearguard? He was trying to keep his hands from shaking, struggling to bring his rifle to bear when he heard gravel sliding down the edges of the foxhole. Instinct took over, and his body snapped around.

"Be cool, Tommy. It's just me." Bill Greene slid down into the trench. "Take it easy man; you're wound pretty damned tight."

"Sorry, Billy." He paused. "This is crazy, man." Greene had been Handler's classmate at the Academy. The two couldn't have been more different, but they'd gotten along from the start. Greene graduated number one in the class, while Handler struggled every step of the way. He knew he'd have never made it without his classmate's constant help, but in the end he did graduate…and made a best friend in the process.

"I came to get your sorry ass. We're bugging out. You don't want to get left behind, do you?"

That got Handler's full attention. "Fuck no. I'm with you, buddy."

"Let's go." Greene stared out over the burnt grasslands and shattered trees extending out behind them. It had been a stretch of idyllic farmland and orchards a few days before, but the fighting had turned it into a scorched desert. "There's some cover to the east, Tommy. Let's make for that wrecked house." He was pointing as he spoke, and he slapped Handler's armor to get his friend's attention.

"Got it, got it." Handler was in pretty bad shape, but Greene was determined to pull his friend through.

Greene was damned scared too, but he was doing a better job of controlling it. "From the house we can make it over that small rise." He kept reminding himself what they repeated in training. Stay focused, and master the fear…or your chances of ending up dead go through the roof.

Handler didn't say anything. He was standing right next to Greene, waiting.

"You good, Tommy? I need you to get your fucking shit together." Greene smacked his friend's armor again. "You with me, brother?"

"Yeah, I'm with you." He sounded a little better, not great, but Greene figured his friend had managed to push the panic back a little.

"Alright…let's go." Greene ran out into the open, zigzagging, heading toward the shattered farmhouse 80 meters from their position. Handler felt a hitch, a second's hesitation, but he overcame it and launched himself into the field, following his friend.

He could feel the suit compensating for his exertion, increasing the oxygen content of his breathing mix and injecting high protein energy formula into his bloodstream. It all helped… he could feel the alertness, the mental focus. He knew he'd be completely exhausted by now without the drugs.

He was running. They were halfway there, maybe a little

more than that. Then he saw it. An enemy soldier, partially hidden behind the remnants of a burned out transport. He was raising his rifle, taking aim at Billy.

Handler's body moved on its own, seemingly with no direction from his brain. His hands snapped up, pulling the assault rifle to firing position, toggling the thing to full auto as he did. It seemed to happen in slow motion, though it was a fraction of a second in reality. The next thing he knew, he was firing, the assault rifle ripping through almost a hundred rounds in less than three seconds.

The hyper-velocity projectiles, driven at 8,500 kps by the nuclear reactor on his back, ripped into the remains of the transport, tearing a large section to shreds. At least 20 of the projectiles hit the enemy trooper behind, slicing his body in half and almost vaporizing his torso.

Handler didn't stop…he just kept running, diving headfirst behind a pile of rubble where part of the building had collapsed. He was terrified, elated, confused. He felt his stomach lurch, but the suit detected the muscle contractions and injected an anti-emetic before he could throw up more than a little spray.

He sat behind the jumbled pile of charred wood and shattered masonry and stared straight ahead, trying to catch his breath. His mind was racing, and sweat was pouring down his body. Realization came slowly. He'd killed a man. And he'd saved Billy. Where, he thought…where did that come from?

"There you go, Tommy!" It was Greene, panting hard, voice strained. He'd come a hair's breadth from getting wasted, and he was just realizing that his friend had saved his life. "Well, I guess I just got paid back for every test I coached your sorry ass through!"

Chapter 4

Presidential Palace
Washbalt Metroplex
Earth, Sol III

"Gavin, I appreciate your getting here so quickly. I'm afraid I'm going to need your help. You'll have to drop everything else and focus on this new problem." Francis Oliver had been President of the Western Alliance for 29 years. An enormously arrogant man, he generally expected to be obeyed without question. But there was something different in his demeanor this time. He was scared…and he didn't know what to do.

Stark sat facing the president, looking across the massive walnut desk. His expression, entirely manufactured, was one of reverent respect, though he was secretly enjoying the fear he saw in Oliver's eyes. This great and powerful man, a bully who had bested all his political rivals for decades…he could feel it all slipping away, Stark thought with a silent laugh. If he only knew the real truth.

"Of course, Mr. President. We must all do what we can in a crisis of this sort." His tone was perfect…concerned, supportive, anxious to help. Stark could sling some serious bullshit when he wanted to.

"Gavin, I know you are familiar with the situation, but things are starting to spiral out of control." He paused, struggling to find the words.

I've never seen him this disoriented, Stark thought…he really has no idea what to do.

"To date we have been unable to determine what caused the

complete communications blackout at Wolf 359. I dispatched two scout vessels to investigate, but we lost contact with both of them as soon as they entered the system."

He's rambling, Stark thought…he knows I know all of this already.

"The other Powers are becoming extremely aggressive. They all have vessels in Wolf 359 under repair at the shipyards. They are accusing us of an attempt to seize those ships."

"Which is understandable, sir." Stark spoke slowly and clearly, with his best poker face. "It would be an advantageous plan if our intentions were to renew hostilities." He paused deliberately, silently counting to five before continuing. "Particularly if a move was also made on the foreign contingents in Grand Fleet. No doubt that is what they fear." He hesitated again, as if he was considering what to say. "Of course, such complaints would also be an effective cover for an enemy to hide their own attack against the shipyards. Seizing the vessels docked there and completing the repairs would provide an aggressor with a large pool of warships." Another pause. "Coming on the heels of the losses in the war against the First Imperium, that could place one of the Powers, or an aligned group, in a very strong position…possibly an unbeatable one."

"Your analysis is flawless, as always, Gavin." Oliver shifted nervously in his chair. "But what we need is hard information." He slapped his hand on the desk in frustration. "The only thing we know for sure is that it's not us."

Stark nodded solemnly. "Of course, sir."

"But we have no way to prove that to the other Powers… assuming it's not one of them behind it all." He stared down at the dark-grained wood of the desk before his eyes darted up and found Stark's. "We have no idea what is happening in that system." He hesitated. "I must know if this is some renegade First Imperium force or some natural disaster…or if…" He paused again. "…if one or more of the Powers are making some sort of move against us. I need to know, Gavin. Are you sure you don't have some intel…anything? Perhaps something you initially discounted as unimportant?"

Stark felt a mix of anger and amusement, though none of it affected his expression or demeanor in the slightest. I don't miss things, you arrogant fool, he thought. "Mr. President, I am not in the habit of bringing you alarmist reports assembled from unconfirmed data." He paused, eyes focused on Oliver's facial reactions. "I am certain you realize the sheer volume of information that passes through Alliance Intelligence on a daily basis. The vast majority of it turns out to be of no significance."

"Yes, Gavin, I understand. And normally, I appreciate your filtering, but at this moment I need to know if there are any indications...any at all...that one or more of the Superpowers may have attacked Wolf 359. I must decide within hours if I am going to allow the other Powers to contact Grand Fleet through Commnet, and I have no idea if this would serve to relive tensions...or simply enable an enemy to gain another advantage on us."

Stark paused. "Well, sir..."

"Out with it, Gavin." Oliver was impatient, edgy. "I understand it may be raw."

Stark had an uncomfortable look on his face. "Yes, sir. Please understand that this is extremely incomplete. I urge you not to make any precipitate decisions based upon it." He hesitated for a few seconds, enjoying the tense look on Oliver's face. "We have several communications intercepts we are currently studying. While they do not specifically reference Wolf 359, they do appear to be military in nature."

Oliver's eyes opened wider. "Intercepts? Intercepts from whom?"

Stark let out a soft sigh. "From the Central Asian Combine, sir. We believe they originated from C1's military liaison division." He paused for a few seconds and added, "Possibly even from Minister Li's private office."

"So it could be the CAC behind this?"

"Mr. President, I must urge extreme caution in drawing conclusions from data of this sort." Stark's tone was urging, almost pleading, for restraint. "There are numerous possibilities, most of which are entirely innocuous."

"But these intercepts you have...they could indicate some type of CAC operation in Wolf 359?" Oliver wasn't listening to Stark's pleas for caution.

"There is no direct link to Wolf 359, sir. All we have are fragments, bits and pieces we have reassembled the best we could. We are still analyzing the data, trying to match it up with other communications that might shed more light on the true subject matter. It is extremely time-consuming work, sir."

"But the CAC could be behind what is happening, correct?" Oliver's mind was fixated.

Stark sighed. "Yes, sir." He paused, watching Oliver's expression closely. "That is one of many possibilities."

"What about the Caliphate?"

"Mr. President, at this time I cannot even conclusively state that the CAC has made any hostile moves against us." He paused, letting Oliver think for a few seconds. "Perhaps..." He let his thought hang unfinished.

"Perhaps what, Gavin? Don't hold anything back. I need to know everything you know...even wild guesses." The tension in Oliver's voice was rising. He was in a bind. If he allowed the other Powers to communicate with Grand Fleet, he could relieve the tensions brewing over Wolf 359. But if the CAC or Caliphate were already engaged in hostilities...what would they order their ships to do? Would Garret find himself the target of a surprise attack from his own former allies?

"Sir, I was just going to say that frequently when we uncover one piece of evidence it sheds light on other, more mundane, data that we previously reviewed." He changed his expression, appearing to be deep in thought. "It is possible that if we are able to verify a CAC operation, we can go back and discover that the Caliphate is also involved." He put up his hands. "But I must remind you again, sir...this is all unconfirmed supposition at this point."

"I understand, Gavin." Oliver took two deep breaths. "If I asked you for your recommendation, would you suggest I allow Commnet access or refuse it?"

"Well, sir..." Stark leaned back, acting as if it was a difficult decision. "At the very least, I would advise you to stall. If there is any type of hostility brewing, we can't have Admiral Garret blindsided, can we?" Not yet, at least, he thought.

"Thank you, Gavin. I am inclined to agree."

Good, Stark thought. He didn't think Oliver was going at approve access, but he wanted to be sure. "Sir, if you'll excuse me, I really should get back to Intelligence headquarters. We're going to have to get you some better data than I was able to give you today, and the sooner I can get over there and crack the whip...well, you know, sir."

Oliver stood up and extended his hand across the table. "I agree completely. Your insight was most helpful, and I look forward to a timely update."

Stark stood up, reaching out to grasp the president's hand. "I am very glad to be of help, Mr. President." He turned and walked toward the door.

"Gavin?"

He turned, looking back. "Yes, sir?"

"I need every resource you have on this. It is your highest... your only...priority right now. Understood?"

He nodded. "Of course, sir. I assure you that everything I can muster is going into this project." If you only knew, he thought.

Oliver nodded. "Keep me posted."

Stark felt a small rush of relief as he opened the door and stepped into the outer office. He didn't think handling Oliver would be difficult, but it was always hard to tell with such ego-driven personalities. A soft sell was essential. It was important to allow him to believe he'd made the decision.

Everything was going according to plan, but when his operative reported that Gwen Monroe was urging Oliver to open the Commnet system to the other Powers, he had to intervene. Allowing the Powers to speak with their task forces would reduce tensions...exactly what Stark didn't want now.

Problem solved, he thought as he walked through the security checkpoint. A little invented com chatter could work wonders. His people had put it together in less than an hour, but it was top quality. It would stand up to any inspection. If Oliver's people looked at it, they'd be completely convinced it was real.

Perfect, he thought, allowing himself a smile as he stepped into the lift.

Roderick Vance sat in the near darkness, staring at the readout for the third time. His red, exhausted eyes burned from overuse, and the pain in his head felt like it was sawing its way through his temples. Vance wasn't one to doubt what he saw for himself, but this was quite a shock. "My God," he muttered softly, "how could this have been hidden for so long?" He shook his head slowly. "How did we keep missing this?"

He knew he was alone, and his office was probably the most secure location anywhere in human space, but he instinctively looked around anyway. What could this be, he thought...what does it mean? Vance had one of the most capable, analytical minds mankind had ever produced, but he had no idea what was going on...or what to do about it. He knew the implications of the figures flickering on his screen, however. This was something big...and that had to mean trouble. One thing he was damned well sure...something had to be done.

He sat quietly, staring, thinking...oblivious to the minutes turning slowly to hours. The reddish Martian day gave way to the crystal clear night, but Vance was still nailed to his chair, wracking his brain for ideas. He considered all possible angles, but he kept coming up blank. He needed help, but couldn't think of anyone he could trust...at least not anyone in a position to aid him with something of this magnitude. He needed to exert extreme caution. If word got out, the fallout would be disastrous. But inaction wasn't an option either. Even if he didn't divulge anything, it wasn't going to remain hidden much longer before it collapsed in on itself. And took everything else down with it.

He trusted Augustus Garret and his inner circle as much as he did anyone, but they were still far out on the Rim. It would take Vance a couple months to reach them, even in a Torch at full thrust...and there was no way he could be away for that long. Not now. It was very unlikely they could help anyway. Vance didn't doubt there would be a need for military action at some point, but first he had to figure out what the hell was going on. And Garret, Cain, and the rest were soldiers without compare, but they weren't spies.

He already had his own people investigating, but he didn't kid himself. He'd uncovered a plan of exquisite intricacy that had clearly been years in the planning…perhaps even decades. His agents were good, but they weren't going to have this figured out any time soon. And he had to be careful…it was possible his own people could unwittingly blunder and blow the cover of the whole thing before he was ready. That would be a disaster.

His eyes drifted back to the screen, his hand moving slowly, scrolling from page to page. It was a thing of beauty, whatever this was, and he couldn't help but admire the mind that created it. Someone had been diverting more than the entire gross domestic product of a Superpower and obfuscating the theft with a bewildering array of accounting tricks and faked documents. So far he had no idea where the resources had been channeled. He couldn't even find a trace.

The amount of missing funding was staggering. It had been brilliantly disguised, hidden by thousands of bogus transactions. Vance couldn't even imagine the level of planning and the flawless execution this had required. The fraud was a work of artistry, but the deficit was real. Trillions of credits were just… gone. He had no clue where they went or why they had been diverted, but he had a good idea who was behind it. "Stark," he whispered to himself, the hatred thick in his hushed voice. It couldn't be anyone else.

He didn't know what Stark was up to, but he knew what was going to happen when the whole thing blew up. The Western Alliance would be bankrupt within an hour, and the world economy would follow. The aftershocks would take down the Martian Confederation's markets too. There was just too much trade and interparty risk. The best case scenario would be the worst depression in history. More likely, it would be far, far worse. Mars and the distant colonies might ultimately weather the storm, but the terrestrial Superpowers, perpetually on the verge of insolvency already, might well collapse entirely. Even the underclasses of Earth, beaten into meek submission for more than a century, would rise up when there was mass starvation.

His hand moved slowly to the com unit on his desk. He knew who he was going to call, but it was going to take him a few seconds to finish convincing himself. He wasn't happy about it, but he couldn't think of anyone else with enough resources to help him in any serious way. If she wanted to, that is.

"Get me a secure line to Minister Li."

Chapter 5

Columbia Defense Force HQ
Weston City
Columbia, Eta Cassiopeiae II

Jarrod Tyler stood in the middle of the control center, watching the data feed over the duty officer's shoulder.

"We have more ships transiting, sir." Lieutenant Stillson's voice was high pitched, but she spoke calmly, evenly. A veteran of the rebellion, she'd impressed John Marek enough to secure a commission and a permanent billet in the new Army of Columbia. "So far we've got 36 vessels in all…mostly transports, but there are six heavy cruisers too."

Tyler sighed softly. That was more than enough to take on Columbia's defense grid. The colony was one of the wealthiest and fastest-growing in human space, but it had been devastated in the Third Frontier War and again during the rebellions. The cost of rebuilding everything twice had strained its considerable wealth, and the Confederation Agreement had stripped away the subsidies from Alliance Gov, leaving the planet to rely solely on its own resources. A space-based defense grid was enormously expensive, and the planned array of satellites and orbital fortresses was less than 20% complete.

"Put the army on full alert, lieutenant. All reservists are called to active duty." He stared at the screen for a few seconds. "Activate the defense grid." He knew he was virtually sentencing the orbital crews to death. They couldn't win…and their chances of successfully ejecting from their fortresses during combat were poor. He almost ordered the forts abandoned, but he quickly disregarded the idea. He needed every advantage if he was going to put up a fight against whatever was coming, no matter what the cost.

"Alert orders issued to all units, sir."

"Very well, lieutenant." Tyler stepped back toward his own console. "Projected time until enemy is within attack range?"

Stillson's hands moved over her workstation for a few seconds. "Based on current velocities and deceleration rates, the computer projects an attack on the orbital facilities in 22 to 40 hours." She was staring at the screen as she spoke, updating the calculations as she did. "Landings projected 2 to 11 hours after conclusion of orbital engagement."

Great, Tyler thought…best case is less than two days. He was barely going to have time to get the army mobilized…and only if he had all the resources he needed. "Get me President Collins." He turned and hopped up the half staircase to the metal catwalk that surrounded the control room. "In my office." He ducked through an open hatch into his small workspace. "Close." The AI obeyed, and the door zipped shut behind him.

"President Collins on your line, sir." It was Stillson on the com. She could have let the AI announce the connection, but it was the president and the planetary military commander. She figured she should handle it personally.

"Thank you, lieutenant. Connect."

"Jarrod, any more news?" Lucia Collins was the President of Columbia. She had been John Marek's VP, and she'd held the office since the day he abruptly resigned and returned to the Marine Corps to fight the First Imperium.

"I'm afraid nothing good, Lucia." His voice was grim. He'd tried to retain a confident tone out in the control room, but there was no point pulling punches with Collins. She had to know what was coming. "The orbital battle's a lost cause."

"No chance at all?" There was still a little hope in her voice. She'd known Tyler a very long time, and she knew he tended toward the pessimistic.

"None." His voice was firm, without the slightest trace of doubt.

There was a short pause. "What about the ground defenses?" The hope was still there. Collins knew the orbital defenses were incomplete and understrength, but the army was a different story. The regulars were leavened with ex-Marines and veterans of the rebellion. Columbia had the best colonial army in human space; she knew that much. The quality of the reserves was spottier, but there were a lot of them. Ten years military service was mandatory for all able-bodied citizens. The planet had suffered too much over the last generation, and those who'd come of age during war and hardship had drawn a line. Two occupations were enough. They swore the next enemy that tried to invade Columbia would take the planet over their dead bodies. Now that resolve was going to get its test.

"You know the army's in much better shape." There was still doubt in his voice. "But it all depends on what kind of troops are in those ships." He paused, wondering again who was approaching his world. "If they're like the Feds were, we've got a great chance." The Federal forces in the rebellion had been mostly detachments from the terrestrial army...troops lacking both powered armor and meaningful combat experience. "But if those ships drop 10,000 Janissaries or something like that, we're in deep shit." It occurred to him he should be a little more circumspect when speaking with the planet's head of state...but then he'd known Lucia Collins since the two of them had driven their parents crazy sneaking out at all hours to go hunting Columbian swamp rats.

"Still no guesses on who they are?"

He let out a frustrated sigh. "No, Lucia. Nothing. I'm stumped."

She was quiet for a few seconds, just the sound of her breathing into the com unit. "Are you requesting the Transfer?"

The Columbian constitution was the guiding document of a republic born of blood and fire. Almost half of its 12,400 words covered matters of defense, and at the heart of it all was the "Transfer," the assignment of full executive powers to the commander of the armed forces. Based on the ancient Roman custom of bestowing temporary dictatorial power in a crisis, it was intended to insure that the planet had the strongest possible leadership in war.

It was a radical provision, especially for the constitution of a young planet normally bristling at any hint of overbearing government or heavy regulation. But the Columbians had seen half their people killed in war over 20 years, and they'd twice rebuilt their capital city. Strong defense had become ingrained in the culture in an almost fanatical way.

Tyler sighed. He knew it was the appropriate time, but he still wasn't comfortable accepting such power. "I don't know." It was all he could say, and it was nothing but the truth.

Collins came close to a small laugh. "You know the constitution as well as I do, Jarrod." Her voice was mildly scolding. "You helped write the thing. You're supposed to ask for it… not wait for me to give it to you." She stopped, but then added, "And you know damned well this is the time it was intended for."

He took a deep breath. She was right. When he'd helped draft the provision, he hoped it would be a lot more than six years before it was invoked, preferably long after he was gone. But Columbia was about to face yet another threat to its survival. "President Collins, pursuant to Article Three, Section Two of the Columbian Constitution, it is my duty to inform you that the Republic is faced with a dire threat to its survival. In accordance with my duties as commander of the armed forces, I hereby request that you vest in me full and unlimited executive powers over all civilian and military authorities of the Republic for the duration of the crisis."

"General Tyler, I have duly received your request and your accompanying report on the threats facing the republic." Tyler had recited his portion exactly as specified in the constitution, and she was going to do no less. "Having reviewed the threat, and finding it a grave and credible danger to the survival of the Republic, I hereby grant your request and invest in you full and unlimited executive powers for the duration of the crisis." Her voice was emotional. When she'd taken the oath of office, she hadn't imagined herself as the president who would first have to utter those words.

"Thank you, Madame President." Tyler recited the rest of the ceremony set forth in the constitution. "I promise to respect these powers you have granted me today and to take all steps necessary to preserve the Republic, and when this crisis is past, I solemnly swear to set aside the executive authority granted to me today and return willingly to my position as military commander under full, reconstituted civilian authority." The constitutional provision was an odd construct, allowing as it did for the president to bestow on another individual powers far in excess of those she, herself, wielded.

"Good luck, Jarrod." Her voice was soft, sad. Collins and Tyler had never been romantically involved, but they'd been close friends as long as either could remember, and she had a lot of affection for the gruff soldier. "The prayers of everyone on Columbia go with you."

Tyler was going to say something, but he realized she'd cut the line. This was a difficult day for her too, he reminded himself. He sat at his desk, quiet and somber. He felt the same as he had a few minutes before, but he knew he wasn't. His power now was absolute, at least in theory. When would it feel different? How would he use the authority?

He had a dark feeling about the coming invasion. His gut told him things were going to be bad. Very bad. But he was sure of one thing...whoever thought they were going to swallow up Columbia in one big bite was going to get a bad case of indigestion.

Jedidiah Lucas was moving up and down the trench line, checking and rechecking his lines. The veteran sergeant already occupied a lieutenant's billet, but now two reserve formations had been added to his platoon of regulars. He'd never been responsible for so many soldiers, and he was tense.

His permanent forces were powered infantry, though their suits were old and obsolete, surplus units from the inter-war period. But even in 40-year old armor, he'd put his people against anyone with the guts to come down to the surface and fight it out. Some of that was bravado, but he had some reason to be proud as well.

The reserves were a different story. They were decent troops, and at least half of them had combat experience during the rebellion. But civilian life sapped readiness quickly, and they weren't even close to a match for his regulars. Their equipment was substandard too. They had decent partial body armor, but nothing powered. Without nuclear-powered fighting suits they couldn't handle the hyper-velocity coilguns his fully-armored troops wielded...and that meant a lot less penetrating capability if the enemy was powered infantry. The slower muzzle velocity of the standard assault rifles necessitated a larger projectile to cause the desired damage on impact. That meant 50 rounds to a clip instead of 500, which contributed to an overall firepower differential of at least 80%. Simply put, the powered units weren't just better protected...they could outshoot the reservists by a wide margin. That would be true of invading powered infantry too.

They didn't know what the enemy had, but they were about to find out. The ground stations had detected the incoming landers 12 minutes before. They'd be on the ground any time, and shortly after that, Lucas and the rest of the Columbian defenders would have a better idea of what they faced. And what kind of chance they had.

An analysis of the landing pattern suggested a move on Weston from the east. That meant they'd be coming right at Lucas' entrenched defenders. "I want all you to keep your eyes on those scanners." He was on the unitwide com. He knew his people were scared, but he be damned if any of them were going to do less than their 100% best. "Anybody falls asleep at the switch they're gonna have to deal with me."

The com crackled with an incoming message on the command line. "Sergeant Lucas...Captain Charles here."

"Yes, sir. Lucas here."

"Your people ready, Jed?"

"Yes, captain." Lucas could hear the tension in Charles' voice. The captain was another veteran from the rebellion who had transitioned into the new army. Lucas didn't think Charles had expected to be back in the field this soon any more than he had. "I have all the reserve units in the rear until we can see what we're facing." He had a bad feeling about what was going to come out of those landers.

"Alright, Jed. Stay sharp. It looks like they're coming our way."

"Yes, sir." He was nervous, but he shoved the doubts aside. They were unproductive, and he didn't have time for that now. "We're ready."

"It looks like you were right, sir. The landing pattern suggests an attack on Weston." Stillson was focused on her scanner, relaying data to Tyler as soon as she got it. It was no surprise that Weston was a primary target, but the enemy was coming in close, apparently forming up for an immediate drive on the capital. That was a bad sign. A precise landing close in to an objective was a tricky piece of soldiering, something only veterans would usually try.

"Advise Captain Charles." Tyler's voice was unemotional. His game face was on. Maybe it was his new powers...or maybe it was seeing his world threatened for the third time, but he'd never felt harder resolve. If these people wanted Columbia, he was going to make them bleed for it. "Tell him I want his people 100% ready."

"Yes, sir." She relayed the message. "General, sir!" She sounded upset, confused.

"What is it, lieutenant?"

"Sir...the landing craft." She hesitated, looking back at her screen confirming what she already knew. "They're Gordons, general."

Tyler's head snapped around. "Gordons?"

"Yes, sir. Confirmed."

What the hell, he thought...what is going on? The TX-11 Gordon landing craft had been used by the Alliance Marines for 25 years. They'd been partially replaced in recent years by the newer, larger TX-15 Liggetts, but it was still an active Marine system, and he'd never heard of them being used by anyone else.

Could there be some kind of mistake? No, he realized. Whatever troops were on those landers, their naval escorts had pulverized the orbital forts without so much as a perfunctory demand for surrender. These weren't Marines; they couldn't be. They were enemies.

Still, the invaders were using Gordons. He had no idea how that had happened, but he knew it meant one thing for sure. "Lieutenant, advise all units that the incoming enemy first wave consists entirely of power infantry." The Gordons were open sleds, designed to land troops in self-contained powered armor units. No one unprotected would survive the trip to the surface.

"Yes, sir." Stillson scowled, angry at not realizing that herself. "Attention all units." She spoke into the main com, addressing every soldier on Columbia. "Incoming enemy forces are powered infantry units. Repeat, enemy forces are entirely powered infantry formations."

Tyler stood almost entirely still, silent, thinking. How are we going to do this? He was hesitant to guess at enemy strength, but based on the number and size of the transports, it looked like his people were dealing with at least 10,000 powered infantry…and maybe as many as 20,000. The more he thought about it, the more he felt his helplessness grow. There was no way his army was going to turn back a force of that strength. Confidence and courage could accomplish a great deal, but eventually, mathematics asserted itself.

He felt himself pushing back against the growing despair, defiance rising up within him to counter his fear. He had total power…he could do anything, employ any means he deemed necessary. What, he wondered, would he be willing to do…how far would he go?

He turned and walked back into his office. Stillson was watching, but she stayed silent. She was scared of what was coming, but she was grateful, at least, that she wasn't in Tyler's shoes. She couldn't imagine the pressure on him.

"Close the door." He snapped at the AI, walking toward his desk as the hatch whooshed shut. He moved around the edge of the worktable, flopping down hard into his chair. What are you willing to do, he thought again…how far are you willing to go to win this fight?

"Display file Omega-12." He leaned back in his chair, eyes closed as he massaged his forehead.

"File Omega-12 is classified subject to level 7 protocols." The AI had a slightly mechanical sound to it, but it was more the cadence of the words rather than the tone of voice. "Voice recognition confirmed, Tyler, Jarrod Scott, General, ColCom. Please provide secondary passcode for final access."

Tyler let out a deep breath. "Access code alfa-7-foxtrot-whiskey-delta-3-3-8-papa."

"Access code approved. Displaying file Omega-12."

A series of columns scrolled down his screen. He opened his eyes and leaned forward, looking at the first few rows. "Yes," he whispered softly to himself, "how far will you go if it comes to it? What are you willing to do for victory? Will you destroy Columbia to save it?"

His eyes focused on the file now displayed on his screen, and he started reading softly to himself. "Inventory number 17034A – Fission-triggered lithium deuteride warhead, yield 2.14 mt, A4 missile delivery system, quantity 7. Inventory number 17034B – Fission-triggered tritium warhead, yield 214kt, portable battle-field delivery system, quantity 22. Inventory number 17034C…"

"Keep that fire going. You guys are doing great." Lucas hopped over the small berm and into the shallow trench. "Now I want you to angle that fire more to the left. The troops in sector D are getting slammed."

"Yes, sarge." Tony Paine swung around the heavy auto-cannon, guiding the barrel as his gunner moved it left.

"A little more." Lucas was watching the line of fire as it flashed across the field. The fire from the auto-cannons looked almost like an old time idea of a ray gun. The atmosphere super-heated the hyper-velocity projectiles almost immediately, creating an orange glow all along the line of fire. "Perfect." He put his hand up, signaling for Paine to stop.

Lucas turned, starting to climb back up and behind the trench. The battle was young, but things were already hot. His people were holding their positions, but barely. He'd been running back and forth for three hours, micromanaging, adjusting every emplacement and encouraging his soldiers' faltering morale. "You're doing great, guys." He'd already told them that, but he figured a quick repeat couldn't hurt. "You gotta hold here, you understand me? Until you get orders otherwise." A short break. "No matter what. I'm counting on you both."

"Yeah, sarge, no problem." It was Private White this time, sounding almost cheerful. He was a natural-born gunner, and he'd been sweeping the field clean with the massive auto-cannon. His blood was up, and he was ready for the fight. It hadn't even occurred to him yet to be scared or worried about the battle.

"You got it, sergeant." Corporal Paine was a little less enthusiastic, but he sounded solid. "You can count on us."

"I know I can." With that, he cut the line and hopped over the edge of the trench...off to the next trouble spot.

"C'mon, your motherfuckers!" White was firing the heavy gun on full. He must have taken down 50 of the enemy in the last ten minutes or so.

Paine was watching, prepping another ammo reload. The gun was redlining on temp. Reggie really needs to slow it down, he thought. He almost told the gunner to take a break, but he stopped himself. Reg White knew that auto-cannon like it was part of his arm. He'd get everything he could out of it, and there wasn't a chance in a million he'd blow the thing.

White was a little crazy, but he was a natural soldier. He'd have been a sergeant at least by now, and maybe an officer, but when he wasn't firing his gun, he was getting into one kind of trouble or another. Paine still had a hard time making himself give the more experienced soldier orders and, despite his higher rank, he relied heavily on the older man for advice.

"They're gonna break through in the center." White spoke calmly, with a firmness that suggested he didn't have a doubt about what he was saying. "It doesn't matter what Sergeant Lucas said...we're gonna get the bug out orders in a minute or two."

Paine looked up from the ammunition box he was opening. "You think?

"Yup." He kept firing at full as he spoke. "Two of the other heavies are out already. Haven't fired in more than ten minutes." Paine was talking about the other heavy hyper-velocity SAWs along Lucas' section of line. There were only four to start, so if he was right, there was only one other one still operating. And that meant trouble for the whole line.

Paine was always amazed at White's ability to track what was going on halfway across the battlefield. The guy would make a great officer, he thought…if he could just learn to keep his mouth shut and stop picking stupid fights.

"Well, now I know why you're redlining that thing."

White laughed. "Yeah…She'll hold out for another minute or two, and I doubt we'll be here longer than that." His voice was terse, distracted. He was focused on taking down as many enemies as he could. "Can you get one of those flash cooling modules ready just in case?"

"Sure." Paine reached into the resupply canister. There were three of the small cylinders. The cooling modules were charged with nitrogen slush. They were designed to rapidly cool the gun while it was in the field.

"We've only got three of these things. This fight doesn't look like it's gonna end any time soon."

"Yeah…that's why I've been holding off. If we can get away with not using it now we'll be glad later. But if we don't get the recall in the next minute or two we're gonna have to pull the trigger on it."

Paine nodded, more for himself than to communicate anything. "What do we do when they're gone?"

"How the hell do I know?" White was suppressing a laugh. "Crack our suits and piss on the thing?" He paused for a few seconds, staring at his tactical display. At least five minutes had passed since Lucas left. "OK, maybe I was wrong about that recall." He stopped firing, looking out at the gun's barrel. "We better crack that thing…"

"Attention Company C." The incoming command message shut down his person to person transmission. "All personnel are ordered to pull back immediately to designated secondary positions." He couldn't place the voice on the com...somebody from HQ, he guessed. "Repeat, Company C is ordered to withdraw to secondary positions immediately."

Paine slammed the cylinder back into its slot and closed the resupply box. He knew White was going to say it...he was just waiting.

Reggie pulled the auto-cannon down into the trench, folding its extensions into their retracted positions. "Let's get this shit packed up and outta here, Tony." It was quiet for another half minute, while they expertly packed up the heavy weapon and prepped for the retreat. The gun was harder to move when it was so hot, but White was still glad he'd saved the cooling module.

"Ready?" Paine threw the supply box over his shoulder onto the specialized rack strapped to the back of his armor. He doubted he'd even be able to push the thing without the strength enhancement from his servo-mechanicals, but the 400kg was manageable for his suit.

"Good to go." White had the gun itself mounted on his back. The thing was big, sticking half a meter over his head. The suit could handle the weight, but the asymmetry of the weapon made it hard to carry comfortably, especially under combat conditions. An inexperienced gunner could easily end up flat on his back, but White wore the thing like a second skin.

"Oh...and Corporal Paine?"

"Yeah, Reg?

"Told you so."

Chapter 6

AS Pershing
Entering Sandoval System
Delta Leonis IV

"This just keeps getting worse." Garret was sitting at the head of the conference table, a sour expression on his face. They'd been inundated with urgent communiques as soon as they emerged from the warp gate into Sandoval's system. The messages contained nothing but bad news, most of it very bad.

"We've got six systems confirmed under attack." Elias Holm had been reading the summary the admiral's staff put together for the meeting. He was sitting at the other end of the table, looking no happier than Garret. "And another four that have ceased all communications. We can only assume they have also been invaded."

"Things have gone well beyond a manageable crisis." Garret slammed his hand down on the table. "All of Alliance space is under attack, and we have no fucking idea who is behind it all." Garret rarely swore, but he was extremely frustrated, and the pressure was getting to him. The last few months had been the most difficult of his life, and he was worn down and brittle. Those close to him knew something dark and ugly was gnawing at him, and that sooner or later it would burst free.

The scale of the attacks had escalated dramatically in the seven weeks it had taken Grand Fleet to return from the Far Rim. Garret agreed with Cain...the likeliest answer was treachery by one or more of the other Powers. But he still had a lot of doubts, and no matter how many hours he thought about it, he couldn't make it add up. He just couldn't see any of them pulling it off, not after the losses they had all taken fighting the First Imperium.

He hoped his analysis was correct, that it wasn't any of the Earth nations. He couldn't even imagine the catastrophic implications of war between the Powers after all the loss and bloodshed of the First Imperium conflict. But he was rapidly running out of alternative explanations. When it was only one or two systems, he held out hope they were dealing with rogue First Imperium forces or even some type of criminal or terrorist activity. But the sheer scale of the problem had pretty much discounted anything but an organized effort by another Superpower...or, most likely, more than one. And that would mean full scale war.

Erik Cain sat quietly, listening, a dejected look on his face. He'd gone into the Grand Alliance with great skepticism, as prejudiced against old enemies as anyone in the Corps. But once battle was joined, he changed his mind, embraced his new friends...even led the way for others to accept a new way of things. By the end of the war he'd become a role model for cooperation between old adversaries. Now he was angry with himself for letting his guard down. You had no excuse, he thought to himself...you knew better. Now he wondered what would happen when he found himself facing some of those new friends across a battlefield. What would he do? What would they do?

"We must move past hoping this is something else and accept the fact that it is extremely likely we will soon be at war with one or more of our former allies...powers that have vessels in this very fleet." Camille Harmon spoke coldly, with no emotion. She'd performed her duty with ruthless efficiency since her son had been stranded in First Imperium space with Terrance Compton, and no one had seen the slightest sign of any emotional response from her. How long she could keep her anger and grief suppressed was anyone's guess. "We cannot know what Powers will be opposed to us or if we will have any remaining allies, so I strongly suggest we prepare a plan utilizing only our own resources." She paused. "Which, as you all know, are extremely inadequate to the task at hand."

Harmon had addressed the matter more starkly than any of the others, but no one could disagree with her. The room was quiet for a minute, all those present deep in thought and not sure what to say. It was Cain who finally broke the brief silence. "Admiral Harmon is correct. It is time for us to stop fooling ourselves and wishing things were different than they are." His tone was thick with disgust. "This should not be a surprise to us." Cain had initially doubted it was one of the other Powers behind the attacks, but no longer. He cursed himself for naivety, for believing that the governments would ever allow peaceful coexistence...whatever the warriors did. We'll always be puppets, he thought, biting down on the seething anger his mind dredged up, forever jerked around on our masters' strings. Now we will go into the field to kill our friends, once again at the behest of our political masters. "Tell me, when the Grand Pact first came into existence did any of you think it would end differently? I mean truly, honestly, notwithstanding whatever you may have convinced yourselves later? Any of you?"

The silence in the room was his answer...it hung thick in the air. Finally, Holm leaned forward, staring down the table. "Erik and Camille are right. We are on our own, and there's no point sitting here complaining about resources we don't have. We've got what we've got, so let's get started deciding how to use that and stop wasting time whining about things we can't change." He glanced over at Garret. "Problem one...the fleet and the disruption that may occur when the allied contingents receive orders from their governments. Augustus, do you think..."

"I have secretly placed the Alliance naval units on alert." Garret interrupted before Holm could finish. He knew the Marine general was going to suggest the very thing he'd already done, and he figured it was past time everyone present knew.

He felt guilty for his mistrust of men and women who'd bled alongside his people...who'd shown nothing but loyalty, courage, and a willingness to follow his orders. Thousands of those naval crew had died serving under him...and more than 20,000 were trapped in the X2 system with Admiral Compton and his Alliance personnel. More likely they're all dead too, he thought grimly. For a while he'd held out the hope that Compton had made it out of there – somehow - but he didn't really believe it. Even Terrance Compton wasn't that good.

He wanted to trust those men and women, but that didn't stop him from taking precautions. He did trust them, after a fashion. It was their governments he doubted. He thought well of most of the commanding officers, but he wasn't about to trust in their committing treason out of loyalty to him. They were, for the most part, disciplined and dedicated military personnel. If they were ordered to attack the Alliance units, Garret didn't think they'd like it one bit. But they would follow their orders, most of them at least. And a surprise attack on Alliance Grand Fleet units would be catastrophic.

"I intend to disband Grand Fleet at Sandoval." Garret took a deep breath. "We probably have allies out there, and I'd damned sure like to keep them with us, but until we're certain, it's too big of a security risk." He paused. "And it's not just the danger of being attacked. We know we're going to be outgunned and outmatched wherever we fight. Unpredictability is the only advantage we have – what we do and where we deploy our forces. We could lose that to one spy in the fleet."

"I think we all agree with your logic, Augustus." Holm panned around the table after he spoke. Everyone else was nodding silently. "You did what had to be done. There was no other alternative."

Cain sighed. "I'll be the one to say it." He looked up and leaned back in his chair. "We need to approach this coldly, analytically." How many times, he wondered, have I said something like that? I was a human being once, one with real feelings… what the hell happened to me? "We're not going to be able to go to the aid of every planet under attack." He hesitated for a few seconds, before continuing, more for everyone else's benefit than because he was uncertain. "I suggest we start making a list of those we're going to aid and the ones we're going to cut loose." Cain would have phrased it differently a few years earlier, but he was exhausted, and he had no patience for bullshit. Why not call it what it was? The worlds that weren't important enough would go to the bottom of the list, just as they had during the Third Frontier War. The people on those colonies would be rated less valuable, less important, because there were fewer of them or they had no super-heavy metals or their system lacked a valuable warp gate nexus. They would live the longest under enemy rule, endure the worst atrocities. Cain had been on the front lines for the liberation of many of those planets, and he saw firsthand what years of occupation did to people.

"Armstrong has to be at the top of the list." Holm spoke slowly, deliberately. Normally, he would have put a different slant on Cain's remarks. He tended to be more optimistic by nature, but he was as disillusioned now as Erik. "It's a must hold…especially since it looks like we've already lost the shipyards at Wolf 359."

Cain nodded. "Yes, Armstrong has to be our priority." The planet was a middling-large colony, certainly not the biggest or wealthiest. But it housed the combined headquarters and training facilities of the Alliance military. Armstrong also had the Marine Training Center at Camp Basilone and the Academy… and the thousands of trainees in those facilities were likely to find themselves in the battle lines long before they completed their programs. "The enemy has to go for Armstrong."

Garret glanced down at his 'pad, confirming what he already knew. "Yet we have no reports of enemy activity in the system." He looked up, first at Cain then at Holm. "I understand hitting Wolf 359 first, especially with all the damaged ships there to be captured. But why wasn't Armstrong next?" He paused. "Militarily, it's a no-brainer." There was confusion in his tone… and suspicion.

"It's a trap, a diversion." Cain's voice showed no surprise, no anger…just simple acknowledgement. "They're waiting for us to make a move. They have to know that's the first place we'll look to secure. They must be planning something to use that to their advantage. It's the only thing they can accurately predict." He looked around the table. "It's what I'd do. At least I'd try to build a strategy around that knowledge."

"You think they want to ambush the fleet?" It was Camille Harmon. "Could they have enough force to take on all the Alliance units from Grand Fleet?" She paused. "They have to know our approximate strength."

"Or maybe they needed their own naval units from Grand Fleet before they could mass enough strength." General Holm didn't usually get involved in debates on naval tactics, but they were all blazing new trails now. He knew they would need to work together even more than they had before if they were going to get through this new crisis.

"No." Augustus Garret silenced the room with one word. "I think Erik is right, but it's not about them getting enough strength to beat us." He looked at Harmon then at Holm. "We have the biggest Grand Fleet contingent, so waiting only serves to give us more incremental power than them." Unless it's 2 or 3 of the Powers working together, he thought...but if that's it, we're screwed anyway.

Garret inhaled deeply, holding his breath for a few seconds before exhaling. "No. It's not a trap...it's a diversion." He turned and looked at Cain. "They want us to deploy the whole fleet to defend Armstrong. That way, they'll have a free run at the rest of Alliance space. By the time we realize no invasion fleet is coming, they'll have every other worthwhile colony sewed up tight."

"So we don't take the bait." Harmon's reply was fast but tentative. She didn't look convinced, but she'd learned long before not to doubt Garret's judgment. "We go after them elsewhere... leave Armstrong to itself."

Garret was silent, thinking about what she said, considering a response, but Cain beat him to it.

"I don't think so, Camille." He glanced at her then stared at Garret. "First, we're not sure we're right. We might just end up giving Armstrong away for no reason. And even if we're right, that doesn't mean the enemy won't change plans if we leave the planet open. You can never know if your adversary will take the bait and willingly step into a trap. Any tactician worth a damn would have two plans…one if the enemy acts as expected and the other if he doesn't."

Garret was looking back at Cain, nodding. "I think you've got it right, Erik." The excitement in his voice was building. Garret was physically and emotionally exhausted, but nothing pumped adrenalin into his bloodstream like the feral reaction he got when he was planning a way to defeat his enemies. "If we move the fleet to Armstrong, they'll stay away…or maybe launch a small diversionary attack. They'd take our naval strength right out of the campaign without firing a shot."

He looked down the table for a few seconds then back to Cain. "But if we don't take the bait, we leave Armstrong lightly defended…then they will hit it. I guarantee they're watching, observing…waiting to see what we do." He paused. "They'd like to take out Armstrong…it's extremely valuable strategically. But it's not worth everything…and tying down most of our naval strength is even more of a win for them."

"So what do we do, sir?" Harmon's voice was soft, tired. She was a gifted commander, but she knew she wasn't anything like Garret's equal. The only naval officer she'd ever known with even a chance to make that kind of claim had been left behind, trapped in the X2 system along with her son and 40,000 of Grand Fleet's people.

Garret was silent for a long time. He had an answer to Harmon's question, but he wasn't happy with it. Not one bit. He panned his eyes around the room, but he settled his gaze on Cain. "Erik, I have a plan, but I'm afraid I will be asking a great deal of you and your people."

Cain stared right back at the Alliance's supreme military commander. Everyone else wore a confused expression, but Cain's eyes bored knowingly into Garret's. "I understand, sir."

"You want to defend Armstrong on the ground." Holm was sitting bolt upright in his chair. He was a few seconds behind Cain in his realization, but he was putting it all together as he spoke. "And pull the fleet out to hit the enemy elsewhere. You want to sucker them in…lure them into an attack on Armstrong and fight it out on the ground, while the fleet fights elsewhere."

Garret was nodding silently. He was still staring at Cain, his eyes a plea for forgiveness. He knew what the ground battle on Armstrong would be without naval support. The Marines were most likely going to be heavily outnumbered without the Janissaries and other allied contingents. They'd be trapped on the planet, fighting an enemy that would probably control local space. It would be a siege. There would be no resupply for them, no reserves...while the enemy would be able to bring in anything they had. He knew what Cain's people had just been through in the First Imperium War, and he didn't know how he could bring himself to ask this of them. But that was exactly what he was going to do.

"This entire enemy strategy feels like something developed by a force weaker in naval units than land forces." He paused. "They could have made a fast thrust for Armstrong, but they didn't. Why? Because Armstrong has the strongest orbital defenses, and their naval forces were already stretched too thin." His eyes darted between Holm and Cain. "So what do they do? They figure maybe they can use Armstrong as bait...to keep our fleet occupied for a while so we're out of their way elsewhere."

"So we don't cooperate. But we don't let them have the planet without a fight either." Cain's eyes didn't move a millimeter while he spoke. "You think you can hunt down and destroy their naval forces piecemeal while we're fighting on Armstrong. That's your plan, isn't it sir?"

Garret nodded slowly. "Yes, Erik. My gut tells me we can match or beat their strength in a series of naval fights...as long as we keep the fleet concentrated into a couple of strong task forces. Then it's search and destroy...anywhere their naval forces show themselves, we go after them." He paused again. "I'm afraid your part will be the toughest." He knew what had to be done, but it was still difficult to say it.

"Don't worry about it, sir." Cain even managed a tiny smile. "You should know by now that Marines always do the job." He was trying to let Garret off the hook a little. The admiral didn't need more guilt, more pain. There was no one who had served mankind more than Augustus Garret. Cain and his Marines would do what had to be done, and the last thing he wanted was Garret shouldering the guilt for it all. "You give us a ride to Armstrong and don't worry about anything else. We'll take care of everything, admiral. It'll be just like the Line."

Of course, Cain thought, the Line was no picnic...barely half his people made it off Sandoval, and he'd had a year to prepare and all the industrial capacity of mankind feeding him supplies. This time he'd be lucky to get enough time to dig a few foxholes, and the supply situation would be close to critical from the start. Cain was far from sure his people would make it through this fight, but that was irrelevant. The job had to be done, and he was going to do it. And he made damned sure not to let any of his doubt show.

Garret looked across the table, an odd expression on his face. Cain knew it was gratitude...and thanks. "We're just speculating anyway." He finally turned from Cain and looked down the table toward Harmon and Holm. "All of this is subject to change anyway. If any of our..." He paused, a sour look on his face. "...wild guesses...turn out to be wrong, we'll have to deal with it on the fly."

"Sir, what about James Teller and his people? And Admiral Davis?" Cain was talking to Garret, but his eyes found Holm's. "We can't just abandon them. We know Teller landed on Arcadia. His people could be in the middle of a fight right now. We need to get help to him." They could all be dead by now too, he thought, but he pushed it aside.

Holm nodded but didn't say anything. He just glanced over at Garret.

Garret was silent, a pained look crossing his face. "No." His voice was grim, cold...like a hammer on an anvil. "We can't abandon them. We've left enough of our people behind already." He took a deep breath, holding it for a few seconds before exhaling loudly. "But I don't know how we're going to do it." He hesitated again, looking first at Holm and then Cain. "It might be a good place to force a naval showdown. If we're right and they are weak on ships, maybe we can force them to deploy a big chunk of their strength...and destroy it. If we can attrit their fleet strength, we might be able to achieve some level of local space superiority in some of the key systems... and severely cripple their ability to support and reinforce their beachheads. It will be a long time before we can mount invasions of all of the occupied worlds, but meanwhile the isolated garrisons might start dying on the vines." Another pause, longer this time. "That is, if we get there before they can put all the captured ships into service." His voice trailed off into a troubled whisper. "Once they do that, it may be us with the weakness in naval strength."

Garret sat quietly for a few seconds before continuing, and everyone else tried not to look like they were staring at him. "If Admiral Davis is still alive, we might be able to rescue him with a naval assault. But if the enemy has a significant ground force, how do we aid General Teller?" A planetary withdrawal of a disadvantaged force under fire was an exercise in controlled suicide, and everyone at the table knew it. The only way to save Teller's people – if they weren't all dead already – was to land and retake the planet...or at least achieve some level of stalemate. And that required another ground force...one they simply didn't have.

"Maybe we could divide..."

"Forget it, Erik." It was Holm who interrupted first, but Garret's mouth was half open as well. "It'll be a miracle if you can hold Armstrong with every Marine on this fleet. Split them up and we'll just have two bloody failures."

Cain nodded. He knew they were right. But the thought of leaving Teller and his people trapped on Arcadia made him sick to his stomach. "We have to do something."

Holm sat still, looking down at the table. "You worry about Armstrong, Erik." There was a firmness growing in his voice. "Leave Teller and Arcadia to me."

"You have an idea, Elias?" There was a hint of surprise in Garret's voice. He hadn't been able to come up with anything himself.

"Yes." He slapped his hand down on the table. "I'm going to get us another attack force."

"How?" Cain was confused. He had no idea where the general planned to get more troops, but Elias Holm wasn't one to make pointless gestures. "Where are you going to find the forces you need?"

"I'm going to get more Marines, Erik." Holm sounded confident. "Retired Marines. I'm going to bring them back to the colors."

Cain shook his head. "But, sir, we already called back almost all the retired vets to fight the First Imperium."

Holm smiled. "You're talking about veterans from the Third Frontier War, Erik." He paused, allowing a small laugh to escape from his lips. "The guys I'm thinking of are a bit...older."

Chapter 7

Saw Tooth Gorge
Red Mountains
Northern Territories, Far Concordia
Arcadia – Wolf 359 III

Kara peered around the granite outcropping, looking across the gorge at the enemy positions 2 kilometers distant. The two armies had been staring at each other for almost a week now, each dug in on its side of the canyon. The mortar fire had been heavy for a while, but her people had strong cover, and they were heavily fortified. Casualties had been light. Now the bombardment was significantly weaker, more of an annoyance than a real threat. She figured the enemy was having trouble supplying themselves so far out in the wilderness and decided to stop wasting ammo.

The enemy didn't seem to be in a hurry to try to force their way across the gorge. They were probably waiting for reserves and supplies. She was pretty sure her people could hold…for a while, at least…though they would run out of food and ammunition before the invaders did.

She didn't have a reliable read on the enemy force occupying the far side of the gorge, but it was definitely weaker than she expected. She had assembled virtually every surviving member of the armed forces…even the remnants of the Arcadia City police forces. Every Arcadian trained to carry a gun was with her in this rocky refuge, yet it looked like almost three-quarters of the invading force was absent. Where were the others? Thousands of troops were missing. Where were they? That strength should be available to finish off her people, but it was nowhere to be seen. The invaders didn't need anything like the missing force to completely pacify the rest of the planet. Why chase her army into the wilderness with a fraction of their available numbers?

Ed Calvin came skittering down a rugged path just behind her. He'd been up on one of the jagged summits that soared above the top rim of the canyon. The three small peaks completely commanded the area, and Kara had ordered all of them heavily fortified and garrisoned with her heavy weapons teams. They offered an excellent line of site down to the enemy positions on the opposite side. She could cause quite a ruckus over there whenever she decided to burn some of her precious ammunition.

"How'd you do?" She swung around as she spoke.

"Not too bad." He turned back and looked up at the peak. "We've got the place turned into a fortress. If they try to come across at us, they're going to have one hell of a time of it."

And they'll still get across, she thought darkly. This whole exercise was about making it too difficult, too costly...enough to discourage them, buy time. If the enemy really wanted to take her position, they could bring another 2 or 3 thousand troops from Arcadia City and do the job right. They'd pay a cost, but they'd win the fight.

"What happened?" He'd been trying to hide a limp as he walked toward her, but she noticed it.

"Oh...nothing." She knew he was lying...she could see he was in considerable pain. "Just twisted my ankle. I'll walk it off in a few minutes."

Bullshit, she thought to herself, but she just looked at him and smiled.

"How about the com? Any luck?"

He frowned. "No. The jamming's too heavy...even up top." The enemy had been blocking all communications, preventing her from contacting anyone...or even determining if there was any other active resistance. The satellites had all been destroyed or taken by the enemy, leaving her people completely cut off.

"So we can only guess at what's going on?" She phrased it like a question, but she didn't really want an answer.

"For now, at least." He looked down at his feet, kicking a small stone as he spoke. "But what could be going on?" He didn't expect an answer either. "We've got everybody up here who can manage a weapon."

She turned back, looking across the gorge again. "I don't know, Ed." She paused, squinting as she stared at the enemy position. "But that…" – she pointed across the canyon – "… is nowhere near all of the force they landed." She turned back and looked at Calvin. "We fought three times that number at Yardley Pass, and even that was only part of their army." She shook her head. "So where are the rest of them? They don't need anywhere near that much strength as garrisons to watch the population. And we may be a poor excuse for an army, but we're still an active force in the field." She paused. "Why aren't they sending more troops after us? Why don't they have enough strength up here to end this now?" Another pause. "Come on, Ed…you know they could have taken us out by now if they had more troops over there."

Calvin was silent for a few seconds. Finally, he shook his head. "I just don't know, Kara." He looked over her shoulder toward the enemy. "Everything you say is true." He sighed heavily. "But for the life of me, I can't think of anything that could have thousands of their troops tied down."

"Look out, Billy." Tommy Handler was crouched behind a pile of debris, the remnants of a storage shed or other small building. He'd been in an intense firefight with two enemy troopers, but he'd just taken out the last of them. He took the chance to scan the tactical display, and he saw the threat to his friend's flank. "You've got bogies working around you." He shook his head, trying to clear away the growing fuzziness. The fatigue was setting in again. He'd been running on pure adrenalin for the last ten minutes, and now his arms and legs felt dead. "There are three of them, buddy. Far side of the main house."

The two privates were all that was left of their fire team.

They'd lost the SAW first…the weapon and its two-man crew were obliterated by a heavy mortar round two days before. Handler had been the first to get there and look for survivors, but he couldn't find a piece of anything bigger than a baseball.

They'd just lost the corporal an hour before. He'd been pinned down by half a dozen enemy troops in a narrow ravine. Handler and Greene finally broke through to him, but they were too late.

They were falling back…again. They'd been retreating almost non-stop for a week, and it didn't look like they were going to hold here either. There were just too many of the enemy…and they were too damned good. The Marines hated to acknowledge they had any equals, but whoever these guys were, Handler had to admit they were damned close. Their equipment was identical…and they had a lot more of it.

"Thanks, pal." He sounded tense, out of breath…scared. Bill Greene had graduated at the top of the last Marine class, which meant he was almost certain to make corporal if he made it back from this mission. But training and the field were two different things, and Greene was struggling. He turned quickly, moving to counter the attackers trying to flank him.

Handler, on the other hand, had barely made it through training. He'd have probably washed out if the base Commandant hadn't seen something in him and massaged his test results to squeak him through. But since hitting dirt on Arcadia, Handler had taken down at least a dozen enemies, and he'd saved his friend's life twice. It didn't matter how you selected recruits or what training methods you used; there was a mysterious factor, a spark of something inexplicable that separated a natural warrior from the well trained and equipped facsimiles. Tommy Handler had it. The Commandant had sensed it, and the cherry Marine's performance on Arcadia validated that confidence.

Handler took a quick look at the tactical display. There was nothing approaching his position, at least nothing close enough to be an immediate threat. He was worried about Billy, and he didn't like his friend's chances against three enemy soldiers coming at him. He snapped his body around, rolling out into the open, hugging the ground and scanning for new cover. There was a rusted out wreck of an old vehicle, some type of farming equipment, he supposed. It was about 20 meters ahead, and it was in a good spot to support Greene.

He told the suit AI to give him a stim. He was just too tired and too sore, and he needed to be sharp now. What a first mission, he thought...I'm not sure how much longer I can make it in this suit. He actually knew the answer to that question. Missions were usually planned to limit deployments to a week before Marines got a chance to pop their suits and the armorers had a chance to do some diagnostics and resupply the units. But forces had been in action for more than a month without a break, and the official word was the suit could sustain a Marine indefinitely. The miniature fusion plant could power the thing for a century or more, at least on minimal life support, and the nutrition system was good for two months, at least.

How long a man could stand to drink recycled urine and sweat and subsist on injected protein and energy formulas was another question. Going past two weeks in a suit, the major concerns were psychological, not physical. Marines thought of themselves as invulnerable, but there was a limit to what they could take...just like any other human being. Awareness and mental acuity declined abruptly after about ten days. That could be balanced out for a while with drugs, but there were limits there too. Mental breakdowns became a concern after two weeks and a major threat at three.

It was ripe in the suit, Handler knew that much. The recycling systems were highly efficient, but after a week, the armor started to smell less like a fresh and clean environment and too much like Tommy Handler. He'd figured a hundred different ways to twist his body and rub against the suit, but he'd have given his left arm for one good chance to scratch himself.

He crawled behind the shattered vehicle. Looks like some kind of tractor, he thought. He laughed softly at himself. He didn't know a damned thing about farming. For all he knew, the vehicle was a melon picker.

He peered out around the end of the wreck, glancing at the

tactical display. Here they come, he thought…they're gonna make their move now. The enemy soldiers were crouched low behind a shattered masonry wall. They were just sitting there, but Handler knew they were about to go after Billy.

"Load grenade." Handler snapped an order to the AI. "Flashbang." Most of the guys named their AIs. It seemed like a pretty good idea to him, but he didn't have time to worry about it now. Maybe later. One day, if he ever got to climb out of the stinking foulness of his suit…and maybe even take a shower. Perhaps then it would seem more important to name his digital assistant.

He heard a loud click as the round snapped into place. The grenade launcher was built into the right arm of his suit. It could throw a 6 kilo weapon as far as 3 klicks, but this time he only needed 800 meters. He angled his arm, using the tactical display to aim.

"Cut your fire, Billy." Greene was shooting at his attackers, but he didn't have a good line of site, and his rounds were just smashing the masonry into smaller chunks. "I'm gonna hit 'em with a flashbang, and then I want you to swing out to your right. Find someplace where you've got cover and a better shot." He paused, finessing his targeting as he did. "You got me, Billy? I want you to haul ass as soon as I give the word."

"Yeah, Tommy." Greene sounded overwhelmed…grateful to his friend for the guidance. "Whatever you say, man."

Technically, Greene outranked Handler, and he should have been giving the orders. The two were both privates, graduated into the Corps on the same day, but as valedictorian, Greene had been given the number 4 slot in the team and Handler number 5. But Handler's natural ability had surfaced, and he had taken charge. Greene was struggling to get through his first battle, and he was content to follow his friend's commands.

Handler held his arm steady, checking his aim again. He pressed the firing lever and felt his arm recoil as the electromagnetic catapult sent the grenade on its way.

The flashbang wasn't going to take any of the enemy troops down; he was pretty sure of that. It was hard to seriously hurt a fully armored trooper with any grenade...at least unless you went nuclear. But the flashbang rounds had a different purpose. Named after ancient stun grenades, the weapons were designed to create severe interference at the point of impact, effectively blinding anyone within 30 meters. One of the newest systems to come out of General Sparks' weapons lab, the flashbangs were a variation on the Caliphate's smoke shells, and they covered the target area with a superheated, radioactive steam that virtually shut down all scanning and detection systems for 2-3 minutes.

Handler watched the grenade land. It exploded with a muffled sound, and the area all around the enemy troopers was obscured with a sickly green cloud. The steam was infused with tiny metallic particles, and the sunlight gave it a vaguely sparkling appearance.

"Let's go, Billy." Handler lunged out from his cover, into the open field between him and the enemy. He swung far to the left, zigzagging, approaching his targets in an irregular pattern. The enemy troopers were firing wildly, but he could see immediately they had no targeting. He held his own fire...he didn't want to give his position away. He ran up a small hill and threw himself over the crest.

He glanced at the tactical display. He had nothing on the enemy...the flashbang was blocking his scanners just as effectively. But Greene was outside the affected area, and Handler could see his friend moving quickly around the enemy's other flank. It looked like he'd found some debris that offered him decent cover and a good line of site.

Handler pulled his assault rifle from his back, extending it in front of him, aiming at the enemy's last known location. He had no idea if his foes had moved, but he hadn't detected anything emerging from the affected area, so if they had, they didn't go far.

"OK, Billy." He flipped the rifle to full-auto. He knew he was going to have to start worrying about his ammo supply soon, but not now. "Fire."

He moved his weapon across the entire obscured area,

focusing on the spot where the enemy had been deployed. He could see on the display that Greene was firing too. He had no idea if they were hitting anything, but the return fire had stopped. He heard the auto-loader slam another clip into place. That meant he'd already sent 500 hyper-velocity rounds into the steam cloud.

He fired through half the second clip and stopped. "Hey Billy, hold your fire. The flashbang's dissipating. There's no one firing back. Let's hold up and see what's in there."

He stared at the tactical display, watching it flicker as his scanner began to penetrate the dissolving steam cloud. There was still no hostile fire. "I'm going in, Billy. Stay sharp and cover me."

Handler dashed out over the crest of the hill, sprinting the distance to the enemy position. There were wispy remnants of the steam from the flashbang, but it was mostly gone. He ran up to the wall, pressing himself against the side opposite the enemy troops. He spun around, rifle at the ready. There were two figures lying on the ground. One was obviously dead, the top half of his armored body torn apart. The other was motionless, and when he looked closely, Handler could see that three rounds had torn right through his chest.

He turned his head quickly, looking in every direction. He caught some movement along the ground, something disappearing behind a chunk of shattered plasti-crete. He lunged forward, toward the mound of rubble.

The next few seconds seemed to play out in slow motion. He saw the movement again, behind the pile of smashed bricks now, rifle moving out. His body seemed to react on its own, instinct taking over. He jumped hard, propelling himself almost two meters up as he lunged forward.

He heard the rounds smashing into the wall behind where he'd been standing half a second earlier. The ground was coming at him fast and he angled his shoulder, landing with a text-book combat roll. His own rifle snapped up, firing. He'd set it on semi-auto to save ammo, and his first three round burst hit the edge of the collapsed wall, sending a spray of dust and shattered rocks into the air.

His momentum carried him forward, and he caught a glimpse of his enemy. He was wounded, that was clear, but he was pulling up his own weapon, firing a burst in Handler's direction. The rounds slammed into the ground next to his leg, scaring the hell out of him, but not causing any damage.

His finger depressed the trigger again…and again. Two bursts of hyper-velocity projectiles ripped through the atmosphere, covering the ten meters to his target in an infinitesimal fraction of a second. The first three went high, leaving a faint glow in the air over his adversary's head. The second burst was lower, more on target. One round clipped the opposing trooper's arm, and the second one smashed into his shoulder, ripping a huge gash in his armor and sending a cloud of blood and shattered bone into the air. The trooper fell to the ground, twisting almost 360 degrees and landing on his back. His rifle slipped from his gloved hand and fell next to him.

Handler's instincts were still in control. He leapt to his feet, pushing too hard and almost tumbling forward face down. He got control of his balance and stepped quickly, standing over the man he'd just shot. He looked down at the stricken soldier. The wounds were bad, that was clear…but they weren't necessarily mortal. The suit had a tremendous capability to stabilize even grievous injuries, and if he got medical attention quickly enough, he had a good chance to make it. But war was rarely that simple.

Handler knew what he had to do. He didn't like it, and his mind rebelled against what his training and combat instincts told him was essential. He couldn't handle a prisoner now, especially not one who couldn't walk. And he couldn't leave him either. He was badly hurt, yes…but the Marine fighting suit was a multi-faceted weapon. If Handler turned his back, even for a second, there was a chance his adversary could take him down. All it would require was a slight move of the hand…perhaps not even that. A whispered command to the suit's AI might do the job. No, he didn't have any choice.

He could hear Greene on the com, shouting to him, and he

could see the small icon on the tactical display moving toward him. He raised the rifle quickly. He knew he was only doing what he had to do…but for some reason he didn't want his friend to see it. He turned off his mind, letting his raw guts control his actions. He looked away, only hearing the three rounds blasting out of the assault rifle. He froze for a second, slowly looking back, seeing what he had done. The soldier was still in place, but his chest was just…gone. Handler had fired 3 dead on heart shots.

"You OK, Tommy?" Greene was almost there, hopping over a pile of shattered debris.

Handler was still frozen. This wasn't the first man he'd killed, or even the fifth. But it was the first he'd shot from so close… and the only one he'd seen moving, looking back at him, before he did. He wanted to drop his rifle and run away…or fall to his knees and empty his stomach. But he knew his duty was here on this battlefield…and intravenous feeding and the anti-emetic drug cocktail made vomiting a non-option too.

Slowly, deliberately, he forced himself to move. He turned sluggishly toward his friend, just as he was rounding the edge of the demolished wall.

"Hey Tommy…you OK, pal?"

Handler looked up at his friend. "Yeah, Billy." His voice was throaty, raw. "I'm OK." He knew he was lying.

"It's our only chance, Jim." Mike Barnes was crouched down below the twisted metal framework. The complex had been a refinery or some other kind of processing plant, but six hours of infantry combat had reduced it to scrap. Teller's people had put up a hell of a fight, but the enemy had extended their line and threatened both flanks. It was time to bug out…before they were completely cut off. Barnes wanted to pull their people back, into a large complex of abandoned mines south of the capital.

Teller sighed hard. "It's the most defensible position, no question about that." His voice was heavy with doubt. "But if we move in there, we'll never get out. We'll lose all mobility, and the battle will become a siege. They'll just cover the entrances and wait us out. You know our supply situation." His tone was grim and getting worse as he continued. "Unless they get sick of waiting and decide to come in after us." He paused. "The position is a strong one, but they've got the numbers to dig us out if they're willing to take the casualties."

"What else can we do, Jim?" Barnes didn't like it any better than Teller. But he couldn't think of an option. "If they had any airpower at all, we'd be dead already. But they've still got us hemmed in. That mobility isn't helping us anymore. They've got too much manpower...they can keep us bracketed and close the circle. What have we got? Five days? A week? Then they'll have us surrounded...but we'll be out in the open and not dug into the mountains."

Teller was frustrated. When he'd gotten the distress call, he figured he could back up the local army and defeat whatever force had invaded the planet. Now he was angry at himself...for recklessness, for arrogance. He'd let his pride do his thinking, confident that his Marines could best any foe. But the forces occupying Arcadia were as well trained as his people, or at least close to it. And their equipment was identical. The campaign had been like a battle against shadow Marines, but the enemy had five times the numbers. Now his people were facing total defeat, and he had nothing to show for it. The local army was nowhere to be found...Teller assumed it had already been destroyed. His people hadn't made a bit of difference. He'd thrown away over a thousand fully trained and equipped Marines. For nothing. Erik Cain had pinned stars on his collar, and trusted him completely. Teller knew he'd let his mentor down.

"Jim?" Barnes slapped his armored hand against Teller's suit. "What's it gonna be?"

His troops were in wholesale retreat now. He was out of time. He had to decide. "The mines." He spat out the words, his voice thick with anger. "Pull everyone back to the mines."

Chapter 8

C1 Headquarters Building
Wan Chai, Hong Kong
Central Asian Combine, Earth

Li An sat quietly at her desk, bourbon number three in her hand. It was late, past 2am, and the lights of Wan Chai still blazed behind her. She knew what was happening out there. The Central Asian Combine enforced a very conservative code of conduct on its residents, but for those in positions of power it was pure façade. In Wan Chai and the other wealthy playgrounds of Hong Kong, the privileged and powerful engaged in every manner of hedonism and debauchery. Indeed, exploiting the vices of various government functionaries had always been one of her favorite tools. Li An wasn't squeamish by any means...she wouldn't hesitate to slowly dissect a troublesome subject down in the lower level interrogation rooms to get what she needed. But why go to the trouble when sex, drugs, and blackmail could do the job so much more efficiently?

The vast majority of the CAC's people lived in extreme poverty, as they did in all of the Superpowers. There was a small middle class of sorts, the same as in the other nations. The engineers and scientists and other educated types a modern society required had to be given some level of privilege over the masses, but few of them could even guess at the virtually unlimited luxury the power brokers in government enjoyed.

Li An herself was no stranger to a plush existence. The bottle of bourbon she was well on her way to polishing off cost as much as the average CAC family earned in a year. Still, by the standards of the other Committee members, her tastes had always been simple. Work had been her life, and C1 was her monument. The intelligence agency was modeled in her image. What will happen to it, she wondered, when I am gone?

If there's anything left at all, she thought darkly. The world was at a crossroads, and Li An was one of the few who truly understood the danger. Things were poised on the edge of a knife...they could spin out of control at any moment. The Alliance had refused to allow the CAC, or any of the Powers, to use the Commnet system to contact their units with Grand Fleet. Then, the scouting force sent to Wolf 359 to investigate what was happening in that troubled system disappeared without a trace. The ships transited, and that was the last anyone heard from them. International tensions soared further, and accusations of foul play flew back and forth between diplomatic missions.

She looked down at the tablet on her desk. The report it displayed was good news...at least it would have been if it had come earlier. Grand Fleet had returned to Sandoval. Other than casualties incurred fighting the First Imperium, every vessel was intact. Augustus Garret had formally disbanded the fleet and thanked all the personnel for their service. Just like that...all the national contingents were back from the Rim and on their way to their bases, safe and sound and under their own commanders.

She drained her glass and set it down, reaching for the bottle. This was exactly what she'd needed two weeks ago. It would have relieved tensions considerably. Now it was close to useless, serving only to mock her. She'd argued as hard as she could... and even hinted at some of the secrets in her file, but she hadn't been able to convince him. Despite her efforts, Huang Wei ordered a secret mobilization of the CAC's terrestrial armed forces, and two days later the Caliphate did as well.

She laughed bitterly to herself as she filled her glass again. Those old fools, she thought, then laughed again, noting they were all younger than her. Li An couldn't remember hearing anything as stupid as a secret mobilization. She hated Gavin Stark with a fiery passion, but if Huang Wei thought the Alliance's spymaster was going to miss two Superpowers mobilizing their forces, he was an imbecile. He probably knows already, she thought, as she put the glass to her lips.

When the new reports first arrived, she considered trying to halt the mobilizations. But that genie was already out of the bottle. She couldn't be sure the Alliance wasn't already responding, and she had no way to know how they would react even if the order was reversed. The CAC could easily find itself unprepared, facing an Alliance at a high state of readiness. She didn't want a war on Earth, but it would be even worse if she interfered and the CAC was unable to defend itself against an attack. She didn't think victory in such a conflict was going to be much of a prize, but defeat was unthinkable.

"Minister Li?" It was her assistant on the com. C1 was a 24/7 operation, and one of her people was always on duty outside her office.

She tapped the com panel. "Yes, Bai?" She was annoyed and surprised at being disturbed at this hour. "What is it?"

"I have Chairman Huang on your line."

Now that's a surprise, Li thought, moving her hand to the com unit. "Good evening, Mr. Chairman." Huang was usually in a drug induced stupor and on his second or third young girl by 2am. "How can I be of assistance?"

"Good evening, Minister Li. I am sorry to disturb you at such a late hour."

"Not at all, Mr. Chairman. In fact, I am still in my office."

"I've been reading the reports from the returning fleet units." His voice was a little shaky. She couldn't tell if it was fatigue or the effects of his evening's earlier activities. "Obviously, I am gratified that our forces have returned without incident. We may have to revisit some of our recent strategic decisions in the coming days."

Damned fool, she thought...he doesn't realize he's taken us down a road we can't easily escape. "Yes, sir." She didn't elaborate. There was no point, and now wasn't the time anyway.

"However, I have another concern that I wanted to address at once." His tone was a mix of anger and suspicion.

"What is it, Mr. Chairman?" She knew Wei was a paranoid sort, apt to see threats where there were none…and recent events had done nothing to calm his mania.

"Have you read the individual officers' reports?"

She wasn't sure where he was going. "Yes, sir. I've read everything." Of course, she thought…what the hell do you think I do here all day?

"It is my opinion that many of them are rather effusive of Admiral Garret and some of the other Alliance military personnel. Disturbingly so. Wouldn't you agree?"

She suppressed a laugh. Li An was used to seeing threats everywhere, but this particular insanity hadn't even occurred to her. But she'd been around long enough to know the phrase, "wouldn't you agree" was a trap when uttered by a paranoid superior. "Of course, Mr. Chairman. The loyalties of our command staff are always of concern." Her face was a mask of exhaustion and disdain. What a waste of time, she thought. "If you would like me to place these officers under enhanced surveillance, I would…"

"I believe we need to move quickly and decisively on this, Minister Li. While I am relieved that our fleet units appear to have returned safely, the situation is still very fluid. I consider the possibility of Alliance perfidy to be a major concern. Indeed, if Admiral Garret has suborned the loyalty of our fleet commanders, we can derive little assurance from the return of the ships. Perhaps the Alliance believes it can control those taskforces through the defection of the commanding officers." The stress was becoming more pronounced in his voice. "I would like you to prepare a plan to immediately remove all officers whose loyalties are suspect." He paused. "Many of the Caliphate personnel have expressed similar disturbing sentiments with regard to Admiral Garret and his associates. I have arranged a call with the Caliph tomorrow to discuss the matter at greater length."

Li An had provided him the Caliphate communiques as well as the CAC ones. C1 was a highly effective organization, and her people had easily intercepted the messages sent to New Media. The Caliphate was a CAC ally, but that didn't mean C1 didn't spy on them as aggressively as they did the Alliance or the PRC.

She forced back a sigh. "May I suggest, sir, that you do not tell the Caliph that we intercepted his fleet communiques?"

"Of course not, Minister." His voice had an edge. She was reminding him not to be careless, and he didn't like it. "I will simply advise him that I have concerns about some of our officers and suggest that he take a closer look at his own."

"Very well, sir." She knew the whole thing was a waste...of time and of experienced, loyal officers. More than a waste... this wasn't going to help the morale or readiness of the armed forces, not one bit. Huang was being foolish and paranoid. It wasn't as simple as he seemed to think for a fleet commander to lead his force over to the enemy, even if he was disposed to do so. But she could tell he wasn't going to let it drop and, innocent or not, she knew she couldn't just fire officers of such high rank. She'd have to bring them up on some kind of charges, at least... or simply institute a purge, accusing them all of treason and classifying the entire affair. It was going to be messy no matter how she handled it. "I will put a plan in place immediately, sir." She'd ruthlessly sacrificed thousands over her career, and the innocence of the victims had never been a major consideration. But this time it didn't seem the same. Maybe it was age, or simply exhaustion...but she felt something different. Was it pity for the victims? Or guilt? It didn't matter. Li An would do what she had to, no matter what. She didn't have to like it.

"Thank you, Minister Li."

There was a wildness in Huang's voice, she thought...this has all been too much for him...the paranoia is taking over. "I am pleased to be of any service, Mr. Chairman."

Huang cut the line. Li leaned back in her chair, draining her glass and setting it down on the desk. She glanced at the chronometer. It was almost 3am. If she left now she could get a couple hours of sleep and a shower before she had to leave for her shuttle.

She had no idea what Roderick Vance wanted to discuss with her. The head of Martian Intelligence was enigmatic, to say the least. Enormously wealthy, he appeared to be utterly incorrupt-

ible as well. Despite years of trying, she'd never been able to
uncover any vices or secrets she could use against him. He was
just about the only man of any importance in occupied space
whose C1 file was almost empty.

He was extremely intelligent too, though she wasn't sure he
was a match for Gavin Stark. The Alliance's master spy was like
no one she'd ever encountered. She hated Stark and knew he
was a monster, but she had to acknowledge the evil bastard was
a genius.

Li and Vance were unlikely compatriots. The Martian Confederation was far more closely aligned with the Alliance than
the CAC, and that meant Vance was usually on the other side.
But he understood, as Li An did, that Stark was his own entity.
His loyalty was to himself only, and his schemes were as likely
to damage the Alliance as aid it. All that was certain was they
would serve Gavin Stark.

Li and Vance worked together during the Alliance's rebellions, and they managed to give Gavin Stark a rare and bitter
defeat, shattering his plans to seize total control over the colonies. Stark had been quiet since then, disturbingly so. He was
clearly up to something – something big, she suspected – but
her every effort to penetrate his security had proven to be a failure. Perhaps Vance knows something, she thought hopefully.

She stood slowly, achingly, flipping off the desk light as she
did. Her legs felt weak, and the pain in her joints was getting
worse. She knew her body was failing her, but there was an odd
little smile on her face. Maybe, she thought to herself…maybe
I will get the chance to deal Gavin Stark one last defeat before
I die.

She walked slowly to the door, wondering again what information Vance had…and looking forward to one last great battle
of wits with an old enemy.

Chapter 9

Astria City
Planet Armstrong
Gamma Pavonis III

Cain walked swiftly down the street, his aides almost jogging to keep up with him. It felt odd to be back on Armstrong…to be on any normal colony. Someplace he could just walk into a restaurant and order a sandwich or a cup of coffee. It had been years now since Cain had been somewhere like this, a civilian environment…someplace that reminded him there were people in the universe who just lived their lives normally. He found it a pleasant diversion, a reminder of what he was fighting to preserve, though he knew he was only there to change it, to save it…probably by destroying it.

He had been on Sandoval when the population there was being evacuated. He remembered the empty cities standing like ghost towns, deserted streets and abandoned buildings silent, save for the occasional patrol passing through. Now those cities were radioactive ruins, one of the many sacrifices made to stop the First Imperium. No one would live there again for generations. The scattered refugees, the former occupants of Sandoval…they could seek some miserable scrap of solace, at least, in the thought that the battle had been a great victory, one that had turned the First Imperium back from the heart of human space. Cain shook his head imperceptibly, thinking what cold comfort that must be.

Since the holocaust of Sandoval, he and his Marines had called the ships of the fleet home, except for the time they spent on Sigma 4, fighting another death struggle with the legions of the First Imperium. That had been an enemy world, at least, not another Alliance colony to destroy. But now he was back on friendly territory, and the situation was eerily like that preceding the Battle of Sandoval.

Things were different on Armstrong, though. Almost all of the population had been evacuated from Sandoval, but that was impossible now. Cain didn't have the ships or the time for anything like that. He'd have to win this fight while trying to keep over a million displaced civilians alive. Erik Cain's way of war had always been total, but now he was thrust into a different role. If he held onto an Armstrong that had become a lifeless rock, its people buried in the ashes of their homes, could he see that as anything but utter defeat?

His forces were different too. On Sandoval, he had a carefully assembled army, including contingents from the other Powers, but his Marines were alone on Armstrong, and they were no freshly organized expeditionary force, but the shattered remnants of the bitter fighting on Sigma 4. He had no reinforcements, no substantive refit…just the exhausted survivors of one of the most murderous battles ever fought.

The force assigned to Sandoval had been one of the best supplied and provisioned armies humanity had ever put into the field. The Marines defending Armstrong had nothing but the remaining ammunition and equipment from the Sigma 4 campaign.

None of that mattered to Cain. He'd gone through the strange transition that overtook him whenever he went into a fight. Normally calm and easy-going, the call of battle changed him somewhere deep inside. Erik Cain the combat commander was cold, focused, ruthless. He didn't let pain and suffering affect his judgment under fire. He saw only two options in combat…total victory or utter defeat. And for Cain, defeat meant death. Anything short of that, and he would still be fighting… and he expected everyone under his command to operate in the same way.

"Isaac, I want these people out of here now." Cain was waving his arm around, gesturing to the buildings of Armstrong's capital city. "What the hell is holding things up?"

Cain had originally made Merrick his chief of staff because it was the position he felt least problematic for an intelligent and gifted officer who lacked sufficient training in powered armor for a field command. It had been somewhat of a "make do" arrangement when he conceived of it, but it turned out to be a huge success. Merrick was extremely competent with organizational tasks, and his personality meshed well with Cain's hard-edged battlefield persona. They worked together seamlessly on Sigma 4, and now Cain couldn't imagine trying to get by without him.

"We've met some…ah…resistance from some of the civilians." Merrick's voice was halting. He knew this wasn't going to go over well with Cain. "Many of them are refusing to leave their homes."

Cain stopped abruptly and turned to face his chief of staff. It was at times like this Merrick wished they were wearing armor, however uncomfortable he found it. At least he wouldn't have had to see the expression on Cain's face. He'd have sworn the temperature dropped ten degrees around the commander-in-chief.

"I know I didn't just hear what I thought I did, General Merrick."

Merrick almost tried to explain that the people were reluctant to uproot themselves and move into makeshift shelters when they didn't even know if there was going to be an attack. No enemy force had been detected. The concern that an invasion was coming was pure conjecture. Merrick understood how the civilians felt, but he knew Cain wouldn't…or if he did, he wouldn't care. Not for the first time, he wondered what it was that happened to Erik Cain when he transported down to a battlefield. Was it some unfathomable pool of raw, iron will from which he drew his merciless strength? Aboard ship or in base, Merrick considered Cain one of his closest friends, a good-natured guy with an offbeat but fun sense of humor. But in the field, he felt he didn't know the man at all. He respected him - and he would follow him against the legions of hell - but the difference was stark, almost indescribable. Fighting with Erik Cain felt like following the god of war into battle.

"I've taken steps to address the matter, sir." He was hoping Cain would let him handle things. He didn't think Erik would order the recalcitrant civilians shot or anything quite so drastic, but he figured there was a good chance he'd have them dragged out of their homes at gunpoint. Merrick thought he could manage a less disruptive solution, while still accomplishing the goal. "I'll see it done, Erik. You have my word."

Cain started walking again. His face wore the usual scowl, but there was a hint of a smile there too. He knew exactly what Merrick was thinking. He didn't have time for such nonsense, but he trusted his chief of staff, and if Merrick was willing to accept the extra effort to go easier on the population, so be it.

"Very well, General Merrick." The amusement in his voice was mostly hidden, but Merrick caught it anyway. "I will leave the matter to you. But we are going to begin prepping these buildings for the battle in three days, so that's how long you've got."

"Yes, sir."

"What is the status of the recruit battalions?" Cain had ordered all the Marine trainees at Camp Basilone organized for active service. There were three battalions formed from trainees who had received their fighting suits and three unarmored ones made up of earlier stage recruits. Teller had already cherry-picked the recent grads and some of the senior classes, and now Cain was taking just about every boot the Corps still had in training. The well had now been sucked bone dry. It would be years before fresh newbs could be recruited and trained enough to take the field with anything like the skillset expected of a Marine. What Cain had was what he had...for the battle on Armstrong and whatever came next.

He shut down the Academy as well, diverting some of the cadets into command positions for the new battalions and the rest into a group of special action teams. Cain had organized the original teams during the Third Frontier War, and they'd proven their worth in the fighting on Carson's World. Despite their successes, they suffered heavy losses and didn't survive the post-war demobilizations. Now Cain was restarting the program. This time every member was a veteran non-com who'd been selected for officer training. In an army with a significant number of inexperienced personnel, the teams would be a razor's edge of hardcore vets he could use wherever he needed it.

"The new teams are ready to go." Merrick had all the information ready. "The powered battalions are 72 hours from full readiness." He turned and looked at Cain. "We had to arm most of them from our stocks. They had mostly training weapons at Basilone."

Cain frowned. That wasn't good news. His supplies were low enough already, without the added drain. "Well, I guess there's no way around that. I thought they would be better supplied." Cain made a face, remembering how the Corps had stripped every depot to mount the invasion of First Imperium space. "Though I probably shouldn't have."

"We're in OK shape on supplies, even after arming the recruits." Merrick was trying to sound a little more optimistic than he felt. "Garret cleaned out the ships and gave us everything he could find. I don't think there's so much as a pistol or spare clip left on the fleet." He paused, sighing softly. "If it's a long fight, we're going to have a logistics problem, but we'll be good for a while. Supply is probably not going to be the first crisis we deal with."

Cain nodded. "I suppose not." He walked quietly for a few seconds. "How about McDaniels' people? How are they shaking out?"

General Erin McDaniels commanded the Obliterator corps. The massive fighting suits had been developed as an answer to the First Imperium's Reapers, and now they were Cain's one big advantage. From the limited intel he had, Cain expected the invaders to be close to a match for his Marines. But he'd heard nothing to suggest they had anything remotely like the Obliterators.

"They're all settled in." Merrick's voice was tentative.

Cain had ordered the Obliterators deployed in hidden locations. They were the one thing he had for which the enemy might not have a counter, and he was going to keep that power dry…and hidden…for as long as possible.

"But?"

"Captain Slavin's people have been working around the clock, Erik, but we've only got 378 units ready for action as of this morning." Cain had attacked Sigma 4 with 3,000 Obliterators. Losses had been heavy, but he'd figured at least a thousand of the units could be put in the field immediately. Less than 400 was a hugely disappointing number. The 4-meter tall suits were a new weapon system that had been rushed into service during the war, and maintenance was proving to be a considerable problem. The lack of spare parts was truly hamstringing the effort to get damaged and malfunctioning suits back into action. Cain's force had over 1,000 salvageable Obliterators, possibly even 1,200-1,300, but the process of getting them ready for action was slow and laborious.

Cain sighed. "I knew we were going to have problems, but that's below even my low range estimate." He stopped and turned to face Merrick. "Isaac, I know they're working like crazy, but they've got to do better than that. I need you to ride them harder."

Merrick nodded. "I understand." He wasn't sure what he could do, but he'd try.

Cain started walking again. They had a lot more prep work to do. He was going to make sure that Armstrong was as heavily defended as humanly possible, even if he had to work his people to death doing it.

"How about the minefields…" He pointed off toward the east as he kept walking.

"General Cain, sir?" Captain Claren's head was poking through the partially open hatch. The room was dark, save for a shaft of light shining in from the hallway.

Cain turned his head and looked toward the door, squinting. He hadn't been asleep, but his eyes weren't adjusted to the light yet. He didn't get much rest during campaigns, but he'd long ago realized that it was easier to pretend to sleep from time to time than to have his staff nagging him 24/7 about it. Plus, he enjoyed the solitude. Even if he wasn't actually sleeping, he found it restful. The ghosts were there, of course, as always, but they didn't really torment him anymore. Somewhere along the line, he'd made a peace of sorts with them. Now they were just there, with him all the time, as if simply waiting patiently for him to join them.

"What is it, captain?" He spoke slowly, softly. He could see how nervously his aide peered into the room. Why, he thought, do I scare them all so?

"General, I'm very sorry to bother you, but we have multiple contacts at the warp gate. Vessels inbound...warships and trans-ports." He paused. "We do not have a breakdown yet."

Cain sat up, his hand behind his head, rubbing his neck. "Place all forces on full alert." He threw the blanket aside and swung his legs over the edge of the bed. "And get me Com-mander Gimble at Orbital Command."

"I took the liberty of contacting the commander, sir." Claren motioned toward the com unit on the table next to the bed. "He's waiting on your line, general."

Cain nodded approvingly. He was proud of his people. He knew he didn't always appreciate them enough or tell them as often as he should, but he doubted there had ever been a bet-ter military organization anywhere. Erik Cain didn't think most people were worth a damn, but knew he had more than his share of outstanding ones.

"Very well, captain." He glanced at the com unit. "Assemble the staff for a tactical briefing in 20 minutes." He glanced back at Claren. "And tell the control room I'm going to want those force breakdowns by then." His tone almost dared the staff to offer excuses instead of the reports he wanted.

"Yes, sir."

Well, Cain thought, it looks like Augustus called it. Many of the Marines...and almost all the civilians...had doubted any attack was coming at all. But that question, at least, seemed to be answered.

"And captain...have them send up a couple sandwiches. If we're going to fight another mysterious enemy, I might as well do it on a full stomach."

"Yes, General Cain." Claren saluted and ducked back into the hall, the hatch sliding shut behind him.

"Lights." Cain barked the command to the room AI, and the track along the ceiling activated. He turned toward the table, extending his hand and slapping the control on the com unit.

"Commander Gimble? It looks like we've got some company on the way."

Gimble stared at the tactical screen. He commanded the most powerful orbital defense force of any human colony, but without fleet support, he knew it wasn't going to be enough. With no warships of his own, all of his forces were static...and that ultimately meant they were easy targets.

"Enemy approaching on projected vector, Commander Gimble." Taylor Jones was fresh out of the Academy, but Gimble had been impressed with the young officer's poise and ability. He was proud of all of his people. The battle fleets usually got the best recruits, and Orbital Command typically had to settle for second rate officers and crew who didn't quite make the cut. But Gimble was an exception, a gifted officer who was prone to an exaggerated set of side effects from warp gate insertions. A lot of people suffered dizziness and nausea during transits, but Gimble got so sick he was incapacitated for hours. He'd tried to adapt, but fleet service just required too many transits, and he'd eventually given up, finding a home in Orbital Command. Admiral Garret had recognized his ability immediately and tapped him to command the defenses of the main military nexus at Armstrong. In turn, Gimble had assembled and trained a staff far superior to the average group of fortress jockeys.

"Very well, ensign." Gimble was staring at a pair of white spheres on the display, Armstrong's two small moons. There was a chain of blue icons around each of them...missile fortresses Garret's ships had towed from their original posts orbiting the planet. "Send updated enemy positioning data to the platforms behind the Twins. Direct laser pulse communication. Tell Lieutenants Long and Harris that we're severing all comm. From this point on, they are to act on their own initiative."

The early colonists on Armstrong hadn't been able to agree on names for the planet's two satellites. They were called by various informal names for years, but eventually The Twins became the dominant designation for the two nearly identical moons. It was finally made official, almost 30 years after the initial colonization.

It had been Cain's idea to tow several fortresses from Armstrong orbit and position them behind the Twins. Garret endorsed the plan the second he heard it, and his ships did the job before pulling out of the system. Gimble was less sanguine about the whole thing and a little annoyed at the usurpation of his authority. It just took power away from his main defense. But as usual, Cain's mind was focused on the cold, brutal mathematics of the situation. Gimble's people were doomed anyway...a few might get to their escape pods and flee to the surface, but they had no chance to defeat the flotilla closing on the planet. But if the enemy was careless, those missile forts hiding behind the Twins might go unnoticed...and get a chance to fire at some transports. Any troops Cain's people killed in orbit were that many less they had to face in the field. And Armstrong would be held or lost on the ground.

"Place all stations on red alert, Ensign Jones." Gimble leaned back in his chair and closed his eyes for a few seconds. He knew he probably only had another couple hours to live. He was scared, certainly, but something else too. Relaxed wasn't the word, of course, but resigned, maybe? He wasn't sure what to call it, but he knew what he had to do, and that was all that mattered...and in that realization there was peace of a sort.

"Transmit warhead activation codes to all weapons." He had just armed over 100 gigatons of nuclear weapons. "Instruct tactical AI to update missile firing solutions."

"Yes, sir." Jones' hand moved over the control board, executing Gimble's commands. A few seconds later: "All warheads armed and ready, sir."

Gimble sighed as he stared at the display. His people had ID'd some of the units inbound. There were two capital ships, and one had been positively identified as Concord. That decisively answered one question. Whatever force was inbound, it was definitely related to the one that took Wolf 359. Concord had been under repair at the shipyards there after sustaining heavy damage during the Line battles. This was the first confirmation that at least some of the ships at Wolf 359 had been captured…and that meant, whoever this enemy was, they had gained considerable naval power. If it was one of the Superpowers, and they managed to get all the captured ships into service, Garret wasn't going to have the superiority he was hoping for.

"Firing solution complete, sir. I'm sending it to your console." Jones' voice was sharp and crisp. "Tactical AI recommends beginning firing sequence in one-seven minutes, sir."

Gimble had been considering holding fire, launching just before the enemy warheads were reaching his platforms. That would maximize his own targeting and inflict heavier damage on the incoming vessels, but he'd have to withhold most of his defensive fire while his own missiles were in the point defense zone. It would be a dangerously aggressive plan, but one that made a strange sort of sense. His defenses were going to be overwhelmed anyway, so why not take as many of the bastards down with him?

"Lock in AI tactical plan." He let out a long exhale. He knew his own instincts were right, but he just could bring himself to leave his people defenseless…even when he knew those defenses wouldn't be enough to make a difference. Cain would have done it, he thought to himself, not sure if he was ashamed or proud of differing with the commander-in-chief's cold-blooded decisiveness.

"Tactical plan locked in, sir." Jones glanced at the chronometer. "Projected first wave launching in fourteen minutes… that's 1-4 minutes."

Alright you bastards, Gimble thought, feeling the anger rising inside him…if you want to get to Armstrong you have to come through us first.

Chapter 10

Five Forks
Western Continent
Planet Tranquility
Omicron 9 System

Sam Thomas reached around and wiped the back of his neck with a small cloth. It was midsummer, and he'd been out in the fields since dawn. Thomas was over 80 years old, but with the rejuv treatments and his natural constitution, he looked like a fit man in his late-40s. He had a few old injuries that gave him some pain now and then, but that was from a lifetime ago. Despite a little chronic soreness, he still had almost limitless energy. He'd long been wealthy enough to passively manage his holdings, but he still spent every day in the fields, directing the work on 30,000 hectares of fertile farmland. He wasn't the kind of man who could sit around the house all day. Inactivity would make him crazy inside of a week.

He was on his way back from the north section, heading down the winding path that led to the house. This was his favorite spot on the farm, an idyllic stretch of grapevines and apple orchards, crisscrossed with small creeks and shallow ponds. He always imagined this was what rural New England had once looked like, centuries ago, before war and pollution had turned the pristine woods and mountains into the contaminated and garbage-strewn wastelands of his childhood.

He'd sent his transport ahead, deciding to walk back the 8 klicks. It was just too nice out to sit cooped up in the ATV, breathing sanitized, climate-controlled atmosphere when a beautiful, unspoiled world offered fresh air. He might be a little late for dinner, but he didn't care. They'd wait for him.

The walk had been a pleasure, though he had to admit to himself he was getting a little tired. Age was wearing lightly on him, but he wasn't immune to the passage of time. He knew one day he'd have to slow down, cut his workload. But today isn't that day, he thought. Not yet.

His body tensed as he came up over the last rise before the house, old senses tingling, flashing a warning. Something was going on. He wasn't sure what, but things were…off. He couldn't see anything amiss, but his instincts were almost never wrong. He slipped back below the hillside, turning and heading toward a series of outbuildings just south of the house.

He moved quickly and quietly, keeping himself hidden behind the hill. He knew every centimeter of the ground, and he swung around the end of a large storage shed and typed in an access code to open the side entry. He ducked inside and looked around, making sure he was alone. He stepped up to a large plasti-steel door on the far wall. There was a small display with a keypad on the wall right next to it. He walked up and punched in a series of numbers. The hatch slid open slowly, revealing a room with racks of neatly stacked weapons.

Thomas slipped into the storeroom, grabbing a pistol and shoving it in his belt. Then he ran his hands down a rack and selected a heavy assault rifle. He took the weapon and a pouch with a dozen clips and slammed a cartridge into the magazine. He stepped back outside, looking around again as he tapped a code into the keypad to close the door.

The approach to the house from the storage complex was mostly hidden, covered by a fold in the ground and the trees of a small orchard. He crept up close and peered cautiously through a window. There was a man at the kitchen table. He wasn't close enough for Thomas to get a good look, but the old farmer knew right away it was no one who should be there. He moved slowly, carefully toward the back of the house, quietly entering the access code. The door opened quickly, and he burst inside, aiming his weapon at the unidentified visitor's head as he did.

"For Christ's sake, Sam." The figure turned slowly, looking right at Thomas. "You're even grouchier now than I remember. I didn't think that was possible."

Thomas stood still for a second, a stunned expression on his face. "Elias Holm, you old dog." He lowered his rifle and let a broad smile replace his usual scowl. "What the hell are you doing here?"

Holm returned his mentor's smile, but it quickly faded on his lips. "I wish it was a social call, Sam." He stood up, extending a hand. "I'm afraid we need to talk."

Holm couldn't remember when he'd had a meal so good... or killed a bottle of Scotch so exquisite. Sam Thomas didn't get many visitors, and he couldn't stand most of the ones he did. But the ornery old Marine was downright thrilled to see Holm, and he'd insisted on breaking out the best. Any Marine could expect to find a warm welcome at Colonel Sam Thomas' house, but Elias Holm was like a son to the old warhorse.

"I followed the whole First Imperium situation, Elias." Thomas extended his arm, pouring the last of the Scotch into Holm's glass. "Your boy Cain did some impressive soldiering there, I'll tell you that much. He's quite a character, isn't he?"

"You've got no idea, Sam." Holm had just decided he'd had enough to drink, but he reached out for the newly-filled glass anyway. "He's like no one else I've ever known. The kid's smarter than both of us combined, my old friend." Holm smiled, thinking, you know you're old when you start calling 50-year old Marines kid. "Erik Cain is the greatest natural military genius I've ever encountered. Except maybe Augustus Garret." Cain had the tenacity to stick with a plan through anything...a focused pigheadedness that helped him persevere through whatever trials he faced. And he was one of the trickiest sons of bitches the old general had ever known. But Holm had never seen anyone able to read an enemy's thoughts like Garret. He'd seen Garret and Cain developing a symbiotic relationship over the last couple years, working together extremely well, even in the most difficult situations...almost like they could read each other's minds. He often felt like the two of them had left the other senior officers behind, rapidly leaping ahead with their planning faster than Holm and the others could keep up.

That didn't surprise him at all…the two of them had more in common with each other than with anyone else in the high command. The rest were good officers, well trained and devoted to duty. But Cain and Garret were creatures of war. Holm wondered if either one of them could live with the absence of conflict. Both of them hated the suffering and death, he knew that. But he couldn't imagine those magnificent minds without the need to constantly strategize and plan. Would they go mad from the inactivity, or would they find another outlet for their brilliance when peace came. If it ever came. That was an eventuality that seemed unlikely any time soon.

"Well that campaign on Sandoval was one for the books." Thomas spoke softly, pulling Holm back from his introspection. He drained the last few drops from his glass, looking at light refracting through the thick-cut crystal. "I think it even topped us on Persis. What do you think?"

Holm was silent, his mind drifting away again, this time back across the years, to another battle, long ago. A sad look moved across his face, but after a few seconds a little smile crawled back onto his lips. "Maybe so, Sam. We didn't have to face the First Imperium back in those days." He paused. "But we did our share of fighting there. I still remember Persis. Every day."

"Me too, old friend." Thomas set his glass down gently. "We lost a lot of good people there. Marines that shouldn't be forgotten, whatever else we wish we could forget. Not ever."

"Not ever."

The two of them were silent for a few minutes, ghostly old faces moving across their eyes. Friends they'd lost years before.

Thomas leaned back in his chair. "So, my friend. I don't get many visits out here, and I can't tell you how good it is to see you." He smiled warmly at Holm. "But you came here for something other than shooting the shit with an old fool Marine…I'm pretty sure of that. Why don't you spill it?"

Holm almost laughed. Thomas had always been very direct, and he was amused to see age had done nothing to change that. "I'm afraid we've got another problem. Another battle, I mean."

Thomas sat still, his face showing not a hint of surprise.

"You mean the attacks on Alliance colony worlds?"

Holm stared at his old friend, a stunned look on his face.

"Come on, Elias. Did you think I wouldn't hear about something like that?"

"I should have known better." This time Holm did laugh. "I don't know how I figured any piece of gossip would escape your ears."

Thomas let out a hearty laugh. "I like farming, Elias, but you can't imagine that's enough to keep me busy, can you?" His broad smile slowly slipped off his face, leaving a deadly serious expression in its place. "So tell me what I can do for you, old friend? You know you just have to ask."

Holm sat uncomfortably, a frown coming over his face. "Sam, I think whatever is happening to Alliance colony worlds is a more extensive problem than we thought at first. A very serious one." He looked up from the table, making eye contact with his companion. "There are over 20 worlds affected now. Whatever informational network you've got out there, I'm sure you haven't heard that."

Thomas had a hard face to read, but it wasn't difficult to tell he was surprised by what Holm had just told him. "My God, Elias...any idea what we're dealing with?" He looked right into his friend's eyes. "One of the other Powers? More than one?"

"Maybe." Holm's tone had become darker, more somber. "We really don't know, Sam." He took a deep breath. "But I know we need help. We can't deal with this ourselves." He paused again. His eyes had been wandering around the room, finally staring down at the table, but now he looked up at Thomas. "Things are much worse than you know. The Corps is shattered."

Thomas breathed in deeply, exhaling loudly. "The Corps is forever, Elias. You know that better than anyone. It always finds a way."

"I've always believed that, Sam." He was still looking into Thomas' eyes, and the old man could see the weakness. Holm had held the Corps together through rebellion, Alliance Intelligence plots, and the brutal war with the First Imperium. But he was close to his wit's end now.

"We lost the Academy during the rebellion…all those cadets, officers who never took the field. And the casualties we've suffered…Carson's World, Farpoint, Sandoval, Sigma 4. Persis was a nightmare, but it was one battle…followed by peace. But now we've been bled dry."

"Where is your strength deployed now?" Thomas' voice had changed in tone. He'd sounded like an old man before, reminiscing with a friend. But that was gone now, and he spoke with the cold rationality of a Marine officer.

"I sent Cain to hold Armstrong." Holm nodded as he spoke. "He's got just about everything battle-ready with him." He paused. "It's not a lot. It'll be a miracle if he can fight off a major attack."

"Cain's in the miracle business, Elias. You know that better than anything. He's earned our confidence by any measure imaginable. You gave him the forces you had…now let him do his job."

Holm nodded. "You're right, Sam. It's just that I keep putting him in impossible situations."

"And he handles them," Thomas interjected. "Save the guilt for later." He paused. "So what else is urgent?"

"Jim Teller's on Arcadia. At least I hope he's still alive. We haven't heard anything since he landed, trying to liberate the colony."

"I've never met Teller, but from what I've heard, he's a good man."

Holm sighed. "One of the best." He paused. "And I have to find the forces to mount a relief expedition. I just don't have the manpower." He looked at Thomas again. "Sam, I need your help. If I don't find some trained troops somewhere, a good Marine and his people are going to die, unaided and abandoned…and one of the most important colony worlds will be lost."

Thomas nodded, seeing where Holm was going. "I'm still handy with a rifle, Elias, but I don't think one old man is going to make a big difference."

Holm smiled grimly. "You're not one man, Sam. How many Marines have retired to this planet? You and I both know every one of them will follow you anywhere."

Thomas had been one of the first colonists on Tranquility. He'd spent more than 30 years of hard work building one of the largest farming complexes on the planet. Tranquility had initially been settled by retired Marines leaving the service after the Second Frontier War, and Colonel Samuel Thomas had been – and remained - the most prominent member of that group.

He'd taken everyone in the Corps by surprise with his retirement. Thomas was one of the great heroes of the Second Frontier War, and most people figured he was on a path that would take him to the Commandant's chair. But it wasn't to be. Something had changed for him during the fighting on Persis, something elemental. He was angry, disillusioned, wanting nothing except peace and solitude. He'd left with the quiet dignity he felt befitted a Marine, but privately he swore he'd never again raise a sword for the Alliance government. And for 30 years he hadn't. Tranquility even remained quiet during the rebellions, and Alliance Gov left it alone. No one was looking to pick a fight with thousands of cantankerous ex-Marines.

"Elias, most of the younger guys already left Tranquility to go back to the Corps." Thomas was thinking as he spoke. "All I could offer you…if anyone even listens to me…is a pack of old men and women."

"If they're old like you, I almost pity our enemies." Holm nodded slightly as he spoke. "Sam, we say it enough, but now I need to ask you to show me they're more than just empty words." He felt a pang of guilt. He had no right to question Sam Thomas' devotion to the Corps. The man had done his service already…far more than his share.

Thomas sat quietly for a minute, a distant look in his eyes, as though he was awash in old memories. Holm was one of the few people who knew why Thomas had left the Corps, and he understood just how much he was asking of his old friend.

"If I had any other options, Sam, I wouldn't be here." Holm spoke softly, sadly. "You deserve to be left alone, to enjoy your retirement and all you fought and worked for."

Holm could see the change in Thomas' eyes. There was sadness there, but something else too. Fire. He could see the tension in the older man's arms, the tautness, the energy coming from someplace deep within.

"I will do what you ask, Elias...recruit as many of the old warhorses as I can." He slapped his hand down on the table. "They're not just words, and you know it well, General Holm." He looked at his friend with a withering stare. "Once a Marine, always a Marine."

Chapter 11

Alliance Intelligence HQ
Washbalt Metroplex
Earth, Sol III

Stark sat quietly at the table, reading the reports on his 'pad as he finished breakfast. He wasn't much of an eater in the morning…just some dry toast and a small bowl of fruit. He didn't usually eat in his office, but things were starting to move quickly, and he'd spent the last couple nights there, grabbing a few hours of sleep before getting back to work early in the morning.

Project Shadow was moving along perfectly. All stage one objectives had been secured with the exceptions of Arcadia and Columbia, and it was only a matter of time until they fell. The Arcadians had been relieved by a small Marine contingent, an unexpected twist, though it was a weak force, enough to cause delays, but too little to turn the tide.

The Columbians were the other ones really defying expectations. He was beginning to think he'd underestimated them. The planet had suffered greatly during both the Third Frontier War and the rebellions, and Stark was coming to realize those experiences had toughened them up considerably. He couldn't help but laugh as he read the report. For all the constant whining about freedom and self-determination from these colonials, the Columbians had given their top military commander dictatorial powers. Everybody wants freedom, he thought, until they're scared…then they want someone to take care of them. He laughed derisively. It wasn't going to help them, though. His forces were too much stronger. The fight might go on a little longer, and casualties would be higher, but Columbia would fall. It had to fall. He was going to need the planet and its resources intact for stage three.

Now it was almost time for stage two. He'd given Augustus Garret only two options that made any sense…deploy his fleet to protect Armstrong, or keep his forces mobile and try to hold the planet with ground troops alone. Garret was a genius, prone to unorthodox strategies, but he would still choose a course of action that was strategically sound. As brilliant as he was, he made his decisions meticulously, and in his current position, that greatly limited his options. Another thought crossed Stark's mind, a dark one that brought a smile to his face. Stranding Terrance Compton and his people behind the Barrier had to hit Garret hard. If anything, he'd be less daring than usual, opting for a safer course. Augustus Garret knew space combat better than any living human being, but unraveling the psychology of adversaries was Gavin Stark's particular brand of genius. Garret might be brilliant at naval tactics, but he was too soft when it came to his people, a weakness Stark did not share. Everyone was expendable to Gavin Stark…nothing mattered but power. His power.

Now it was starting to look like Garret was leaving Cain and the Marines on Armstrong and pulling his ships out. Stark sighed. If he'd been given the choice, he'd have ceded Armstrong in return for tying down Garret's fleet. Naval strength was always the weak spot in Project Shadow, which is why he'd chosen Wolf 359 as the first objective. His people were getting the repaired ships into the line as quickly as possible, but if it came to a straight up fleet engagement against Garret any time soon, Stark was far from confident of victory. He had a number of backup plans for dealing with Garret, but he'd have preferred if the son of a bitch had just parked himself at Armstrong and stayed there for a few months.

Even with his own weakness in naval strength, it wasn't Garret that most worried Stark. Erik Cain was the one he was truly concerned about. Not because he was smarter than Garret; he wasn't. But he was crazier. Cain was the more dangerous opponent because he was less predictable. By all accounts he was as wracked by guilt over expending his people as Garret...but he still did it. Again and again. He would sacrifice huge portions of his force and do things that seemed stupid, foolish...all to gain the element of surprise. Erik Cain didn't fight to win...he fought to obliterate his enemies, to destroy them utterly. As far as Stark could tell, Cain would do anything to win. Anything at all. And he would never stop, never surrender. That was a dangerous man. Stark would do anything, sacrifice any number of lives, to win. Cain was the closest counter to that his enemies possessed.

But now he was where Stark wanted him. Cain was a threat anywhere he went, but stuck on Armstrong fighting a protracted battle, he was contained. Stark didn't fool himself about the casualties his forces were likely to sustain fighting against the Marines' blood and guts commander. But it was worth it to know where Cain was...and to keep him from interfering anywhere else. Stark didn't really need Armstrong, but his adversaries did. His attack there was more of a diversion than anything else. If he took the planet, so much the better. He would deprive his enemies of their main base. But just keeping Cain and the bulk of the Marines' remaining strength there was its own victory, regardless of the final resolution. Stark wanted the battle as bloody as possible...Armstrong would be the graveyard of what remained of the Marine Corps. Win or lose, there would be so few of them left, they'd never interfere with his plans again.

Plus, he had an ace in the hole on Armstrong. He wasn't counting on Alex Linden. He'd once let himself believe she was as coldly sociopathic as he was, but that hadn't proven to be the case. His trust in her had been an uncharacteristic weakness. Stark rarely let anyone affect his judgment, but Alex's sheer sexual magnetism was like nothing he'd ever encountered before. Even though he'd been consciously wary of her, his subconscious proved to be susceptible to her charms. Stark wasn't one to let his prick make decisions for him, but Alex was a wildcat like no woman he'd ever encountered. He doubted she'd ever failed to seduce any man into doing her bidding…or any woman for that matter.

He'd been careless with her, but it wouldn't happen again. Reuniting her with her long lost sister had been a mistake, and the ancient submerged emotions had caused unexpected behavior in his former protégé. He'd done his best to shock her back to her senses, to remind her of the rewards of success and the penalties for failure and betrayal. Now she would have a chance to fulfill her longstanding mission to assassinate Erik Cain. Whether she would do it or not was yet to be seen.

If she did, the battle on Armstrong would be over that much sooner. Without Cain, the Marines would have no chance against his forces. Success wouldn't affect her fate, though. Alex Linden was far too dangerous to leave alive. Whether she killed Cain or not, Stark had no intention of letting her leave Armstrong. He couldn't tolerate anyone who affected his judgment, reached whatever fragments of human emotion remained in his sociopathic mind. And he wouldn't let himself underestimate her. Alex was a viper, and a brilliant and unpredictable one at that. He wouldn't put it past her to kill Cain as ordered and then come back to Earth and try to assassinate him. He wasn't going to give her the chance. No, she would never get off Armstrong.

"Number One, the package has arrived." The voice on the com was cool, unemotional. His new operatives were working out very well. He wasn't sure they had the sophisticated cunning of his veteran field agents, but they were serving their purpose. And they were as secure as possible. They had no backgrounds, no pasts, no unknown weaknesses. They couldn't be blackmailed, seduced, or bribed.

Stark wasn't about to divulge any of the details of Shadow to anyone who didn't need to know. And that included nearly everyone in Alliance Intelligence. With a very few vital exceptions, no one but Stark's new Shadow Team knew anything about the ongoing project.

"Very well. You know what to do." A smile crept onto Stark's lips. The package hadn't been easy to obtain. Unauthorized nuclear materials weren't all that difficult to find, but this batch was very special, and Stark's plans required absolute secrecy. The uranium was from Yosan, one of the CAC's major resource-producing colonies. And it didn't exist, at least not on the production records of the Yosan Mining Corporation.

Certain types of procurement were an art form, and Alliance Intelligence had its share of artists. Unfortunately, the agents who executed this heist so expertly wouldn't have much time to enjoy the rewards of success. The drug was time-released, with a critical reaction period that varied with body chemistry. Some would last a few days, others would be dead by evening. By the weekend, all living links to the theft would be gone, including Agent J, who'd just reported the package's arrival. Stark had always hated loose ends, but he was taking it to an extreme with Project Shadow. Ten years of planning, of herculean effort… it was finally coming to fruition. He wasn't going to take any chances.

The package from Yosan was crucial to stage two, and he felt a small wave of relief that it had arrived. U-235 was basically a commodity, at least with regard to its ability to reach critical mass and trigger a nuclear reaction. But there were subtle differences, and with enough effort, a skilled team could trace the residue from an explosion to the source of the key element.

Stark leaned back and smiled. He wouldn't be part of that investigation. He'd be dead…one of the victims of the CAC plot to destroy Alliance Intelligence headquarters. But he was confident his people, enraged at the attack against their HQ, would quickly trace the fissionable materials to Yosan…and the CAC. His successor would declare Plan Omega immediately, and every Alliance assassin would target a list of designated C1 operatives. It would be total war between the intelligence agencies…and probably between the Superpowers as well. Augustus Garret would find himself ordered to attack the CAC's fleet… and even if he refused, it wouldn't be long before Hong Kong sent its forces against him, forcing the issue. With Garret distracted, Stark would be able to complete stage two by consolidating control over the major Alliance colonies.

The Caliphate would probably ally with the CAC. If they did, Garret would be outnumbered and cut off from his major bases. It would be an almost impossible situation, but Stark didn't underestimate the Alliance's brilliant admiral. He was betting Garret would find a way to win, despite his disadvantages. Stark smiled. Augustus Garret would perform one last service for Stark, clearing away the CAC and Caliphate navies. Then the Shadow forces would dispatch Garret's battered survivors…and Gavin Stark would be on the cusp of total control of human-occupied space.

He drained the last few swallows of coffee and turned to look through the window. There was a smile of satisfaction on his face as he looked out at the towers of the Washbalt Core. He felt a bit odd looking at the familiar skyline. It was something he enjoyed doing, staring out at the kilometer-high spires of the city…but not for much longer, he thought. He didn't expect the Alliance's capital to survive stage three. Total war between the Superpowers was the final act of the great play he was mounting. It was a radical step, one that would almost certainly involve hundreds of millions of casualties. He was about to unleash an unimaginable horror on mankind, but he thought of it only coldly, in logical terms. He would rid himself of the troublesome ruling classes, and sweep away the vast slums full of useless Cogs, those who were nothing but a liability to a modern society.

Yes, he thought, the Superpowers will destroy each other, as they almost did a century before. This time there would be no pact, no treaty to stop the slaughter. Stark would see to that. This time, they would fight their war to its conclusion… and that finish could only be the total collapse of every one of the Superpowers.

It was a plan of vast and unfathomable scope, one that could be the product only of a mind utterly devoid of conscience and human emotion. But it was the only way Stark could be sure there would be no adversary strong enough to interfere with his plans. When Earth's nations had ground each other into dust, Stark would release the rest of the Shadow Legions, almost a million troops, fully-armored and trained to the standards of the Marine Corps. His soldiers would quickly sweep away any battered remnants of the Superpowers' forces…and Gavin Stark would achieve what no human being had ever accomplished. He would be the absolute and unchallenged ruler of all humankind…both on Earth and throughout space. Then he would rebuild the shattered Earth in his own image, an ordered society controlled so rigidly it would be inconceivable for his authority to ever be seriously challenged. Men would do as he commanded, think as he commanded.

His smile widened as he contemplated his ultimate victory, blissfully unaware of the madness consuming him, destroying whatever tiny scraps remained of his humanity.

Chapter 12

Orbital Defense Perimeter
Planet Armstrong
Gamma Pavonis III

A warhead exploded in space. Like most of the bombs used by warships in combat, it was a 4F, a multi-stage fission-fusion-fission-fusion model, a more sophisticated version of the basic design used since the 20th century. When the missile reached the desired detonation point, a highly efficient conventional explosion compressed a shell of U-235, initiating a chain reaction. The initial stage was boosted, with strategically placed packets of tritium gas situated where compression would ignite supplemental fusion reactions.

The localized fusion released neutrons, vastly increasing the efficiency of the fission and increasing the yield enormously. A significant portion of the energy produced was channeled to the primary fusion stage, compressing it, vastly increasing the temperature until a fusion reaction ignited. The fusing hydrogen released enormous additional quantities of high-energy neutrons, which triggered a secondary fission reaction in the normally stable U-238 of the bomb's casing. This energy, in turn, was channeled to compress and heat a second fusion stage, repeating the process. In substantially less than a second, all stages had detonated, producing a combined yield of 573.4 megatons.

The warhead was 6 kilometers from Gimble's HQ fortress. On land, an explosion of this magnitude would have utterly destroyed any physical construct at such a short distance, but in space, without an atmosphere to carry heated air or a shock-wave, the destructive range of the warhead was much lower. A detonation at 6 kilometers was best characterized as a near miss, and the weapon inflicted only minor damage. It bathed the heavy shielding of the orbital station with neutrons and gamma rays, producing a few local penetrations. In those areas, electronic equipment was overloaded and exposed crew received heavy doses of radiation, incapacitating at least and, in many cases, lethal. There were a few secondary explosions inside the fortress, but that was the worst of it.

Gimble sat in his command chair, following the progress of the battle. He hadn't expected to survive this long, but he was still there, and his battlestation was better than 70% effective, despite the massive bombardment. The enemy was going to overwhelm his forces, but it was going to be numbers, not skill that sealed his fate. They may have captured Alliance warships, he thought, but their personnel are nowhere near the proficiency of Garret's navy. His platforms were stationary targets, and despite their extensive point defense, a fleet that size should have taken them out in one barrage, perhaps two. They were in the middle of the third now.

"Prepare to fire all remaining missiles." Most of his forts had already flushed their magazines, but the heavy platforms had one volley left…and Gimble wasn't going to let any of it go to waste. "Concentrate all fire on Concord." It cut at him to fire on an Alliance ship, even if she had been hijacked and crewed by the enemy. But he knew taking out a battleship would hurt more than anything else his people could do. And she was already in rough shape, one of her reactors down and her defense systems highly compromised.

"All platforms report remaining missiles armed and ready to launch." Jones didn't sound as calm as he had before, but for a rookie two hours into an all-out battle, he was holding up pretty well.

"Launch immediately." Gimble gave the order coolly. He was watching the wall of missiles coming at his stations, and he wasn't about to risk losing any weapons in their launchers. "Cut point defense fire in missile transit corridors."

Jones turned to look at Gimble for a second. His expression was doubtful, but he didn't say anything. After a brief pause he replied, "Yes, sir."

Launching a full missile volley required disabling much of a station's point defense to allow the friendly missiles to escape the interception zone. Laser turrets would continue to fire, directed by "friend or foe" targeting systems, but the defensive missiles and shotguns would be silent. They weren't precision weapons, and they were as likely to take out the station's own missiles as the incoming warheads.

Gimble leaned back. He caught a sigh before it escaped his lips. His crew didn't need to see his negativity. The warheads now approaching carried his death with them, he knew that. His and hundreds of his people. He couldn't do anything about it, but he decided no more than necessary would die.

"Ensign, issue Code 2 evacuation orders to all personnel except point defense crews, laser battery gunners and support specialists." The laser crews would get their shots at the enemy if the station survived the incoming barrage. And the point defense would try to buy them that chance. Gimble didn't know if any of them would make a real difference in the battle, but duty compelled him to pursue every option to inflict damage on the enemy. Their jobs sealed their fates. But he was out of missiles, and he couldn't see any reason why those crews…or some steward from the mess hall…had to die.

"Yes, sir." Jones hesitated, surprised. There were no provisions in the regs for a partial evacuation. Crews were authorized to abandon ineffective battle stations, but to leave their friends and comrades behind to die while they climbed inside the escape pods? It didn't feel right. "Code 2 evac in progress, sir."

Gimble sighed…and this time it burst right past his lips. He knew his people wouldn't feel right about leaving some of their number behind, but he was damned if he was going to let them die just so they could feel like they were doing their duty. The station was doomed, and absolutely nothing would be served by keeping the non-essential personnel aboard.

"And ensign…issue the order to all stations." He paused, watching Jones lean over his workstation, transmitting the command. He stared at the young ensign. "That means you too, Ian." He waved his hand across the control room. "All of you. Report to the escape pods immediately. The AIs and I can manage this old rust bucket."

Every eye was on him, but not a crewmember stirred. The control room was silent, except for the soft voices of the AIs making various reports.

"Now!" Gimble slapped his hand hard on the side of his chair. "When I give an order, I expect it to be obeyed!"

The control center crew jumped to their feet, and began moving slowly, reluctantly toward the exit, eyes still fixed on their CO…the man who was saving their lives, even as he sacrificed his own.

"Go!"

The slow move toward the hatch continued, each officer looking back, taking one last glance at their commander before stepping into the corridor.

Gimble didn't return the glances. He stared straight ahead at the tactical display. He didn't know if they'd make it off and to the surface safely, but if they did, he suspected they were far from out of danger. General Cain would almost certainly draft them for some type of duty…and knowing the Marine general's reputation, that could be defending the command post, armed with nothing but frying pans. Gimble didn't know what kind of force was going to land, but he knew Erik Cain would defeat it…or every man and woman on Armstrong would die in the fight.

"It looks just like one of our landings." Cain was speaking softly, to himself more than anyone else. "And where did they get all those Gordons? Who the hell are these guys?" If Cain didn't know better, he'd have sworn he was watching a Marine division landing.

"Sir, the last of Commander Gimble's 'non-essentials' are accounted for. That makes over 1,000 safely evacuated." Isaac

Merrick was standing behind Cain. He thought the C in C hadn't noticed him, but Cain had been watching him since he walked into the room. No one snuck up on Erik Cain. Twenty-five years of battle reflexes and a lifetime of paranoia had given him a tremendous awareness of the space around him.

"Good." Cain's voice was soft, somber. He'd watched Gimble's station blown to bits an hour before. He and his remaining crew fought like caged devils to the last, and one thing was certain. No one else made it off that fortress. Still, the orbital commander had saved a thousand of his people without degrading combat effectiveness. All in all, Cain thought grimly, not a bad last order.

Cain turned to face Merrick. "Let's get them all down to medical before everything goes crazy. Have them all checked out and cleared for reassignment." He paused for an instant. "And download their duty files into the tactical AI. I want recommendations for alternate duty." Cain knew Gimble's people had been through a lot already, but he didn't have the luxury of wasting 1,000 trained personnel. He suspected this fight would come down to the wire, and he was determined to hold Armstrong at all costs. All costs.

He waved for Merrick to go and see to the disposition of Gimble's crews himself. The former federal general nodded and turned to walk back toward the door. He and Cain meshed so well, they barely needed words to communicate.

"Hector, get me an updated strength estimate on the landing." Cain's AI had been with him since he'd left the Academy...more years ago than he wanted to think about. They'd had a somewhat dysfunctional, but highly productive relationship over that entire time. Cain hadn't really noticed, but his electronic assistant had performed exactly as it was designed to, changing to suit the Marine's needs. It had molded to Cain's personality...and evolved over time. The snarky, mildly obnoxious persona that had engaged the young junior officer had slowly changed to a calm and supportive assistant...a match for the older, grimmer Cain.

"It is still difficult to model a specific strength, but assuming

4-6 waves comparable to the first, I would speculate that we are facing a corps-sized force at minimum." Hector's tone changed slightly as he delivered the report.

At least 35,000 troops, Cain thought, shaking his head slightly. Nearly twice what he had...and almost certainly better-supplied. He wondered if the whole force was powered infantry. Certainly the entire first wave landing in those Gordons was fully armored.

"Hector, get me Jack Winton on the line."

The AI replied promptly. "Yes, general." A few seconds later: "Admiral Winton on your line."

"Jack, how's it going down there?"

"Better than you expect, Erik...I'll bet you that much." Winton's tone was cheerful, self-satisfied. "All you needed was a real pro on the job."

Winton had been a transport mogul of sorts on Columbia before he got swept up into the rebellion there. The years of bitter fighting and deprivation had changed him, and he couldn't bring himself to go back to his old life. His daughter, Jill, had suffered terribly as well, spending most of the war in one of the federal concentration camps. She'd endured all she could take, and then she went mad...ultimately leading a group of escaped prisoners on an indiscriminate, murderous rampage. By the time he found her she was almost catatonic, and completely unaware of what she'd done.

Sarah Linden sent her to the hospital on Armstrong for psychiatric care, so when Admiral Garret offered Winton a job there as the navy's chief of logistics, he jumped at it. He'd spent the years since helping with Jill's recovery and honing the navy's supply systems to a razor's edge.

"Numbers, man...I need numbers." Cain almost laughed at his own mock-annoyed tone.

Winton let out a soft chuckle. "Please, mon général, pardon your wayward servant." He paused, but only for a second. He knew Cain was joking, but he also knew the Marine general was not a patient man. "How does 1,177 operational Obliterator suits sound?"

Cain couldn't keep the smile off his face. "It sounds pretty damned good, Jack. I could run down there and kiss you." A short pause. "Great job."

Cain had put the navy's logistical wizard in charge of the rehab operation on the Obliterators. His own people had needed, as he was inclined to put it, "a good kick in the ass." Winton provided that…and he'd scrounged up every type of part or supply the effort required. There seemed to be no material or device Winton couldn't find under some rock someplace on Armstrong.

"Thank you, Erik." Winton and Cain didn't know each other well; their battlefields had been different ones for the most part. But Winton had a lot of respect for the Marine, and he smiled at the general's praise. "We've got them all hidden, as you requested. I had to split them up, but they're all in underground bunkers and shielded against scanning." He hesitated for a few seconds. "When you're ready, they should be one hell of a surprise."

Maybe, Cain thought, his caution outweighing his hope. "Possibly, Jack. But remember, we have no idea who these people are, and it is hardly a secret that we had Obliterator units with us. We can't even guess at what this enemy knows, or what intelligence gathering capability they have." Cain sat silently for a few seconds, thinking. "If we hold the Obliterators back long enough, they may assume we don't have any left…even if they know about them. But a small tactical surprise is all we can reasonably hope for, I'm afraid."

Winton answered after a brief silence. "Still, it's a lot of extra firepower, surprise or not."

"It is that." Cain let a small smile creep across his lips. "And I guarantee the enemy will underestimate them. Not many people have seen upclose what they can do." Especially with Erin McDaniels in charge, he thought. The talented officer had become the foremost expert – the only one, really – in commanding Obliterators on the ground. "And I suspect we will all be surprised at how hard they can hit regular infantry without a bunch of Reapers to deal with."

"General Cain, the leading units of the first wave are projected to land in four minutes." Hector's voice was calm, unchanging.

"Gotta go Jack." Cain was already staring at the tactical display, watching the formations approaching landfall. "I'm counting on your people to keep our supply situation under control. I know you're navy, but I'm officially designating you a Marine now."

"I'll keep your boys and girls fed and armed, Erik." Winton's voice was a little forced...he knew the supply situation wasn't good, especially for a protracted campaign. "Whatever I have to do."

"Thanks, Jack." Cain was already sliding his hands over his 'pad, issuing small repositioning orders to some of the front line units. "I'm gonna hold you to it." He cut the line. "Hector, get me Colonel Brown."

"Colonel Brown on your com, general."

"Coop, are your people ready to go? Looks like we're back in the shit."

Chapter 13

Columbia Defense Force HQ
Weston City
Columbia, Eta Cassiopeiae II

"Die, you scumbag motherfuckers." The tone in Reggie White's voice was almost one of glee as he raked the advancing enemy troops with the heavy auto-cannon. The invaders were fully-armored, wearing Marine fighting suits, but the massive hyper-velocity rounds tore them apart anyway. White and Paine had been falling back steadily with the company, but at each place they'd stopped to fight, he picked a perfect vantage point to maximize his fire. He'd twice run out of ammunition, but General Tyler had been working wonders getting supplies to the front lines…a task that had to be getting easier as the army got pushed back closer to its logistical hub in Weston City.

He was in a foxhole dug into a small hill, less than a kilometer from the city limits. The army had been fighting well, bleeding the larger and better-equipped enemy force. But they were still getting pushed back. They were losing the battle…slowly, perhaps, but still losing.

Corporal Paine was hauling another heavy magazine into position. It wasn't difficult in armor, though he doubted he could have budged the thing without his suit. Paine and White were a great team with the auto-cannon. The two were close friends, and they managed their odd situation well. White was by far the better soldier, a natural warrior who moved across the battlefield like a force of nature. But Tony Paine wore a corporal's stripes while his friend was only a private. Reg White had a temper and a disrespect for authority that had wreaked havoc on his military career.

"We're getting the fallback signal."

"I hear it." White was still firing, ignoring the recall. "I wanna finish this magazine." White tended to consider orders something akin to suggestions.

Paine pulled back the ammunition canister he'd been about to load, reconnecting it to the rack on his armor. It was a cumbersome job. He had to affix it correctly and then sort of back into it until it snapped into place.

The recall signal sounded again. Paine could see the rest of the platoon was pulling back already. "We better get going, Reg." Paine was all for getting as much fire off as possible, but he didn't like the idea of being so far out in front of the unit, especially when they were pulling back.

"With you!" White almost shouted his reply, firing off one last burst before ejecting the spent magazine and snapping up the legs of the auto-cannon. He hooked it into the harness on his own armor, a task as cumbersome as Paine's had been with the ammo reloads. "Get going, Tony. Move your ass. I'm right behind you."

Paine took one more glance at the display, worried that they'd waited too long. But there was a small dent in the line of approaching enemies. White's fire had been so heavy and accurate, the advancing forces had instinctively flowed to the sides, around the edges of his primary kill zone. He slapped his hand on White's armored shoulder and launched himself hard toward the rear.

The ground was open, and the elevation rose gradually for the first 100 meters. There was no cover, nothing to do but run for it. White felt the legs of his suit digging into the soft clay, pushing off with nuclear-powered force to propel his armored body forward. He couldn't run full out, not without bounding up off the ground and giving a perfect target to the enemy, but he could still do at least three times the speed of an unarmored man. He could cover the 100 meters and get up over the hillside in 3 seconds. But that was one second too many. He was looking at the top of the hill as he ran. He felt naked, exposed. He was encased in his suit, sealed off from outside sensations, but his scanner told him enemy fire was zipping all around. Almost there, he thought, just another few steps.

He felt it just before he reached the crest. It was an odd sensation…pain, he supposed, but for so brief an instant he wasn't sure. The suit's trauma control system was more rudimentary than those in the newest Marine armor, but it was still highly effective at dealing with battlefield wounds. It filled his bloodstream with a cocktail of drugs…painkillers, blood coagulants, antibiotics, mood enhancers. He knew he'd been hit, but with the suit's intervention, it wasn't that bad.

It was his shoulder. It didn't hurt, not really…it seemed almost normal after that first instant. But then he realized he couldn't feel it at all or move it. He could hear a hissing sound… his suit administering the self-expanding foam that would serve as both bandage and sutures, stopping the bleeding and stabilizing the wound. It filled the entire arm of his suit, holding the stricken appendage immobile, encased in sterile packing.

His legs felt weak, and he stumbled to his knees…still a few meters short of the relative safety of the hill's reverse slope. He gritted his teeth and pushed hard, dragging himself slowly back to his feet. Then he felt a hard impact on his shoulder, and he was falling forward, stumbling over the crest and onto the ground behind the crest.

White was alongside, still shoving his friend onward, pushing him to the ground, down below the ridge and into a covered position. "You alright man?"

Paine felt a little disoriented, but he recognized White's voice. "Reg…yeah…I'm OK." He wasn't sure how OK he was, but he was alive, and that would do for now. "Thanks for the assist."

"Anytime." White was checking Paine's arm. As a private, he didn't have access to his friend's med system monitors through his display, but he could check the readouts on the outside of Paine's suit. "Maybe think about ducking next time, alright?" He chuckled softly, trying to keep up Paine's spirits.

"Yeah." Paine's voice was getting a little stronger. The suit had the bleeding under control, and it was starting to give him a small dose of stims. "I never thought of that."

"You're gonna be fine, Tony." White's head was moving back and forth between the monitors and Paine's arm. "You fucked your shoulder up pretty good, pal, but it's nothing the docs can't fix."

Paine twisted his body up into a seated position. "We're a long way from any docs, Reg." He straightened up. He was feeling more alert, and his arm was only numb, mildly distracting, but nothing he couldn't handle. It was all drug-induced illusion; he knew that. But it was good enough for now. "We can't stay behind this hill, so help me up, and let's get the hell out of here."

White reached down, supporting Paine's left side as he staggered to his feet. "The only place you're going is the field hosp..."

"Bullshit." Paine interrupted. "You'd never come off the line with a bum arm, and I'm not gonna either. You might have to help me with the reloading, but I can still haul this magazine around."

White opened his mouth to argue, but he changed his mind. Paine was right...the army was fighting for its life, and it needed the best everyone could give. "Alright, man." He tapped Paine's armor on the back. "You're a better soldier than I thought." He smiled to himself, but it quickly slipped off his lips. "Now let's get the hell outta here."

Tyler stood staring at the main display, his cold eyes focused, unmoving. The underground bunker was a lot smaller than the main HQ, and the command staff was cramped and uncomfortable. They had been at battlestations for days, and the room reeked of sweat and stale air. The trash receptacles were overflowing with discarded packaging from combat ration packs.

Columbia's absolute ruler had been silent, reluctant, not wanting to issue the orders to complete the evacuation of the capital. He made sure to project nothing but utter certainty and relentless strength for the benefit of his staff but, in truth, he was conflicted and uncertain.

Should he pull his forces back? Conventional wisdom said yes. He was outnumbered and outgunned, and his troops were catching hell. If he pulled back and played for time, he could ease some of the pressure they were under.

But that's a fool's game, he thought…what's the point of buying a few more weeks if the outcome is the same? No… if he retreated, his army wouldn't find a better position. His people would be relentlessly pursued and defeated piecemeal. And that was something he wasn't going to allow.

"Sir, Eastern Brigade is falling back to defensive positions on the outskirts of Weston." Stillson's voice pulled him from his dark thoughts. He was proud of her…she was holding up well. Like everyone else in HQ, she was exhausted and strung out on stims, but she still managed to sound sharp and crisp. "Colonel Vernon reports heavy casualties."

"Very well, lieutenant." Tyler's voice was soft, distracted. "Vernon is to deploy on the perimeter of the city." He paused. "His orders are to hold at all costs."

Stillson hesitated. "Yes…sir." She'd expected Tyler to order Weston evacuated. The civilian population had been mostly withdrawn already, but the army was dug in everywhere. It seemed pointless to her. She didn't see how they had a chance to hold the capital, and a protracted house to house fight would only destroy the twice rebuilt city."

"I want the civilian evacuation completed at once. No more bullshit." Most of the inhabitants were already gone, but some diehards had refused to leave, and Tyler was out of patience. "Anyone puts up a fight, Major Rentz' people are to hit them with stun blasts and carry them to the transports. He is to be done in an hour…and I mean every civilian gone…I don't care if he has to start shooting people." He paused to add emphasis, though no one who heard him doubted the sincerity of his words. "Then he is to position his regiment in support of Colonel Vernon's defensive line and act as a general reserve." He looked over at Stillson, his eyes glaring. "Understood?"

"Yes, sir." She didn't hesitate again.

He had decided. He was going to fight it out in the capital. His army would stand here…until the bitter end. The war would be decided in and around Weston. If defeat was the fate of his forces, it would happen here, not along some miserable line of retreat. If victory was not to be his, the city itself would be his army's pyre. Either that or…

"Put Captain Crillon's force on alert. Code Black." His eyes were still boring into hers. "Get him on my line. Now."

Stillson swallowed hard. "Yes, sir." Her hand was shaking as she worked the com station, connecting to the army's nuclear artillery commander.

Jack Worth didn't move…he hadn't budged, hadn't twitched, for over an hour. The rest of the brigade had bugged out… as far as he could tell, they were dug in along the perimeter of Weston City. But Worth was hunting, and nothing would interfere with that. He'd find a way, some way, to get back to the brigade when he was done, but first he was going to take down his target. However long it took.

The MZ-40 sniper's rifle was the ultimate tool of the surgeon of the battlefield. Auto-cannons and rocket launchers were outstanding tools for mass killing, dealing out indiscriminate death, but the MZ-40 was a more elegant weapon. Almost half again as long as an assault rifle, the slender-barreled MZ-40 was the bane of senior officers and crucial specialists. In the hands of a skilled sniper, the AI-assisted weapon could take out a target up to 8 klicks distant. And Worth was one of the best.

He'd been stalking his prey for two days. He was a regimental commander at least, and possibly a brigadier. It was hard to tell without knowing the enemy's organizational structure. Either way, he was a choice target, and taking him out was likely to disrupt the enemy's operations more effectively than killing a hundred privates would.

Patience, he reminded himself. Worth had been a Marine, and his mentor there had been a veteran sniper with ten years' experience. Patience. It was what he pounded into Worth's head, over and over. Not marksmanship, not fancy rifles. Patience. Take the time to select your target. Learn his habits…

choose your spot. Plan your effort well...then wait. For as long as it took.

Worth had taken the training to heart. The target was the highest ranking officer he'd been able to identify, and he'd watched his routine for two days. The marked officer inspected this unit every day, and when he did he was visible from here.

Worth was in place, hidden, half-buried in the soft clay behind a pile of boulders. He hadn't fired...shooting now would give away his location. He hadn't even moved. He just waited. It's almost time, he thought. The target should be here soon.

He saw the motion, a small cluster of armored figures approaching. His visor was on Mag 8, and he had a crisp view of them despite his location almost two klicks away. He stared, looking at each figure in turn, trying to identify his target. It was hard to distinguish ranks in powered armor, and officers did nothing to make it any easier. Most armies forbade saluting on the battlefield, and officers' armor was indistinguishable from the suits worn by enlisted personnel. Officer rigs were more sophisticated, with enhanced AIs and communications, but they were identical outside. Anything else would have been a death sentence when facing veteran adversaries.

That's him, Worth thought suddenly. It was a combination of factors...where he stood, how he was gesturing. It was a guess, but it was the best he had. His eyes squinted, lining up the shot. He had the AI set to compensate for the wind, so he was taking a straight shot. Powered armor could do wonders to save a wounded soldier. He needed a dead center headshot to be sure of a kill.

The target moved suddenly. His head turned, and he was looking at something to the rear. He was pointing, probably chewing someone out on his com. Worth was even more certain this was his man.

His finger tensed on the trigger, just like he was trained. Slow, steady pressure, barely enough to overcome the resistance, then...Crack!

The hyper-velocity round cleared the distance to the target almost instantly. Worth saw his victim's head explode into a shower of shattered metal and red mist. "That's a fucking kill." He hissed under his breath, as he popped off another dozen shots into the group. It was time to get away, and he had a better chance if they all had their heads down.

Jed Lucas watched the two blips on his tactical display. Paine and White, he thought…last again. Reg White was the biggest pain in the ass he knew, and he spent half his time wishing the discipline problem was someone else's. Then he looked at the kill numbers, and he remembered the cantankerous soldier was a virtuoso with that auto-cannon. He handled it like it was part of his body, and he'd taken down so many of the enemy, their advances were breaking around his strongpoint, trying to avoid the withering fire. For the last day they'd been trying to get him with mortars, but he picked well-protected positions and moved around often. The son of a bitch was driving them crazy…even more than he did Lucas.

Lucas' people had been in the center of the line since the landing. Casualties had been high, but General Tyler kept feeding him reinforcements. Fewer than half the people he'd started with remained in action, but he was still at full strength. How long the general could keep finding reserves was another question, one Lucas wasn't going to think about now.

They were back on the outskirts of Weston digging in. They had constructed fallback positions here when the enemy first entered the system. They'd hoped to keep the fighting farther from the beleaguered capital, but the enemy was too strong. He'd have sworn he and his people were fighting Marines, but he wouldn't let himself believe these attackers had anything to do with the Corps. He'd been in the line with the rebel forces seven years before, when General Jax and a group of volunteer Marines landed on Columbia. He didn't have a doubt the rebellion would have collapsed without that aid and, as far as he was concerned, the Marines were nothing short of heroes.

He wasn't sure all his soldiers felt that way, though. There were whisperings and conspiracy theories making their ways through the ranks. The invaders wore Marine armor and came

down in Marine landing craft. They maneuvered like Marines…
they fought like Marines. He understood why his troopers had
doubts…but he also knew he'd put down the first son of a bitch
who had the balls to talk shit about the Marines in his presence.

The rest of his people were already in their positions, and
White and Paine looked like they were going to make it back,
despite waiting until well past the recall signal to break off.
Maybe that slug in Paine's arm would teach the two of them
a lesson. Probably not, he thought…but there's always hope.
He'd considered ordering Paine off the line, but if the corporal
thought he could stay, so be it. Lucas couldn't afford to disrupt
his most effective pair of killers.

The icons on the display were heavier on the left side of
the line. Paine and White were on the extreme right, and Lucas
was betting the enemy would come hard on the left. They'd
taken out both auto-cannon teams on that flank and shot up
the squads there pretty badly. But they'd have a surprise waiting. Tyler had sent up two new heavy auto-cannons from the
reserve, and Lucas had deployed them together on the left. One
thing he knew for sure…if the enemy came at that end of the
line they'd run into one hell of a shitstorm. And if they came on
the other flank they'd have to deal with Reg White.

Chapter 14

Warehouse 27 - Tang-Tze Imports
Shanghai Industrial Zone
Central Asian Combine
Earth, Sol III

"I want to thank you for coming, Mr. Vance." Li An's voice was frail.

Vance had been shocked to see how much weaker she was than the last time they met. That was only a few years ago, he thought, surprised to find himself feeling a touch of sadness. Li An had been an adversary more than a friend, but he couldn't help but have an odd sort of respect for her. "It's the least I could do, Minister Li." Vance offered her a smile. "After all, you did come to me last time."

She led him around a large stack of shipping boxes. There was a small portable table set up, with two folding chairs and a single lamp. The warehouse was immense, but it was dark and completely silent. Vance had told Li they needed to meet in complete privacy and secrecy. Looking around, he was confident she'd taken his requests seriously.

"Yes, Mr. Vance. It was a pleasure visiting Mars again. I was there several times in my youth, and the development that has occurred since that time is nothing short of remarkable." She paused for a few seconds. "While our nations have their philosophical differences, I must confess that the Confederation has become something of an economic powerhouse. Your people are to be commended for their industry."

"You are welcome anytime, Minister. Perhaps next time there

will be less need for secrecy, and you can enjoy our amenities."

A fragile smile crept onto her thin lips. "I'm afraid I have seen my last of your fascinating world, Mr. Vance. Time marches on for all of us, and for me it has gone most of its way." Li An's age was one of the great mysteries of the intelligence community. There were a dozen commonly circulated guesses…all of them wrong…and all lower than the actual figure.

"That would be tragic, if true." Vance pulled out one of the chairs, looking over at Li An. "Please, Minister. I'm afraid I cannot stay long, and what I have to tell you is of extreme importance.

She nodded and walked toward Vance, taking the seat he offered. "By all means, Mr. Vance. I am at your disposal." She was extremely curious about whatever problem had brought the head of Martian security – and one of the richest men in the Confederation - to the CAC in total secrecy.

The Confederation and the CAC had typically been suspicious neutrals toward each other in the ongoing rivalries between the Powers, but Vance and Li An were both aware that, despite the stated neutrality, the Martians would side with the Alliance rather than allow the CAC-Caliphate bloc to attain hegemony. That made the two of them, if not enemies, at least something close to that. Yet once before, Li An had provided Vance with vital information. Her discovery that Gavin Stark was holding Augustus Garret hostage, and Vance's subsequent use of that knowledge, had probably saved the rebellions on the Alliance colonies from being crushed. Her interference, subtle as it was, had also destroyed Stark's plans to take total control over the colonial worlds, repaying the hated Alliance spymaster for many past grievances.

"I'm going to come straight to the point, but first, I must have your word that nothing we discuss will leave this room. I am hoping you will assist me in investigating this situation, but no one…" - he stared hard into her eyes – "…no one…can know what I am about to tell you."

"You have my word, Mr. Vance."

Vance sat in the other chair. Li An met most people's definition of a monster, and he couldn't begin to guess how many people she'd killed and tortured in her long career. But as far as he knew, she'd always kept her word once she'd expressly given it. There was a form of honor, even among spies.

"My people have discovered several...how shall I put it? Anomalies? Discrepancies? All regarding Alliance governmental spending." He pulled a miniature 'pad from his breast pocket and slid it across the table. "I must ask that you review this with me here, as it is highly sensitive, and I am reluctant to see copies made." He knew he was trusting her...if she really wanted to, he was sure she could have a hundred agents descend on the warehouse in an instant and take whatever she wanted. "As of now there is just this copy and one other I have hidden in a secure location. This data is not stored on any network or computer system subject to any conceivable security breach."

Li An nodded. "Very well, Mr. Vance. I take your concerns to heart." She'd never seen the cold, analytical Martian spy so nervous about anything.

"You may confirm all of this with your own analysis of the data, but I will summarize it for you now." He was glancing at the 'pad as he spoke. "Quite by accident, my staff and I have discovered a series of inconsistencies in Alliance economic benchmarks." He looked up at Li. "Simply put, it appears that for a number of years...at least 5, and perhaps as many as 8-10, an enormous percentage of Alliance government funds have been diverted...somewhere."

"Somewhere?"

He sighed softly. "My people have been unable to ascertain exactly where this funding has been utilized. The entire process is shrouded in a massive web of dummy agencies and false documents."

"How much money are we talking about?" Li An was a little surprised that Vance would come all the way to Earth to meet with her over some Alliance financial irregularities. All the political masters on Earth stole as much as they could, and if the Alliance had produced someone more gifted at graft than the others, what did it matter?

"This is a rough estimate." He hesitated, looking at her, making sure she was paying close attention. "Our best guess is a cumulative total equal to 350-600% of annual Alliance GDP."

The room was silent. Li An was just staring across the table, looking very much like she thought Vance had gone mad.

"You heard me correctly, Minister Li." Vance spoke slowly, forcefully. "Over the last decade, approximately three and a half to six times the annual GDP of the Alliance has been siphoned off to some unknown purpose."

She sat a few more seconds before she was able to force words from her mouth. "How is that even possible? Such a thing couldn't go unnoticed."

Vance nodded slowly. "That is exactly what I thought when I first came to this conclusion. I would ask you to review the summarized data on the 'pad before you discount what I am telling you." He pushed the small tablet the rest of the way across the table. "This has been an ongoing fraud, one that was brilliantly and meticulously constructed. Secrecy has been maintained through an ingenious series of falsified documents, phony government agencies, and phantom revenues."

Li An would have walked out if she had been sitting opposite anyone else. But Roderick Vance was no fool, nor was he a time waster. If he was sitting in this warehouse, there was something to what he was saying, however insane it sounded. She reached out and slowly picked up the 'pad. She stared at the screen, reading silently.

Vance sat quietly, watching Li An page through the document. After a few minutes she stopped reading and looked up.

"You have confirmed that all of this is accurate?" Her voice was deadly serious, all trace of her earlier frailty gone.

"I wouldn't be here if I hadn't."

"This is difficult to believe." She hadn't read much of the data, but even the few pages she'd scanned had been enough. Virtually the entire economy of the Alliance was one massive fiction…and it had been so for at least six years. She stared across the table at Vance. "The implications of this are staggering. It is astonishing that this secret has held so long…but time is quickly running out."

"My projections vary from three weeks to six months, but in half a year max…and probably much sooner…the entire scheme will collapse, taking the Alliance economy with it."

Li An was trying, with very limited success, to keep the shocked expression off her face. "And it will bring down the rest of the world economy with it in a matter of minutes."

"Seconds." Vance's tone was grim. "I suspect the chain reaction will be almost instantaneous." He looked over at Li An. He'd known this for a few days, and he understood how shocking it was to her.

"This will be the worst economic disaster in history." She glanced back at the 'pad, swiping through another few pages, skimming the contents. "I can't even begin to speculate on where this could lead."

"It will almost certainly cause widespread revolt in every Superpower. When the economic infrastructure breaks down entirely, there will be widespread starvation. Even your well-controlled and carefully monitored lower classes will riot and rebel when there is no food."

Vance knew the economic disruption would hit Mars hard too, but his world wouldn't suffer the same level of social disruption as the terrestrial Powers. The Martian Confederation didn't have a significant underclass, and its population was tiny compared to its wealth and economic output. It had strictly controlled immigration for a century, allowing entry only to skilled professionals, while the Superpowers all had vast legions of oppressed and uneducated workers.

"It will go farther than that." Li An's voice was flat, emotionless. She was imagining the nightmare that would unfold. "It will lead to war, and that will hasten the decline." She paused, looking down at the table. "This could finish the destruction of civilization the Unification Wars failed to complete."

"So you will help me unravel this mystery?"

Li An looked up at Vance. Whatever she had seen fit to do in her career, Li was a patriot. She'd certainly done all she could to build her own power base, but most of her efforts were focused on insuring the CAC remained a strong and viable power...and she shuddered at the thought of all that being in vain. She imagined all she knew, Hong Kong, Shanghai...all the great cities rebuilt since the Unification Wars...lying in ashes again.

"Of course, Mr. Vance." The soft light from the lamp made her moist eyes glisten. "I will do everything humanly possible."

Vance nodded gratefully. "I came to you because I have exhausted all my available resources. I am hopeful that your people have come upon useful information in their day to day duties...data they didn't realize was important because they lacked the knowledge you now possess." He took a deep breath. "We don't have time for a lot of new intelligence gathering, so I would start by tearing apart your existing files. It's hard to believe something of this scale didn't leave any ripples that were picked up by your surveillance activities. Your people just had no context to recognize them as important." He paused. "We both know the CAC spies on the Alliance much more aggressively than my people do."

"I will devote all of C1's resources to this at once."

"I am very grateful." He hesitated, then decided to continue. "I would also point out that the impending economic disaster may well be the least of our concerns." Li An stared at him quizzically, but she didn't say anything. "A sum of money approaching a year's total output of the entire planet is missing." He stared at her, and he knew his mask of calm was slipping away. "That is more than petty corruption. It went somewhere, for some purpose we don't yet understand...and that can't be good."

The room was utterly silent, Vance and Li An just staring at each other. Finally, she opened her mouth, and a single word escaped. "Stark."

Chapter 15

Saw Tooth Gorge
Red Mountains
Northern Territories, Far Concordia
Arcadia – Wolf 359 III

"Cease firing!" Kara's voice was raw and shrill as she screamed into the comlink. Her people were going through way too much ammunition, blazing away at full auto all across the line. The enemy was already running, and she didn't have anywhere near enough supplies to sustain this level of fire.

The enemy attack had been unexpected. The opposing forces had been fixed on their respective sides of the canyon for three weeks, just staring across at each other. She had a pretty good idea the enemy's logistics were fairly strained, but her own supply situation was downright dire. She was going to have to put her soldiers on half-rations very soon…and the ammunition stockpile was even worse.

The enemy's move had been a feint, a spoiling attack to see if her army's morale had crumbled enough that they'd run at the first sign of an assault. Well, she thought, they got their answer. Their forces had barely started down the ragged paths leading from the canyon's edge when her entire line opened up with withering fire. She didn't figure the invaders had given her ragtag army much respect, but they got a lesson they wouldn't soon forget. They turned tail and headed back almost immediately, and by the time they got back to cover, they'd suffered 200 casualties.

Her people kept up their fire after the pullback started, gunning down the retreating enemy soldiers. She didn't have any problem with that – she'd have shot every one of them herself if she had the chance – but they just didn't have that kind of ammo to waste. She'd told them over and over again to fire the minimum amount necessary to turn back an enemy attack. But their blood got up in the battle, and it took her shrieking into the comlink three times to get them to stop.

"I know the troops used too much ammo, Kara, but those bastards won't soon forget what they got today." Ed Calvin came hobbling up behind her, the elation in his voice obvious. "If they think that force over there is enough to finish us off, they are very much mistaken."

Kara turned to face her number two. Calvin knows better, she thought. But she realized that he, like her - like many of her troops, the ones who'd battled their way through the rebellion - fought with the ghost of William Thompson looking over their shoulders. Defeat was as unthinkable to them as it was to her. They had all loved Thompson intensely, and their loyalty was absolute. He had almost single-handedly held them together during the worst days of the revolution. Losing the republic he'd given his life to create, a mere seven years after its founding, was unthinkable to them.

Calvin was grinding his teeth as he spoke. He wouldn't admit he was in significant pain, stubbornly insisting he could barely feel it. The "nothing" in his foot turned out to be two broken bones and a sizable section of torn ligaments, and he'd flatly refused to use up any of the army's limited supply of painkillers.

A tiny smile crossed Kara's lips. Calvin reminded her of Thompson in a number of ways…certainly he was nearly as pig-headed as her lost love. "I know, Ed. We all want to gun down every last one of them." Her voice was mildly scolding. "But if we run out of ammo, we hand them the army, the war, and Arcadia." She motioned around her, toward the army's positions. "Is that what they want? What you want?"

He sighed. "No, of course not, Kara." His voice was sullen, apologetic. "You're right. We may have to ration ammunition allotments after all." They'd discussed that before…reducing the supplies to the troops on the line and keeping a larger central reserve. But that strategy had risks too. If the enemy launched a full scale attack and the troops on the line were caught without enough ammunition, it could be catastrophic.

She stood silently for a moment. "No, not yet." She took a deep breath. "Let's put this on the small unit commanders… make them responsible for controlling ammunition usage." She looked up at Calvin. "We've got good people, Ed. We just need to figure out how to really get through to them."

He was nodding. "I agree, Kara." He hesitated. "And I think you should do it." He felt odd, pushing the responsibility off on her. Officially, he was the army's commander and Kara was just some civilian tagging along. But he knew she was the heart and soul of the army, the inspiration for all the men and women under arms…including himself. No one could get through to the soldiers better than she could.

She smiled, though it took considerable effort. This wasn't what she wanted…the responsibility, the adoration. She wasn't a soldier, and she certainly never expected to find herself in de facto command of an army. She accepted it because she owed it to Will…because she loved Arcadia and wouldn't see it fall while there was breath in her body. She accepted it so her son had a chance at a future free of constant war and suffering. "Set it up, Ed. On the com in 30 minutes. All officers and sergeants commanding platoons."

Calvin stood straight up, not exactly at attention, but something very close. "Yes, Kara. In 30 minutes."

She nodded and turned slowly. He stood and watched her walk away. She does what she has to do, he thought, but she doesn't really understand…she thinks she's here by accident, trying to protect Will's army or her father's republic. "It was Will's army, but not anymore." Calvin whispered softly, sadness and hope mingling in his voice. "It's your army now, Kara…and it will follow you anywhere. This is your destiny."

The rough, rocky plain was littered with armored corpses. Three times the invaders had launched themselves at Teller's troops dug into the mountains…and three times they'd been repulsed with heavy casualties. The Marines had their backs against the wall, but they were fighting like devils. They were trapped and low on supplies, but they didn't falter, not for an instant.

Teller's command post was deep in the abandoned mine complex. It wasn't a very cozy spot, without significant ventilation and highly contaminated by radioactive ores and toxic residues of the mining operation. His people had done their best to turn the place into a fortress, but they'd had no time to make it comfortable. Teller would have loved to have a place he could let his Marines pop their suits, even for a few hours, but it was out of the question. The rad levels in the deep corridors would give an unprotected man a lethal dose in less than ten minutes.

He could hear the sound of metal boots stomping hard on the rocky floor of the access tunnel. Mike Barnes walked into the command post and stopped, snapping to attention and saluting crisply…at least as crisply as possible in armor.

"Cut the saluting nonsense, Mike. Let's just say battlefield conditions apply…" - he looked around the room, making a waving motion with his arm – "…even if we're technically out of line of sight here." Teller had been a hardass for military formalities as a junior officer, but he'd seen too much since then to give a shit about that sort of nonsense.

"Yes, sir." Barnes walked across the room, a medium sized cavern that had been dug out by plasma torch, he guessed. "The enemy has pulled back, sir. I estimate their losses at approximately 300. We had 7 killed and 11 wounded."

Teller sighed softly. "How many of those 11 will survive? We're trapped in these poisoned tunnels…the medics can't even take the wounded out of their suits in here."

"Jim, we'd probably all be dead if we'd stayed on the surface. At least in here we've repulsed three all-out attacks with a casualty differential of at least 10-1."

Teller nodded. "Yes, this is a strong position." He sighed again, clearly unsatisfied.

"What is it, sir?" Barnes could see Teller was concerned

about something.

"Alright, Mike, let me know what you think of this." He cleared his throat. "The enemy doesn't have any armored vehicles or air power. We don't either, but it's because we had to scrape up what we could while the rest of the Corps was off fighting the First Imperium." He paused and turned to face Barnes. "Why don't they?"

Barnes hesitated for a few seconds before answering. "I don't have enough data to give you a good answer, but if you want a semi-educated guess, I'd say they have limited transport."

"Exactly what I came up with." Tanks and aircraft required enormous transport capacity to move from planet to planet. Even large inter-planetary forces tended to field extremely limited quantities of these weapons, and it was entirely plausible a force with an inadequate number of transport vessels might have none at all. "So why no nuclear weapons?"

"Well…again, if I had to guess, I'd say they want the planet intact. That they're here for the long term…as conquerors."

"I agree again." Teller tapped a control switch, and a tactical display appeared on the main screen. "But that's not a physical constraint like too few transports. That's a discretionary prohibition they could drop at any time."

"I'm not sure what you're getting at, Jim."

"Look at the display." The screen showed a rough schematic of the mining complex. "Put yourself in the enemy's shoes. The high command wants you to take the planet intact, so they deny permission for nuclear strikes. We've done the same thing more than once."

Barnes was nodding subconsciously as he listened. He agreed with what Teller was saying, but he wasn't sure where the whole thing was going.

"Then you run into a heavy enemy strongpoint, a position like this one…almost impossible to take in a head on assault. At least a conventional one. What do you do?"

Barnes thought for a few seconds before answering. "Well, if it's a situation like this, I'd cover all the exits and starve them out."

"A siege?" Teller seemed to be rambling a bit, but his voice was totally focused. "Of course...that's what I'd do too. Your enemy is dug in with limited supplies. Powered armor can recycle piss and shit with remarkable efficiency, but they can't hold out forever without resupply." He angled his head, looking up at Barnes. "So you lay siege."

Barnes didn't say anything...he just looked down at the seated figure of Teller, wondering what the general was getting at.

"So you're going to starve them out. Having made that decision, do you send in a heavy assault? And, after it turns into a bloody mess do you send another? And another?" His volume was rising, not quite a shout, but loud nevertheless. "Because that's what they've done. Does it make sense to you?"

"No, not really." His voice was tentative...then realization crept into it...firmness. "Unless you had serious time constraints. Some deadline to completely pacify the planet."

"Or maybe you're concerned about pinching out the defenders before they are reinforced." Teller softened his tone. "Holm and Cain and the rest of the Corps will get back from Sigma 4 eventually. And these guys need to have the planet totally under control so they can mount a defense if the Corps invades and tries to take it back. Otherwise, they'll have hostiles behind their backs, while three-quarters of their strength is tied up manning siege lines around an enemy fortress out in the middle of nowhere...far from the inhabited areas of the planet."

"OK...I agree with everything you're saying." Barnes' voice was steady, but there was confusion there too. "But what does that have to do with nukes?" Even as it came out of his mouth, realization was starting to set in.

"What do you do in the situation we just laid out? If you were at the top?"

There was a short pause before Barnes blurted out his answer. "I'd authorize a nuclear attack on the mountain. It's far away from anything useful, and a localized attack won't materially damage the planet. These mines are even played out. There's nothing worth a damn for 300 klicks around here."

Teller stood up slowly, looking right at Barnes. "So unless we make the extremely baseless assumption that a large invasion force trained, armed, and equipped to Marine standards lacks any nuclear arsenal whatsoever…"

"We better expect a nuclear bombardment." Barnes finished the thought. "We might be able to go deeper, get our command and control down to a survivable level, but the guys manning the defenses will be sitting ducks. And if we pull them down too, the enemy will just follow us, and we'll have a running battle underground. That'll just be a bloodbath for both sides…and their numbers will tell."

Teller reached out and put his gloved hand on Barnes' shoulder. "But if they've got some 50 megaton bunker busters in their supply train we're just…"

"Fucked." Barnes finished the thought again.

The general stood in the center of the control room, his enormous bulk clad in a charcoal gray duty uniform. He was a massive bear of a man, and overweight besides. His figure dominated the room, almost oppressively. He was staring at the tactical readout on the main screen, considering the situation on the ground.

Raphael Samuels had been the Commandant of the Marine Corps, a position he had only been able to obtain with the aid of Gavin Stark. He hadn't been fully aware of the form that aid would take until two of his rivals for the position turned up mysteriously dead. Then it was too late to go back.

That deal with the devil came back to haunt him, leading him farther down a path controlled by Stark, one that eventually forced him to become the greatest traitor in the history of the Corps. His treachery brought considerable rewards, including enormous wealth and a spot on the Alliance Intelligence Directorate. Now he was the field commander of another fighting force, the Shadow Legions. And the most hated figure in the history of the Marine Corps.

"Is this report reliable?" Samuels was surprised. He didn't see how Elias Holm had managed to put another strike force together, not with the strength Cain had taken to Armstrong. The Corps had been gutted by the rebellions and the war against the First Imperium. There just weren't that many Marines left to fill the ranks.

"Yes General Samuels." Like all the Shadow troopers, his aide was utterly disciplined and well-trained, if a little deadpan and boring. They were just like the Marines, he thought, but without the difficult personalities. There was uniform quality across the ranks, an almost unrelenting sameness, even between officers, non-coms and privates. They were extraordinarily competent, but they were missing something, the spark that powered true brilliance. He doubted they would produce any Erik Cains or Elias Holms, but he'd put their rank and file up against any outfit the Marines cared to send his way.

Damn, Samuels thought, bringing his attention back to the current campaign. If we're going to have to defend against another Marine landing, I want Teller's people dealt with first. His troops were already fighting both the remnants of the native army and Teller's force…the last thing he wanted was a third front.

The Marines were an unexpected factor. James Teller may have run off half-cocked and gotten himself in trouble, but he'd also thrown a wrench into Samuels' plans. The entire incursion had been a complete surprise, allowing Admiral Davis' task force to fight its way to the planet and cover Teller's landing. The naval units had since been overwhelmed and destroyed, but the Marines on the ground had put up a stubborn fight, drawing strength away from the pursuit of the Arcadian forces. Samuels' troops had contained the natives, but they'd had to divert most of their strength to face Teller's army, leaving insufficient forces to finish off the Arcadians. Now they were up into the really rough terrain, and it was going to take a lot more effort – and a good portion of the troops currently facing Teller - to root them out of the hills and destroy them. Unless he got rid of the Marines immediately and reinforced his troops facing the Arcadians, he'd end up with that third front for sure.

He sighed. Arcadia wasn't supposed to be this difficult.

He'd expected to be long gone by now, the planet conquered and pacified. Instead, he'd been tied down in orbit dealing with the fallout from Teller's intervention instead of accompanying the strike force heading for Armstrong as planned. And that force was going to fight Erik Cain…if there was someplace he needed to be, it was Armstrong. If there was going to be trouble somewhere, he'd expected it would come from the Corps' stone cold killer himself.

Maybe, he thought, Admiral Liang could beat back the invasion force and prevent Holm from landing. He clung to that hope for a few seconds, but he knew it was unlikely. Garret had not taken the bait to remain at Armstrong…he was on the loose somewhere. His ships would almost certainly accompany Holm's transports. And Admiral Liang would never risk the Shadow Fleet in a straight up fight with Garret's full strength. Indeed, he'd already begun withdrawing all of the damaged ships that could be moved so they wouldn't fall back into Garret's hands if he retook the Wolf 359 system. Stark had been very clear that Liang was to be extremely cautious with the Shadow naval strength, and both Samuels and the admiral were scared to death of Garret and what he might do.

So Samuels had to assume Holm would get through and land his forces on Arcadia. He'd have to beat them on the ground. His hands felt cold and clammy as he rubbed them together. His ego wouldn't allow him to realize how scared he was at the prospect of facing Elias Holm. Samuels was a capable general, but one whose ambition and narcissism had too often overridden his judgment. But his rational mind knew Holm was a brilliant general, one whose skills he could never match. One thing he knew for sure…he wanted every possible advantage in the coming fight.

He turned toward his aide. "We need to blast Teller's people out of that fucking mountain." He spoke loudly, angrily. "I'm authorizing ten 75 megaton warheads for use on the position." Stark had told him to avoid going nuclear if possible, but he hadn't forbidden it…and Samuels couldn't think of another way to finish off Teller in time. The mountain was in a remote area, and its destruction wouldn't damage anything productive or populated.

He was tense, his hands balled up into fists at his side. "Attack to commence at once."

"Yes, sir." The aide stood rigidly at attention and snapped a textbook salute before turning and walking swiftly from the room.

"What the hell are we doing back out here?" Handler was crawling forward, trying to stay below the tiny fold in the ground. The whole force was breaking out, abandoning the entrenched position and exiting the mines on the far side of the mountain.

"I don't know, Tommy." Greene was right behind his friend. The whole company was strung out in single file, crawling through the boulder-strewn badlands. "But I'd rather be here than with Simonson's group." Captain Carl Simonson had drawn the rearguard. His people were kilometers away from the rest of Teller's command, holding the original position and trying to look like the whole force. It was a crucial mission if the army was going to successfully get away without crippling losses, but not one with great survival prospects.

Handler pushed his arm forward, twisting his body hard to move himself ahead. His suit was on reduced power...all part of the plan to stay undetected for as long as possible. That made crawling slow and tiring work.

"You think we'll make the objective before they spot us?" Greene's voice was strained, his breath labored from the exertion.

"I doubt it." Handler sounded slightly better, but he was also tiring quickly. "It's what? Another four klicks?" He paused, taking a deep breath as he did. "That's two, three hours at this speed?" They'd been crawling for kilometers, heading toward a rocky ridge with orders to occupy and fortify the position. From there they would cover the withdrawal of the rest of the army. Then it would be their turn to hold until the last of Simonson's people made it past.

They crawled almost another klick, one slow, aching meter at a time. Handler reach out again to pull himself forward when his arm lightened considerably. It took him a second to realize his suit had gone to full power. He glanced at the tactical display. Troops were pouring out of the tunnels, running at full speed. They were spotted immediately, and sporadic enemy fire began raking across the open fields.

"Simonson's people. What the fu…" Handler never got to finish his question.

"Attention all forces…Code Orange. Repeat…Code Orange." It was Teller's voice on the com. "All personnel are directed to take any available cover immediately."

"There's your answer, Tommy." Bill Green's voice was tense, edgy…but he was holding it together. He and Handler were still rookies, but they both knew Code Orange meant an imminent nuclear attack.

Handler was looking around, eyes darting from his visor to the tactical display and back again. "Behind that hill," he shouted on the unitwide com, pointing. "Take cover behind that hill."

He slapped Greene's armored back and took off, running as hard as he could without bounding up too high. He glanced at the display…he didn't have any command authority, but most of the platoon was following him anyway. The hill was pretty steep, and the reverse slope would provide decent protection, even against a nuclear shockwave. The crest ran almost parallel to the old position, giving the maximum possible cover if ground zero was the mountain stronghold.

There was sporadic fire as they ran. The enemy wasn't pursuing…most of them were breaking off and heading for their own cover. Still, they were picking off a few of the fleeing Marines as they ran. Handler saw one go down. It was a corporal in one of the other squads.

He was rising now, running up the hillside…almost to the crest. He saw another casualty on his display. Then another. He threw himself over the top of the hill to the shelter of the reverse slope.

He'd pushed off too hard on the final lunge, and he lost his footing and tumbled down the steep hillside. He reached out, the gloves of his armor digging into the muddy ground, slowing his fall. He ended up at the base of the hill, lying on his back. He saw Marines hopping over the crest...dozens of them...maybe a hundred. It looked like the whole company, at least, had followed him.

Then his visor went dark. At first he thought he must have damaged his suit, but one glance at the readouts told him what had happened...and an instant later he heard the first massive explosion. Then another. And another.

He lay still, instinctively trying to force his body lower, into the ground itself. He could hear the titanic winds, feel the shockwaves radiating out from the mountain. The ground shook hard, and he felt his body rocked back and forth in the soft mud. The hillside was shielding him from most of the effects, as missile after missile impacted into the ground, each unleashing thermonuclear fury on the mountain fortress.

His visor reactivated. It had done its job, saved his vision from the blinding flashes of the detonations. The last of the warheads had exploded, and his AI restored his view of the outside. The visor was still heavily shaded, but Handler could see the scene unfolding before him.

He was lying flat, looking up at the top of the hill. Beyond, in the direction of the mountain, there were huge, billowing plumes, smoke and fire, rising sixty kilometers into the reddish sky.

Chapter 16

CAS Kublai Khan
Approaching Planet Shintai
Omicron 11 System

Fleet Admiral An sat quietly on Kublai Khan's flag bridge, watching his staff efficiently performing their duties. A pall hung over them all, one that dampened the joy at defeating the First Imperium invasion and returning home. The CAC's Grand Fleet contingent had left almost half its ships and crews behind. Some had been destroyed in battle, but most were trapped when Admiral Garret detonated the massive alien bomb in the warp gate, stranding hundreds of ships…and thousands of naval crew…in the X2 system.

It had been two months, but the pain was still sharp. In many ways, he thought, it would have been easier if the lost ships had just been destroyed in battle. That feeling didn't make sense…at least there was a chance the stranded fleet had found a way to survive. But he realized it was true nonetheless. For those who returned without friends and comrades, there was no closure, just an open wound, and a constant uncertainty.

It felt strange to be back in CAC space. For three years An Ying and his people had fought alongside Augustus Garret and the Alliance fleets, waging a desperate battle to turn back the deadly forces of the First Imperium. Now they were back where they had started, almost as if nothing had happened, though he doubted things would ever be quite the same. The last few years had changed them all, in ways he suspected none of them could fully understand.

An had spent all his long career fighting against the Alliance and its allies, and now he felt a bit lost, confused. Augustus Garret had proven himself not only a brilliant naval commander, but also a courageous and trustworthy ally. An was well aware of the political forces driving relations between the Superpowers, and the virtual inevitability of renewed rivalries. He wondered whether the knowledge that mankind was not alone, that there were immense dangers waiting out in space, would alter the trajectory of international relations, or if his beloved CAC navy would once again find itself facing off against Garret and his people.

His initial hope had since given way to pessimism. There was already tension between the Powers…no open war yet, but An could see that the conflict with the First Imperium had done nothing to eliminate old rivalries and suspicions.

He'd prayed for one thing…that if his navy was forced once again to go to war against the Alliance, it happen after he was gone. He didn't want to see such a tragedy, and he vastly preferred death to sitting in his chair issuing the orders for the fleet to move against their new friends. He would give those orders if he had to…he'd served the CAC navy for 80 years, and his loyalty was absolute. He would follow whatever commands Hong Kong issued…no matter what it cost him personally.

"Admiral, six vessels have just transited via the Beta-16 warpgate." Commander Qin had proven to be a talented aide. An fully intended to see him promoted to captain and given a good command when they returned to base. "Two Luhu-class courier vessels and four Kilo-class light transports."

An looked down at his own screen, reviewing the same information Qin had just provided. That's strange, he thought…I wasn't expecting any contact yet.

"Incoming message, sir." Qin was staring at his workstation, relaying the communique as it came in. "To Fleet Admiral An Ying, from Ambassador Lin Tao. We have been dispatched by the Committee to provide a fitting welcome for the heroes of the recent war. We will be presenting decorations to you and your senior commanders, and we bear a proclamation of thanks from the Committee, to be entered into the service records of every crew member in the fleet."

An leaned back in his chair. It was odd, he thought, that no word had been sent ahead of this delegation. His ships had been back within the CAC's interstellar communications network for days now. For that matter, he wondered, why not wait until the fleet was back at base?

"Thank you, Ambassador Lin." An felt a strange discomfort, but he ignored it. Nothing like the First Imperium crisis had ever happened before, and he told himself he shouldn't be surprised at an exaggerated response by the Committee. Ceremony had always been important in the CAC, and this time the Committee members had actually been afraid for themselves instead of simply moving chess pieces around a board. Perhaps it wasn't surprising for them to overdo it a bit. "I look forward to greeting you."

An tried to put his concern aside, but his doubts continued to nag. He didn't know any ambassador named Lin Tao. He stared at the floor for a few minutes, wondering again why he was so unsettled. He hardly knew every functionary from a well-connected family the Committee might draft as an envoy.

An turned to face Commander Qin. "Projected time until docking?"

Qin leaned over his screen for a few seconds. "We are close to their entry warpgate, sir. Estimated time to match velocity and dock, 46 minutes."

He stood up slowly. "I will be in my quarters, commander." He turned and walked toward the door, glancing up at the chronometer. The older he got, the longer it took to wedge himself into his dress uniform.

"Is everyone clear on the plan?" Xu Wei wore the ceremonial dress of a CAC ambassador, all silks and embroidery...but beneath was a skintight suit of flexible body armor and two miniature auto-pistols strapped under his arms. His entourage, all attired as diplomatic functionaries, were outfitted the same way, as were the teams on the other five ships. Xu was part of the Black Dragon Corps, Li An's most elite team of assassins, and he was there not to celebrate and reward old An Ying, but to execute a purge against him and his command team. Xu didn't know what An had done…he didn't know if the old man had done anything at all. That didn't matter to him. C1's director had ordered a purge, and that meant An Ying was already dead. Xu and his team were just here for the formality of stopping the old admiral's heart from beating.

The proscription list had 47 names on it, officers currently posted on six different ships. All were expecting to receive medals and citations for their parts in the war against the First Imperium. It was better this way. A bit of deception, and the whole thing would go much more smoothly. It wasn't Minister Li's way to give powerful targets warning. Far too dangerous.

"Docking in two minutes." The ship's AI had a female voice, an interesting choice since there were few women serving on CAC warships.

Xu felt the urge to check his weapons, but he'd already inspected them twice. They were carefully situated, undetectable to anyone looking at him. It took a long time to get them that way, and he wasn't about to dishevel everything so he could do a needless third check.

"One minute to docking."

Xu rolled his head around on his shoulders, trying to force out the ever present kinks. He'd spent far too long in the acceleration couches, and his body was feeling it. Whatever the reasons behind these executions, Li An had ordered it done as quickly as possible, and that meant Xu and his people spent the entire trip being bloated and crushed as the ships constantly accelerated and decelerated.

"Thirty seconds to docking."

He ran his fingers along the smooth edge of the polished wood box in his hand. The finely crafted container held the medals for the ceremonies. His team was going to execute almost four dozen officers from six different vessels. Synchronization was crucial to avoid any unnecessary resistance or disruption, and Xu's people were equipped to maintain the deception to the very last.

The ship shuddered slightly as it docked with the massive battleship. It took a few minutes for the crews of the two vessels to check the seals and get the hatches open, and Xu used the time to get his people organized and ready. They walked through the airlock in single file, and into the massive bay of the capital ship.

Lined up on both sides of the delegation were CAC Marines, standing at rigid attention in their brown and gold full dress uniforms. At the end of the honor guard stood an old man, slightly stooped over, but still stout. He wore the white uniform of a CAC admiral, and his chest was festooned with a riotous mass of medals and ribbons. A cluster of aides and junior officers surrounded him.

Xu walked up to him and bowed his head slightly. "It is a pleasure to be aboard, Admiral An."

The wardroom of the courier vessel Chou had been modified...hastily turned into a fitting space for the awarding of the CAC's highest military citations. Xu's people had greeted Admiral An and his staff aboard Kublai Khan, but the actual ceremony would take place on the diplomatic vessel...as on the other five ships of Xu's flotilla. The last group had arrived on Chou; all of the designated personnel were present onboard.

Admiral An stood in the center of the crowd of officers, wearing an impatient expression. Medals and awards were extremely important to an officer's career in the CAC, but An was old and at the top of the chain of command already. The last thing he wanted to put up with now was more useless pomp. Still, it would be good for the younger officers' careers, and he was glad to see his people recognized for their valor.

The awards were set out on the table. An had seen them already. Xu had brought them aboard during his tour of Kublai Khan, giving the officers a sneak peak during the series of interminable receptions protocol demanded.

Everyone present had drinks in their hands, clustering around and speaking with each other while they waited for the

ceremony to begin. Xu and several of his people had been cir-
culating, chatting with An and some of his officers.

"I can only imagine what it feels like to engage a First Imperium taskforce." Xu had urged An to share some war stories
and, after a bit of prodding and a second drink, the old admiral
was only too happy to oblige. Xu listened patiently before raising his hand slightly. "Now if you will excuse me, I believe it is
time to begin."

Xu walked to the front of the room and climbed two steps
to the top of the small rostrum. He glanced over to the side,
nodding almost imperceptibly as he did. A few seconds later,
two hatches opened on opposite sides of the room, and fully
armed security officers marched in.

"What is the meaning of this?" There was bewilderment in
An's voice...then anger. "I demand you explain this immediately, Ambassador Xu."

"I am afraid, Admiral An, that there has been a change in
plans. By order of the Chairman of the Central Committee, the
16 naval officers present are hereby charged with high treason.
It is further stated that the officers so named have been tried in
absentia and convicted on all counts."

An's face was twisted in rage. The other officers were bab-
bling incoherently or shouting out, protesting their innocence,
but An just stood, almost silent. Two words escaped his lips, a
name, and he spoke it like a curse. "Li An."

"All convicted officers are hereby stripped of rank and position...and sentenced to death." His pretense as ambassador fell
away, and he spoke in icy tones, not an ounce of empathy or pity
for the victims. "Sentence to be carried out immediately."

The agents were moving into the mass of officers, grabbing
them by the shoulders, shoving them to the side of the room.
Each of them was forced down to his knees, facing the wall.
Some of them were silent, resigned to their fate. Others struggled and tried to wrest free of the grasp of their captors. A few
broke down in sobs and begged for their lives.

An agent stood behind the first captive, placing his pistol
against the back of the man's head. Without a word, he pulled

the trigger. The prisoner's head jerked forward as his body convulsed, a spray of blood and brain splattering against the bulkhead.

The executioner pulled his arm back and stepped to the side, positioning himself behind the next target and, with equal lack of ceremony, pulled the trigger again.

It took less than five minutes to execute 15 of the 16. Admiral An stood silent in the center of the room, aware he had no chance of escape and equally unwilling to give Li An or her killers the satisfaction of seeing his fear. He knew another 31 of his officers were being killed on the other ships of Xu's squadron, but he wouldn't let his murderers see his despair either.

"Mr. An…" - the man who had executed the others stood silent and still…it was Xu himself speaking now - "…please kneel." An wasn't technically an admiral anymore, his rank having been stripped from him. He wasn't sure if denying him a death as a naval officer was some special added spite from Li An or if it was just window dressing, designed to add an appearance of legitimacy to her purge. He couldn't recall offending the miserable old bitch in any significant way, so he suspected it was the latter. The head of C1 planned things meticulously. He could only imagine the file she'd invented to justify this massacre.

"Mr. An…" Xu put a little pressure on the old man's shoulder, guiding more than pushing him down.

He bent his head forward. There was no point in saying anything. C1's trained killers were impervious to pleas for mercy. He didn't know whether Li An found or created her reptilian servants, but he knew better than to trade his dignity for a futile attempt to gain a reprieve.

"Let's get this over with." He shoved back the fear and put all his strength into keeping his voice strong and defiant. He tried to hold his body rigid, but his strength failed when he felt the cold of the pistol's barrel against his neck, and a single shiver ran down his spine. He was breathing heavily, eyes closed. Memories flooded into his mind, an odd assortment…95 years of life condensed into a few seconds. He could hear his heart pounding in his ears. It was only 2 or 3 seconds, but it seemed to drag on and on.

Then there was a loud crack, and it was over.

Chapter 17

Great Sentinel Forest
Planet Armstrong
Gamma Pavonis III

The tree was massive, a gargantuan tower a thousand years old, but the auto-cannon's hyper-velocity rounds blasted it to sawdust in an instant. A huge section simply ceased to exist, and the 100 meters above came crashing down, slamming into the ground with an earsplitting crash.

The giant trees produced some of the most sought after hardwood in all of the Alliance, finer than Earth's most exquisite walnuts and African Blackwoods…even before those species had been driven to near extinction by pollution, war, and mismanagement.

Armstrong's great forest was one of the planet's most treasured resources, strictly managed and protected…but now its western half was a battlefield, and the priceless hardwoods were ravaged by the scourge of war. Huge swaths of the deep forest were on fire, the conflagration spreading rapidly in the high winds. On the ground, Marines battled the invaders, the two sides spread out in opposing skirmish lines.

"More reports coming in, sir. Captain Santi's people are retreating." Corvus' tone was sharp. He'd only been halfway through his course at the Academy when Colonel Storm picked him as his aide. The duty came with an immediate commission to lieutenant's rank…and a workload the likes of which he'd never imagined.

Storm was standing right next to Corvus, looking out at the

trees in front of the command post. He nodded, but he didn't say anything, just continuing to stare off into the blackness of the forest.

Colonel Eliot Storm was one of the next generation heroes of the Corps, a protégé of Cain's, just as Erik and Darius Jax had been of Holm. He'd served on the steppes of Sandoval, supporting Isaac Merrick's tank corps. Both the armored battalions and the Marines suffered massive losses in their death struggle with the First Imperium, but they were instrumental in achieving Cain's victory there, and turning the enemy assault back.

Corvus had been there too, a sergeant who ended up in command of a company. His people had been cut off for six hours, surrounded and under relentless attack. By the time the relieving forces broke through, the company was down to Corvus and two other survivors, the three of them manning their own scavenged auto-cannons and fighting like wild men.

After the battle, Storm went with Cain's army to the Rim, but Corvus was sent to the Academy instead. He'd begged to go on the campaign, but Storm and Cain held firm. The Corps was going to need trained officers badly, and Corvus was an ideal candidate to become part of that new cadre.

"Major Danton's 1st Battalion is holding, but he reports heavy losses." Corvus looked up from his portable workstation toward Storm. "He requests permission to commit the 2nd Battalion."

Storm remained silent for another moment. Danton's not a nervous officer, he thought...if he's asking to commit more strength his situation is probably pretty damned bad. "Permission denied," Storm finally croaked.

Corvus hesitated. "Sir…"

"Permission denied, lieutenant." Storm's tone was sharp… not angry, but not inviting additional discussion either.

"Yes, sir." Corvus turned to his com unit and relayed Storm's order. He paused for a few seconds. "What about Captain Santi, sir? His forces are falling back all across the line."

Storm let out a long exhale, so hard it momentarily fogged up the inside of his visor. "Order the 2nd Training Battalion forward." Storm's voice was halting, somber. The training battalions had been formed from the recruits at Camp Basilone who hadn't received powered armor yet. They were partially trained and completely ill-equipped for a battlefield full of powered infantry formations. Sending them forward, he thought, is no better than murder. But he needed every bit of strength he could find. He saw Corvus hesitating again. "You heard me, lieutenant."

"Yes, sir."

I don't like it either, Storm thought, but I just can't commit any more front line units this early...we need to buy some time. We're going to need those reserves...I know it. "This game has just begun, Jeff." He spoke to his aide, his voice conciliatory, understanding. He empathized with Corvus' discomfort. It would be a miracle if 20% of those men and women came back...but that's where he needed them. "Now give the order."

"Colonel Storm's forces are being pushed back through Sentinel Forest, sir." Captain Claren had been Cain's aide throughout the Sigma 4 campaign. He had a good sense of what details the C in C wanted, and he usually managed to report them before Cain asked. "They're giving ground, but slowly."

Cain nodded. "Thank you, captain." He leaned back and sighed softly. He was going to have to reinforce Storm. The forest was massive, and he was counting on it holding up the enemy advance. If they got through the Sentinel, they'd be out on the open plains, less than 50 klicks from Astria. The terrain in the Sentinel was rugged for a major axis of advance, and he hadn't expected this big a push there. The enemy had surprised him, and he cursed himself for his blindness.

He looked down at the large 'pad on the table, checking Storm's unit statuses. He shook his head slowly as he read. Storm had been feeding his reserves in slowly, and he still had a reaction force uncommitted. Cain sighed softly. Storm had used his unarmored training battalion to support his powered infantry forces while he kept stronger units in reserve. Ill equipped for the front lines, the fresh troops fought bravely. They did manage to disrupt the advancing enemy formations, but at an enormous cost. The shattered force was hastily retreating, leaving at least half their number on the field.

Erik sighed again, feeling a pang for those half-Marines, men and women so poorly prepared for what they'd been compelled to do. There was a scowl on his face, but it wasn't anger with Storm for making the decision he did. It was acknowledgement that he would have done the same thing. Cain knew there had been a time when he couldn't treat human lives as variables in some mathematical equation, but he didn't remember it. He had 18,000 Marines and support soldiers and almost a million civilians…all his responsibility. If he had to send 400 men and women to certain death to save the rest he would. War had flags and banners and stories of great valor, but in the end, a lot of it came down to math.

"Hector, get me Colonel Storm."

Claren leaned forward and ran his hand across his 'pad. "On your line, sir."

"General Cain." Storm sounded tired, but overall in pretty good shape, considering what he was dealing with. "What can I do for you, sir?"

"You're planning a counter-attack, aren't you?" Cain could see it in the units Storm was holding back. "I know I gave you a free hand, but you should check in on something like this." He paused for a second. "I might even be able to help."

"Sir…I have been doing the prep, but I was going to ask permission before launching the attack."

"Relax, Eliot, I'm not upset with you." Cain's mind was racing, trying to decide what forces he could pour into Storm's counter-attack. He considered sending a couple companies of McDaniels' Obliterators, but he rejected that idea immediately. He wanted to keep them hidden and release them all in one massive stroke. It wasn't worth showing even a few of them to the enemy until he was ready to make it count.

"I'm sending you 10 of the special action teams, Eliot." He wanted to send more, but he didn't dare spare anything else… not this early in the fight. "Use them as infiltration units on the front of the assault. They're all marksman-rated, and they'll run wild in terrain like that forest."

"Thank you, sir." Storm paused. "General, when do you want me to launch the attack?"

"Whenever you think is right, Eliot. You're on the scene, not me." Cain knew he had a reputation as a control freak but, in truth, he tended to give considerable latitude to subordinates he trusted.

"Very well, sir. Thank you."

Cain cut the line. "Hector, get me General Merrick." He'd sent his chief of staff with Cooper Brown to reconnoiter the ground to the south and east, around the Graywater. The enemy was bringing their third wave down behind the big river. It seemed like an odd place to deploy, and that made Cain nervous. He wanted Merrick's analysis as soon as possible.

"Yes, general." Merrick voice was ragged.

"What is it, Isaac? You sound tense." Cain held off asking anything else…he wanted to know what was going on up at the river.

Merrick paused, trying to decide whether his idle speculations were well-founded enough to report to Cain. "I'm not sure, sir. I just don't like the look of this wave. We were wondering why they were coming down where they'll have to cross the river to move on Astria, but now I'm not so sure they are planning to advance at all. It looks like they've got some heavy equipment over there. I'm launching a flight of drones to get some closer intel to back up my guesses. I'm wondering if this is some kind of divisional artillery battery. It looks an awful lot like one, and I'm thinking it's over there so we have to cross the river to attack it." Merrick knew a lot more about artillery than Cain. He'd served 30 years with the terrestrial army, which was well equipped with weapon systems of that sort. The Marines had small contingents of atmospheric fighter-bombers and lightly-armored vehicles, but there wasn't a lot of heavy artillery used in colonial warfare. It was just too hard to move from planet to planet. The space it occupied was better used to transport more powered infantry.

Cain took a deep breath, holding it in for a few seconds before exhaling slowly. He didn't understand…and that made him even more uncomfortable. "Isaac, I want more than drones on this. Tell Cooper Brown I want a patrol pushed across the river. Now."

"Yes, sir."

Cain looked south, in the general direction of Merrick's position. What the hell, he thought…what are they up to? "I'm not going to let them fool me again," he whispered to himself.

"Keep it moving." Jake Carlson was struggling through the thickets, waist deep in mud. The edge of the river was rough terrain, even for Marines in full armor. He couldn't have moved an inch without his suit, but the nuclear-powered servo-mechanicals pushed his legs through the muck like a backhoe digging into the ground.

Moving a large powered infantry force with supplies and equipment across a river generally required engineers and bridging materials, but a small patrol in armor could cross in a variety of ways. Forces deployed to water worlds were usually equipped with flotation modules, allowing the heavier than water suits to achieve a level of buoyancy. The Marines on Armstrong didn't have anything of the sort, which left them with a stunningly simple option. Carlson and his hand-picked team were going to walk across along the bottom of the river.

It was a perfectly reasonable tactic, though one subject to the vagaries of the terrain on the riverbed. Marine armor could withstand the pressure to at least 500 meters, and the Graywater was no more than 200 at its deepest point. But the geography of the river bottom could make the crossing difficult and hazardous.

"Alright, let's go." Carlson stepped into the river, sliding down the waterlogged mud of the steep bank and under the surface. He could see on the tactical display that his people were following his lead…too fast. They were bunching up, sliding down onto the Marines in front of them. "Slow it down. Give the guys in front of you a chance to move out." The water would reduce the range of the comlinks, but that wasn't a problem for a small, compact group.

Carlson picked himself up and started walking slowly. The river bottom descended quickly, and it was only a minute before it was almost totally dark. Their suits had floodlights, but stealth was important, and he'd ordered everyone to utilize tactical displays only.

His visor displayed an eerie reconstruction of the terrain in front of him. The programming creating the scene was extremely sophisticated, presenting an accurate, but strangely surrealistic, portrayal of the area ahead. He could see rocks and spots where there were steep drops. Anything the AI considered hazardous was outlined with a soft yellow glow.

Carlson walked slowly, turning carefully to avoid the roughest locations. He checked the tactical display every few minutes...everyone was following behind, more or less in formation. He toggled the display to a wider view. They were about 60% of the way across.

There was a shimmering yellow line across the entire display as he continued. It was a ledge, a small cliff where the depth abruptly dropped 30 meters. Shit, he thought, extending the display to the left and right, checking for an easier spot to cross. Nothing. The drop extended as far off to both sides as his scanner could reach.

"All personnel." He spoke on the unitwide com, not entirely managing to hide his frustration. "We have a trench of some sort ahead of us...about 30 meters deep. There's no way around...we're going to have to jump." And, he thought, unless the other side rises more gently, we're going to have to climb back up. "I want 100% concentration, Marines." He knew he could lose people here if they weren't careful. "No screw-ups. Any of you take your eyes off what you're doing and get killed, you're going to have to deal with me."

Carlson repositioned the tactical display, giving him a better look at the terrain at the bottom of the trench. Not too bad, he thought, as he looked as the computer reconstruction of the mostly flat ground.

He positioned himself carefully along the ledge and leapt out, pushing himself far enough to clear any protrusions along the cliff wall. He fell quickly. If his force had been equipped for aquatic operations he would have had compressed gas jets to slow his movement and adjust his positioning. But he had none of that.

He braced for impact. His left foot came down first, on top of a small rock. His right foot hit an instant later, and he felt his body shifting, falling. He spun around, throwing his arms out in front of him, absorbing the force of the impact.

"Status?" He snapped out the inquiry to his AI.

"Armor is fully functional, Captain Carlson. No damage."

He pushed himself back up to his feet, stumbling forward, clearing the area immediately below the ledge to make room. He flipped the tactical display back onto his visor as he took a dozen steps forward. His people were coming down now. Four were already following him from the landing area, and half a dozen more were pulling themselves back to their feet.

He walked another 20 meters or so, giving a wide berth to those still coming down. It took another few minutes, but all his people made it. There were no major injuries and just two small incidents...both insignificant damage to exterior sensors on suits.

The rest of the crossing was uneventful. There was a small climb, about 15 meters, and a gently rising slope the rest of the way. Carlson was the first to poke his head above the water, and the second he did, fire erupted from positions just in from the river's edge.

Carlson ducked down and pushed himself forward against the muddy riverbank. "Incoming fire." He shouted a warning on the com. "Everybody get to the bank and stay low."

He listened. It sounded like two assault rifles firing. We must have run into a couple of scouts, he thought, pissed at the bad luck. He looked around his position. The bank of the river was providing cover, but he wasn't going to get line of sight to the targets unless he popped up from his protected position. He knew his adversaries were in the same boat...and the clear option for both of them was the same. "Grena…"

He heard the whistle just as he started to shout the warning, and the explosion cut him off. The frag grenade was a bit long, exploding about 15 meters behind his position. A huge plume of water rose around the explosion, and a few of his people took minor hits from the shrapnel, but nothing serious.

"Load flashbang." He fired off the command to the AI, and the round snapped into place almost immediately. Grenades were a tough weapon to use against armored troops. You had to practically drop a frag on the target's head to be sure of a kill. But Carlson had something else in mind.

He stared at the tactical display. The AI downloaded the enemy's positional information into the launcher's targeting system. Carlson extended his arm, taking his own aim, and then he pressed the firing lever.

His arm snapped back from the recoil as the grenade blasted out of the launcher and toward the target. Another enemy round impacted as he did, just short of the river this time. Half his force got splattered with mud, and one of his people took a minor wound to the arm.

"Onto the river bank and fire on my command." He gripped his own rifle as he shouted the order. He heard the muffled explosion of the flashbang and checked the tactical display. Right on target.

"Now!" He thrust himself up over the bank, struggling a bit with the slick mud. As soon as he was on top he opened up at full auto. He was banking on the sensor-scrambling grenade to distract the enemy long enough for his people to take them out. They couldn't see or scan anything through the thick green cloud the weapon released, just as Carlson's own sensors were unable to get a read on anything inside. But there were at least ten of his Marines on the bank now, sending thousands of rounds into the compact area.

"Cease firing." If we didn't get them with that, we're never going to, he thought. "Rodriquez, Thompson…move out and make sure they're dead."

He watched the two Marines head out, quickly but cautiously.

There was no fire from the enemy position as he watched his people disappear into the slowly-dissipating cloud. A few seconds later, Rodriguez trotted out. "Clear, sir. Two dead bogies. No other contacts."

"Very well, Rodriguez." No contacts now, he thought, but it won't be long…those two must have warned half the invasion force.

He glanced at the tactical display. "Alright, boys and girls… we're gonna split up into five teams and do a quick scouting job." He knew he didn't have much time before they'd have a hundred bad guys on their asses. "Find out everything you can, but watch out for enemy contacts…and get back to the river in 20 minutes." He knew he should just turn around and go back now. His mission was compromised. They were still at the riverbank, and the enemy knew they were there. But Cooper needed this intel…and Erik Cain did too. It was his job to get some idea of what was going on…and he wasn't going to let General Cain down.

He turned right and then left, looking over his Marines. "Twenty minutes, you understand me? If you're not in the river in 20 minutes, I'll come find you and shoot you myself and save the enemy the trouble."

"It's confirmed, sir." There was confusion in Merrick's voice, an underlying uncertainty. He knew the enemy force was a heavy battery, but he still didn't have a guess why it was there. "It looks like a battalion of infantry too, dug into defensive positions around the guns and along the riverbank. Carlson's scouts ran into heavy resistance just in from the river." His voice became somber. "Only half of them made it back."

Merrick paused, but Cain was silent, so he continued with his report. "I pushed another flight of drones east, around the southern end of the Sentinel." Cain's force didn't have any air assets…and their satellites had all been destroyed or co-opted. Drones were just about the only intel gathering resource they had left, and Merrick had the last few of those. "They shot them all down, but one got close enough to get some disturbing images."

"What?" Cain's voice was showing his impatience.

"Sending the images to you now, sir. This is southeast of here, below the Sentinel Forest. Behind the troops facing Storm's people." The line went silent for a few seconds, Merrick transmitting the images. He was getting better with his powered armor, but it was still taking longer than it should.

Cain didn't criticize his chief of staff. It had taken him years of intensive training – in a controlled environment - to master his fighting suit. Merrick had broken his cherry with his armor in the field, with little chance to practice under training conditions.

"What the hell is that?" Cain was staring at the image displayed inside his visor. "They're building bridges?"

"That's what it looks like to me, sir." Merrick cleared his throat. "I'm sending you more shots. It appears that one bridge may be complete and already in use."

The image was loading as Merrick spoke, and Cain froze when he saw it. There it was, a long pontoon bridge spanning the river. All along its length, and stretching as far as the drone's image reached, was a column of armored soldiers marching northward.

"Shit...they must have landed another wave outside our scanning range." Not for the first time, Cain recognized the disadvantages of ceding total control of local space to an enemy. He'd have given his left arm for one functioning satellite or scoutship in orbit.

"Why would they have heavy artillery? Why go to that much trouble?" Cain's thinking shifted to the western edge of the front. "They must have a specific plan. Otherwise, they'd never have committed the transport capacity." Cain was talking to himself as much as Merrick. He was looking down at the tactical map as he spoke. The plains north of the Graywater were the obvious spot for a landing. From there it was less than 50 klicks to Astria, with only moderately difficult terrain and few naturally defensible positions along the way. To the east, the river curved far to the south, running just below the lower end of the Sentinel Forest. Right where the enemy was building its bridges.

"What's the range on those guns, Isaac?" Cain could just as easily have asked Hector, but he knew his chief of staff had seen these kinds of weapons in actual use...even if only in training exercises.

"About sixty klicks. With Armstrong's atmospheric density and gravity, I'd bet close to 70, actually."

"Projected maximum effective range is 67.6 kilometers." Hector interrupted, having concluded the accurate information was important to Cain.

"More than enough to bombard Astria." He paused. "And maybe the refugee camps just north of the city, for that matter." He paused. "They want to force us to attack those artillery positions to shut those guns down." God, Cain thought, what I wouldn't give for one of the air wings we had on Sandoval.

"Across the river?" Merrick asked the question, but he wasn't expecting an answer. "We're going to need to mass a lot of strength to force the crossing...and it's going to be a bloodbath." He paused. "They're trying to attrit us. That's why they have a battalion dug in. They know we'll lose heavily taking out that battery...far more than they will. It will increase their numerical superiority...and losing the guns won't really hurt their main strength."

"That's only part of it, Isaac." Cain was thinking as he spoke, and the firmness in his voice grew with his realization. He remembered accounts of an old battle...mid-20th century. It was a rematch of an earlier conflict, and the defenders expected the invaders to come on the same route they had before, the only open way. The rest of the border was covered with a forest widely considered impenetrable to the tank-heavy armies of the day. But the attackers did come through the woods, and they surprised the defenders and smashed through a weak part of their line, flanking the rest of their army and seizing their capital. Blitzkrieg, they called it...lightning war in the language of the victors. "They want to tie down as much of our force as possible along the open river...a diversion while they drive their main force through the Sentinel and get on our rear before we can react. They'll take Astria and roll up the whole army."

"Do you really think they can get their main force through those woods?" He paused, his mind reviewing the possibilities. "If that's true, it means Eliot Storm will be facing a lot more strength that he's expecting." Merrick's tone was matter-of-fact. "We better reinforce him. Fast."

Cain felt his blood run cold. Storm's counter-attack could begin at any time…and his advancing forces would run head on into the massive enemy formation coming across the river. It would be a disaster.

"Hector, get me Colonel Storm. Immediately."

Chapter 18

CWS Suleiman
En Route to Fleet Base Two
Samarkand System

Ali Khaled was silent, listening intently to everything the mysterious visitor had to say. The Supreme Commander of the Janissary Corps looked calm, like a man listening to a list of choices in a restaurant. That was nothing but a testament to Khaled's iron control over his reactions. Inside, his anger raged like a fusion core.

"Is Mr. Vance certain of this?" Ali Khaled had come to know the Martian spymaster during the First Imperium War. The Janissary officer had always hated and mistrusted intelligence operatives, but he found it difficult to group Vance with the others. An enormously wealthy man, Roderick Vance could have lived a life of unmatched luxury instead of one of crushing work and constant danger, yet he was always at the forefront of every crisis, and his efforts consistently seemed designed to reduce international tensions and human suffering. At one point or another, Khaled realized, he'd begun to trust the Martian. "I mean no chance of a mistake?"

"He is certain, Lord Khaled. Our senior operative in the CAC made the initial report, and our...ah...we have been able to confirm through Caliphate sources as well." Bryce Trent was a skilled agent, one of the best in the Martian service. But even he felt tongue tied trying to tell a Caliphate lord about data obtained from Martian double agents in his own government. Intelligence became an even more difficult game when the lines between friends and enemies blurred. "I fear we were not able to warn Admiral An in time. Unconfirmed reports suggest that he and a large number of his officers have already been executed by C1 agents."

Khaled just looked back at his visitor, thinking about his old CAC ally. Old An had been a pain in the ass at times, and grouchy always, but he had been a good man...and he deserved far better from the government he'd spent a lifetime serving. Trent had characterized the report as unconfirmed, but he'd never have mentioned it unless he knew it was true. An Ying was dead. And if Trent was right, Khaled would be soon as well. Unless he took action now.

"I want to offer my sincere thanks to Mr. Vance...and to you for making such a difficult and dangerous journey to bring me this news." Khaled didn't know what he was going to do yet, but he appreciated the chance to choose for himself...even if it was only a choice between committing high treason or meekly accepting disgrace and execution. He stood up. "Let me get you back to your ship. I don't imagine time is on our side right now." Khaled's rank allowed him the prerogative of having unexplained visitors, but if he was the target of a purge, it was possible he was already under enhanced surveillance. Whatever happened, he didn't want to put Trent at further risk or cause any blowback on Vance. He owed them both, and Ali Khaled paid his debts.

"Thank you, Lord Khaled." Trent rose and offered a slight bow before turning toward the hatch.

Khaled stepped alongside. "I will walk you to your ship." *And once I see you safely on your way,* he thought grimly, *I will go see Admiral Abbas...we have much to discuss.*

"Admiral, I know this is a shock, but I felt an obligation to inform you as quickly as possible." Khaled was sitting across a small table from the Caliphate's number two naval officer. His demeanor was as calm as it had been with Trent, and every bit as fake as well. His iron control was overpowering his fear and rage at the moment, though the prospect of a group of assassins on the way to execute him was sobering, to say the least.

Abbas glared back across the table. The admiral had an incredulous look on his face, but there was doubt there too. He'd known Khaled for more than thirty years and, while he and the Janissary commander didn't particularly like each other, they did have a sort of mutual trust and respect. Abbas certainly took anything Khaled said seriously. But he was getting this news second hand, and he had a harder time accepting that the Caliph would act so precipitously against him and the other officers on the list. The fleet admiral was a member of the hereditary nobility, and he had a different perspective than Khaled, who had been born in the gutters of New Cairo.

"Lord Khaled…" - there was skepticism in Abbas' voice, but Khaled could hear concern as well…even fear – "with all due respect, don't you think the word of some Martian spy is a very thin pretext for believing something of this magnitude?"

Khaled nodded almost imperceptibly. "Indeed admiral, your concerns echo my own." He paused for a few seconds, staring hard at Abbas. "Yet, I find it very difficult to simply disregard a warning of this type from Roderick Vance. You fought in the First Imperium War from beginning to end. Did you ever find him to be anything less than totally committed to aiding us? Was any of his intelligence ever inaccurate?"

"No." He paused. "But when we were facing the First Imperium, Vance's own survival was on the line. I wouldn't have expected treachery then."

Not entirely true, Khaled thought with mild disdain. Abbas had been quite vocal about his reservations early in the war. He'd questioned Vance's intelligence many times…and each time the Martian's information had been proven to be absolutely accurate. But now wasn't the time to win debate points. Khaled might command the Janissaries, but Abbas was in charge of the ships carrying them. He hadn't decided himself what he wanted to do, but without the admiral he had no real choices. He could remain and face whatever was coming, or he could take a small transport and skulk out of the system. That was no choice at all…Ali Khaled would do many things, but sneaking out of the system and leaving the rest of his senior officers to face death wasn't one of them.

"Admiral...I understand your doubts, but I submit that Mr. Vance's warning cannot be dismissed out of hand." Khaled looked around him as he spoke, an involuntary response. Privacy was crucial...they were essentially discussing the possibility of committing treason. Constant surveillance was a fact of life in the CAC, both in the military and in civilian life. But Khaled had to trust Abbas. If the fleet admiral didn't know a safe spot on his own flagship, they were screwed anyway. "What do you propose we do?"

Abbas opened his mouth and closed it again. He didn't know how to respond. He couldn't imagine throwing away a forty year career and a lifetime of allegiance to the Caliph on the word of a foreign spy. But he knew it would be too late if he waited. By the time he had proof of the purge, all would be lost. "I don't even know if the fleet would accept treasonous orders." Abbas was well-loved by his crews, but he'd be asking them to abandon country and family, to go rogue, become a force without a country...just to save him and a few dozen other officers. "Most likely we would have dissension. It could come to civil war in the fleet." The Alliance had faced similar situations during their rebellions. Abbas remembered well how he had laughed at such folly and wondered how the Alliance commanders could have allowed it to happen. Now he felt suitably chagrined. "Can you be sure the Janissaries will follow you down such a path?"

Khaled inhaled deeply. The question demanded a thoughtful answer, not a quick, ego-based response. "Most of them... yes." The reservation in his voice was obvious. "All? No. It is possible there could be fighting among the Ortas. But I am certain I can retain control of the corps."

"I cannot guarantee the response of the fleet with such certainty. So, even if we decide to take drastic action, we cannot be sure of success. We may achieve nothing beyond being arrested by our junior commanders and delivered to our assassins in chains."

"Many of those officers are themselves on the list, admiral."
Khaled spoke slowly, matter-of-factly.

"If they believe any of this, Lord Khaled." He paused, taking a deep breath. "I'm not even sure that I do."

The two sat silently for several minutes, each deep in thought,
each trying to reason out a course of action that made sense.

"What of our families, Lord Khaled?" Abbas spoke softly,
as if raising a topic he'd rather forget.

He's leaning toward doing something, Khaled thought. He's
only worried now about what will happen to his family. "I have
no family, admiral. My mother died when I was 12, so over-
worked and poorly cared for, simple influenza killed her." Years
of indoctrination were peeling away inside Khaled, and bitterness and anger long buried were re-emerging. "I have no one
else. My father I never knew. Whether he was one of my mother's employers who raped her or some vagrant on the streets
of New Cairo who seduced her, he was long gone before I was
born." He breathed deeply, a defiant look taking over his face.
"My family are my Janissaries, admiral." After another pause:
"Including 11 men on that purge list."

Abbas sat quietly, looking across the table at Khaled, seeing the anger in his face. He felt his own fury rising as well.
Decades of loyalty were being repaid with treachery. The injus-
tice of it tore at him. "Very well, Lord Khaled." He spoke with
resignation. He'd made a decision. "I am with you. How do
you propose we proceed?"

Khaled sighed with relief. "First, we must choose the men
on the list we know best…the ones we truly trust. Then we…"

"Admiral Abbas, this is Commander Qin on the flag bridge,
sir." Qin sounded nervous. Bothering the fleet admiral when
he'd left specific instructions not to be disturbed took considerable courage. "I am sorry to interrupt you, sir, but we have
unscheduled ships transiting through the warp gate. They are
broadcasting diplomatic IDs." Qin paused, listening to something in the background. "Incoming message, sir. They say they
are a delegation from the Caliph here to congratulate us and
welcome the fleet back to friendly space."

Abbas didn't answer…he flipped the lever to mute the com-link. "Well, Ali…" - his voice was softer, friendlier – "I'd say the odds of Mr. Vance's warning being accurate just increased exponentially." He sighed. "The relevant question is, what do we do now?"

"What can we do?" Khaled's voice was dark, without hope. "We're out of time."

Abbas stared back at the Janissary commander, his eyes blaz-ing. "Almost out of time. Almost." He flipped the comlink back on. "Commander Qin, shut down all incoming frequen-cies except fleet battle coms. And jam those ships." His hands were on the table, curled up into fists. "Immediately. They are hostiles."

"Ah…yes, sir." Qin sounded confused, but there was no doubt, no hesitation in Abbas' tone.

The admiral looked over at Khaled, who was nodding, his morose expression gone, replaced by an iron stare. "And com-mander…" Abbas paused, but only for an instant. "All capital ships are to load missiles and prepare for immediate fire."

Chapter 19

AS Pershing
Transit + Three Minutes
Wolf 359 System

Augustus Garret sat in the center of Pershing's flag bridge, his eyes focused like lasers on the main battle display. His staff were at their posts, bathed in the eerie red light of the battlestations lamps.

The fleet was blasting hard into the Wolf 359 system, moving at 0.08c. Garret expected the enemy to cut and run, and he was determined to send as many of the bastards as he could to hell before they had the chance to get away. He had a reasonable expectation of finding enemy ships here, and he knew he'd just be facing them somewhere else if they got away. Another system, another battle.

He'd sacrificed maneuverability for speed, and that meant running the gauntlet past whatever defenses the enemy had waiting just beyond the warp gate. At 8% of lightspeed, his ships wouldn't be able to make any quick vector changes. "Scanner teams...report any contacts immediately. Even a twitchy feeling in your leg." Every detection resource in the fleet was on full power, straining to make contact with anything that lay ahead of Garret's speeding warships.

"No contacts yet, sir." Tara Rourke sat bolt upright at her station, her own eyes glued as firmly as Garret's to the display. Garret could hear her heavy breathing from 3 meters away.

Not that we'd find well hidden defenses anyway, he thought... not at any appreciable range. If the enemy had deployed a belt of laser buoys or stealth missiles, the weapons would be at minimum power, doing their best imitation of empty space.

Garret remained silent, his mind considering and reconsidering the tactical situation. The enemy had been here in force two months ago; that was a certainty. If they hadn't had a significant fleet, Admiral Davis wouldn't have lost contact. But anything past that assumption was pure guesswork. Garret didn't think the enemy would want to abandon the shipyards unless they were sure they faced a stronger force, so he expected a fight of some sort. That was an educated guess, at least…perhaps even a probability. But if he was right about the enemy's limited naval strength, he didn't think they'd stay around for a death fight with his fleet. They'd turn tail and run, save what they could.

"Warp gate scanners detected, sir." Rourke's voice pulled him from his deep thoughts. "Two minimum, admiral."

"Very well." Ok, he thought, one thing is for sure…whatever enemy forces are lurking in the system, they know we're here. At least they would when the lightspeed transmissions from the scanner buoys reached them…wherever they were waiting.

"Commander, confirm missile team readiness." Garret had gone through the warp gate at red alert, and he had no idea how long his crews would have to remain at that high state of readiness. When an alert went on for too long, the edge began to wear off. He frequently ordered spot checks and diagnostics, more to give his crews something to do than because he was concerned about equipment status. Those who haven't experienced it tend to think of space combat as fast, explosive. But it is mostly a test of endurance, of stamina and the ability to remain focused despite exhaustion, fear, and boredom.

"Yes, sir." Rourke passed the order to the fleet with a tiny smile on her face. She knew very well why he issued it. Most of the veterans receiving the directive knew as well. Still, the make work would help them stay focused…even as they realized that's what it was intended to do.

The flag bridge was quiet as Pershing and the rest of the fleet moved deeper into the Wolf 359 system. There were no transmissions…from Arcadia or from the shipyards. Garret hadn't really expected any, but he couldn't help but feel a bit disappointed.

"Captain, sporadic unidentified contacts." Rourke spoke loudly, the edginess obvious in her voice. "AI projection, 87%." She turned to face Garret. "Laser buoys, sir."

Garret quietly exhaled. It shouldn't be a surprise, he thought. We knew they took the shipyards, and there was a damned production line there building the things. The x-ray laser buoys had only been deployed against the First Imperium…no human ship had faced an attack from one. But they'd all seen the deadly power of the new weapon system.

"Calculate range and projected firing point." His voice was crisp, professional. Garret almost relished combat now. It was something that came naturally to him, and when his mind was occupied with battle, he didn't think of…other things. "All angel dust launchers, prepare to fire." The anti-laser reflective particle interdiction system had been commonly called angel dust since before Garret had stepped aboard his first space ship. The clouds of tiny metallic particles were highly effective at dispersing the strength of a laser blast…if they were positioned correctly. It was a difficult system to use, requiring an odd combination of mathematical acuity and clairvoyance. Lasers moved at lightspeed, making it impossible to react to a shot once it was fired. Angel dust crews tried to guess when and where an attack would come from. If they were right, they could aim the torpedoes to intersect the laser's path, providing excellent protection to the targeted ships. If not, their efforts were fruitless. The clouds of angel dust would float pointlessly in space, while the deadly spears of light ripped into their targets.

Garret didn't know if they would work at all this time. There were x-ray lasers on those buoys, and the normal reflective materials would be nearly useless against them. General Sparks had revised the payloads of the angel dust torpedoes to increase x-ray reflexivity, but the new system had never been tested in combat conditions.

"Yes, admiral." A few seconds later: "Angel dust crews at

full readiness, sir. Should I lock in the AI firing plan?" The fleet tactical computer calculated a recommended pattern to counter its expectation of incoming fire. Most commanders tended to utilize the AI plan. But Augustus Garret wasn't "most" commanders.

"Negative." Garret was staring at his screen, hastily entering revised parameters. "Upload these revisions." He swiped his finger across the screen, sending her the file. They're going to fire early, he thought to himself...they know how powerful these weapons are, and they'll be anxious.

"Multiple additional contacts, sir." Rourke was getting excited, and it was showing in her voice. "Fleet units, admiral."

"Very well." Garret sat motionless, feeling almost nothing. Have I really become so cold and efficient, he thought, that I can't even feel a wave of fear before battle? He knew the answer, but he wasn't ready to accept it. Not yet.

"Fire laser buoys." Liang's voice was hoarse and strained. He hated going into a fight buttoned up in the acceleration couches, but he didn't have any choice. Goddamned Garret, he thought. Liang hadn't expected the Alliance admiral to come charging recklessly through the warp gate at 8% of lightspeed. Liang had to build some velocity, and he had to do it quickly.

"Yes Admiral Liang." Commander Horace-103 replied immediately.

Dammit, Liang thought...they all sound the same. His crews weren't all Shadow warriors, but most of them were. It wasn't easy to crew a bunch of warships...veteran spacers weren't exactly sitting around reading want ads, and the Shadow personnel filled a lot of chairs. They were completely competent... better, probably, than his other personnel. But they creeped the hell out of him.

Liang was stunned when Stark first told him of the Shadow plan and even more so when the Alliance spy came right out and offered him command of the fleet. The former CAC admiral had spent almost ten years confined in Alliance Intelligence headquarters, living in extremely plush conditions, but virtually a prisoner. Li An had sworn to execute Liang after his failures in the Third Frontier War, and it had been a source of humiliation to her that she'd been unable to do so. Even with Liang under lock and key, Li An had made two credible efforts to get someone on the inside to do the job for her.

Stark had taken Liang in and protected him mostly to piss off the old bitch, as he called Li An, but when he conceived the full extent of the Shadow plan, he knew he'd need a trained naval commander. He didn't kid himself…Liang was no match for Garret, but he wasn't a fool either. He was capable and experienced…and the most trustworthy candidate Stark was likely to find, being motivated as he was not just by greed, but by the near certainty he'd be killed if Stark withdrew his protection.

Liang had been doubtful the plan was possible, but Stark insisted it would…and he had accomplished everything he'd set out to do so far. His army was occupying worlds throughout Alliance space, and his machinations had brought the Powers to the brink of open war. Liang shook his head as lay half-crushed in the acceleration couch. Stark truly is a genius, he thought.

"We're getting damage reports back from the laser buoys, sir." Horace-103 in the same relentless tone. "Moderate effectiveness only, admiral. The Alliance fleet seems to have had great luck in positioning its angel dust torpedoes."

Luck, my ass, Liang thought…fucking Garret's a genius too. He'd faced the Alliance admiral before, with uniformly disastrous results. His fall from power and grace had come at the hands of Augustus Garret. Still, he'd expected the x-ray units to perform better against the angel dust, but it didn't seem that had been the case.

"Prepare to commence missile launches immediately." The distance between the fleets was at the extreme edge of effective range, but Liang was thrusting away from Garret's force. His missiles would have to accelerate just to overcome the intrinsic velocity of the launch platforms. Time would only exacerbate that disadvantage. "I want all external ordnance launched. Racks are to be jettisoned immediately after fire. I want a second wave ready to launch fifteen minutes after the first." Most ships carried externally mounted missiles that increased their magazine capacity by 25-40%. It took time to properly eject the mounting systems holding the missiles in place, especially under high acceleration. Significant calculations were required to insure the jettisoned racks wouldn't become a collision hazard to any of the fleet's vessels. Rushing the process was dangerous, but it had to be finished before any internally-carried missiles could be launched. And fifteen minutes was definitely rushing.

"Yes, admiral." A short pause, then: "External missiles launching in 60 seconds."

Liang stared up at the small screen above his head watching the seconds tick off the chronometer. Well, Augustus Garret, he thought...here we go again.

"External racks flushed, sir." Rourke snapped out the report. "Mounting disengagement in progress."

Garret nodded. He wanted to get as many volleys launched as possible before he had to engage his point defense systems. His fleet wasn't heading directly toward the enemy force, but it was close enough to give him a big advantage in the missile exchange. Their weapons would be struggling to overcome negative intrinsic velocity with respect to his ships, while his own missiles were coming out of the launchers at 0.08c.

Ideally, he'd be decelerating now, but he wanted his crews at their posts during the fighting, not wrapped up and half-crushed in the couches. Ships could fight under those conditions, but it degraded anyone's performance...even that of Augustus Garret and his vaunted Alliance navy. He could slow down later. His trajectory was good enough for the missile exchange, and he very much doubted the enemy would let him get close to energy weapons range anyway.

"Updated damage report?"

The laser attack from the buoys hit a few of his ships hard, but Garret had timed the angel dust launches perfectly, and Sparks' new reflective materials had performed extremely well against the x-ray weapons. Two of the battleships had major damage, and a destroyer had been nearly vaporized, but he knew it could have been much, much worse. He suspected one of those buoys could destroy a capital ship with a single direct hit, and he was glad to postpone the day that theory got its test.

"One of Cromwell's reactors is offline, sir, and she has heavy casualties." Rourke hated casualty reports, and it showed in her voice. "All other vessels report 85% or higher operational capacity and full battle-readiness."

"Very well, commander." Garret leaned back in his chair. Cromwell, he thought…the old girl's done enough…we really shouldn't be asking more of her. The oldest capital ship in the Alliance fleet by 30 years, Cromwell had been somewhat of a lucky ship, surviving far longer than any other vessel of her day. She should have been in well-deserved retirement in the strategic reserve by now, but there was no reserve anymore. Crisis after crisis had driven the navy to the edge, and anything capable of carrying weapons had been kept in service. Cromwell wasn't a match for a modern battleship, but there was more to war than counting weapons. Garret considered himself fortunate to have her under his command, and he was pulling for her damage control crews to save her once again.

"All primary units report mounting disengagement complete, admiral."

Garret glanced at the chronometer. Seven minutes, fifteen seconds. He let a brief smile cross his lips. He drove his crews hard, but it was times like this that it really showed. No other naval force in human space could match that time.

"Commence second missile launch immediately."

"This is your last chance, general." Liang was exhausted with Samuels' indecision. "If you wish to join your ground forces on Arcadia, we will cut acceleration and launch your shuttle. But it was to be now."

Liang was angry and frustrated enough without having to deal with this reject Marine Stark had placed in command of the Shadow ground forces. The fleet had taken heavy damage, much worse than he'd anticipated. They were already leaving one battleship behind. Toshiru had been a PRC vessel badly damaged in the fighting at Garrison. She'd been nearly fully repaired when Liang's forces seized the shipyards, and he'd put the vessel into service almost immediately. Now her reactors were both down and she was streaming air. There was no chance her crew would complete repairs before Garret's ships caught up and destroyed or captured her.

He had one thought now…getting out of this system while he still had a fleet. Garret's people had been good when he'd last faced them during the Third Frontier War, but they were like razors now. War against an enemy like the First Imperium had killed many of them, but it had honed the survivors into a weapon the likes of which he'd never seen. Stark thought he had everything figured out, but Liang was starting to wonder if he hadn't underestimated this adversary. Liang still had a lot of force under his command, but he didn't know how he was going to defeat Garret. All he could do now was postpone that inevitable showdown.

"No." Samuels tried to hide the fear in his voice, but his efforts were in vain. "I will go to Armstrong."

"As you wish, general." Liang cut the line. "Yes," he whispered to himself. "You don't want to be left behind, cut off with your troops and blockaded." His face was twisted with derision. "So you will go to Armstrong instead…and face Erik Cain." He couldn't stifle a laugh, at least as much of one as 30g acceleration would allow.

"General Holm's transports are inbound to Arcadia at 0.02c. Projected orbital insertion in two hours, forty-three minutes." Rourke's voice betrayed her fatigue. She'd been on duty for almost two straight days, and in the acceleration couches for most of the week prior. Garret had as well, but somehow he seemed immune to exhaustion.

"Very well, commander." He was as tired as Rourke and the rest of the staff, but he refused to let them see it. He didn't crave the hero worship…in fact, he hated it. But there was no arguing its usefulness and effect on morale. Men and women would follow the invincible Augustus Garret into places that would freeze their blood if they were under any other commander. "Advise Blackhawk to begin deploying com satellites." Garret didn't know if Holm's hastily-assembled strike force of retirees would be enough to turn the tide on the ground, but he was going to do what he could to help. His ships had already destroyed the enemy satellite network, severely crippling their communications. Now his ships would string a new series of com satellites, giving Holm and his people planetwide transmission capability once they landed. If Teller's Marines were still holding out somewhere on the surface, their Corps-standard transponders would find the new satellite network immediately. They would be able to tap in, vastly improving their own communications and connecting them with Holm's new force.

"Incoming message from Admiral Arlington's task force, sir. She reports no enemy contacts." Rourke looked up from her workstation toward Garret. "The system is clear, sir."

Arlington's group was the last of the scouting parties Garret had dispatched. It had taken a week to complete the scanning job and insure there were no enemy forces hiding anywhere. Fleets traveled hundreds of lightyears through warp gates, but movement between transit points was at non-relativistic speeds...and a solar system was one goddamned big space to cover.

The enemy fleet had been defeated and driven from the system, but he still had no more information on who they were. The battleship Toshiru and the other damaged ships had self-destructed before his people could board them, and the shipyards had been mined with thermonuclear charges. Trillions of credits of construction had been consumed in an instant, leaving nothing but a slowly cooling plasma where the largest shipyard in human space had been.

Garret felt strange about covering Holm's landing and then evacuating the system, leaving the Marines on their own. But it was unlikely the enemy would come back anytime soon, and he couldn't afford to tie down too much fleet power in one place. With the shipyards gone, there was nothing of value in the system but Arcadia, and the enemy ground forces were still in place...and presumably in control of most of the planet.

There wasn't much the fleet could do to help the Marines once they were landed. Arcadia was an Alliance world, and that ruled out any orbital bombardment. For better or worse, the Marines would have to try to retake the planet on the ground…meter by meter.

He'd tried to convince Holm to wait until he could gather more force. He was landing with just over 1,000 Marines, most of whom hadn't seen action in 40 years. Garret had a bad feeling about the whole thing…but he understood. General Teller had gone down there, and as long as there was a chance he and some of his people were alive, Elias Holm had to go in. It was his duty, just as pulling out of the system was Garret's. Like defending Armstrong was Cain's…and staying behind in the X2 system had been Compton's.

Garret was beginning to hate duty. Certainly, she was a harsh mistress, one who seemed unceasing in her constant demands. In a few hours he would direct the landing of Holm's strike force…a few days later he would begin pulling the fleet out, hunting down the enemy force they'd already wounded. Holm and his people would be left on Arcadia, to live or die on their own.

How many more friends, he wondered, would this new war cost him?

Chapter 20

Paradis
Seventh Arrondissement
Paris, Europa Federalis
Earth – Sol III

Roderick Vance sat at a small table next to the fountain. Paradis was one of the most exclusive cafes in the Europan capital, indeed, in the world. Only the elite politicians and their most influential cronies walked through its celebrated doors. Vance was in his element, traveling in his cover as a Martian mogul and industrialist. It wasn't so much a cover as a part of his real life... Vance was one of the wealthiest men in any of the Powers, and he legitimately headed his family's massive conglomerate. He was in Paris to conduct real business...which was the perfect cover to meet Li An's emissary.

He'd have preferred to meet the CAC's intelligence master herself, but they both agreed it was too dangerous. Even those who knew Vance was also the Confederation's top spy were aware that he frequently conducted private business as well. He would draw no undue suspicion sitting at a café in Paris, but if he was spotted within 100 kilometers of Li An, it would be obvious he was wearing his hat as intel chief.

It's a shame, he thought...I'd like to see her again. He'd been an adversary of Li An far more frequently than an ally, but he found her to be a fascinating woman. Her moral code differed wildly from his own, but he had come to enjoy her company and respect her intelligence. He would have been happy to see her one more time. But it was very unlikely they would meet in person again.

"Mr. Vance?" A tall, thin Asian man stood next to the table. He spoke English with no discernible accent, and he was impeccably dressed.

Vance rose and extended his hand. "Mr. Fung." He gestured toward the empty chair. "Please...join me."

"I am sorry I am late." In truth, he wasn't late. Vance was habitually early to any meeting, especially those dealing with security matters. "I must confess, I saw this as both an opportunity to meet with you and a chance to get to Paris for a few days." He looked around. "Beautiful city."

"Yes, it is." Vance detested meaningless chitchat, though he knew it was necessary. In this case, however, he agreed completely. Europa Federalis didn't function very well as a Superpower, but Paris was a magnificent metropolis...at least the inner core. The slums around La Courneuve and other rundown areas were notorious.

"Unfortunately, I had some difficulty clearing security." The visitor pulled the chair from the table and lowered himself gracefully into it. "I'm afraid I haven't seen international tensions this high since the last colonial war."

Vance nodded in agreement but didn't say anything.

"I trust we can come to an agreement." Fung turned the subject to business. "We are very interested in regular importation of stable super-heavy elements from your sources."

Fung was one of Li An's agents, of course, but he also ran one of the CAC's megacorps, one with which Vance had done considerable business. He'd gotten the job over half a dozen more senior personnel, something very rare in the CAC, where seniority was the usual determining factor in advancement. That had been two years earlier. Vance was impressed with Li An's forward thinking in preparing for future dealings with him before any crisis actually existed. She'd put Fung where he was to facilitate contact with him just in case she needed it. She had a reputation for being meticulous, and he realized it was well deserved.

The waitress came over as soon as Fung sat. She was very

pretty, her uniform form-fitting, with a short skirt and very high heels. The fashions and behavioral codes of Europa Federalis were considerably more libertine than those in the straitlaced CAC or the conservative Confederation. "May I get you anything, sir?"

"Perhaps you'd care to share this bottle with me, Mr. Fung?" Vance gestured toward a slender decanter, almost full with a deep red wine. "It is something special, a pre-Blight Bordeaux. An indulgence, I'm afraid, one I find I can't resist when I'm in Paris."

Fung smiled and nodded slightly. "Thank you, Mr. Vance. You are most kind." To the waitress: "Just another glass, please."

"Yes, sir." She smiled and glided toward the bar.

"I am glad we were able to schedule this meeting, Mr. Vance. Our business relationship has always been satisfactory, but I find that despite all our technology, there is no substitute for sitting face to face across a table. It may not be logical, but there is something to sharing a meal, shaking a hand…especially before embarking on an endeavor of this size." His eyes held Vance's for a few extra seconds.

He's telling me they found something, Vance thought… something significant. Something urgent.

The waitress reappeared with a second crystal goblet, placing it gently in front of Fung, pausing for an instant to give both men a better view of her as she leaned over the table and filled the glass from the decanter. "Would you gentlemen care to order lunch?"

"Perhaps in a few minutes." Vance glanced up and smiled. "I think we're fine with this…" – he held up his glass – "…for now."

She nodded and smiled before turning and walking away, giving them both an extended view of how short her skirt really was.

Vance smiled again, amused by the differing customs of the Powers. Europa Federalis, while as repressive a government as any other, was very open with regard to sexual matters. It was always amusing…Paris seemed like one massive adult resort, but it actually made intelligence gathering more difficult. He suspected the CAC and Confederation had just as much going on, but it was behind closed doors. Mistresses and concubines were generally kept hidden, as his extensive blackmail files attested. Sex remained one of the top tools of the spy trade, as he suspected it had always been...both for bribery and coercion. But in Europa Federalis, the powerful indulged quite openly, indeed, even competing informally to have the most beautiful mistresses. Such an environment virtually eliminated the effectiveness of blackmail, at least regarding sexual matters. Any Europan politician would welcome that sort of attention.

"Indeed, Mr. Vance, I do not believe I have ever tasted such a delightful wine." Fung put his glass on the table. "You must give me the name and vintage so I can acquire some for my own cellar."

"I'm afraid it's not generally available, Mr. Fung." Vance set his own glass down. "The pre-Blight vintages are almost extinct. I have a small cache they keep for me here. I'm afraid I have already hunted down and purchased every available bottle. However, I will be happy to send you one to celebrate our transaction." His voice changed, became almost imperceptibly more serious in tone. "Speaking of which, do you have the proposed figures for me?"

Fung's hand slipped inside his jacket, and he placed a small data chip on the table, sliding it toward Vance. "I think you will find this proposal acceptable." He paused for a few seconds. "My board is quite impatient for your response. I will be in Paris for another day. Is it possible you can review this today and give me a response before I leave?"

"Of course, Mr. Fung." Vance looked down at the small chip. She must have found something important, he thought, if she's so anxious for my input. "I will review your proposal this evening and provide you with some feedback. Perhaps we can breakfast together tomorrow, say 9am at my hotel?"

Fung nodded. "That would be most satisfactory, Mr. Vance. Thank you."

"Of course, you realize I will have to review this in greater detail with my own board before I can offer anything final."

"Certainly, Mr. Vance. I appreciate even your preliminary feedback."

Vance nodded and raised his hand slightly, signaling to the waitress. "For now, why don't we enjoy our lunch?" Vance wished he could leave immediately and read Li An's report on the data chip, but his cover demanded he waste time on banal playacting. "The Bouillabaisse is particularly excellent."

Stark glanced out the window of the private shuttle. It was leased through a dummy corporation...several layers of them, actually. It had been built for the highest levels of Corporate Magnate and Political Class users, and no comfort had been spared in its appointments.

Stark was uncomfortable, nevertheless. He was used to his own shuttle, but the time had come to leave that behind...along with so many other things. Project Shadow had been proceeding satisfactorily, and now it was time for stage 2. Gavin Stark would be dead soon, buried in the radioactive rubble of Alliance Intelligence HQ...at least that's how it would appear. The Alliance and the CAC would probably be at war within a week, their long-atrophied ground forces creaking into action, beginning the dance Stark had so carefully choreographed. How long, he thought, before all the Powers were at each other's throats? He'd projected 3-4 months, but that was the one part of the plan he had to admit was pure guesswork. But he knew how all the nations functioned, and he was sure war would come.

Things had gone well so far. Garret had been a problem, of course, just as Stark expected. But soon he would have the CAC fleet to deal with...and probably the Caliphate's too. War on Earth would spread to space immediately. The ruling classes, threatened at their very doorsteps as they hadn't been in over 100 years, would panic...they would act rashly. They would seek to gain advantage anywhere they could. If not tools of victory, the colonies they seized would be bargaining chips in mitigating defeat at the negotiating table. At least that's how those in charge thought. Stark expected it would be rather more difficult to put a stop to total war, even when defeat was imminent. When cities were nuked into rubble and the lower classes were rioting and rebelling, it would take more than a few dozen diplomats filling rooms with CO_2 to pull things back from the brink.

He did a mental tally of the strength of the combined CAC and Caliphate fleets. Despite their loss in the Third Frontier War and the ample displays of Garret's genius since then, he had no doubt they would simply add up hulls and assume they could win the fight in space.

That's right, Augustus, he thought with wicked delight…I will pull back all my ships and leave you alone once they attack. Fight the CAC and the Caliphate, and destroy them with your tactical brilliance…I will be most grateful for your help. "Then bring your battered survivors back to me," he whispered to himself. "Even Liang Chang will be able to defeat your handful of broken ships limping back without supplies or refit."

Stark and Garret had tangled before. Stark smiled thinking back at the defeats Garret and his allies had handed him. Wouldn't the great admiral be amused, he thought, if he knew how vital to my plans he was?

He'd gone to great lengths to precipitate war between the Powers. He needed war. Without the fleets destroying each other, Shadow would leave Stark ruling only the Alliance colonies, and his naval units would be no match against those of the rapacious other Powers. No, Stark wasn't after partial power… he wanted it all, to rule not a group of colonies, not a Superpower…but all mankind. He wouldn't leave anyone with the strength to oppose him.

War on Earth was essential to his plans. He needed a high intensity conflict in space, one that would force the navies to fight to the last and not just fence with each other over moderate targets…and if cities on Earth were being bombed into rubble, the Powers would order their space-based forces into endless combat. Nothing would cause the escalation he needed like combat on Earth itself.

A terrestrial conflict would clear away the Powers and their massive armies. His armored Shadow warriors were vastly superior to anything the Earthly nations possessed, but he couldn't match the tens of millions of soldiers, the legions of main battle tanks, the sea-going battle platforms and waves of atmospheric aircraft. No...he needed the Powers to destroy themselves first. He had them on the brink, and in a few days he'd push them onto an irrevocable path to destruction. Then his forces...fresh, undamaged, would take control of the smoking remnants...and Earth and all of human space would be his.

"Prepare for takeoff in 30 seconds." The ships' AI had a female voice, soft, comforting.

The soothing nature was lost on Stark. He hated space. He'd been from one end to the other of mankind's interstellar dominions as a young intelligence officer, but his hatred had only grown. The colonists were a bunch of unruly loudmouths who didn't know enough to do what they were told. And there wasn't a colony with any real level of urban sophistication. Most of them, he thought derisively, were more like some county seat, where farmers hauled their harvested wheat and prize pigs to market. At least they were compared to a true metropolis like Washbalt.

He didn't know if any of Earth's cities would survive the coming conflagration...he rather doubted it. But a price had to be paid for progress, and cities could always be rebuilt. It was one of the unappealing aspects of his grab for power - that he would have to do without the comforts of a true city for a while – but if he had to rough it for a few years, so be it.

Stark let out a breath as the acceleration of liftoff pushed him into his seat. Heading into space is another price I have to pay, he thought. Things were likely to get bad on Earth...very bad. It was too dangerous to try to manage Shadow from any terrestrial location...even the Dakota site. No one would go in or out of there - or even send a communique – until he gave the coded order to release the reserve legions. His presence would increase the threat of detection...and he didn't want to take a chance on getting stuck on Earth when things got really bad. Better to run the program from the off-planet command post.

Stark wasn't usually sentimental, but he found himself looking out the small window, catching one last glimpse of the Wash-balt skyline in the distance. He'd lived there all his adult life. All the restaurants he liked, the women he visited, the apartment he'd finally gotten just the way he liked it…he was leaving it all behind, probably forever. He knew it could be a long time before he saw Earth again, and when he finally did, he doubted he'd recognize it. But whatever was left of it would be his… and his alone.

"What the hell are you up to, you psychotic maniac?" Vance stared at the screen, amazed at the intel Li An had managed to scrounge up in such a short time. My God, he thought…could it actually be Stark behind both the coming financial apocalypse and the unexplained invasions of Alliance colony worlds?

Li An's data was enormously incomplete. With a routine intelligence matter, she'd never have released it until she could confirm more of the details. But both she and Vance were beginning to believe this was a life and death situation, and the slightest scrap of information…even a decent hunch…was important.

There were two references to South Dakota in the reams of raw intel she had sent over. Both were related to what appeared to be large expenditures of the missing funds. There was a third possible money trail, very vague and convoluted, that might also lead to that site.

"South Dakota?" Vance thought out loud, the confusion evident in his whispered tones. A state in the American section of the Alliance, it was a backwater, largely undeveloped and dot-ted with hotspots where old U.S. missile bases had been targeted during the Unification Wars. "What could be in South Dakota?"

Vance was usually disciplined, but now he found his mind continually wandering. Nothing Gavin Stark could do would surprise him, but he was having trouble grasping the idea of a plan so vast it could consume more than the GDP of a Super-power for 5-10 years. He was mystified as well at the brilliance of the cover up hiding the missing funds for so long. It was almost as if Stark had managed to create new money out of thin air. The truth was rather more problematic, however. The funds were all illusion, and the deception was finally about to fail. In a few days, weeks at the most, trillions of credits of financial obligations were going to be revealed as frauds, fabrications. Economists had been debating financial collapses for centuries, but now they were about to get the biggest of them all. It would be a miracle if it didn't lead to all-out war and the destruction of the terrestrial Superpowers.

Could that be part of his plan, Vance thought? "What would Stark gain by throwing Earth into Armageddon?" His whispers were deep and hoarse. He reached over to the pitcher on the table and filled a glass with water, draining two-thirds of it almost immediately. "What would he gain?" he asked himself again.

There was nothing he could do about the economic situation. He didn't think there was any way to undo that damage. He had a team working on it, just in case, but he wasn't at all hopeful they would come up with anything. They were quarantined on a small research facility on Deimos, no contact with the outside world except a one way beacon to signal that they discovered something. Vance hated locking up his own people like prisoners, but he couldn't chance a leak that could trigger the collapse any sooner than it was already going to happen. And, while he didn't expect them to develop a workable plan, he had to try, at least.

This mysterious Dakota site, he thought…that's a different matter now, isn't it? If he could locate it, it might be just the lead he needed to figure what Stark was up to.

Of course, he thought, scolding himself for getting prematurely excited, it could be anything…it might even be a phantom…part of the fraud. Or "it" could be a lot of its, scattered all over the place. He had no idea. But he was damned sure going to find out.

Chapter 21

Great Sentinel Forest
Planet Armstrong
Gamma Pavonis III

The fire was heavy…and it was getting worse. Major Danton was up on the forward line, directing the advance. Colonel Storm had launched his planned counter-attack, committing the last of the reserves and throwing the enemy back with the ferocity of the assault. Danton's 2nd Battalion had been one of those just-activated formations, and now his entire regiment had pushed forward. The newly released strength turned the momentum to the Marines, and they had driven the enemy back 2 klicks. But now the advance was slowing…a lot sooner than he'd expected. Resistance was thickening, and his own casualties were spiking rapidly.

Fuck, he thought…where the hell are they getting all these troops? He'd had a pretty good read on the forces he was facing and the casualties his people had inflicted. But he couldn't reconcile with the reports he was getting now…or the scene right in front of him. The enemy forces were far larger than he'd expected, and it felt like they were getting stronger and stronger, even as they fell back.

"Major Danton, Lieutenant Davison here, sir." The officer on the other end of the com sounded like he was 15 years old. Danton knew part of that was just him feeling old. It was getting harder and harder sending these kids into battle. Too few of them came back.

"What is it, Davison?" It took him a second to place the

name. He was part of the training battalion Danton had assigned to back up Captain Santi's forces…third or fourth in line of command, if he remembered correctly. Fourth, he confirmed, as he checked the OB on his tactical display. An acting lieutenant only, like all the officers in the junior training battalions.

"Captain Santi's dead, sir." Davison sounded shaky, his voice cracking as he spoke. "Captain Glantz and Lieutenant Solomon too." He paused, breathing loudly into the com. "I'm…I'm in command, sir."

"Get a grip on yourself, Davison." Danton spoke sharply, almost harshly to the panicked young officer. He empathized with Davison, but he needed to get through to the kid. Fast. He needed everyone's best right now.

"Yes, sir."

He sounds a little better, Danton thought…at least I think so. "Now report." He snapped out the command firmly.

"They're running, sir." His voice was quickly losing the tiny burst of confidence. The whole battalion, sir. I can't stop them."

Danton muted the connection and snapped at his AI, instructing it to show him Davison's position on the tactical display. "Fuck," he whispered under his breath as he saw the small blue icons streaming away from the line. He'd never seen a Marine battalion in wholesale rout…but then these weren't really Marines. They were underclassmen from Camp Basilone, recruits who hadn't completed half their training and who'd been pushed forward totally unarmored against first class powered infantry. They were running now, but that didn't tell the whole story. They'd held for a good while – longer than Danton had a right to expect – and they were leaving almost half their number on the field.

He unmuted the connection to Davison. "Lieutenant, fall back with your troops." He paused, looking at the map projected inside his visor. "Attempt to rally them at…" - he was still looking at the screen, trying to find a place far enough to the rear where Davison had a chance to reform his terrified recruits – "…Blackwood Hill." That was almost ten klicks back. He knew Davison didn't have a prayer of stopping the rout any-where closer to the front. But he didn't have time to worry about Davison's people now. He had to figure out how to plug the hole in his line before the entire advance collapsed.

The armor felt odd, the inner membrane cool against her bare skin. Sarah Linden hadn't worn her fighting suit for years, but Admiral Jacobs had flatly refused to let her land any other way. Neither side controlled the space around Armstrong…it was a kind of no man's land where a small destroyer squadron could temporarily claim local superiority. Far too dangerous to allow the Corps' senior medical officer to hop into a regular shuttle. He didn't like the idea of her and her people landing at all, but he insisted outright that if they were going, they were doing it fully armored in Gordon landers.

The acceleration from the launch catapult took her back through the years. There's no feeling quite like that, she thought, as she struggled to get her breath back. Sarah had spent most of her career in the medical branch, first in years of training and then as an active surgeon on some of the worst battlefields where men and women have fought. But everyone in the Corps started as a combat soldier, and it had been no different for her. She'd only made two battle drops, and both of them were rou-tine missions…nothing like the bloody nightmares she'd seen as a surgeon. But the feeling of descending through the upper atmosphere of a contested world was something you never forgot.

Very little intel had gotten out from Armstrong, but she was sure Erik's army was in a hard fight. Cain won battles – perhaps better than anyone in the history of the Corps – but his victories left huge numbers of shattered Marines on the field, broken men and women who deserved the best care the Corps could give them. Sarah had lagged behind Cain's army this time, tend-ing to the wounded from his last battle. But now she was here, and she'd be damned if anything was going to keep her from caring for the shattered Marines she knew were waiting down on the surface.

She didn't have any equipment...just 40 of her best people. But Armstrong wasn't some miscellaneous colony world. It was the home of the Marine Corps, and the hospital there was the biggest and best equipped anywhere in human space. She knew the facility itself would be off-limits...most of the fighting would be around the capital city of Astria, and Cain would almost certainly have evacuated all non-combat personnel. But he'd have moved all the portable equipment as well, and she was sure the staff would have set up a series of well-stocked field hospitals.

Her visor flipped open as the Gordon continued its rough ride to the surface. The zigzag pattern was a precaution. There'd been no sign of any enemy ground to air fire capability, but Jacobs insisted on the full assault landing profile. And that included a pattern of sudden, random movements designed to defeat targeting AIs. Sarah was glad she'd insisted all her people follow the 36 hour intravenous feeding program the combat Marines used. They weren't used to being bounced around quite so roughly.

Jacobs had tried to convince her she wasn't needed on the surface at all...that the hospital staff was perfectly capable of caring for the wounded. She didn't argue with him; she simply told him she was going. One look at her expression was enough to convince him he'd never change her mind.

She understood his point of view, and he was probably right, at least to a certain extent. But she also knew her place was down there with those Marines forced to go into battle again, so soon after the last war. And with Erik. She might not see him at all...she knew he'd be neck deep in command duties. But she needed to at least be on the same planet, fighting the same battle. And if he was wounded and she wasn't there to help him...to save him...she'd never be able to live with that. *I'm almost there, Erik,* she thought as the lander swung hard to the side...*I'm almost there.*

"We've got fires in the south sector too." Captain Claren was gesturing as he spoke into the com, trying to direct the civilian emergency crews. "Move it…I need two teams there now!"

Cain had sent his aide to direct the firefighting effort in Astria, but he didn't have any other manpower to spare. The civilians were doing an excellent job, but they weren't used to being ordered around like Marines. They weren't accustomed to being shelled while they fought fires either, but they were holding up.

The enemy artillery had begun the bombardment six hours earlier. They were trying to goad Cain into launching a ground attack across the Graywater. Claren almost snickered, though there was nothing funny about the situation. But if these people, whoever they are, he thought, think they're going to push Erik Cain into doing something he doesn't want to do, they're in for a rude awakening.

"If Cain comes across the Graywater at you, it's because he wants to…and that's not going to be a good day for you." He was talking to himself, expressing the same feeling that permeated the army. Cain was a harsh taskmaster, a ruthless butcher, an almost inhuman warrior…but to a man, the Marines considered him invincible on the battlefield. If Cain was at their head, they were resolute…they might not survive the fight, but they'd never taste defeat. It was an attitude Cain hated, though he didn't hesitate to use it to extract the maximum effort from his people. He was a confident officer, and an experienced leader, but Erik Cain had no illusions about invincibility. He stepped onto every battlefield knowing defeat nipped at his heels.

Claren's display flashed red…new fire. "Incoming." He shouted to the emergency crews, already diving for cover as he did. The civilians hesitated an instant before following his lead, their lack of combat reflexes showing.

The first explosion was on the outskirts of town, a mostly abandoned area containing nothing but empty warehouses. The second hit closer, right in the middle of a high-end residential area. Those who lived there had been evacuated, but Claren knew the blast would start more fires…and right in the center of the city this time. The conflagration would spread in all directions if he didn't get to it soon.

"I need crews 3 and 4 ready to move out in two minutes." He
yelled into the com, wondering as he did if the civilians would
come out of their hiding places and follow him. He felt nothing but admiration for these emergency workers, but he'd have
given his left arm for a company of armored Marines. "We've
got fires in the Park West district, and we need to get them under
control now. He lunged out from behind the plasti-steel girder,
waving his arms for the crews to follow.

He was watching them move slowly to follow when the area
behind him was suddenly engulfed in flame and smoke. The
force of the explosion threw his armored body hard against a
wall. He felt a stabbing pain…then the flow of drugs that shut
it down. He was lying at the base of a large building, disoriented, but he quickly realized he wasn't badly wounded. It's
just my arm, he thought, trying to twist his body around and
get up. The workers who'd lined up behind him were just gone.
Without armor they'd been blown to bits by the exploding shell.

Despite what happened, the rest of the crews were coming
out from their cover. They weren't Marines, he thought, but
they had their own courage. He was proud of them, as much
as he was of his own comrades in arms. He saw three of them
running over to him, rushing to his aid, screaming and waving
their arms…just as the wall collapsed and buried him under ten
tons of rubble.

Alex Linden sat quietly on the cold ground, leaning against
the wall of one of the portable shelters. She'd been trying to
reach Cain when the Marines poured into Astria and started
evacuating everyone. She almost tried telling one of the officers she was Sarah Linden's sister, but she stopped just before
it came out of her mouth. This was no time for carelessness.
She had no idea where Cain was, or how many of his people
would be around him. He'd seen her on Carson's World during
the final battle of the Third Frontier War, and he'd probably
remember her. If she told him she was Sarah's sister he would
be immediately suspicious. She'd only have one brief opportunity…and none at all if Cain was surrounded by his Marines.

Perhaps he won't remember, she thought, dismissing the hope in an instant. Betting her life on Erik Cain forgetting something seemed terribly unwise, especially since he'd been startled at her resemblance to Sarah. No, there was no chance he wouldn't recognize her. And that made this operation a knife's edge proposition.

It had been a hard decision to move forward and try to kill Cain. Her old resolve, the emotionless way she approached things, was gone. She'd carried immense anger and resentment toward the sister she thought was dead, blaming her for the nightmare that had destroyed her family and cast her into the violent ghettoes as a child. That rage had driven her, made her the relentless killer who had risen to the highest levels of Alliance Intelligence.

Finding Sarah alive…actually seeing her, spending time with her…it cracked the foundation of that deadly resolve. It was easier to blame a shadow, a memory, than an actual flesh and blood sister. For the first time in her adult life, Alex Linden was confused, unsure what to do…even how she felt.

She didn't want to kill Cain. She didn't have any quarrel with him herself, and she didn't want to cause Sarah the pain. But it wasn't that simple. Underestimating Gavin Stark would be an enormously foolish thing to do, and Stark had ordered her to assassinate Cain. She didn't really believe Stark would forgive her past failure and take her back into the fold…she knew she'd have to kill him if she was going to survive. But that would have to wait. There was no way to get to him now. And if she didn't kill Cain soon, she knew Stark would retaliate. He'd have her killed…and probably Sarah too. Alex wasn't going to let that happen. Not to Sarah. There had been so much anger toward her sister, so much bitterness over the years. Oaths of hatred she'd sworn when she was doing the things she had to do to survive. But everything was different now…the anger was still there, but there was something else too. Sarah was the only link Alex had to a family she thought she'd lost long ago. Whatever she felt, she knew she couldn't let Sarah die.

Erik Cain was a different matter. There was no animosity, no anger, no desire to kill the celebrated Marine. But there was no other way. She had enough of the cold, analytical resolve left to decide that Cain had to die.

She knew he was going to be hard to reach during the battle. She didn't have any solid intel on what was happening to the south, but she expected the fighting was raging. With Cain's reputation, he could be anywhere from the main HQ to leading a squad on the front lines.

She rose slowly to her feet, walking toward the perimeter of the camp. Well, she thought, wherever he is, I'm not going to find him in here. She walked toward one of the perimeter fences. The camp wasn't a detention facility, but it was surrounded by modular wall sections. The guards – mostly Astria police – were patrolling, trying to keep people from wandering off where they could get caught in the fighting or lost in the wilderness.

She wandered near the wall, trying not to draw attention to herself. She found a spot behind a row of portable storage sheds that blocked the view from the rest of the camp. With one quick move, she leapt over to the wall and upward, grabbing onto a hinge between sections. She was about to pull herself up and over when she heard it. Someone had walked around behind the sheds.

"Excuse me, Miss."

She didn't have to turn to know it was one of the guards.

"Please come down from there. You may get injured." His voice was soothing. He obviously thought she was a normal civilian, and the confinement and stress had gotten to her. "It is dangerous outside of the camp."

She held in a sigh as she hopped down to the ground. She'd really hoped to just slip away. Alex Linden was questioning many things she'd believed, but she was still a veteran assassin and intelligence operative. Her reflexes acted on their own, while her conscious mind debated what to do. She pretended to fall forward, and the guard instinctively lunged, catching her.

The motion was blindingly quick. He didn't have a chance to realize what was happening...even that anything at all was happening. She twisted, arms around his head, snapping his neck in an instant. She felt the body tense then go limp, and she released her grip, letting the dead guard slip to the ground.

She turned and jumped back on the wall, without so much as a look back, and threw herself up and over the top. Her feet slapped hard on the ground as she landed, and she ran over a small hillside, getting herself out of sight of the camp.

For an instant, a thought drifted through her mind...I can't even picture the face of the man I just killed. It was something new, the kind of thing that had never troubled her before, not in all the countless times she'd killed. She felt a rush of sadness, and something else...was it guilt? She paused for an instant, quietly thinking. Then a frown took over her face and she exhaled hard. No time for this, she thought, shaking her head and putting it out of her mind as she ran to the south... toward the fighting.

"I want prisoners." Cain's voice was loud, not quite deafening, but heading that way. "I have made that clear. Why don't we have any?" He paused for an instant, but continued his tirade before Merrick could speak. "Not one. Not even one!" There were half a dozen officers in the command post, every one of them pretending to be focused on something other than the commanding general's conversation with the chief of staff.

"General..." Merrick had just had the same go around with Colonel Storm, though he'd been the inquisitor on that one, not the hapless recipient of a superior's frustration. The fighting had been raging in Sentinel Forest for two days. The Marines had over 2,000 casualties, and by all accounts they'd inflicted far more than they'd taken. Yet not one live prisoner had been captured. And Erik Cain wasn't happy about that. "...all field units have been advised to collect live prisoners." He paused, his face twisting, as if he had a bad taste in his mouth. "We have preliminary evidence to suggest that the trauma control systems of the enemy's fighting suits have been modified to inject a fatal dose of barbiturates to non-ambulatory wounded personnel."

Cain had turned to look at the main display, but his head

snapped back to face Merrick. He had a formidable reputation for cold-bloodedness and for applying the brutal mathematics of war, but the thought of any army murdering its own wounded was beyond anything even Erik Cain could imagine. "Is this wild conjecture to excuse the lack of prisoners, or do we have real evidence?"

"Information is still sparse, general." Merrick's voice didn't project any doubt. "I don't have anything conclusive, but if you are asking my opinion based on what I have been told, there isn't much doubt."

Cain's face froze into something elemental. He didn't know where these soldiers had come from, whether it was one or more of the Powers behind this…or some other unknown adversary. But whoever or whatever it was, Cain decided then and there… it didn't need to be defeated. It needed to be utterly destroyed, crushed so completely that even memory of it would fade.

"I want to know who we are fighting, Isaac." Cain stared into his number two's eyes. "I want to know now."

"I want to know too, Erik." Merrick held up under Cain's icy stare, making him part of a small, elite group. "I just don't know how to find out."

"And I want prisoners, Isaac." Cain spoke with a resolve as solid as granite. "No matter what it takes."

Chapter 22

Saw Tooth Gorge
Red Mountains
Northern Territories, Far Concordia
Arcadia – Wolf 359 III

"Kara, we're picking up transmissions on the military fre-
quencies." Ed Calvin was standing outside her tent, shouting
excitedly.

"What?" Her voice was soft, groggy. She'd been having
trouble sleeping and just drifted off an hour before. "What kind
of message?" The tent flap opened, and she walked out wearing
rumpled fatigues, her coat draped over her shoulders.

"A general query for any Arcadian forces still in the field."
He saw the suspicious look forming on her face. "I know, I
know…I didn't respond. I wanted to talk to you first." He
paused uncomfortably. "But what could the enemy gain if it's a
trick of some kind? They know exactly where we are. As long
as we don't divulge any specific status info, what can it hurt to
answer?"

Kara stood silently, looking back at Calvin. She was still
waking up, her mind clearing slowly. Caution had been her first
impulse, but Calvin was right. They had nothing to lose. "OK,
Ed." She nodded slowly. "Let's answer and see what this is
all about." She wriggled, sliding her arms into her coat as she
began walking toward the communications tent.

Calvin walked alongside, following her the 30 or so meters
to the com center. He blew into his hands, the breath visible
in the cold morning air. Winter was coming on fast, and up in

the mountains it was going to be hard on the army. They had a couple nuclear-powered heaters that would last the winter, but they wouldn't do the job alone, and there wasn't nearly enough fuel to run the conventional units until spring. They'd been worried mostly about food and ammunition, but it took more than that to sustain thousands of soldiers indefinitely.

Kara threw aside the flap of the com tent and ducked inside. "Are we still getting transmissions?" She stared down at Captain Larson, the senior com officer in the army. A junior technician had been on duty, but when the receivers started blasting out transmissions, she called Larson immediately.

"Yes, commander." Kara didn't have a formal military title, and the troops had been uncertain how to address her with the proper respect. Eventually, commander became the standard form of address, though it had spread organically and wasn't based on any formalized commission or comparable military rank. "The same message keeps repeating. It is coming from orbit, and the broadcast is in Alliance standard code."

"Prepare to transmit a response. Set for translation to Alliance code A." Kara slid to the left, making room for Calvin to come all the way inside.

Larson moved his hands across his screen and flipped a small lever. "Ready, commander. Just speak into the microphone."

"Transmitting unit, this is Arcadia One responding to your query. What are your intentions?" Kara spoke slowly, clearly.

There was silence on the line, the tense seconds ticking slowly away. Kara was nervous. As suspicious as she was, the hope that some sort of relief had arrived lurked in her thoughts.

"Arcadia One, we are in receipt of your transmission."

Kara let out a soft sigh. Maybe, she thought…maybe there really is help on the way.

"We are able to provide you with resupply. Please provide your coordinates and a manifest of what you require."

Kara's suspicions flared up again. She wasn't about to give the enemy any intel on her supply situation. "Mute that." She whispered softly to Larson, who flipped a lever and nodded.

"What do you think?" She was turning to face Calvin. "You

think they're trying to pump us for info? Maybe it's the enemy, after all."

Calvin looked uncertain. "There's no way to know, Kara. If it is a relief force, this is what they would do...but it's also how the enemy would try to fake us out." He took a deep breath. "Even if they are friendlies, the enemy could still intercept our communications. There's no guarantee they haven't broken Alliance codes."

Kara looked down at the ground for a few seconds. "The enemy knows where we are, right?" Her head snapped up to look at Calvin. "No harm in giving out coordinates, at least."

"No...I can't see any downside in that. But if we give them a manifest of supplies we could be telling the enemy what we have...and more importantly, what we don't have. If they knew we were as low on ammo as we are, they'd probably be more aggressive."

She nodded. "I agree." She turned toward Larson. "Lieutenant, open the line again."

The com officer flipped another lever. "You're mic is live, commander."

"Arcadia One here. We will transmit our current coordinates immediately." She nodded to Larson, who sent the locational data.

"Cut the transmission." Kara had an odd expression on her face, stern yet hopeful. Was it actually possible that a relief force had arrived? She took a deep breath. She'd know soon if they were friendlies...if her people had a chance to get out of these mountains alive.

He'd forgotten how intense the jarring could be. It had been years since Elias Holm had taken an assault lander down to a target planet. His rank had relegated him to the follow up waves and the more comfortable heavy shuttles that transported supplies and equipment...along with the upper echelon command.

He found it exhilarating, a feeling that quickly came back to him, along with memories from dozens of past assaults. The Gordon zigzagged wildly, following a pre-programmed evasive course. He'd almost ignored the Marine standard 36 hour intravenous feeding period before launch, but now he was glad he'd relented and followed it. He thought of himself as too much of a veteran to lose his lunch on a landing, but the human digestive system wasn't built to endure this kind of punishment. Not without a little preparation and a good dose of pharmaceuticals.

"Sam, how're you holding up?" He spoke into the command com, checking up on his 83 year old comrade in arms.

"Just fine, Elias." Thomas snapped back his reply. "Don't you worry about me, you young punk. I've ridden worse than this. These things are like luxury shuttles compared to our old rides…and Arcadia's a pleasure palace compared to some of the hells I've fought on."

Holm laughed. Thomas was a character, there was no question about that. But he was right too. The Reynolds landers he and Thomas had used during the Second Frontier War bounced around a lot worse than the more modern Gordons. Back then, Holm had proven to himself you could vomit even when there was nothing in your stomach…despite a horse's dose of anti-emetics.

There was no fire from the ground, but the landers ratcheted around anyway, following the same evasive program they would have if a hundred surface to air missiles were coming at them. Carelessness killed Marines. Holm had said it countless times, trying to beat it into the heads of little puppy jarheads… and more than a few combat vets too…guys who should have known better than they did. But he'd almost ignored his own advice. Until Sam Thomas scolded him.

Holm was nervous about the mission, worried about the retired vets he'd recruited back into service. Once a Marine, always a Marine…it was the Corps creed. But is there never a time, Holm thought, when someone has done enough? When they've earned the right to be left alone, to run their farms or sit in their easy chairs? He'd brought over 1,000 Marines here, men and women who'd done their service before most of James Teller's people were born. Some of them would die here…maybe all of them. Did he have a right to lay this at their doorstep, to pull them away from hearth and home and back to the horrors of the battlefield after so many years?

His guilt walked hand in hand with his pride, his solemn respect for the men and women the Corps produced. When Thomas had spread the word, the veterans poured onto his farm, answering the call without a second thought. Other Marines were in trouble…that's all they needed to hear. Even as he hated himself for calling them back to the colors, he waxed with admiration and respect for these veterans who answered, who came without hesitation to rally to his cause.

"Touchdown in 60 seconds." The soothing tones of the AI pulled him from his introspection. He couldn't really move, bolted into his armor, but he could see the landscape below. They were coming down in a broad plain, not too far from Teller's reported position, just north of a huge inland sea.

Holm had never been as relieved as he was when Teller answered the fleet's query. Rounding up the retirees and dragging them to Arcadia weighed on him a bit less heavily now that they'd confirmed there were live Marines to rescue. Whatever happened, however the battle ahead turned out, Holm and his band of veterans were here to aid their brothers and sisters. However brutal the fighting…no matter how many died, that made the effort worthwhile. Marines aiding their comrades didn't stop to do math, they didn't weigh the costs of going in. They just went.

"Thirty seconds to impact." Holm heard his rifle whine, the nuclear reactor on his back feeding power into its circuits. A few seconds later there was a loud crack…the landing struts extending from their retracted position.

"Alright, Marines…" Holm was speaking into the forcewide com, feeling a little silly nursemaiding these warriors, most of whom had been veterans when he was swabbing the bathrooms back at Camp Basilone. "…we don't expect any resistance at the landing zone, but I want everybody ready anyway."

He felt the upward jerk of the landing jets firing, then the mildly stomach-churning sensation of the ship dropping the last ten meters to the ground. An instant later the landing gears hit dirt, and the locking bolts released their hold on his armor.

He jumped forward a meter or so, pulling his rifle from its harness and looking out toward the perimeter of the LZ. He scanned around his ship, seeing mostly the other landers. There was no enemy in range…no incoming fire at all. Holm had chosen this position carefully. It was close to Teller's people, but not too close. He didn't want to expose his aged veterans to an opposed landing. Better to march 50 klicks than to get shot to pieces climbing out of the landers.

"Alright, Sam, let's get everybody formed up and on the move." Holm had made Thomas second in command. It felt strange giving orders to his old commander, but Thomas didn't seem to have any problem following them. It had been a long time since the old colonel had been in the field, and Holm wasn't the young officer thrust prematurely into command that he'd been the last time he shared a battlefield with Thomas. This Elias Holm had more than four decades of combat experience.

"Already getting them formed up, general." Thomas sounded sharp and crisp, like the almost 40 year period separating him from his last battlefield was merely an instant. "Let's go pull Jim Teller's ass out of the fire."

Handler was crouched behind a pile of twisted metal, looking out over the pockmarked prairie. He wasn't sure what his makeshift cover had been before it was blasted into an unrecognizable mess. A drilling rig, perhaps? It didn't really matter, he thought…it was decent protection. He was out on point, watching for any enemy move from the north.

After the retreat from the mountain, the battle had become a fluid one. Teller ordered the entire army — what was left of it — into extended formation. The enemy had gone nuclear, and that had changed things. It had been a unique target, and they hadn't used any specials since, but Teller ordered nuclear battlefield protocols anyway. He'd lost almost 100 of his people in the first attack…Marines who hadn't gotten far enough from the mountain to survive the massive blasts of the heavy nukes. He wasn't about to risk another disaster like that.

The enemy had been hot on their heels for days, attacking almost continuously. Handler didn't know what had ignited such urgency. He was about as far from the top of the organizational chart as he could be, but even grunts in the field usually had some idea of what motivated their enemy. Now it all made sense. General Teller had made the force-wide announcement. A relief force had landed. That's why the enemy had gone nuclear. And that's why Teller was worried they would again.

So, Handler thought, they wanted to take us out before they had a second army to deal with. "Well, fuck you all," he muttered with considerable venom. Handler was a training camp slacker who was finding his true self on the battlefield, and one lesson he was learning all too well…hatred for the enemy. He'd started going through the motions, executing on his training. He'd been almost robotic at first, following one instruction after another, like a computer. But then he saw friends and comrades die at the hands of the enemy. Now there was more than training at work. He relished every enemy he took out, savored the vengeance as he massacred those who had pursued and killed his brothers in arms.

"Anything out there?" Bill Greene ran up from behind. He sat down hard behind Handler, releasing the large cargo canister from his back.

"Nope. Nothing at all. Looks like they had enough." Handler didn't really believe that. The enemy was as good as the Marines, or at least nearly so. Wherever they came from, Handler had to acknowledge these were elite troops he and his brethren were facing.

"Maybe they're dealing with the landing." Morale had soared with the news that reinforcements had arrived, and Greene was no exception. "For all we know, the rest of the Corps landed on their asses."

"Maybe." Handler was considerably more circumspect than his friend. It was possible, he guessed, that an overwhelmingly powerful force of Marines had landed, but he doubted it. If an enemy force of this quality was fighting on Arcadia, there had to be other trouble spots too. Perhaps war had broken out between the Powers. No, he thought…the best we can reasonably hope for is enough strength to gain a stalemate.

"You don't sound convinced." Greene wasn't letting his comrade's concern bring him down. "But it looks like the enemy pulled back. That must mean something." He was digging into the cargo container as he spoke, pulling out assault rifle cartridges and stacking them next to Handler.

"Call me cautious." Handler reached to the side, grabbing the clips one at a time and snapping them into the slots on the outside of his armor. His eyes stayed focused on the flat ground in front of him, never wavering.

"What the hell happened to my under-achieving best friend?" Greene was trying to suppress a laugh as he spoke. "When did you turn into another Blood and Guts Cain?"

"This isn't training anymore, Tommy." There was an edge to Handler's voice, a seriousness that hadn't been there before. "It's life and death. And we've…" He hesitated for an instant, staring at his display then he switched his com to the HQ line. "Major Barnes, sir…this is Private Handler on scouting duty. I have multiple enemy contacts on my scanners sir. It looks like another assault coming in." He paused, just for an instant. "A big one, sir." He snapped a new cartridge into his rifle's magazine and looked out over the prairie.

Chapter 23

Alliance Intelligence Facility Q
Dakota Foothills
American Sector, Western Alliance
Earth – Sol III

The moon shone brightly above the rugged hills and jagged ridges of the Dakota backcountry. Major Garth would have preferred to wait for a moonless night, but Vance had made it clear…time was of the essence. They had to go in immediately. Garth couldn't even imagine what resources Vance had employed to smuggle the whole team into the Alliance undetected. This must be beyond urgent, he thought grimly, as he stared at his display, making sure everyone was in position. He exhaled hard, pushing back the feeling of dread that was trying to bubble up from inside him.

His people had been well-briefed. They all knew what to do, and they'd been ordered to maintain communications silence unless it was an emergency. They were looking for something, an Alliance facility of some sort. Whatever it is, Garth thought, it's damned well hidden.

His troops were the best the Confederation had, trained both as commandos and intelligence agents. Red Team Beta was the senior formation in the Confederation's ground forces…and they had been since the Alpha team had been wiped out on a mission so secret, as far as anyone but the Council was concerned, they'd simply vanished into thin air. Rumors persisted that there had been a single survivor, but if that was true, no one had ever seen him.

Alpha team's colors had been cased and the unit retired, the only honor Vance could give to troops lost on such a secret mission. Now Red Team Beta was on another operation, one just as vital…perhaps even more so. Vance had addressed them himself before they were inserted, and it was obvious from his demeanor that whatever they were looking for, it was immensely important. None of them had ever witnessed Roderick Vance anything but coldly efficient, but this time they'd seen fear in his eyes.

Garth moved quietly along a small rocky spine, crouched low behind the meter and a half wall of stone. The team had the newest prototype armor, equipped with every device Martian science possessed to thwart detection, including the still-experimental Mark 10 camouflage. But he wasn't taking any chances. All the tech in the world wasn't an excuse to get careless.

"Lieutenant Tobin, take point." His visor was up, and Tobin was standing right next to him. It was low tech, but it was the most undetectable way for them to communicate.

"Yes sir." Rick Tobin was a humorless sort, and he sounded like a martinet when he spoke. Garth knew otherwise. Tobin had been a highly decorated platoon commander during the fighting on Garrison. Though twice hit himself, he ran a gauntlet of First Imperium fire three times, carrying back his wounded troopers. When they finally got him to the field hospital, he'd been hit five times and, despite the best efforts of his suit's trauma control system, he was nearly bled out.

"Be careful, lieutenant." Garth was speaking softly. His people hadn't detected any contacts, but there was no point in shouting, just in case. "Avoiding detection is your top priority." Garth didn't know how realistic that was. If there was something around here as important as Vance seemed to think, there was no way they were sneaking in undetected. Still, they had to try.

"Yes, major." Tobin nodded and snapped his visor down as he turned and trotted over to where his team had assembled.

Garth looked out over the scrubby prairie. What could they have out here? What could have gotten the normally ice-cold

Roderick Vance so unnerved? Garth shuddered just thinking about it.

"Colonel, I am monitoring multiple surface contacts." Lieutenant Jackson-315 spoke steadily, almost robotically. "Minimum 20, sir. Possibly more."

The control center was almost silent, save for an occasional beep from one of the computers. There were a dozen officers present, quietly manning workstations positioned around the perimeter of the circular room. They worked with cool efficiency, managing the complex and its detection and defense systems. Facility Q was the largest base ever constructed by mankind. Its underground tunnels and rooms spread under 40 square kilometers of desolate South Dakota wilderness.

"Alert the duty company." Colonel Anderson-17 sat like a statue, unmoving, his chair set upon a raised dais in the center of the room. This could be an innocent contact, he thought... local ranchers looking for strays or something similar. Indeed, that's most likely what it was. He had to be cautious...sending a company of armored guards to shoot up the countryside was a last resort. His primary orders were to avoid any type of contact that might threaten the facility's secrecy. Most likely, this was nothing requiring a response. Still, he couldn't take any chances. "Prepare to intercept on my command."

"Yes, sir." Jackson-315 snapped off the response, his fingers already dancing across his control pad. A few seconds later: "Gold Company leader reports ready, colonel." He paused, only for a brief instant. "Awaiting your orders, sir."

Anderson-17 remained silent, considered the situation methodically. If he blasted a bunch of locals who'd wandered into the quarantined zone, it would be a mess to clean up later. One ranch hand getting lost and disappearing in the wilderness wouldn't draw attention. Twenty people missing would kick off a search...even if they were only Cog ranch workers. Number One had been very clear about maintaining the facility's secrecy. Starting a firefight and wiping out a pack of locals wasn't exactly low profile. Anderson-17 was as coldly fearless as the rest of the Shadow Force, but that courage didn't extend to matters involving the Commander. He had a deep fear of Gavin Stark, just like all the Shadow soldiers. He'd wait and watch. For now.

"There are definitely contacts here, sir." Tobin had moved out in the open, allowing him line of sight to contact Garth with a direct laser communication. The energy of the laser was detectable, but far less so than a standard com line.

There was something in Tobin's voice. Garth couldn't quite place it. Not fear, exactly…at least not only fear. Astonishment? "Talk to me, lieutenant. What are you reading?"

"I'm only getting intermittent signals, sir." The scanner he was using was the leading edge of Martian R&D, a quantum leap over any existing systems. It was also one of the most classified devices in human space. Nothing short of the present crisis would have compelled Vance to release it from the underground lab where it had been tested…and protected by a division of Confederation regulars. "There's all kinds of shielding here. Without these new scanners we wouldn't be reading a thing."

"What are you getting?" Garth was getting impatient. "Let's go, Tobin. Talk to me."

"Sorry sir." Tobin's tone was still distracted. "Sorry, major," he repeated. "I am getting readings over a large area, sir." He looked up from the screen he'd been focused on. "If this is all one complex, it is the biggest thing I've ever seen. We have intermittent contacts over 40 square kilometers."

Now it was Garth's turn to stand in stunned silence, though only for a few seconds. "Forty square kilometers?" It was all he managed to spit out.

"Yes, sir. If this is all one base, it's massive."

"Any indication of entry points?" Garth knew the answer before he even asked.

"Negative, sir." Tobin turned to look over at Garth. "We're barely getting any readings at all."

Garth sighed. Vance had been clear about the importance of this mission. His people had already accomplished a great deal simply validating the Martian spymaster's concerns. What-

ever it was they had found, there could be no doubt this barren
stretch of wilderness was the home to an enormous construct
of some kind.

"Sergeant Barrick." Garth snapped into the com, again by
direct laser link.

"Yes, major?" The response was immediate. Barrick was
a veteran's veteran. The armored figure turned at once to face
Garth and trotted over toward the major's position.

"Take one of the privates and fall back to the rally point."
They had a satellite uplink hidden there, and he was determined
that Vance would know what they had found, even though they
really knew very little. Garth suspected even the simple confirmation that an enormous facility existed would be valuable to
Vance. "I want you to transmit a message back to Control. And
remember, direct laser communication only until you get to the
uplink."

Garth had every intention of trying to gain access to the
mysterious facility...and no illusions about the chances of any
of his people making it back out. But whatever happened, he
had to be sure Vance at least knew they'd confirmed the presence of...something. With luck, Garth figured he'd be able to
follow up with more information once they scouted things more
closely. If not, at least his people wouldn't die for nothing.

"Yes, sir." Barrick's voice was as impassive as usual.
"Thurber, report to me at once." Garth could hear the veteran
sergeant snapping his orders to one of the privates.

Garth flipped to Tobin's line. "Lieutenant, transmit the full
data set from the scanners to Sergeant Barrick immediately." He
paused. "Everything you've got."

"Yes, sir." Tobin's reply was immediate.

Garth flipped back to Barrick's line. "Sergeant, Lieutenant
Tobin is transmitting the scanner readings to you. It is impera-
tive that you get all of that data up to the satellite. I'm sending
you the frequency for the priority channel. Use it."

"Yes, sir." Barrick was silent for a few seconds. "Sir, I
already have the data from Lieutenant Barrick. Request permission to move out, sir."

"Granted. Get going." He paused briefly, the com channel still open, then he added, "Good luck, sergeant." He closed the link and took a deep breath. Now it was time to try to sneak inside the biggest base he'd ever seen...just him and 36 commandos. He flipped the comlink back to Tobin's frequency. "Lieutenant, I need your best guess on where to look for an entrance to this...whatever." He inhaled deeply. "We're going in."

Chapter 24

Great Sentinel Forest
Planet Armstrong
Gamma Pavonis III

The Obliterators crashed through the forest, moving quickly, knocking aside some of the smaller trees as they passed. General McDaniels was in the forefront, pushing her people hard. Cain's orders had been clear, and the urgency in his voice had been unmistakable. He hadn't wanted to release the Obliterator's this early, but he was out of options. All hell was breaking loose in the Sentinel. Colonel Storm's command was being overrun, his lines a shattered wreck, pierced in a dozen places. If McDaniels didn't execute her flank attack on the left, half the army would be nothing but shattered remnants.

The forest was far from ideal terrain for her people and their four meter tall suits of armor. Was it just armor, she thought… or were the massive suits really small vehicles? She wasn't sure where the Obliterators fit in terms of military categorization. But whatever you called them, they were having one hell of a time getting through the dense woods. Still, McDaniels was determined to push her people through. The Sentinel had been considered virtually impassable to large bodies of infantry – until the enemy marched north in force, laying that myth to rest. Cain's response was typical. If the enemy could march thousands of powered infantry through the clusters of massive trees, then his people could do one better…and move over a thousand of the massive Obliterators south. When McDaniels pointed out the difficulty, Cain simply expressed his confidence in her and repeated his orders, urging her to move as quickly as possible. She knew there was no point in arguing. She'd have to find a way to get through the forest.

From his position on the far right, Cooper Brown had been burning through scouts trying to reach the bridges and get a read on the enemy strength moving across the river. With the satellite network destroyed and no air power, there'd been no way for Cain to know how many waves the enemy had landed to the south, outside the range of his ground detection. Brown's efforts hadn't produced much besides dead scouts, and what intel he was able to get was grim. He hadn't managed to push anyone across the Graywater, but his people had confirmed long columns of enemy troops moving across the bridges. Cain resisted as long as he could, but in the end he had no choice. He issued the order and sent the Obliterators into the battle. McDaniels would have followed Cain anywhere, but she swore under her breath when he ordered her people into the dense forest. He assured her she could execute the maneuver, and to her surprise, she had. Once again, Cain had been right. What seemed impossible wasn't, and her forces were about to emerge into the open country just north of the river. It hadn't been easy, but her people had seen it done.

Cain's order was further vindicated when Admiral Jacobs' naval squadron burst into the system and did a complete scan of the planet. They dropped a new network of scanner buoys in orbit and destroyed the enemy satellites. Suddenly, Cain's intel was back on line, and the data coming in was alarming. Storm's people were outnumbered at least five to one, and more enemy forces were pouring northward toward the forest.

Erin McDaniels had served with Erik Cain throughout the First Imperium War, and she was the first – and only – commander of the Obliterator corps. She knew better than any living Marine exactly what these things could do with the right tactics. She even felt something approaching confidence that her people could stabilize the situation. But first she had to get through the forest and cut the bridges over the Graywater.

Cain had ordered her to widen her approach march, trying to

take advantage of the enemy's loss of its own satellite observa-
tion. The tactic made sense, making her people harder for the
enemy to detect…but it also delayed the attack, allowing more
enemy troops to cross the river and leaving Storm's forces to
hold off the overwhelming advance alone. Cain's response had
been simple when she raised that issue. "They'll hold," was all
he had said, though the silence that followed told her there was
far more going on in Cain's head than simple confidence. He
could appear cold and unfeeling, but she knew a part of him
died with every one of those Marines on the line who fell.

"Captain Jager, your people will be in the lead." She had her
force on radio silence, and she'd jogged forward to get a direct
laser com line to Jager. "When you come out of the forest you'll
be 5 klicks east of the first enemy bridge. I want you to execute
a sharp turn, advance, and launch your attack."

"Yes, general." Jager, like the rest of her Marines, was frustrated with the difficult march and straining to get at the enemy.

They didn't know the odds they faced, and McDaniels didn't
see any point in telling them. They were ready for the fight…
and they would give all they had. She knew that for certain.
"And Captain…" - her voice hardened, her own resolve stiff-
ening – "…when you go in, just keep pushing forward." She
paused for an instant, exhaling hard. "I'll be right behind you
with the rest of the corps."

General Anderson-3 stood in the rocky sand along the banks
of the Graywater. The forest ran almost to the water's edge,
maybe 700 meters of muddy marsh sitting between the river and
the towering trees of the Sentinel. His forces were advancing,
moving across the pontoon bridges and into the dense trees…
toward the front, where the enemy lines were starting to collapse. The Marines fought like hell, but Anderson-3 had a huge
numerical superiority, and he kept throwing fresh units at them,
slowly, surely blunting their advance and then pushing them
back. Now, victory was in his grasp. It was time to launch an
all-out attack and break them.

He'd lost his satellite intel, the unfortunate result of the arrival of an enemy squadron. At first, he'd been concerned that the newly arrived ships would land Marine reinforcements, but they'd only sent down a handful of landers...nothing that would seriously affect the battle. Other than the loss of his satellites, little had changed. His forces had numbers; they had momentum. He just had to push forward, driving relentlessly against the outmatched enemy until they finally broke.

Anderson felt something...satisfaction, perhaps? As with many sensations, he had trouble fully understanding it, identifying its source. He knew he had false memories...not truly invented ones, perhaps, but not his own either. He could vaguely remember leading forces on other worlds...wispy images of places his conscious mind knew he'd never been. He couldn't really comprehend it all, but that was OK. He didn't have to understand...he just had to do his duty. Still, it was unnerving at times, distracting. A strange hole in his mind, one that nagged at him, especially when he had time to think.

"Colonel, it is time for your people to advance."

Colonel Anderson-45 snapped to attention. "Yes, sir." His response was crisp and immediate, but he didn't salute. It came to him from the place in his mind where his training was stored. Regulations said no saluting this close to the enemy. Snipers, he realized. They could be hidden in the woods, looking for high value targets.

He nodded slightly then turned and trotted off, issuing orders to his regiment's officers as he did. His people had just crossed the river. They were already formed up and ready to advance, but he double-checked anyway. It seemed superfluous, but that's what the manual required, so that's what he did.

The regiment was in line of battle, 3000 strong, all along the edge of the great forest. His mission was clear. His force would smash through the wavering enemy lines and pursue the exhausted Marines north, staying with them, not giving them a chance to rally or regroup.

He was confident his force could do the job. The enemy lines were already buckling. They were trying to fall back, to disengage and regroup. But he wasn't going to give them the chance.

It felt odd, moving forward, about to launch the attack. Strange, unfamiliar feelings rose up from within. Was this fear, he wondered? Or was it simply heightened sensitivity, his body's reaction to the danger ahead? He had wispy memories of combat, though he'd never been in battle before. Strange, he thought...all this is familiar, though it is my first time going into combat. He pondered the strange sensations for an instant then something, some mental discipline deep in his mind, forced his thoughts away from the esoteric, back to the task at hand.

"Regiment, prepare to advance." He spoke loudly into the unitwide com. "Forward." He walked quickly, determinedly into the dense woods. Into combat.

Cain stared at the display, silent, rigid as a stone monument. There is was, right in front of him...courtesy of the string of satellites Admiral Jacobs had left in orbit before he pulled out of the system. Jacobs' force was small, just an escort for Sarah and her medical teams. He didn't have any reinforcements for Cain's army, but he was able to restore the orbital surveillance network...and give him back his eyes on the battlefield.

Those eyes showed him a stark reality. For once, things were worse even than Cain expected. After the enemy had blinded him by destroying his satellites, they had landed wave after wave of reinforcements. They came down in the middle of the undeveloped wilderness far to the south, and they quickly destroyed the few monitoring stations, leaving Cain and the Marines completely blind as more and more troops landed. He'd added it up three times, coming to the same conclusion. His people were facing over twice as much enemy strength as they thought. There were at least 50,000 invaders on Armstrong's surface, thousands of them still marching north toward the primary battlefield. Which meant everything his people had fought, all the enemy formations they had identified...they were less than half of what they truly faced.

Casualties were already high, and the staff of the Corps hospital in Astria was working around the clock caring for the wounded. Things had been under control until the enemy bombardment forced Cain to order the facility abandoned. The wounded were evacuated and moved to makeshift field hospitals to the north. That meant rougher facilities and more shortages of equipment and supplies. And that meant more of his people would die.

Sarah would quickly take charge of it all…he knew that much. And the wounded would benefit. She had tremendous experience working in the difficult conditions of field hospitals during a battle. She would work tirelessly and ride her people without mercy. Her presence would save lives, he had no doubt about that. The wounded Marines deserved nothing less.

Cain had been happy to see her, of course, though he'd only been able to spare a few minutes for the reunion. Nevertheless, a part of him wished she hadn't come. He couldn't explain it fully. He hated the long separations, missed her every day she wasn't with him…but there was something else, something darker in his mind. He didn't really like himself on the battlefield. He knew there were two incarnations of Erik Cain, drastically different from each other…and the battlefield commander was by far his darker side. He didn't want her to see him that way, to watch him turn into the icy cold monster that sent thousands to their deaths.

The cold, ruthless combat commander, who'd gone from victory to victory and blazed a trail of glory across human space – it was an impressive image, but in Cain's mind it was pure fiction. No, he thought, the larger than life hero is bullshit, the product of peoples' need to idolize leaders. To what was left of Erik Cain, the man, the persona that strode so tall across these battlefields was a butcher, a stone cold killer, a monster who should be locked away forever. He was a man who sent his loyal troops to their deaths again and again, who'd sacrificed his best friend to his own arrogance. Perhaps, he thought, he had only become what was needed to face the endless strife that afflicted mankind. But that didn't help him like himself, and it didn't change what he was. And he was at a loss to explain how Sarah could love a creature like him.

He looked around the control room, shaking himself from his introspection. What am I doing here? His thoughts were grim, dark. The battle will be decided in the Sentinel…and along the river. He'd allowed the enemy batteries to smash Astria nearly to rubble…all to divert strength to the decisive combat. Would it be enough? He didn't know, but he was sure of one thing. Whatever happened, he'd be on that line with his Marines when it did.

"Captain Claren, I'm suiting up and moving forward to get a look."

Claren's face wore a mask of horror, but the loyal aide knew better than to argue with Cain. The general was like a force of nature in battle, and nothing he could say would make any difference at all. Or perhaps one thing…

"Request permission to accompany the general." Claren stood rigidly at attention. "I fear we need every man, sir."

Cain stopped and turned to look back at Claren. He was about to tell the aide to remain behind and keep him advised from the scanning reports…but he paused, his eyes settling on Claren's stony expression. The young officer had been in a very close call in Astria, but in the end, his armor saved him from serious injury. He had a few scrapes and bruises…not bad considering a building had fallen on him. The suit was a total loss, but Claren had been able to find a new one that fit from the army's dwindling supplies.

"Very well, captain. Suit up." He turned around and strode from the room, his face grim. He didn't really expect to come back, and he hadn't wanted to take Claren with him. But his aide was a Marine, and a good one at that. He didn't have the right to force him to stay behind, and he knew it.

"Forward. All units." McDaniels' voice was raw, hoarse. Her people had been in action nonstop for 36 hours. "To the bridges!" They were almost there. One more good push; that's all it would take.

The tiny strip of land between the river and the forest was packed with troops, her people in their massive Obliterator suits pushing forward, slowly driving the disordered enemy back. It was a bloody affair, one costly attack after another, the invaders fighting like devils but not able to endure the firepower of the Obliterators.

She was down to half strength, but she knew at least some of that was just suit damage. The almost four-meter tall suits could be disabled without the operator even being hit. She'd been monitoring the data feed on her display, and it looked like about half her "casualties" were just wrecked suits. Still, that meant a quarter of her people were dead or wounded, and they were kilometers from the nearest aid station.

"I'm with the lead elements, general." Her comlink crackled to life, the voice of her exec, Colonel Clarkson coming through. "We're 500 meters from objective A." There were three bridges spanning the Graywater, each separated by about 300 meters. "We've got incoming fire from the bridge as well as the shore."

"Very well, colonel." She felt a rush of adrenalin. Almost there, she thought. "I'm sending you reserves now. I want an all-out attack here. Forward to the bridges." She knew time wasn't on her side. Her people were taking partial enfilade fire now, and it would just get worse as they advanced. The enemy had a lot of strength south of the river. Her people were inflicting more damage, but she was going to run out of troops first. They had to clear those bridges and get between the enemy forces on each side of the river. Fast.

She switched her com frequency. "Captain Horgan, move your troops forward and reinforce Colonel Clarkson."

"Yes, general." The response was almost immediate. Horgan was one of her best officers, and his company was a crack formation, the successor unit to the original company of Obliterators.

She started moving forward, waddling back and forth to keep from bounding up in the air as she jogged. She was going in with her people. This was the final push. "Now's our time, people." She was shouting into the unitwide com. "Forward to the bridges!" She clicked a switch and deployed her dual autoguns as she advanced. "Forwa..."

She felt the impacts, slamming into her, pushing her back. It was surreal, almost slow motion at first. Then the pain. Searing agony. She'd been hit, at least 3 or 4 times. It was an enemy auto-cannon on the bridge, a lucky shot at this range. She held her scream until she cut the comlink, but then it forced its way out. Anger, frustration, pain…terrible pain. She struggled, sweat beading on her forehead. No time for this, she thought. Work to do. She gritted her teeth, took a deep breath and flipped the com back on. "Forward!"

Storm was crouched in a trench – more of a foxhole, really, and a shallow one at that. He was scanning the small clearing, waiting for the enemy to move out into the open. His people had been falling back, reforming every few klicks and trying to hold for at least a few hours before retreating again. He was choosing positions carefully, trying to maximize the damage inflicted on the advancing enemy. He was making good use of the cover, but he knew once his people were driven from the forest it would be over. They were massively outnumbered, and the enemy was as well trained as his Marines. If they were forced to fight in open country, he knew it would be over in a few hours.

He couldn't even keep track of the casualties anymore, but he knew all his units were below half strength…and some a lot worse off than that. There were probably a few Marines still in the fight with damaged medical scanners or transmitters. Still, no matter how he looked at it, his forces were gutted.

He rolled his eyes up, glancing at his tactical display. There were small blue rectangles stretched out in a rough line through the woods…his forces. Clusters of red symbols were moving toward his much thinner blue line. There was about a kilome-ter and a half between the two positions. In the open, they'd already be engaged and, even in the dense woods, it wouldn't be more than a few minutes before the fighting started up again. He'd reviewed the ground behind this location. They had one, maybe two fallback positions, and then they'd be out in the roll-ing grasslands south of Astria. Then they'd be fucked.

"Colonel Storm, enemy forces are advancing on my position." It was Corporal Wimmer, one of the forward pickets. "I think they're moving to the left, sir."

"Very well, corporal." Storm flipped his com channel. "Sergeant Kelton, any activity in your sector?" Kelton was posted on the extreme right.

"Negative, sir." The response was immediate and definitive. Not for the first time, Storm felt a rush of pride for his people. They were in deep shit, and they all knew it, but their discipline and competency were unaffected. "All quiet here."

Shit, Storm thought...they're trying to flank us. He scolded himself. He'd been expecting them to plunge straight ahead into the teeth of his defenses. The First Imperium War had been as hard a fight as Storm had ever seen, but it had been the enemy's technology and numbers that made it so. The tactics of the First Imperium master computers had been rudimentary... predictable and lacking in creativity. He didn't know who this new enemy was, but he realized he was going to have to adapt to dealing with an adversary nearly as unpredictable and skilled as his own Marines.

"Lieutenant Davenport, move your strike force to the extreme left flank."

"Yes, sir." Julia Davenport was another veteran of the First Imperium War. Most of his people were. "Keep your eyes open, Julia. I think the enemy is trying to flank us." After five years of fighting a technologically superior robotic enemy, his people all needed a crash course in dealing with human foes again.

"Understood, sir." A short pause. "Moving out now."

"I want a report if you see so much as a leaf flutter over there. Understood?" Storm didn't really need any confirmation, however. He'd already come to a conclusion. The enemy was going to hit the left hard. Well, two could play at that game. He flipped his com channel again. "Captain Barrington..." – Barrington commanded two strike forces on the extreme right - "the enemy is about to attack our left. You are to advance and assault their exposed left." He hoped it would be exposed, at least.

"Yes, sir."

Two can play at this game, not just..." He paused...he didn't know what to call this enemy. They were human, and they had the same equipment and doctrine as Alliance Marines. That was all he knew. And he didn't think Erik Cain or any of the rest of the high command knew much more. He shook his head. That's not my problem now, he thought, forcing his thoughts back to the battle. Whomever they are, wherever they came from, they're here. That's all that matters.

"And, captain...I need you to hit them hard. You'll be out-numbered, so the first few minutes are crucial."

"Understood, sir."

Yes, Storm thought. Barrington knows just what I need from his people.

Anderson-45 was running up and down his lines, rallying his troops, driving them forward against the relentless fire. He'd thought he had the Marines broken more than once, but each time they'd fallen back a few kilometers and formed another line. He'd lost a third of his troops, and the regiments on either side were even worse off. The enemy was suffering too, but no matter how many his people killed, the cursed Marines simply refused to break. They made his troops pay in blood for every bitter step and then pulled back to another position.

Now they'd broken off again, slipping farther to the north after blooding his battalions yet again. It was beyond frustrating. Every time he thought he had them, they slipped away, found a newer, stronger position. And each time they broke contact they managed to slip out of engagement range, forcing him to reform his forces and pursue.

He knew his troops were good...but there was something these Marines had that his own people lacked. He wasn't sure what it was, and he didn't know if he'd understand it anyway. But it was more than the skill of the troops. It was leadership. Anderson-45 followed every regulation, every bit of training. He led his regiment with flawless competence. But the commanders he was facing were better, more unpredictable. The Shadow Corps was one of the best fighting formations in human space...Anderson-45 knew that. But as close as the legions had come, the Marines were better still.

It didn't matter. It wasn't going to save them. He had reinforcements moving north even now, and he knew the Marines had none. The enemy would make this a costly affair, but in the end it wouldn't change a thing. And they were running out of forest. Another few kilometers, and they'd be out in the open. Then Anderson-45's numbers would tell.

"OK Marines, listen up." Cain's voice was unmistakable on the com. He was addressing every man and woman in Storm's shattered command, and in his voice they heard a strength, a firmness that drew from them every ounce of stamina and determination they had left. "We're going to hold this line." He paused, and when he continued his voice was louder, more determined. "We're going to stand here, and we will fight to the last man. If we do not turn the enemy back on this line, there won't be anyone left to retreat." He paused again. He was rallying these battered Marines. Every one of them knew they had their best chance if they held their ground, didn't allow themselves to get pushed back into the open. But they were exhausted...and many of them were wounded. Men and women were still human, no matter how well trained they were, how many times they'd been in battle. They had a breaking point, and when they reached it, reason went out the window. Cain wasn't sure he fully understood his complex relationship with his Marines, but he knew one thing for sure. When he stood with them, shoulder to shoulder, they would hold firm if the devil himself was charging through these woods. "And I will be here with you. My rifle will fire with yours." Another pause. "And together we will hold this line!"

He couldn't hear them all, but he knew they were cheering. Men were simple creatures, really, and Erik Cain knew how to work them up, drive them forward, probably to their deaths. He wasn't sure he understood it, but he'd seen it in action enough times to know it was true. And he knew they would draw strength from his presence, from knowing their general was here in the thick of things, fighting alongside them.

"They're coming, sir." It was Storm again, confirming what Cain already saw on his monitor. The next enemy wave was a klick away and moving fast. And it was a big one.

"Blow those bridges now." McDaniels gritted her teeth as she yelled to her forward units. The pain was almost unbearable, but she was trying like hell to ignore it. She knew she wasn't going to make it off this battlefield, but she had work to do, and she'd be Goddamned if she wasn't going to see it done before she died.

She winced again. Shit luck, she thought. The rounds had hit her square in the chest, and, by luckless chance, they'd wrecked her trauma control system too. She could feel the slickness of her blood pouring out of the wounds and down her body, and she endured the pain, without so much as an aspirin from the shattered circuitry of her suit's destroyed med unit.

She was close enough to watch her people prepping the demo. They'd paid heavily to take control of the bridges. Her advance elements were hard at work, laying the heavy charges. She wasn't just going to cut the bridges, leaving an easy repair for the enemy engineers. She was going to obliterate them. She would leave nothing to fix. And then her people would form up along the bank...and blow the living shit out of any enemy force that tried to rebuild.

She coughed, tasting the metallic blood in her spittle. Colonel Clarkson would be in command by then, she thought, a whirlwind of emotions struggling to escape from the back of her mind. She was grateful she could focus on finishing this job. Otherwise, she'd have nothing but the fear. She was holding it together, her training and experience mostly in control. But the terror was there too...stark and black, crawling around the edge of her thoughts. She knew death was staring her in the face. McDaniels had never been particularly religious, but now she wasn't sure what to think...to expect. She'd seen thousands of

Marines die, and the old adages were true. Lying in the mud, their lives slipping slowly away, many found God. Whether it was something real…or just the last mental defenses of broken and dying men and women, she didn't know. She didn't even know what she believed herself.

"The charges are set, General."

She shook herself back to the moment. There was a voice on her com. It was Captain Carlyle, the chief engineer. "Very well, captain." Her voice was hoarse, hard to understand. She cleared her throat hard, spitting out the bloody saliva. "Get your men out of there so we can blow those things."

She turned, moving back toward the woods. She coughed again, still trying to clear her voice. "All units, retreat to the wood line immediately." She got the command out clearly…at least she hoped she did. She staggered back herself, stepping a few meters into the forest and turning to face the river.

She felt the fatigue taking control of her, weakness in her limbs, her joints. The suit did most of the work, especially an Obliterator, and she knew that was the only reason she was still standing. She waited two minutes, trying desperately to stay focused, to avoid her mind drifting off into gauzy daydreams. Finally, she flipped the comlink back on. "Captain…detonate the charges."

Cain knew as soon as he heard her voice, and his stomach clenched. McDaniels was reporting the destruction of the bridges. Her people had done it…they'd blown all three, bought the army a chance to stabilize the lines in the Sentinel. And just in time. Somehow Storm's tattered and weary Marines had beaten back the last assault, but Cain knew the next would be the final one.

He'd known McDaniels' objective wouldn't come cheap, but now he was starting to understand the full price he had paid. That she had paid.

My people…" - she coughed, and Cain could hear the fluid sounds from her pierced lungs - "…are dug in along the riverbank, sir." Her voice was weak. There was fear there, and pain…but satisfaction and pride too. She'd done what Cain had sent her to do. She'd completed her mission. And possibly saved the entire army.

"General McDaniels, report to a field hospital at once." His expression was grim. The command was an empty gesture, and he knew it. The nearest aid station was kilometers away, through the dense tangle of the Sentinel's woods. McDaniels would never make it.

"It's OK, sir." He could hear her labored breath. She knew it was too late, just as Cain did. "Don't worry about me. Just send these bastards to hell."

"Erin…" Cain's voice was struggling. He was trying to keep his solid, emotionless demeanor, but the grief was welling up inside him. Another friend, he thought…another trusted comrade I sent to her death. "…I can't tell you how magnificently you performed with the Obliterators." His voice was raw, edgy. "I can't even begin to count how many Marines your people have saved. Or how we could possibly have survived the First Imperium War without you." Cain took a deep, forced breath, taking an instant to regain his grip on himself. "You are one of the finest Marines I have ever known."

The com was almost silent for a few seconds, nothing but the rattling sound of McDaniels' labored breath. Finally, she said, "Thank you, sir. Erik. It has been a privilege to serve under you." She coughed, trying to clear her throat again, to force breath down as her lungs filled with her own blood. "Now forget about me, sir…and go win the battle."

Erin McDaniels lay on her back, her hands fumbling with the visor controls. The sky, she thought dreamily…just one more look at the sky. Her fingers were slick with blood, and they slid around the controls, fumbling, finally hitting the lever. The visor snapped open. Her eyes were watery, and her vision was blurry at first, slowly focusing.

The sky was brilliant blue…a beautiful day, warm and clear, with a soft breeze. A fine day for anything she thought…even to die. Her teeth were gritted tightly. The pain was intense, though she could feel it beginning to recede as she drifted slowly away.

She could hear her people clustered around her, feel her body moving as they poked at her, tried desperately to give her first aid. It felt very far off, a haziness to it all. She was proud of her Marines, all of them. She'd created the Obliterator corps; from its infancy she'd been its CO. Cain had put enormous trust in her, turning the new weapon system over to her, relying on her ability to forge it into the weapon he needed. She forced a tiny smile to her lips. She'd done that, she knew. She had repaid Cain's trust and justified his confidence in her. Through the pain and the fear she felt something else. Satisfaction. Pride. She'd done her duty.

The sky was darker now, the sun dimmer, somehow farther away. She couldn't feel her people anymore, couldn't hear anything but the rattling sound of every labored breath. The pain… that was gone too. She couldn't feel anything. Just floating, drifting along…quiet, painless. Nothing but fleeting thoughts, random, drifting in and out of her mind. Then silence, calm, blackness.

"Colonel Clarkson, leave a covering force along the river line and advance north." Cain's voice was raw, angry. As always, he forced his emotions down deep during the battle. All that remained was anger at the enemy, heightened by the need to avenge yet another friend. "General McDaniels' sacrifice is not going to be in vain." He meant that with every fiber of his being, but he was manipulating Clarkson too. He wanted McDaniels' people lusting for revenge, savoring the deaths of every enemy soldier. Some battles required finesse and elegance, but this was going to be a bare knuckled brawl in the deep woods. Under the soaring trees of the Sentinel, the Marines who still survived were going to fight it out with the invaders trapped north of the river. If they won, they'd achieve a stalemate, and the battle for Armstrong would go on, probably after a much-needed lull. If not, the enemy would have their victory…and Erik Cain and his Marines would be dead. He knew it would be a savage fight…

indeed, he would make sure of it.

"Yes sir." Clarkson's voice was thick with vengeful rage. McDaniels had been an enormously popular commander. "Understood."

Cain cut the line and turned his head. "OK, Eliot." Storm was standing next to Cain, and both men had their visors retracted. "Let's get your boys and girls advancing south again. We'll hit this attack as it's coming in. That should surprise these bastards." He paused, the determination growing inside him, becoming something elemental. "We've retreated as far as we're going to."

"Yes, sir." Storm's tone was determined, angry, bitter. "Not one more step back." His people had already rebuffed the last enemy advance, hitting them hard in the flank and disordering their whole attack. He was going to make sure Captain Barrington got the Marine Cross for it too. Though he wasn't sure how much good a posthumous medal could do the fallen hero.

He and Cain stood silently for a moment, staring off into the tangled mass of trees. They didn't have a chance against the force they were about to fight, at least not straight up. But Clarkson and two-thirds of McDaniels' survivors were moving north...against the enemy's rear. It wasn't hopeless. They had a chance, maybe even a good one. As long as the Obliterators made it in time.

Chapter 25

CWS Suleiman
Deep Space
Near the Samarkand System

Admiral Abbas sat quietly on the bridge, an angry scowl on his face. He stifled another cough. Despite the best efforts of the ventilation system, the stink still hung in the air, a combination of smoke and burnt machinery. He was exhausted, his mind almost punch drunk. He decided he'd rather march into a First Imperium fortress armed with a butter knife than relive the last 12 hours.

He tried to ignore the four armed men standing behind him, but it wasn't easy. The armored Janissaries were massive figures, rigid and unmoving. He'd almost ordered them to leave half a dozen times, but he'd held back. He doubted they'd obey his orders anyway. Ali Khaled had sent them to protect Abbas… and he'd given them a strict command to guard the admiral at all times. No one but Khaled could countermand that order. Not with the Janissaries. The silent, menacing figures followed him everywhere. Abbas hadn't so much as gone to the bathroom unprotected. The Janissaries had their own code of honor and obedience. It was all crazy secret handshake stuff as far as Abbas was concerned, but the elite footsoldiers took it seriously. They considered themselves a sacred brotherhood, and they took matters of honor very seriously. They were as bad that way as the Alliance Marines they'd fought for so many years, he thought…maybe even worse.

Things had gone better than he'd had any right to expect, but still, he'd never felt worse in his life. Fighting his own people, watching armored Janissaries gunning down members of his crews…it was almost more than he could bear. He told himself he'd had no choice, but he knew that wasn't exactly true. More accurately, there'd been no other option that would have preserved his own hide. He didn't know why the Caliph had ordered a purge, but Abbas knew he could have just let it happen. Instead, he'd resisted, gone rogue and taken the fleet with him. To save his own life.

No, he thought defensively, arguing with himself, not just my life. The lives of almost three dozen innocent naval officers, all of whom were to be executed if Roderick Vance's information was to be believed. Abbas was usually a skeptical man, but he couldn't convince himself to doubt Vance's intel. If he hadn't acted, 34 of his most loyal and capable officers would be dead right now, their names blackened by false treason charges. He shook his head. Not that he'd been able to save their names. Now they were actually traitors, at least from the government's point of view. But they were also alive. All but the four who'd died in the fighting. He still didn't know how many hundreds of naval crew had been killed in the combat for control of the fleet…a battle fought so that 30 senior officers could live.

He'd thought about keeping the truth from the crews, taking off for the Rim and inventing some cover story until he could figure out what to do. But that was never a workable plan. The fleet was riddled with informers and intelligence agents. He'd identified many of them, but he didn't even try to fool himself…there was no way he'd found them all. The trouble started the instant he took out the incoming vessels, the ones carrying his executioners. He addressed the fleet immediately afterward, but things quickly deteriorated into civil war.

Most of the crews backed Abbas and Khaled. They had gone to the farthest reaches of explored space under these men…and saved all mankind from destruction in the process. When their loyalties were put to the test, they followed the officers who'd led them in combat, the ones who'd brought them back from the apocalypse of war with the First Imperium. But a significant minority, manipulated and driven forward by the implanted intelligence operatives, remained loyal to the Earth government, and the officers of this faction attempted to take control of the fleet. There was fighting on every ship…and later between vessels controlled by opposing factions.

It was over now, all but some residual mopping up. Abbas had ordered the captured intelligence operatives shot, but he didn't know what to do with the thousands of crew members now in makeshift brigs all over the fleet. They were still his people, and their only crime was remaining loyal to their oaths. His ships were understaffed, and he wished he could just release them all and send them back to their posts. But that was impossible. They had taken up arms against him. There was no way he could trust them again, however much he understood their justifications. But he wasn't going to just line them up and shoot them. That was unthinkable.

He flipped a switch on the arm of his chair. "Lord Khaled, we need to discuss some matters. Are you available now?"

"Yes, admiral." Khaled sounded harried, exhausted…anything but available. "I am in conference room B. Please join me when convenient."

"Very well, Lord Khaled. I am on my way." Abbas knew there was nothing convenient about any of it. The Janissary commander was busy coordinating his men throughout the fleet as they stamped out the last rebel elements. Abbas couldn't even imagine the bloodshed that would have occurred if Khaled's troops hadn't intervened. More closely matched, the naval crews would have savaged each other. But when a naval officer with a sidearm ran into an armored Janissary, it was over pretty quickly. It was the elite infantry more than anything that broke the morale of the loyalist crews, and gave Abbas thousands of prisoners to deal with…instead of a fight to the finish that would have left many more dead on each side.

Abbas rose slowly and turned toward the doorway leading to the main corridor, bound for the conference room where Khaled had set up his makeshift headquarters. He forced back a sigh as he heard the clomping sounds of his bodyguards falling in behind him.

Ali Khaled was staring at the monitor as he listened to Farooq's report. Commander Farooq was one of his senior officers, a hero of the First Imperium War. He was on the battleship Ming, standing in one of the landing bays. "Ming is nearly secured, sir." The capital ship had seen some of the worst fighting in the fleet. Her second-in-command had been an officer named Wei Chin. Unknown to Abbas, Wei Chin had also been a senior intelligence operative. He killed the captain almost immediately and assumed command. It took hours of savage deck to deck fighting to reclaim the vessel. Wei was killed early in the battle, but scattered elements had continued the struggle, only yielding when Farooq's Janissaries arrived and turned it from a battle into a slaughter.

"Very well done, commander." Khaled tried to keep the fatigue from his voice, but the result was mixed at best. "Who is in command of the vessel?" The captain had been murdered by the first officer, who had then been killed in the fighting, and Khaled had no idea who was on the bridge.

"Lieutenant Yang, sir." There was a touch of doubt in the Janissary commander's voice. "I believe he was fifth in the chain of command." Farooq paused for a few seconds. "The second officer sided with Commander Wei, and he is now captive along with the rest of the loyalist forces. Lieutenant Commander Shin was fourth in command, but he was killed in the fighting."

"Very well." Ming was one of the CAC's biggest capital ships, and Khaled had more than a few doubts about such a junior officer commanding her. Especially not when there was bound to be more tension among the crews. That's not your problem, he reminded himself...what do you know about commanding spaceships? "I will update Admiral Abbas." And see if he is comfortable with a lieutenant commanding a battleship.

"Update Admiral Abbas about what?" The admiral walked through the just-opened hatch, his Janissary escort hot on his heels. The elite soldiers snapped to rigid attention at the sight of Khaled.

"Carry on, Commander Farooq." Khaled was still speaking into the com. "Advise me when you have completed operations on Ming." Khaled terminated the connection almost immediately, cutting off Farooq's perfunctory response halfway through. He turned to face Abbas. "Hello admiral." He forced a modest smile. "Ming is nearly secured. As you know, Commander Wei is dead, and most of the rebels…" – he wasn't sure that was the right word – "…have surrendered." He paused. "A Lieutenant Yang is in command. I'm afraid all the senior officers were either killed, or they sided with the insurgents." Another odd designation, Khaled thought…by most conventional definitions, we are the revolutionaries, aren't we?

"Yang?" Abbas paused, taking a second to place the name among the hundreds of officers in the fleet. "Fifth echelon?" He exhaled with considerable force. "Four senior officers dead or in revolt." It was a statement, not a question. "I'm glad the news isn't this bad on every ship." He walked over and sat, facing Khaled at an angle across the table.

"No." Khaled nodded, his tone slightly less grim. "I'd have to say we were quite lucky overall. Ming was the only capital ship where the issue was seriously in doubt. It appears that Commander Wei was the highest-placed intelligence operative in the fleet, and he was able to create considerable mayhem. The forces on the other ships were mostly disorganized and relatively easily suppressed." They both sat silently for several moments, reflecting on the heavy losses even on the vessels that had been quickly pacified.

Khaled broke the long silence. "So, Admiral…" He looked intently at Abbas. "…we have a pressing matter to discuss." He took a breath. "What do we do next?"

Chapter 26

Columbia Defense Force HQ
Weston City
Columbia, Eta Cassiopeiae II

Jed Lucas was exhausted. The med system in his out-dated armor wasn't as sophisticated as the units on state of the art fighting suits, but it still had a decent selection of uppers designed to keep an exhausted soldier fighting until the battle was over. The army was rationing supplies, and he'd been try-ing to conserve on his stims. However bad he felt, he knew things were likely to get worse before they got better. But now he tapped the small button to the side of his finger and admin-istered a heavy dose. The enemy would be coming again soon, and he had to stay alert. If he walked into fire and got himself killed, the meds he'd saved wouldn't do him much good.

The Columbians were still pumped up from their small victory. They'd been retreating since the invasion began, but now they were back in their pre-prepared positions just out-side Weston. The enemy had gotten careless and pursued them right up to the entrenchments. That attack turned into a bloody repulse all along the line, and the enemy fell back 5 klicks to regroup. It was a momentary respite, not a lasting victory, but he was grateful for the morale boost it gave his battered soldiers.

The enemy had reinforcements available and an advantage in equipment, supplies, and overall numbers. Lucas knew they'd be back in greater strength with a properly executed attack. Then his forces would be defeated…it was simple inevitability.

The invaders had every advantage except one. Lucas and

the rest of the Columbians were defending their homes. That meant a lot, and it could keep a soldier fighting past the point of normal endurance…but it wasn't everything. Not when the enemy had the edge in training, weapons, armor, and logistics. The relentlessness of mathematics can be bent in warfare, but never broken.

"Sergeant Lucas." The voice of Captain Charles burst loudly through the com. Charles' voice sounded odd…edgy, nervous, but also surprised. "I need you to prepare your forces." Lucas was commanding the remnants of his initial company, plus the remains of two others. "The enemy is preparing to launch another attack." Charles paused for a few seconds, clearly uncomfortable with what he had to say. "When they are one kilometer from your position you are to withdraw through Weston to the western perimeter of the city."

Retreat? Lucas' mind was reeling. He didn't think his people could hold here indefinitely against the enemy's massive superiority, but to simply give up the strongest position they had…and the capital as well? It didn't make sense. "Sir?" Lucas was still trying to absorb what Charles had just said. "Our position here is strong, sir. Are you…"

"Your orders are to pull back, Sergeant. As soon as the enemy is one kilometer from your position. Until that point, you are to maintain full fire." Charles hesitated again, just for an instant. "This is a Code Black operation, sergeant." Another pause, equally short. "As a precaution, you are to observe Code Orange protocols when you occupy your new position."

Lucas felt his chest tighten. Code Black…they were going nuclear. And Code Orange…his forces were to prepare for a possible atomic counter-attack.

"Yes, sir." His response was simple, direct. It was all he could manage. All hell was about to break loose.

Private White was firing small, targeted bursts. The enemy was still 3 kilometers out, and he was starting to worry about ammunition. He'd expected to be resupplied when the company pulled back to Weston, but there'd been nothing. Not a single cartridge. Paine had been on the com with Sergeant Lucas, and even Captain Charles, but he'd gotten nothing but senseless doubletalk. Something was up, but neither Paine nor White had any idea what it was.

White had been about to chew his way up the line of command, but Paine managed to control his friend's anger. For the moment. Reg White had been a sergeant a month before – the third time he'd reached that rank – but a nasty piece of insubordination got him busted back down to private again. *It's a shame he can't control himself better*, Paine thought, not for the first time. White was a natural soldier, but he was also his own worst enemy.

White was crouched next to Paine, continuing to fire intermittent bursts with the heavy auto-cannon. The attack was coming in force, he was sure of that. The enemy had been hasty last time, and they got a bloody nose for their carelessness. But they were well trained and led...they wouldn't make the same mistake twice. White knew he and his comrades would make the attackers pay and pay hard, but in the end he doubted they could repulse them again. There were just too many of them, and they were too well trained and equipped. It might take a few assaults, but they'd force the Columbians back through Weston...and the capital would fall, just like it did during the rebellion. *That wasn't the end of the matter then*, Paine thought defiantly, *and it won't be now*, though final victory in the rebellion had ultimately depended on the intervention of the Marines...and these troops they were fighting looked a lot like those same Marines.

"They're two klicks out, Reg." Paine broke his line of thinking. His voice was a little softer than usual. The trauma control system had his wound packed and stabilized and the pain well controlled. Still, getting half your shoulder shot off was a hell of a shock to the body no matter how many pharmaceuticals the suit pumped into you. He had his monitor set to scan the approaching enemy while White concentrated on picking out individual targets.

"Roger that, Tone." The two of them worked seamlessly as a team, communicating almost telepathically. "I'll switch to full auto at one klick."

"Corporal Paine, you are to withdraw when the enemy is one kilometer from your position." It was Sergeant Lucas' voice, coming in a second after White's. "You will fall back through Weston to designated positions west of the city. Code Black and Orange protocols are in effect. Confirm."

Paine hesitated. We're retreating again, he thought...without even putting up a fight? And going nuclear?

"Corporal!" Lucas' voice was loud, sharp. "Acknowledge receipt of orders!"

"Uh...yes, sergeant. Acknowledged."

The command line went dead. Paine turned slowly, flipping his com back to White's line. "Hey Reg...you're not going to believe this shit."

Tyler was silent, standing in the middle of the control center. His gray uniform was dark and featureless, and the cold stare of his eyes froze anyone who returned his glance. Everyone knew now what he was going to do, though most had just found out. Tyler had been planning this for the last few days, but he'd kept it to himself.

Columbia's dictator hadn't consulted with his officers or staff. He'd been mostly locked in his office since the landings, issuing dozens of orders and staring at maps and OBs around the clock. He knew his army couldn't beat the massive invasion force...at least not unless they were prepared to fight with everything they had. Everything. Despite the consequences.

"General, the enemy is one kilometer from the defensive line." Anne Stillson was trying to disguise her tension, with sharply limited success. The lieutenant had proven to be a capable aide, but Tyler had gone someplace dark, and she recoiled when she tried to follow. She knew the odds, that Tyler's way was the only one that offered any real hope of victory. But at what cost?

"Very well, lieutenant." Tyler's voice was cold as stone. "All units are to retreat immediately."

"Yes, general." She paused for a few seconds. "The army is

retiring as ordered, sir."

Tyler stared at the map of the Weston area displayed on the main screen. His eyes were focused, his body as unmoving as stone. He hoped the units on the line executed their orders promptly. The entire operation was planned on a knife's edge, with no time for mistakes. His eyes fixed on the display, but he wasn't seeing anything. He was just waiting, trying to keep extraneous thoughts at bay. He didn't tread this road willingly, nor without doubts. But he was sure it was the only option. The alternative was a slow and grinding defeat, and the loss of Columbia's freedom. And Jarrod Tyler would see his people buried in the ashes of their world before he would abandon them to slavery and oppression.

He turned his head slowly, deliberately. "Captain Crillon, you may begin."

"All guns, prepare to fire." Lieutenant Kebble's battery was hidden in the Village of Glaston. A small cluster of houses ten kilometers outside Weston, it was in every way an unexceptional place. Every way except the 8 nuclear-armed guns of Kebble's battery hidden under tarps and camouflage netting.

His troopers had been sitting around their guns, waiting for the orders. Their mood was grim. They knew what they were about to unleash...and what the enemy's response was likely to be. Now those orders had finally come.

"Primary target selections confirmed." Kebble's voice was raw, scratchy.

The gun crews rushed into action, pulling the netting away and entering final launch codes. One by one, the sergeant in charge of each gun confirmed readiness.

Kebble just stood and nodded as he got the last confirmation. He flipped his com to the HQ line. "Captain Crillon...all weapons are armed and loaded. Ready to fire on your command."

There was a brief pause. Kebble imagined Crillon turning, looking over at General Tyler for the final authorization.

"You may fire when ready, lieutenant." Crillon spoke slowly, clearly. This was not the time for a misunderstanding.

"Yes, sir." He turned and panned his eyes slowly, staring briefly at each of the eight guns as he switched back to the unit-wide com. "All guns..." He paused, turning to look forward, toward the city of Weston. He lived there. His son had been born there. He'd been driven out during the rebellions and returned triumphantly when that war was won. Weston was one of the finest cities in colonized space, cosmopolitan and graced with some of the most beautiful architecture anywhere off of man's home world. Now he was going to destroy it. He took a deep breath, struggling to find his voice. "Fire."

Jack Worth was flat against the ground, hoping for the best. The first two blasts had been almost simultaneous. He'd been looking away, which was the only reason he still had his sight. His survival prospects didn't look that good as they were, but blind they would be almost non-existent. Burned out retinas weren't exactly an injury you slapped a bandage on and went back into the fight, and regeneration would take weeks. Worse, the only hospital on Weston that could perform the procedure was now on fire at least, and more likely a pile of molten slag.

Worth stared straight into his now-shielded visor, wondering who had gone nuclear. He'd ranged far beyond his designated area of operations, working his way around the enemy flank, hoping to take out as many senior officers as he could. It was a dangerous tactic, one that ran against his usual meticulous patience. But he knew the odds his comrades faced, and the only way he could make a meaningful difference in the fight was to try to chew up the enemy high command.

If the enemy had nuked the positions around Weston, there wasn't a doubt in Worth's mind that General Tyler would respond in kind. That made Worth's position near the outskirts of the enemy HQ a very unhealthy place to be. But where could he go?

He glanced at the expanded display projected on his now blacked out visor. Ten detonations now...no, twelve. All along the eastern edge of Weston. Tiny symbols continued to appear.

Sixteen. Twenty. Then it stopped. Twenty-four nuclear detonations, all along the eastern perimeter of the capital. My God, Worth thought grimly, imagining the devastation the enemy bombardment must have wreaked on the defending Columbian forces.

There was something else in his mind, though. Another possibility. He wondered, could this be us? General Tyler was the toughest man he'd ever met, but would he really sacrifice the capital city to total destruction to spring a trap on the enemy? Worth dismissed the thought summarily…or he thought he did. But it crept back, lingering on the edge of his mind. Was it them? Or us?

242 of 300 The Shadow Legions

Chapter 27

Alliance Intelligence Facility Q
Dakota Foothills
American Sector, Western Alliance
Earth – Sol III

It was the stupidest plan he'd ever heard of…blunt, unso-phisticated, with a pitiful chance of success. He'd probably have busted anyone with the nerve to suggest it all the way down to private…if it hadn't been his own piece of work. But Steve Garth was going to do it anyway. It was the only thing he'd been able to come up with, and he was more convinced than ever that Roderick Vance's concerns were valid. Whatever was down there, under square kilometers of scrubby Dakota grasslands, it was extremely dangerous. If there was any chance, any way at all, to find out what it was, he had to take it.

Tobin's scanner had given them the approximate size of the enormous facility, but that was about all. The shielding was blocking everything else; it was only the experimental new scan-ners that detected anything at all.

Tobin was standing two meters away, looking right at his CO. They both had their visors down, but Garth imagined the expression on the lieutenant's face…a mix of horror and sym-pathy. Surely he must be thinking Garth had lost his mind.

"The device is in position, sir." Tobin was a cool operator, one of the best elite commandos Garth had ever seen, stone cold in every situation the two had faced together. But the worry was still there in his voice. Garth knew he was trying to hide it, but this time his stony resolve failed him, at least partially. Garth understood. The chances were slim his plan would get them any useful intel they could transmit to Vance. They were almost non-existent that any of them would make it out alive.

"Very well, lieutenant." Garth didn't have any illusions about the chances any of his people would get out of this. But he couldn't forget the image of Vance's face during the briefing, the shakiness in his voice. Anything that could scare Roderick Vance was certain to be catastrophic…and if the team could get any additional info, they simply had to do it. No matter what the cost. "Arm the mine. Detonation in 120 seconds."

"Yes, sir," Tobin croaked.

"Attention all personnel…clear the blast zone immediately." He'd already pulled everyone back, but he wanted to be sure. The 5 kiloton burrowing mine had a danger radius of about 0.5 klicks for fully-armored troops. It would be a dirty explosion, and his people would be covered with contaminants. Their armor would be a lost cause, too radioactive to salvage, but they'd be safe inside, for a while at least. Long enough to gather their intel and escape…or die in the fight that was almost certain to follow the explosion.

"Detonation in 60 seconds." Tobin's voice was louder, a little firmer. Garth smiled. The kid was hardcore, he thought, chuckling at himself for calling a decorated elite soldier a kid. Everyone seemed like a kid to him…he'd been in too many fights, seen too many things he couldn't make himself forget.

Steve Garth had given all to the service. He had no family, no one waiting for him at home. No home, even, outside a military base. If he died here, he knew it would just be a hole on an OB. His life was likely measured in minutes now, but he regarded that more as an odd fact than a source of concern. It was his men that troubled him. They were going to die with him, all for the faint hope of getting a scrap of information to Roderick Vance. And if they failed, they would die for nothing. Nothing at all.

Anderson-17 cursed softy to himself, shaking his head. He'd ordered intercepting forces to the surface, but he knew he'd waited too long. He'd let his hope the intruders were a group of lost locals color his judgment. Now he knew it was some sort of incursion…spies, probably. He didn't want to think about what would happen when Gavin Stark found out. Anderson-17 had never actually seen Shadow One, but he'd heard enough to know things were going to be bad for him. Very bad.

His people would wipe out these invaders…he was sure of that, at least. But his scanners had picked up the nuclear mine, and he was far from sure his forces would arrive before it blew a hole leading right into the most sensitive part of the facility. And that would be a mess of epic proportions.

"Colonel, Captain Jarvis-789 reporting. We are emerging from access tubes 7 and 8 and engaging the enemy." Anderson-17 could hear the sounds of battle in the background, the speaker feed from Jarvis-789's armor. "We have located the enemy mine and are…"

The speaker screeched loudly and, an instant later, the floor shook hard, knocking half of the control center crew from their chairs. A dozen alarms started going off, and the com panel went crazy. Anderson-17 was almost tossed to the ground, but he gripped the armrests of his chair tightly and held on, a harsh frown on his face. So much for getting to the mine in time, he thought with disgust.

"I want Sector 34 sealed off immediately." Things were bad enough without letting enemy troops get loose inside the whole facility. Sector 34 was already a problem, but he didn't intend to spend the next few weeks hunting down rogue invaders hiding in the crèche chambers. "Reserve forces to the surface and the affected areas."

"Yes, colonel." Lieutenant Jackson-315 was furiously working his control pad, sending out a flurry of orders.

"I want these invaders wiped out to a man!" Anderson-17 took a deep breath, slowly regaining his composure. "Immediately, lieutenant," he said, more calmly. "Immediately."

Garth was crouched down behind a boulder, beads of sweat pooling at the edge of his hairline, sliding slowly down the side of his face. For the tenth time his arm twitched, a natural urge to wipe his forehead. The impulse was quickly squelched by the recollection that such an act was an impossibility in powered armor. He could hear the enemy rounds slamming into the other side of the giant rock, sending shards of stone scattering all around. It sounded like a whole squad was shooting at him.

The enemy had sent a force to the surface just before the mine blew, and now there were more armored troops pouring out of hidden egress points. His people were almost surrounded, outnumbered 10-1, 20-1…he couldn't even guess. He'd ordered them all to make for the crater the mine had left behind, but most had taken cover where they were and started returning the enemy's fire. It made tactical sense, but it was pointless. Red Team Beta was finished, as good as wiped out. The fact that most of them were still alive was a passing technicality. There wasn't a chance any of them were making it out of this mess. All they could do now was gather the intel Vance needed…the information that would make their deaths mean something more than senseless waste.

"Let's move it out, boys and girls." Garth's voice was calm, steady. He could have been ordering his people to line up in the mess hall. It was pure fiction…Garth was so scared he could barely keep his hands from shaking. But it was what his people needed now. "Into the crater." He gulped a big breath of the oxygen-enhanced air his suit was pumping out and ran hard for the edge of the smoking pit the mine had dug into the rocky ground.

Major Anderson-89 stared at his display. He was in command on the surface, trying to organize a dozen disparate units that had been rushed into the battle. The enemy troops were making for the crater…exactly what he was here to prevent. His orders were clear…keep them all on the surface until they were wiped out. But orders were easier to issue than execute. These were elite troops, commandos of some sort, he was facing. Not so easy to kill.

"Blue Company, advance to the crater. Attack the enemy

troopers attempting to access the facility." He had to cut the invaders off from the crater. Three or four of them had gotten in already, at least into the pit itself, and ten or twelve more were dashing for it now.

The troopers of Blue Company obeyed without complaint, of course, though doing so exposed them to the deadly accurate fire of the dozen or so commandos covering the advance on the crater. Anderson-89 watched on his display as Blue's troops went down in clumps, raked by the invaders' two auto-cannons. Both guns were dug in behind large boulders, shielded from his own fire. He had two platoons working around the flank, but that would take time, and he needed men in that crater now.

At least half of the company was down by the time the Blues reached the lip of the crater...and another four or five enemy commandos had made it down by then. Anderson-89's troops slid down the sides of the still-smoking pit, following the invaders into the bowels of Facility Q.

Anderson-89 was distracted by another report...one of the enemy auto-cannons had been taken out. There was just one strongpoint — and maybe 3 or 4 commandos left. Every other enemy combatant still on the surface was dead. He knew he'd have the area secured in another few minutes. No more than 8 or 9 of them had made it into the crater. They'd be hunted down and killed before they could cause any harm, he thought, not as convinced as he wished he was.

Garth was running as fast as he could. It wasn't easy to move quickly indoors in powered armor without smashing into walls and ceilings. His people were all dead...he was fairly certain of that. All but the two posted on the hilltop with the satellite uplink...the ones he had to contact before the enemy caught and killed him.

My God, he thought...Vance was right. Garth knew now that the intel he had gained was worth his whole unit. It was worth ten divisions. He still couldn't believe what he had seen. Rows and rows of tanks...and in each one, suspended in some kind of yellowish fluid...it was almost too much to absorb.

He pushed hard. He had a wound, more than one. He knew he'd taken a slug in the side, but it didn't seem too bad. His shoulder was throbbing too, and he could feel a strange sensation, like tiny bugs crawling all around the wound. It was the nanobots from his suit's med system, he realized. Beyond stopping the bleeding and buying him an extra minute or two of life, he knew their work was in vain. Still, they were hard at it, trying to repair the damage. Just as well, he thought…that minute might make all the difference.

The surface would be crawling with enemy soldiers, and there wouldn't be any cover…not like in these catacombs. He wouldn't live more than a few seconds when he got out. Maybe, just maybe, he'd get lucky. He was going to jump out of the crater, as high as the leg servos on his damaged suit could propel him. He'd overload the small motors, burn out the circuits. He didn't need to worry about how he'd land…he'd probably be dead, or at least mortally wounded, before he hit the ground. But if he could just get off a transmission, the two troopers manning the satellite uplink might pick it up…and send it before they too were located and killed. He was going to die…and his men were already dead. But he could still give meaning to all of that, make their sacrifices something noble instead of futile.

He realized he was scrambling up the sides of the crater, trying to get near the top. There were enemies here…they were shooting at him. He felt the impacts. More wounds. There was pain, but it wasn't bad. The suit had already flooded his bloodstream with painkillers. His mind was focused…only one thing mattered.

He was near the top. It was a ledge. It felt solid, firm enough for him to launch off. He flexed his knees and jumped.

He was hit. This time he felt his head snapping hard to the side, and his consciousness quickly faded. Blackness covered his eyes. His last thought was that the AI would transmit the message, even if he was already dead.

Chapter 28

North of the Midland Sea
Arcadia – Wolf 359 III

"They're retreating to the north, General Holm." Thomas' voice was deep and gravelly, but Holm could hear the fire in his tone. The old Marine was energized, focused. His last battlefield had been 40 years before, but his combat reflexes were already coming back, and he was pumped up. Holms' Marauders, as the relief force had spontaneously started calling itself, had decisively beaten back an enemy attack against their LZ. Losses were fairly light, but it had been jarring to Thomas when the first of his people was killed. Watching friends die was the one part of being a Marine that Sam Thomas hadn't missed over the past four decades.

"Excellent, colonel." Holm still felt odd addressing the older man formally, but Thomas had already scolded him twice. The old Marine didn't have the slightest problem following his former protégé's orders…it was Holm who was struggling with it. "Pursue, and don't give them a chance to regroup." He'd almost ordered Thomas to stand fast. He was struggling with the guilt of bringing these old veterans to fight on Arcadia, and his first impulse was to hold them back and avoid unnecessary casualties. But they were here to link up with Teller's Marines, and they had to push the enemy back to do it.

Holm had been relieved when Teller answered his initial communications. He'd been afraid there would be nothing but ominous silence in response to his query. His joy was soon tempered when he realized just how badly the Marine general and his force had been shot up. The relief expedition hadn't arrived a moment too soon…assuming they were able to make a difference. Even with the new forces, the Marines on Arcadia were heavily outnumbered. Holm wasn't sure if he'd end up relieving Teller…or if he'd just lead another thousand Marines to their deaths.

There was one unexpected surprise, however. The fleet had made contact with a friendly force up in the far northern mountains, dug in and tying down considerable enemy strength. It could only be the native army, or whatever was left of it. Holm hadn't dared to hope the Arcadian forces were still in the field, but now he realized that Teller's intervention had come in time to prevent the enemy from focusing their full strength to pacify the planet. The two forces were thousands of kilometers apart, but each had effectively prevented the enemy from concentrating enough strength to destroy the other.

Holm took a deep breath and exhaled. Time to get moving, he thought. He turned and walked down the hillside, heading toward Thomas' column, half a dozen armed Marines falling in behind him. The bodyguard wasn't his idea, but the rest of his officers – to a man – had insisted. The Commandant of the Corps had no place marching around a planet's surface with 1,000 Marines, hopelessly outnumbered by the enemy. A number of officers had suggested Holm stay behind on the fleet, and each of them had been treated to the full fury of the titanic temper Holm usually controlled so well. Nothing was going to keep him from leading this campaign personally. Nothing. The Corps was staring off into the abyss, its last veterans dusting off their arms and answering the call. There was no way Elias Holm was going to sit at a desk on one of the battleships while his Marines faced this battle. No way.

"Still only ten landers, commander." The comm officer was staring at the display, as she had been since the incoming landing craft had been detected, and Kara was looking over her shoulder. "They should be on the ground in 3 minutes."

Kara nodded then realized the officer couldn't see her where she was standing. "Very well," she muttered. She had no idea what was coming down. There had been no further communication from the newly arrived fleet since the supply drop two days before. That had been enormously useful, providing her beleaguered forces with weapons, ammunition, food, and medical supplies. Whoever was in orbit, they certainly appeared to be friends. But Kara wasn't going to take any chances. Her suspicion was keen, and she'd had the food checked for contamination and poisons and the weapons for booby traps. Her people hadn't found anything out of the ordinary...and if this was all some elaborate trick, the enemy had vastly strengthened her defenses in the bargain.

"Get Colonel Calvin on the line." Kara spoke softly, slowly.

"Yes, commander." A brief pause, two or three seconds. "Colonel Calvin is on the line."

"Ed, are your people in position?" She knew they were... this was the third time she'd checked.

Calvin stifled a small chuckle. "Yes, Kara." He was amused by her persistence, but also impressed. Kara Sanders was like no one he had ever known. There was a pool of strength in her that ran deep. He knew he'd only seen tiny flashes of it. He was fond of her - loyalty to Will Thompson wouldn't let him admit to himself he loved her - but he also felt she was something above him, almost a living legend, at least to the people of Arcadia. "We're still in position. We've got visuals on the landing craft."

Kara had Calvin and 300 troops positioned to meet the landers. If this was some kind of enemy force trying to catch her by surprise, they'd have a rude welcome waiting for them. The landers were Marine Gordons, but that meant nothing; the invaders had come in the standard Alliance landing craft as well.

She watched quietly, hoping her caution was misplaced, that these ships weren't landing enemy commandos or a 500 kiloton warhead. Her force didn't have any appreciable surface to air attack capability, but she wondered...if you had it, would you have used it? She didn't know, one minute thinking yes, the next, no.

"Enemy vessels landing, commander." The tension in the com officer's voice was increasing. In a few seconds they'd know if they were dealing with friends or enemies.

Kara stared at the screen, listening, waiting. The seconds passed, then a minute…two.

"Kara!" It was Calvin, and she could tell immediately from his voice the news was good. "I'm standing here with Captain Mandrake and a platoon of Marines. And they just told me some very good news."

"Keep firing, Billy." Tommy Handler was crouched behind a pile of shattered plasti-crete. He and Greene had been on the line for 3 days without a rest, trying to break through and link up with the relief force. They were both exhausted, but the arrival of reinforcements had energized all of Teller's Marines, reviving their shattered morale.

"I'm firing. I'm firing." Greene was about ten meters from his friend, standing behind the remnants of a small storage shed. His assault rifle was on full auto, and he was hosing down an enemy trench. He wasn't sure if he'd hit anything, but he was keeping their heads down at least, covering 3rd squad's imminent move around their flank.

"And be careful you don't hit any friendlies." Handler was staring out at the small trenchline ahead, scanning for any of the enemy careless enough to show his head. "We've got to be close to the relief force."

There was no way for Holm's people to securely communicate with Teller's force, so they'd maintained almost total radio silence. But with the newly-deployed satellite network, the Marines had their eyes back, allowing them to get a locational fix on Holm's forces. And they were close. Very close. Only this last enemy position lay between them.

Handler whipped around and fired a few bursts, ducking back into cover before a blast of return fire slammed into the jagged chunks of plasti-crete. Teller's Marines had spent most of their time defending, which had been a considerable force magnifier, allowing them to hold out against a superior enemy for as long as they had. But now they were attacking. The enemy was temporarily on the defensive, trying to stand between the two forces and keep them apart. Handler didn't think 3rd squad's attack was going to go very well, but the lieutenant had given the orders, and there was nothing the platoon's junior private could do to stop it.

"They're going in." Greene didn't sound like he thought any more of the plan than Handler. "I hope they don't get wasted."

Shit, Handler thought…too soon. That line is still too strong. They're going to get massacred. "Eyes open, Billy. Anyone over there shows some forehead, be ready to blow it off. Got it?"

"Got it." Greene's voice was firm, calm. The training class valedictorian had struggled at first to adapt to real service in the field, but now he was finding himself. It wasn't coming to him as naturally as it had to Handler, but he was getting there, slowly, steadily. "There they go!"

Handler was watching on his scanner too. Ten small blue dots were moving slowly across his display, heading toward the enemy position. His eyes darted back and forth from the shimmering tactical display to his visor. He had it cranked up to Mag 10, and he was staring at the enemy trenchline, waiting for any movement.

Suddenly, he saw at least half a dozen enemy troopers peer over the trench. They opened fire immediately, targeting not the advancing troops, but the section off to the left where he and Greene were deployed. He ducked back behind his makeshift cover as a hundred rounds slammed into the plasti-crete rubble, sending clouds of powdery dust into the air. "Fuck." He pivoted, moving around, looking for a place along his front the enemy wasn't hosing down with fire. "Billy, you OK?"

"Yeah, but I'm pinned." His voice was thick with frustration. "I can't get a shot." He was silent for a few seconds. "And the guys are catching hell out there."

Handler had taken his attention from the tactical display, but his eyes flashed back. Four of the blue circles were gone, three of them replaced by small crosses. KIAs. There was a single flashing triangle…a wounded Marine. While he was watching, a fifth circle winked out, replaced by another triangle. Fuck, he thought…we're supposed to be covering them. "Billy, we've got to get some fire on that trench line.

Handler dropped to the ground, lying flat. He crawled to the edge of his cover, holding his assault rifle around the corner, firing blindly on full auto. Fuck, he thought angrily…this isn't doing a fucking thing. "Billy…grenades. Get your launcher online. The grenades were a trajectory weapon. His AI could handle targeting well enough to drop them along the enemy trench, and he could do it all without sticking anything out of his cover and getting it blown off. He doubted he'd kill anyone over there…unless he got a lucky shot. But a whole spread might distract them long enough to help the Marines caught out in the open. He checked the display again…only four left standing, and now they were falling back, carrying the wounded with them. They'd never make it unless he and Greene could give the enemy something else to worry about.

"Let's go, Billy. Launch grenades…all you've got. Now!" Handler held his left arm up, angling to match the small targeting display projected to the side of his tactical map. The launcher was attached to the arm of the suit, a flexible tube connecting it to the small, auto-loading magazine on his back. He lined up the shot and depressed the firing stud inside his glove, holding it down, feeling the vibration as one round after another fired. He moved his arm slowly down the enemy line, trying to space his shots about ten meters apart. He knew he could have just ordered the AI to fire, but he still hadn't gotten used to the personal assistant. It was a blind spot, he knew. Using the AI could save him time…and that could save his life. But now wasn't the time to worry about it, so he filed it away. He'd think about it later. If there was a later.

"I cannot express my admiration strongly enough for the skill and tenacity you have all shown in these difficult conditions." Captain Craig Mandrake had quite won over Kara and the rest of the Arcadian officers. He'd been stunned to find a force this size still in the field, and he was enormously impressed with the actions of the Arcadian army. He hadn't hesitated to make that clear to any who'd listen.

Kara allowed herself a brief smile. "Thank you again, captain. We only did what we had to do." She'd been relieved when the small contingent landed. Fifty Marines wasn't a large enough force to meaningfully turn the tide, but she was still glad to see them. Even more so because it pretty much confirmed that the new arrivals were indeed friendly...and it quickly put to rest the disgusting rumors that they'd been fighting the Corps all along.

"I had hoped we would be able to join your force with General's Holm's army, but I do not believe that is possible, at least not immediately. Now that you are resupplied, it is likely your force can hold this terrain indefinitely, even against an armored enemy. I doubt they are in a position to reinforce their positions here...at least not while they are engaged with both General Teller and General Holm. However, the terrain will also work strongly against you if you attempt to take the offensive."

She nodded slowly. She agreed with everything he was saying. Now that her logistics had improved, she wanted to break out of these mountains...hit the enemy and drive them back. But she knew that was foolish. Even if an attack was successful, the casualties would be staggering. In victory, as surely as in defeat, she would destroy the army she had so carefully preserved these past months. No, she thought decisively...I will not do that. She looked back at Mandrake and nodded. "I am in complete agreement, captain." She took a short breath. "We cannot consider going on the offensive now. All we can do is continue to hold this position and await further developments."

Her eyes dropped slowly, her stare focusing on the sparse, scrubby grass. Stalemate, she thought, dejectedly...not just here, but everywhere. Free Arcadia was hanging on, resisting the final domination of the enemy. But that was all they could do. Holm and Teller were in the same situation as her force. They had finally linked up, but casualties were high, and the enemy still had the superiority in numbers. The Marine generals could hold out...and punish a careless enemy if they got the chance. But they didn't have anywhere near the strength to defeat the invaders and drive them from Arcadia. "Stalemate," she muttered softly to herself.

Chapter 29

CWS Suleiman
Deep Space
Near the Samarkand System

Admiral Abbas stared across the table, his eyes locked on Ali Khaled's. "We must be sure, Lord Khaled, before we commit to such a course of action." The Caliphate admiral – more accurately, formerly of the Caliphate and now the leader of a fugitive fleet – looked exhausted.

"For my part, I am willing to place my trust in our Alliance friends, admiral." Khaled was just as worn out as Abbas, though perhaps he hid it just a bit better. "They have been true to their word in our operations together, and I believe they will continue to behave in that way." Khaled wasn't referring to the Alliance as a political entity, but rather to the specific individuals in command of the fleet and Marine Corps. Still, it felt odd speaking in such terms of men and women he'd thought of as mortal enemies for most of his life.

"Well…" - Abbas moved his hand to the back of his neck, massaging it slowly as he spoke – "…we do not appear, as the saying goes, to have much to lose, do we?" Abbas wondered how the crews would react, but he wasn't overly concerned. By siding with him, they had all branded themselves as traitors. He doubted most of them had thought it through clearly or in such harsh terms…they simply rallied to their commander. But it was too late for them to go back. Nothing but disgrace and execution waited for them on Earth. If Abbas and Khaled threw their lot in with the Alliance commanders, the crews would follow.

Especially after the last few years of successful cooperation.

"The minuscule intelligence we have suggests the Alliance forces are engaged in some sort of conflict." Khaled sat rigidly in his chair, as he always did. "Our last data indicates it is some sort of internecine strife, though there has also been speculation that they are engaged with remnant First Imperium forces."

Abbas frowned. "I doubt it is the First Imperium. Admiral Garret would never have disbanded Grand Fleet if there were any known enemy forces this side of the Barrier." The admiral leaned back, stifling a yawn. It had been two days – or three? – since he'd slept. "On the other hand, it has not been long since their recent rebellions. Some type of internal conflict seems likely. We know very well their interstellar forces have had a difficult relationship with the Earth government for some time."

"I suggest we set a course for the nearest of their Commnet stations." Khaled was moving his fingers across the 'pad embedded in the table in front of him. "We should be able to obtain updated information...and possibly determine a destination where we can join Admiral Garret."

"Avalon," Abbas said, waving Khaled from his search. "Avalon is the closest Alliance world on Commnet." He smiled, amused at the infantry officer's unfamiliarity with the warp gate network. Khaled was used to being ferried around and dropped into whatever inferno needed the very particular skills of his elite footsoldiers. He spent his time readying his men for ground combat, not memorizing warp gate networks. "We can get there in three jumps...a month, maximum. Maybe three weeks if we push hard."

Khaled looked up from the 'pad. "I think we should push hard." He frowned. "The more I think about this, the worse I feel. I was surprised when Garret disbanded the fleet so soon." He looked across the table at Abbas. "I'm starting to think our Alliance friends might be in more trouble than we imagined."

Abbas stared back silently, processing the Janissary general's words. He hadn't thought about it before, but now he was wondering. He considered the Alliance admiral to be the best naval leader in human space, himself included. Augustus Garret didn't do things for no reason…and Sandoval was not where he'd expected the fleet to disperse. Why would Garret want to get rid of the national task forces?

Abbas took a breath and exhaled slowly. "I think you may be right, Lord Khaled." He nodded. "I believe we should go to Avalon immediately. He reached for the com, not even waiting for Khaled's response.

"I'm sorry, Admiral Abbas, my orders are clear." The junior officer was showing considerable backbone. Abbas knew Commnet duty hardly attracted the cream of the Alliance service, but this lieutenant was standing his ground when his tiny station was surrounded by two-thirds of the Caliphate navy.

"Lieutenant, it is our intent to assist Admiral Garret, but to do that, we must first be able to reach him." Abbas was getting impatient, but he was controlling his temper. He couldn't fault an officer for the courage to follow his orders, especially in a situation like this. But he didn't have time to waste either.

"I'm sorry, Admiral Abbas." The young lieutenant's voice was cracking a little, but overall, he was showing remarkable strength of will. "I am not authorized to grant you access to the Commnet system without express approval from Admiral Garret or Command Central in Washbalt."

Abbas sighed hard, flipping the switch to cut the line. He turned to face Khaled, who was standing wordlessly behind him. "I'm afraid your people are going to have to board the station, Lord Khaled."

The Janissary simply nodded, and he tapped the portable com on his wrist. "Commander Salam, your people may embark immediately." Khaled hadn't expected such fortitude from a junior Alliance officer stationed in a backwater system, but he'd been prepared anyway. "Remember, commander…stun guns only." He paused then added, "Even if you take casualties, you are forbidden to respond with deadly force. Remember, we the provocateurs here." He spoke firmly, almost threateningly to his subordinate. It was a tough order to give to any troops… to refrain from lethal action, even against an adversary who was killing your people. But Khaled and Abbas had agreed. They might have to take the com station by force, but neither of them wanted Alliance blood on their hands when they made contact with Garret.

"Yes, Commander Khaled." Salam had a loud, deep voice. "Your orders will be obeyed, my lord."

Khaled felt a moment of pride in his warriors and their discipline. He had no doubt his orders would be followed to the letter, no matter how much resistance the station crew offered. The Alliance Marines were the only troops in space that could match the Janissaries. "Go then, commander. And may fortune be with you."

"You may begin your transmission whenever you are ready, Lord Khaled." The deep voice of Commander Salam boomed from the speaker. "The communications team has programmed the system to relay your message to all active Alliance Commnet relays." The Janissaries had quickly secured the station, suffering a few casualties, but none of them KIA. The station's crew had been subdued with stun guns. They'd wake up with bad headaches, but otherwise no Alliance personnel had been injured. Salam had them all locked up in one of his shuttles, and a Caliphate med team was tending to them.

"Admiral?" Khaled deferred to Abbas. The admiral was the senior of the two while onboard naval vessels, though such distinctions were less official since the fleet had gone renegade. But Khaled was a creature of tradition, and he was still following Caliphate protocol to the letter.

"Thank you, commander." Abbas offered a weak smile. He was less formal than Khaled, but he appreciated the respect his companion in treason afforded him. "Very well, Commander Salam...begin transmitting." He paused for an instant before continuing. "This is a priority transmission for Admiral Augustus Garret from Admiral Abbas and Janissary Commander Khaled. We are transmitting from the Commnet station in the Avalon system...."

Chapter 30

Marine HQ
North of Astria
Planet Armstrong
Gamma Pavonis III

Cain stared out across the scrubby grasslands north of Armstrong's battered capital. The enemy bombardment had done considerable damage, and whole sections of the city were in ruins. But much of Astria still stood, enough, at least, that Cain called it damaged and not destroyed in his log. The enemy had lost heart in blowing the city apart once it was clear Cain wasn't going to take the bait. It had been a fool's game for the invaders. Cain's stubbornness was legendary, and he'd lived up to that reputation. He had refused to become distracted from the main area of battle, no matter how much of the capital was in flames.

The fighting in the Sentinel had been some of the worst Cain had ever seen. The invaders were armed and equipped like the Marines, and clearly trained in the same tactics. There was an eerie feeling to the battle, almost as if the men and women struggling amid the shattered trees were battling themselves. In the end it came to hand-to-hand fighting, blade against blade. The fighting blades were one of the most terrifying weapons a Marine could face. Barely a molecule thick along the cutting edge, they sliced through armor nearly as easily as air itself.

For a while, Cain thought the battle was lost. He was in the line with his Marines, fighting bitterly to hold on in the woods. But they were just too outnumbered, and they were pushed back...closer and closer to defeat. Finally, like the answer to a prayer, the Obliterators smashed through from the south and into the rear of the enemy forces, turning the tide just in time.

It had been a victory, if so costly a struggle can truly be designated as such. Cain's Marines had lost 60% of their strength… but there wasn't a live enemy north of the Graywater. They'd fought with the same determination the Marines had, and in the end, the few remnants that broke and ran met the rest of the Obliterators stationed along the river, and they were slaughtered.

It was a passing triumph…a battle won, not the war. The enemy forces to the south still vastly outnumbered Cain's remaining troops. They were regrouping, trying to adjust to the unexpected reverse they had suffered. But eventually they would move north and attack the forces Cain had entrenched along the river. The Marines were in a good position, but they were battered and low on supplies. Cain had no idea if they'd be able to hold…or if the victory in the Sentinel would prove to be a passing moment of no lasting value.

Cain pulled out of his introspection and turned to face Colonel Storm. "One prisoner. That is all we were able to take?" Cain spoke softly, shivering slightly in the cool evening air. His arm throbbed, despite the meds Sarah had given him. The wound wasn't severe, but his suit had taken considerable damage. The armorer would have it repaired in a few hours, but for now Cain breathed the outside air and felt the wind blowing through his hair. It was still thick with the acrid smell of the fires, though the last of them been extinguished hours before. It is amazing, Cain thought, how the stench of destruction lingers so long. Still, he enjoyed the cool breeze and the freshness of the air. At least it doesn't smell like recycled Erik Cain, his mind added. "Well, it would seem you are to be congratulated, colonel, since you have achieved what no one else has managed."

Storm nodded, so slightly it was barely noticeable. He, too, wore fatigues and not a fighting suit. Though he had, somewhat miraculously, escaped any wounds during the final battle in the Sentinel, he'd been in his armor for 18 straight days. Sarah had insisted he spend at least a few hours – and preferably longer – outside his fighting suit while he had the chance. Marines tended to think of themselves as indestructible, especially in areas like psychology, but men and women started to go a little crazy after being trapped in armor for so long. Storm hadn't argued, at least not much. He knew it would be good to feel the breeze for a while…and the armorer could give his suit a thorough refit while he was following Sarah's instructions.

"We're still studying their suits, sir." Storm's voice was deep. "They are identical to ours in most ways." Storm turned to look into Cain's eyes. How and why the enemy was equipped with complete copies of the Corps' armor and weapons was one of the biggest mysteries and topics of debate in the army. "However, there appear to be a few modified systems." Storm stopped and took a deep breath. He really didn't want to tell Cain what Sarah had told him.

Cain stared back expectantly. "What? Spit it out," he said after a few silent seconds.

"You know I just came from the hospital." He'd been visiting his wounded Marines when Sarah Linden hijacked him and insisted on checking him out carefully. He almost tried to argue, but Sarah's commission predated his, so she was his technically the superior officer. Besides, she was nearly as stubborn as Erik Cain himself and idolized by every Marine. The men and women of the Corps revered their senior medical officer and would refuse her nothing, and Storm was no exception.

"Yes." Cain's voice was a mix of confusion and impatience. "Is there news of some kind?"

"Well, sir. It seems that the enemy's trauma control systems have been modified." His voice was becoming more and more uncomfortable. "They apparently…" He paused again.

"Eliot, what's wrong with you? Just say what you want to say. Modified how?"

"The AIs apparently administer a fatal dose of barbiturates to non-ambulatory wounded, sir." Storm's tone was grim, his voice a mix of shock and anger…consuming hatred for any military force that would murder its own wounded to prevent them from being captured. "That is why we have been unable to take any live prisoners until now. Colonel Linden said our captive's suit was damaged, and it failed to administer the dosage. That's the only reason we got to him alive. A random stroke of luck." He was staring at Cain, seeing the rage in the slowly changing facial lines of the Marine general. "It's just a freak accident that we have him, sir."

Cain's expression morphed into icy death. "Is that confirmed, or is it simply conjecture?" His voice was soft, calm… that strange tone he used when his anger was barely controllable. Many who'd been castigated by his tirades were grateful they hadn't heard the quieter, softer voice…the one that meant Erik Cain was ready to kill.

Storm shifted his feet nervously. "Colonel Linden apparently examined a number of enemy corpses and determined that all of them without immediately fatal wounds had toxic levels of depressants in their bodies." He hesitated again, trying to force himself to return Cain's frigid gaze. "She is continuing her investigation, sir, but it certainly appears to be the case."

Cain didn't say anything, but Storm never forgot the frozen look on his face.

"They're clones, Erik." Sarah Linden was a beautiful women, almost unchanged in the more than 20 years Cain had known her. But now she looked haggard, exhausted. He couldn't even guess how long it had been since she'd slept, but it was obvious she was strung out on stims.

"Clones?" Cloning was illegal, proscribed by the terms of the Treaty of Paris, the peace that had ended the Unification Wars more than a century before. Earth's nations had all experimented with creating clone soldiers, but the process had proven to be far more difficult than scientists had expected. The clones that had been created suffered from a wide range of problems… new diseases, deformities, major neurological problems. Even before the formal prohibition was enacted, most of the projects had been abandoned. "I thought cloning was proscribed."

"It was…is. Whoever we are dealing with is apparently unconcerned with treaty provisions banning the process." She wiped her hand across her forehead, forcing back a yawn. It was time for another stim, but she wasn't going to take it in front of Erik. She knew he was already worried about her, and she didn't want to argue about something stupid. Especially since she was going to take the damned stim whether he liked it or not. Why have a pointless fight?

Cain stood silently for a few seconds. "But these soldiers are in their 20s, Sarah. That means this has been going on for what…25 years? How is that possible?"

She was shaking her head. "No, that's the part I'm still trying to fully understand. I have been able to establish an approximate age of our specimen, however."

"25?"

"Try six years." Sarah was staring right at Cain, her reddish blonde hair a riotous mess around her face. "Maybe six and a half."

"How is that possible?" Cain's voice was questioning, skeptical. His mind wanted to discount what he was being told. But he knew just how intelligent Sarah was…and how methodical. Sarah Linden was not one to jump to unfounded conclusions.

"I can't give you a detailed answer yet, Erik." She ran her hand through her tangled mass of hair. "But I believe that whoever created these clones has discovered some way to accelerate their growth, producing adult specimens in 4-5 years."

"My God." Cain stood frozen in place. "But even that doesn't explain everything. These soldiers are as trained as my Marines…and you know how long that takes. Even if they could grow an adult in a few years, they'd still need to train them."

Sarah turned toward a counter and grabbed two mugs. "I can give you an answer on that too." She put the mugs in the wall dispenser. "At least a partial one." She pulled away the two cups of hot coffee, holding one out to Erik. Coffee was no substitute for the enhanced stim formula she'd been taking. But it was better than nothing, and she'd take what she could get.

"I found an irregularity in the upper spinal column, some type of biomechanical port providing access directly to the brain." Her voice changed slightly. However horrified she was at what she had uncovered, she couldn't restrain her scientific amazement. She was describing a process well beyond existing science, and she found it fascinating. "I can't even begin to explain the specifics of the process, but I can be fairly certain that this is how the training was implanted into the subject's mind. They weren't trained in a conventional sense…they had the memories and reflexes implanted directly into their brains."

Cain took a sip of the steaming hot coffee and set the mug on the counter. "Like copying a program into a computer?"

"Far more complicated a process, but yes, it appears to be something like that. A raw, uneducated clone undergoes this neural download procedure and walks out with all the knowledge of a fully-trained Marine."

"You realize what this means? There is no way we can recruit and train Marines faster than…" His voice trailed off as his mind raced. He still had no idea who was behind this. Another power?

"Yes," Sarah interjected. "Certainly this process would allow the…" – she paused, struggling for the right term – "…production of trained soldiers at a pace we could never match." She paused, not wanting to go on. But she had more to tell him, so she cleared her throat and continued. "It's actually even worse, Erik. Our captive seems to be a regimental commander. The neural download process we are hypothesizing appears to be capable of far more than simply replicating a training regimen. Consider the campaign. Do you feel like you've been fighting against a group of trained but raw soldiers?" She didn't wait for the answer. "These troopers fight like veterans, not new recruits. The enemy, whoever they are, can produce not just trained soldiers, but combat veterans who aren't really veterans at all."

"How is that even possible?" Cain's expression morphed, the realization that Sarah had to be correct taking hold. He'd fought a battle to the death with the enemy, and one thing was certain. They fought like veterans, not raw cherries.

"I don't know yet, but the lack of an alternative explanation suggests it must be." She was a scientist, and she preferred to deal in evidence, not wild hunches. But now wasn't the time for holding back. "My best guess is that whoever is behind this has developed a way to extract information from at least part of the memory center of the brain and to download the data into the mind of a clone."

"Can that be done?" Cain's mind raced at the implications of such a capability.

There is nothing I know of that makes it impossible. While I don't have any idea of the specific process, I believe it is plausible…and also the only realistic explanation for what we have clearly seen. The only alternative is one of mind-boggling complexity. It is almost inconceivable that someone has developed the capability to…" – she paused, struggling for the right wording again – "…program a human mind from scratch." She looked up, meeting Cain's gaze. "I think we can eliminate that as a possibility. As far as we can tell, that is beyond even First Imperium technology.

"But…" – Cain had a horrified expression on his face – "… that would mean…" He stopped, unable to put together the words he wanted.

"It would mean that these clones are copies of actual Marines." Sarah finished Erik's thought. "Yes, I suspect that is the case." She paused, looking back at Cain's stunned stare. "They have also apparently developed a way to parse the information that is transferred, picking and choosing what knowledge and memories are transferred and what is not. For example, the clones 'remember' their training, but not the other aspects of the lives of the actual specimens providing the original memories." Another hesitation. "At least, that's what I've been able to piece together from our prisoner. He has not been enormously cooperative, but neither has he been overtly hostile. I am almost certain he has no meaningful recollections of life as a Marine outside of training or battle…though the host from which his experience was derived clearly would have such memories."

"So, they would have needed actual Marines to create these… soldiers."

Sarah nodded. "Yes." She turned slightly, looking down at the table and picking up a small 'pad. "And that explains other factors we have observed. You have been advised, no doubt, that the enemy soldiers bear a strong resemblance to each other…indeed, many of them are identical."

"Well, if they are clones…"

"Yes," Sarah interrupted, "but they are not all the same. We have identified eleven different - models, for lack of a better word – each apparently derived from a unique original specimen."

"So they cloned more than one original Marine." Cain's face was twisted in a thoughtful expression. "Why use more than one?"

"Because they are of different ranks and specialties." Sarah handed the 'pad to Cain. "Our captive is a colonel, and he calls himself Anderson. Anderson-45, to be exact. There is no way of knowing whether that is the actual name of the original specimen, or simply a designation assigned to a command class of clones. But we have found a number of matches among the dead…six colonels and two generals."

"So the Anderson clones were produced from genetic material of a Marine officer of high rank?" It was half a question, half a statement.

"That is my best guess." She nodded slowly as she answered. "That 'pad has the eleven known classes listed, along with our best analysis of the primary purpose of each." She lifted the coffee mug from the table and took another sip. "There are two classes that seem to be essentially privates, two of corporals and sergeants, and several that are clearly officers at various levels. There are a few we are still uncertain about. They may be snipers or other specialists. Or officers with a different kind of experience, such as siege tactics."

Cain stood quietly, his mind in a state of utter chaos. He'd wondered, of course, about this new enemy, and why they so resembled his own people in tactics, equipment, and skill. But he'd never come close to guessing the shocking truth. "This has to be an Alliance operation." His voice was soft, more shock than anger in his tone." He looked back up, his eyes locking on Sarah's. "Think about it. Perhaps anyone could enlist – or

kidnap – eleven ex-Marines, but this army has the same equipment we do. Our armor, weapons…the Gordon landers." His
face was twisted in confusion, an elemental rage rising within,
barely contained.

"But why?" Sarah's voice was calmer…she'd always controlled her anger better than Erik. "Why would Alliance Gov
do something like this now?" She didn't trust the politicians that
ran the Alliance any more than Erik did, though she tended to
be less paranoid about it. "Even if they wanted to re-impose
pre-rebellion control levels over the colonies, would they do it
now? With Augustus still in command of the fleet? They can't
think he would go along with anything like that…he certainly
didn't during the rebellions."

"I don't know." Cain could feel the anger surging, aching
to escape in a fit of rage. But he just couldn't get it all to make
sense. The attacks on colonies had started months before,
when the whole fleet was still out at Sigma 4. The politicians
on Earth had nearly pissed themselves with fear of the First
Imperium. Would they really start something like this when they
couldn't even be sure the First Imperium forces were truly contained? No, he thought…they're a bunch of cowards…they'd
have never had the guts to pull the trigger on something like
this. Not while they were still worried about the First Imperium. Who then? None of the other Powers could have copied
the Alliance weapons systems so exactly. Alliance tech was the
most advanced…and it wasn't exactly standard practice to share
technical specifications with the other Superpowers. No…it
couldn't be any of them.

Suddenly he knew. It just popped into his mind, and he
was instantly certain who he was fighting. He couldn't even
guess at how something of this scale was even possible or how it
could have been planned and executed. But he was sure of one
thing…as sure as he'd ever been about anything. Gavin Stark
was behind this.

Chapter 31

Martian Command Bunker
Garibaldi Base
Mars, Sol IV

Vance sat watching the transmissions. It was on every Alliance media channel, and they were all saying exactly the same thing. Of course, Vance thought...they're all managed by the government. All the media on Earth was. His thought had started as one of derision, but he had to admit to himself the Martian authorities exerted a considerable influence over the Confederation's own information networks. Vance believed in freedom and self-determination, at least in theory. In practice he'd found it a far more difficult analysis, and he wondered if true freedom was possible...at least for a species as fundamentally flawed as man.

There wasn't any close in video yet...the emergency services personnel had locked down the entire area. But the shots from outside the city were astonishing. The cameras gave a majestic view of the Washbalt skyline, its gleaming kilometer-high towers reflecting the reddish afternoon sun. Except in the main government district. There, a massive plume of smoke and debris rose kilometers into the sky, a roiling mushroom cloud right where Alliance Intelligence HQ had stood.

The reports were still sketchy, but they were saying it was a terrorist attack of some kind, a small nuclear device that had been smuggled either close to or actually inside the building before it was detonated. There were dozens of rumors flying around, and they were saying that a meeting of the Directorate had been in session...and that there were no survivors.

The nuke had been a small one, but even so, it had taken out half a dozen other buildings, mostly mundane government departments. Vance tried to imagine the chaos on the streets of Washbalt, the screeching of sirens, the traffic clogged with emergency vehicles. The coverage wasn't showing any of that, at least not yet. When the Alliance government decided on a response the networks would be flooded with carefully selected footage intended to support that action. Until then, only the most general information would be released.

Vance sighed. He hoped it was a terrorist attack. If it was one of the other Powers, Earth was going to explode into chaos. He found it hard to believe a group of rebels or terrorists had pulled off something of this magnitude; he hadn't gotten a whisper of it from any of his sources. Terrorism had been a serious problem in the 21st and early 22nd centuries, but surveillance technology had crippled most resistance and terrorist groups. The Superpowers were inefficient as political entities, but they were highly effective at rooting out and crushing internal opposition. Vance prided himself on his carefully constructed network of spies, and he couldn't imagine they wouldn't have warned him about something like this.

Of course, he thought grimly, Stark's little financial charade went on for years, and he'd never gotten the slightest inkling of it. Perhaps this was another piece of crucial intel his network had missed.

Just before he got word of the attack, he'd been reviewing Li An's proposed plan for dealing with the facility his people had scouted in South Dakota. Died to scout, he reminded himself. Not one of the commandos he'd sent had survived, but they had managed to send him a report before the last of them was killed. Vance had been worried about the missing funds and concerned about the purpose of the strange Alliance facility, but now he knew the truth. It was worse than anything he'd imagined.

An army of clones, he thought. He had nowhere near the information he needed, but the thought of Gavin Stark controlling thousands of manufactured soldiers scared him to death. Stark didn't do things by half-measures, and Vance knew it had to be part of an overall plan. Anything of this scope with Stark behind it had to be more than a problem, it had to be a disaster.

Unless Stark was dead. He glanced back at the screens, his eyes focusing on the smoke rising above the city. Was it possible? Could this really be some random act of terrorism that rid the world of Gavin Stark? Vance allowed himself one excited moment before he discounted the possibility. That would be a very convenient course of events, he thought. Indeed, it could very well be Stark himself behind this attack. It would be a brilliant way to cover his tracks when the economy collapsed, something Vance expected any day now. No, he wouldn't believe Stark was dead. Not unless he had absolute proof.

And if Stark was on the loose somewhere, figuring out his next step was absolutely vital.

Gavin Stark stared straight forward, anger radiating off him so strongly it could almost be felt in the air. Everything had been going perfectly. Everything! Fucking Vance, he thought bitterly. Facility Q was compromised. How was he going to move almost a million soldiers out of there in the time he had left - however long that turned out to be?

Vance would have trouble following up, he thought, almost in answer to his own question. It was one thing to sneak a few dozen commandos into the Alliance, and quite another to launch a major invasion. No, Vance would have to advise Alliance Gov of the facility's existence and purpose. There would be doubt, confusion…Francis Oliver and the other inept fools who ran the Alliance would argue for days – weeks – before reacting. He hoped they would, at least. Vance was the question mark. The Martian spy was not to be trifled with. Maybe, just maybe he'd manage to force quicker action. That would be a problem.

Stark had backup bases, locations where the duty-ready soldiers could hide, waiting for their moment. But Q was the only facility with functioning crèches. He would lose all the soldiers still in the growth tanks...and he'd have to build a new production facility from scratch. Someplace.

He sighed hard and turned his attention to the latest intel from the colonies. The military reports were far more satisfactory than the unpleasant news from Earth. Almost all the target worlds had fallen. Only Armstrong, Columbia, and Arcadia were still resisting, and his forces outnumbered their stubborn adversaries on each. Casualties had been appalling on all three, but Stark didn't care. Gruesome holocausts suited him fine, as long as his enemies were destroyed. He wished he could just nuke all three troublesome planets, but they were crucial to his plans. He couldn't establish the power base he needed in the colonies without taking the three wealthiest and most powerful planets reasonably intact. There wasn't going to be much left on Earth by the time his plan was complete, and he'd need a functioning and independent empire in space to complete phase three...the re-occupation and rebuilding of Earth as the capital of his own empire, one ruling all mankind.

He couldn't afford any mistakes now. Erik Cain was on Armstrong...and reports suggested Elias Holm was in command of the forces on Arcadia. He still needed Augustus Garret alive to destroy the fleets of the other Superpowers, but the Marine generals had outlived their usefulness. If he moved swiftly now, he could ensure that neither of them left their respective battlefields.

He leaned over and flipped on the com. "Admiral Liang, I want Force B dispatched immediately to reinforce the army on Armstrong."

"Yes, Number One."

The former CAC admiral wasn't a military genius like Garret, but he'd done well so far, Stark thought...at least I'm getting some payback for protecting him all these years.

"And Force A, sir?"

"Force A and the balance of the fleet will proceed to Arcadia, Admiral Liang. It is time to crush the troublesome resistance and secure the planet once and for all."

"What of Admiral Garret's fleet, sir?" The Alliance admiral

had chased Liang's forces out of Arcadia's system two months before.

The gutless shit can't even hide his fear of facing Garret, Stark thought angrily. "Don't worry, admiral." He was trying to hide the disgust in his voice...but he wasn't trying too hard. "I can assure you that Admiral Garret will be otherwise occupied by the time we reach Arcadia."

"Yes, sir. Liang out."

Oh yes, Stark thought. Admiral Garret will have his hands full...doing a service for me. He smiled, leaning his head back and closing his eyes for a moment. If only he could know how vital he is to my plans.

Vance was staring at the reports from the Alliance worlds. In all, 32 colonies had been attacked, and 29 had been fully or nearly pacified by the enemy – now presumed to be Gavin Stark's clone armies. Only three worlds were still contested... Arcadia, Armstrong, and Columbia. The usual suspects, Vance thought. If there were Alliance worlds he'd have expected to put up a fight, these three were the ones.

Erik Cain had fought a brutal campaign on Armstrong, defeating the enemy's main thrust toward the capital in a battle of unimaginable brutality. His shattered Marines were faced off against the remains of the invasion force. The two sides were dug in on opposite sides of a great river. As of the last intelligence Vance had available, the exhausted armies were staring at each other across the water, neither with the will nor the supplies to launch a renewed battle. At least not yet.

Columbia was a holocaust by all accounts. General Tyler, whose dictatorial powers afforded him more options than the other planetary commanders, allowed the enemy to occupy the capital city. Then he launched a massive nuclear attack, turning Weston into one massive trap. The tactic inflicted thousands of casualties on the enemy...at the cost of one of the largest and most cosmopolitan cities in colonial space. The enemy forces were shocked and disordered, and the result was yet another watchful stalemate.

Arcadia was perhaps the most convoluted situation of all. Two small Marine contingents had linked up, creating a force too weak to drive the enemy off the planet, but strong enough to hold out against any attacks, at least for the short term. Complicating the situation further, the native army had somehow survived the initial onslaught. It was trapped in the northern wilderness of the planet where it was tying down significant enemy forces. Vance's intel was incomplete; he couldn't get a clear read on whether the overall situation was another standoff, or if the invaders had enough strength to overwhelm and defeat the defenders.

The remaining Marine forces were all heavily outnumbered, with little or no chance for ultimate victory…at least without some sort of assistance. He'd have normally had faith that the Marines could overcome a deficit in numbers, but now that he knew they were fighting an army of clones - clones of other Marines - he despaired of their chances. Especially if Stark was able to continue producing hundreds of thousands of new troops each year. No…that couldn't be allowed to continue.

His operative had made contact with Li An, sharing with her the intel from Team Beta. He'd desperately wanted to discuss the matter directly with the CAC spymaster, but there just wasn't time. Now he had the report from that meeting, and it was a bombshell. The CAC was going to launch a nuclear attack against the Dakota facility.

Vance knew Li An could move decisively when it was necessary, but he still found himself surprised and impressed. She was doing what had to be done, despite the danger and the inevitable fallout. She was taking the risk of letting him know… and requesting his aid in handling the diplomatic blowback, but she wasn't going to wait long. Stark knew his secrecy had been compromised…the commando raid had hardly been a subtle reconnaissance. But even he couldn't move a facility of this size overnight. If he got the time, he'd cover his tracks…and move his base of operations. That would be a disaster. There was no time to lose. It had to be now.

He couldn't even guess how many of Stark's clones were

already off-world, on or en-route to colony planets…but if the production facility wasn't destroyed, the size of the force currently engaged would pale next to the numbers of new soldiers Stark would put in the field.

He leaned over his keyboard, entering the series of passwords that activated his secure personal com system. No codes were unbreakable…he knew that. But his system generated the most secure encryption known to human science. That didn't mean it was unbreakable, but it was close.

He flipped the switch that locked down his office, physically sealing the door and jamming all other communications. Li An had asked for his help in preventing the CAC's strike from initiating a general war between the Powers. He was certain Alliance Gov had no idea about Stark's plans…or his super-secret base in the Dakota badlands, but he also knew how they'd almost certainly react to a CAC strike anywhere in Alliance territory. He wasn't at all sure he could do anything to forestall the inevitable fallout from the attack, but he would try. Nevertheless, whatever the consequences, Li An's action was essential…even at the risk of war on Earth.

He flipped a switch and held a small microphone close to his lips. "Minister Li…" – he spoke slowly and gravely – "…I have been advised regarding your plan of operations, and I agree completely. I assure you I will assist in any way…"

"My fellow council members, I have called this meeting to address several matters of the utmost urgency." Vance stood at the head of the table, the five other moguls who effectively ruled the Confederation, four men and one woman, stared at him in utter silence. They had come to rely on his ability and to trust him as the de facto, though unofficial, leader of the Council.

Vance was the only one standing, and he walked slowly back and forth as he spoke. None of those present had ever seen Vance so nervous…indeed, the spymaster rarely betrayed any emotion at all. But now he was visibly disturbed, unable to hide his anxiety.

"I will be sharing intelligence of the most sensitive nature and, as always, I must request that nothing I say leave this room." Vance knew the Council members understood, but he said it anyway.

"First, as you are all aware, the Alliance Intelligence headquarters building was destroyed by a crude nuclear device while the Directorate was in session. Apparently, there were no survivors." His voice took on a suspicious tone. "I say 'apparently' because I suspect that is not entirely correct. While I lack specific evidence, based on my analysis of the information available to us – not only of this bombing, but of other matters I will discuss in a moment – I do not believe that Alliance Intelligence Number One, Gavin Stark, was killed." He hesitated, knowing what he was about to say was the wildest conjecture on his part. "In fact, it is my belief that the bombing was orchestrated by Mr. Stark himself."

"For what purpose, Roderick?" Sebastian Vallen was the most aged member of the Council, well past his hundredth birthday. The old man had been a close friend of Vance's father… and of his grandfather before that. "I am not one to doubt your deductions, Roderick, but what would Stark gain by destroying his own headquarters and killing so many of his operatives?

Vance took a deep breath. "Sebastian…all of you…I ask that you let me complete my presentation. When you know the full scope of recent events, you will be better able to judge my conclusions."

"Very well, Roderick. Please continue." A series of nods worked around the table.

"I have reliable intelligence from my sources in the Alliance government that the uranium used in the bomb has been traced to a CAC colony."

A murmur of surprise rippled around the table, but no one spoke. They were staring at Vance, waiting for him to continue.

"For reasons that will become clear as I elaborate further, I do not believe C1 or any organization within the CAC, was responsible for this attack. He panned his eyes around the table. "As you are all aware, several weeks ago, we dispatched Red

Team Beta to investigate a mysterious base located in a remote region of the Alliance." He paused, looking out again at his five colleagues. "What you do not know is that we located this site with the aid of Minister Li and her C1 apparatus."

"Pardon the interruption, Roderick, but do you really feel that Li An is trustworthy?" Vallen had sparred with the CAC's top spy years before, when he had occupied Vance's seat at Martian Intelligence.

Vance looked in Vallen's direction. "Not conventionally, no. Of course not." He paused yet again, trying to find the words he wanted. "I would say that I respect her ability…and I trust my own judgment on whether a matter is adversarial between our nations or of joint concern." He stared at Vallen intently. "I assure you, Sebastian, none of my analyses have been conducted without a full consideration of Minister Li…or what she is capable of."

Vallen nodded, but he remained silent.

"We have conclusively…well, nearly conclusively…determined that Gavin Stark has been producing clone soldiers at this facility." He paused then added, "In enormous numbers. Hundreds of thousands."

"How is that even possible?" It was Katarina Berchtold, who hesitated after her initial outburst. "I apologize, Roderick, but that is an astonishing – and extremely troubling – statement. I wasn't aware that such advances had been made in cloning technology."

"They haven't." Vance returned her gaze. "At least not by any of the Powers. It would appear that Mr. Vance – or associates of his – have perfected a technique for producing clone soldiers, one considerably ahead of previously existing technology." The tension was obvious in his voice. "Indeed, it would seem they are able to produce them at an accelerated rate."

The room was silent. Vance hadn't shared his earlier, unfounded speculations with the Council, so they were getting it all now…without any preparation or time to adapt.

"Is there a connection to the economic issues we have been monitoring?" It was Berchtold again, after a long silence.

"Almost certainly," Vance replied immediately. "It was our search for the missing funds that led us to this discovery." He moved his eyes across the table. "This is something I cannot emphasize strongly enough. This is no small project, no pilot program. It may seem unreal, hard to accept that such a scientific advancement has occurred in total secrecy, but I must remind each of you...60% of Alliance GDP has been poured into this project for at least six years. This is a massive endeavor, a research effort orders of magnitude larger than the Manhattan Project or the drive to put a man on the moon."

"So it would appear you have solved the mystery regarding the irregularities in the Alliance economy. An impressive effort, Roderick." Vallen's voice was as grim as Vance's. "Though it does not appear to offer much hope of averting the inevitable financial collapse."

Vance frowned. "I'm afraid not. I have taken all possible steps to insulate our economy...in total secrecy, of course." He took a deep breath. "But you all know as well as I that the effects, even in the Confederation, are likely to be devastating." He hesitated again, finally adding, "We can only hope the Powers have so much internal unrest that it forestalls them from plunging into war with each other."

The room was silent. Everyone present managed massive businesses, the vast economic empires of Mars' five leading families. They were all trillionaires, though Vance doubted that status would survive the next few weeks' events.

"Have you taken steps to control any internal unrest in the Confederation?" It was Vallen again, his voice like gravel. He was asking about something he'd never expected to be an issue.

Vance looked back, silently at first. "Yes," he said with considerable emotion. "I have deployed army units to all of the cities. I have kept it quiet, but all commanders have orders to deploy immediately to quell any outbreaks of violence or rioting."

The room grew silent again. As the smallest Superpower, Mars had always walked a fine line, maintaining the closest thing to true neutrality that confused politics and constant war allowed.

But internal dissension had never been a major issue. Mars had been founded by the best and the brightest from Earth, and it had maintained a very strict and exclusionary immigration policy. Mars welcomed scientists and educated and productive new citizens who added to the collective whole. The Confederation sympathized with the uneducated masses of Earth, trapped in oppressive squalor…but they didn't want them on Mars. The original settlers of the red planet had founded an oligarchic society where productivity wasn't a goal, but a near-obsession. The policy had been stunningly successful, turning a small colony into a full-blown Superpower and economic powerhouse in less than a century. But the coming collapse was going to be bad…and even engineers and professors rioted when they were starving.

"Well, thank you, Roderick." Vallen spoke softly, somberly. "As always, you have handled things with great skill." He looked around the room. "I move that we all remain at Garibaldi Base, and that we meet daily until these unfolding crises are more contained." He saw the worried expressions around the table. "I am aware we all have considerable business interests to safeguard during this difficult time, but I submit our duty to the Confederation must take the foremost position."

"I second the motion." Berchtold was nodding slowly. "Duty must come first. And, in any event, we can do little more to protect our assets than guide the Confederation safely through this terrible time."

"I think we are all in agreement." Vance looked around the room, nodding at the raised hands. He cleared his throat. "Before I adjourn this meeting and let you all go, I have one more topic to discuss. It is an action I simply cannot undertake on my own. I feel I must have the Council's unanimous approval."

He took a deep breath, then another. The other Councilors were staring at him silently. "I was cooperating with Li An on a plan for the CAC to launch a large nuclear strike on the Dakota base. I believe it is essential to destroy the facility before Gavin Stark is able to relocate his production operation." He looked at each of his colleagues in turn. "In the aftermath of the destruction of Alliance Intelligence HQ, I no longer consider that plan feasible. Whether it is true or not, Alliance Gov now suspects CAC involvement in the attack in Washbalt. We might have calmed the situation after one incident, but if the CAC is seen to have made multiple attacks on the Alliance, it will almost certainly ignite open war on Earth itself.

There was silence, except for Vallen. He looked up at Stark, the two sharing an understanding glance. "So, you want our approval to…"

"To send a fleet to Earth and destroy the Dakota facility from orbit," Vance interjected. "And to do so immediately."

Chapter 32

Marine HQ
North of Astria
Planet Armstrong
Gamma Pavonis III

"Anderson-45? Is that your entire name?" Cain reached out and grabbed a rigid metal chair, dragging it slowly toward the bed.

"It is my full designation." There was a robotic cadence to Anderson-45's speech, but otherwise he sounded normal. His wounds had been severe, but Sarah had stabilized him and treated his injuries. He faced a significant recovery period, but he would survive. He was lying on the cot, his head propped up on a pile of pillows.

"I am General Cain." He sat down, pulling the chair under him as he did. "You can call me Erik."

"You are a primary target." Anderson-45 spoke directly, without emotion. "Cain, Erik Daniel, General." There was no hostility in his voice.

"Do you wish to kill me?" Cain's voice didn't show any anger or concern, just curiosity. The prisoner hadn't made any aggressive moves…and Cain doubted whether he could have even raised his head.

"Wish?" The prisoner's voice changed slightly, the deadpan tone becoming quizzical, questioning. "No, I do not think I wish any harm to come to you. I am a prisoner, and I have not been mistreated. My code of honor requires that I respond to your respectful treatment in kind."

"Is that part of your training?" Cain looked questioningly at the wounded soldier. He was certain that no soldiers trained by Gavin Stark would pay any attention to something so quaint as a code of honor.

Anderson-45 sat quietly, not responding at first. Finally he turned his head slowly and looked at Cain. "No, it is not from my training. I am not permitted to discuss any specifics of my training. That is classified information." He paused. "It is from...elsewhere."

"Elsewhere?"

"Yes. It is from the other thoughts."

Cain glanced toward Sarah then back to the wounded enemy soldier. "Other thoughts?"

"Yes, the background thoughts. Those separate from my training." He turned his head back from Cain, lying still, staring at the ceiling. "The background thoughts are intermittent. They are sporadic, difficult to understand at times. They are often cloudy, hard to retrieve. They are part of the others."

"The others?"

"Yes, the things I remember, but only sometimes. Memories of places I have never been. I have been told they are waking dreams, that they have no significance. But I do not believe this is the case. I can tell...I can feel it. They are somehow real, though I cannot explain further."

"Erik, I think it would be best if Anderson-45 rested for a while. His wounds were quite serious."

Cain nodded. "I think Dr. Linden is correct. You sleep, and we will talk more later."

"Thank you, general." The captured clone closed his eyes and exhaled strongly. "I am quite fatigued."

Cain turned toward Sarah, and the two walked wordlessly through the door and out into the bright afternoon sunshine.

"Let's walk a little." Cain motioned away from the portable structure that housed their only captive. When they had moved fifty or sixty meters he turned back toward Sarah. "OK...we should have some privacy here. What the hell was all that?"

"I suspect it is a side effect of the knowledge transfer process.

When they attempted to isolate the memories that contained the combat experience of the subjects, they were probably unable to completely exclude other thoughts and experiences." Sarah's voice had an odd tone. She was horrified at what had been done, how these soldiers had been created and used so callously. But she was fascinated at the science behind it and anxious to learn more. "Think about what makes a veteran soldier. It's an incredibly complex combination of training, modified by experiences, memories, interactions." She put her hand on Cain's arm. "Think about yourself. Can you segregate the knowledge that drives your command ability from personal beliefs and memories of interactions with other people?"

Cain shook his head. "I doubt it." He forced a brief smile for her. "But my mind is a cluttered mess, so I'd look for a better example."

She returned the smile, though only for an instant. "I'm serious, Erik. This may be very important in learning how to deal with these soldiers. Think about our guest." She deliberately avoided a term like prisoner. "He is strictly abiding by the obvious requirements of his duty. He won't discuss enemy dispositions, plans, strengths, or anything else of direct military significance. Nothing. But on any other subject you could be having lunch with him. He seems to bear us no ill will."

"It does seem odd." Cain's expression turned thoughtful. "What do you think it means?"

"Well, for one he seems to be extraordinarily underdeveloped in many emotional areas. Anderson-45 is perfectly pleasant in a conversation. I get no feeling of any anger, frustration, resentment. We've killed how many of his comrades? He's a prisoner of war, probably the first ever taken from his army. Yet he doesn't seem to care very much." She rubbed her forehead, pulling back a wispy strand of reddish blonde hair. "I'd wager he would fight to the death to protect a comrade but have no significant reaction or emotional response if the soldier was killed. He'd just move on, follow his training logically."

"So you are saying these clones have an almost verbatim copy of the objective aspects of military training and tactics?

You fight to save a comrade not for any emotional reason but simply because that's what training and doctrine dictate?" Cain was beginning to get an idea what she was trying to explain. "But the experience of a veteran isn't segregated as easily from other thoughts…even emotions. If you want a raw recruit, you can make him almost emotionless, but if you are trying to copy a veteran, some other aspects come along with the package."

She nodded. "Essentially, that is what I am saying." She glanced back toward the modular structure. "We have no idea how much emotional…" – she hesitated, trying to think of the right word – "…baggage comes along with the essential knowledge. I suppose that would depend on how advanced the process is, how able it is to dig deeply and finely segregate thoughts and memories. But if I was forced to guess, I'd say considerable unintended information comes along. It is probably deeply suppressed, but it is there nevertheless.

Cain stood quietly, listening to everything she was saying, and he couldn't help but be impressed. He loved Sarah Linden, but that had nothing to do with this. She was a brilliant scientist, the youngest senior medical officer in Corps history. He needed the best from everyone he had, and she was no exception. Right now he wasn't looking at her as a lover or a friend. She was one of his smartest and most capable subordinates, and he needed everything she had to offer.

"Are you saying it is possible to reach them…to negotiate, convince them we are not their enemies?" Cain's tone was skeptical, but only moderately so.

"I suppose…in theory. In practice, we are nowhere close to that. Realistically, we may be able to get some information, develop some tactics to exploit their weaknesses, the…mmm… the blindspots in their thought processes."

"Anything would help." Cain looked down at the ground. There was something in the back of his mind, something unsettling. Were these really enemies? Or helpless slaves created to fight, without the ability to choose or make moral decisions? If they attacked his people, he would try to destroy them, of course, but the usual fury he felt toward his enemies was starting to crack. "Sarah, I need you to learn as much about these... people...as you can." He paused. "I know how you feel about the wounded, but you have to turn control of the field hospitals over to Major Ving." His voice was tentative. He was half-expecting a verbal tirade from her.

"Yes, Erik." She said softly, a touch of sadness in her voice, perhaps, but no argument. "I agree." Her mind was already wandering, putting together theories and guesses to explore further. "And Erik?"

"Yes?"

"It would help if we could get a few more prisoners."

He forced a smile, thinking, I had to kill 20,000 of them to get this one. "I'll do my best," is all he said.

"Are you sure?" Cain's expression was hard to read. There was anger there, certainly, but also confusion...and even sadness. He'd spoken extensively with Anderson-45. The prisoner was a little odd, but that was understandable considering how he had come into being and acquired his training. Overall, Cain had found the captive to be quite likeable, despite the fact that a few days before he'd been leading troops against the Marines. He certainly didn't feel like an enemy, though he steadfastly refused to provide any information on the invasion forces.

Sarah had a blank expression on her face. She'd run the tests three times, wondering for an instant if her exhaustion was clouding her interpretation. No, she thought...it wasn't. Her data was correct. "Yes." Her voice was quiet, sad. "As sure as I can be. Anderson-45's DNA has been modified, probably as part of the accelerated maturation process. The accelerated growth seems to have worked perfectly, though not without causing other damage." She paused again. "The side effects of the program appear to be quite severe. Greatly accelerated aging is the most extreme. By my calculations, Anderson-45 will be too 'old' to serve by age 28 or 29, and he will probably die in his early 30s...at the latest."

"Is there any way to treat this?" Cain wasn't sure why he was worried about prolonging the lives of his enemies. It was sympathy, perhaps, or pity. He was beginning to understand that these soldiers were only pawns, produced to fight as slaves and then die to be replaced by a new batch. Experience wasn't an issue when you could simply download it directly into the mind of a fresh soldier right out of the growth tanks.

Sarah shook her head sadly. "No, Erik. The damage is permanent. Anderson-45 and all of the other clones will have a severely reduced lifespan. With the chromosomal damage, I don't even think rejuv treatments would have an effect. He will die before his 31st birthday...his 32nd at the latest."

Cain stood stone still, his mind racing. His confusion was rapidly turning to anger. He'd seen the brutality of war and fought many enemies. The wars between the Superpowers had seen their share of atrocities, but they had been political conflicts at their core. Even the First Imperium, xenocidal as it was, considered humanity to be the aggressors...and their soldiers were machines, not sentient beings created to fight as slaves. But this was different. Any enemy who would create disposable human beings to wage a war of pure conquest was indefensible. Cain knew in that instant his enemy was pure evil.

"Erik..." - Sarah's voice was distant at first, working its way through his thoughts – "do you think we should tell him?

Cain looked over at her, but he didn't reply at first. Finally, he said, "Yes. He has a right to know. Whatever his masters may think, he is a human being." Is that why you want to tell him, he asked himself...or do you just hope the shock of it all may get him to cooperate more? Cain had no pretensions. He knew that victory came at a cost. Always. And, more often than not, that cost was to become disturbingly like your enemy. Cain knew his motives were different than his adversary's, but he also knew he was likely to do whatever was necessary to win.

He took a step toward Sarah and put his hand on her arm. "Let's go see him now."

Sarah looked uncertain. "Erik, maybe we should wait until he is stronger."

"No," he said, more harshly than he'd intended. "Let's do it..."

The comlink crackled to life, cutting him off. "General Cain…" – it was Claren, and his voice was clearly shaken – "…the warp gate surveillance satellite transmitted a scanning report, and then it was destroyed." The aide's voice was silent, but only for a few seconds. "We have an enemy fleet inbound from the gate. A big one."

Cain felt his chest tighten. He was far from sure he could hold out against the enemy forces already onplanet…if a fresh invasion force landed there was no chance. None at all. He felt a flush of despair then pushed it quickly into the recesses of his mind. Hopeless or not, he'd be damned if his people were going down without a fight. "Get me General Merrick. Now." Merrick was commanding the line along the Graywater…a strong defensive position, but one the enemy could easily compromise with a new landing to the north of the great waterway.

"Yes, sir." There was a pause, 4 or 5 seconds. "General Merrick on your line, sir."

Cain took a deep breath. "Isaac…I need you to get your people buttoned up and moving north. ASAP." He paused then added, "The shit's about to hit the fan."

To be continued in:
Crimson Worlds VIII: Even Legends Die

Crimson Worlds Series

Marines (Crimson Worlds I)

The Cost of Victory (Crimson Worlds II)

A Little Rebellion (Crimson Worlds III)

The First Imperium (Crimson Worlds IV)

The Line Must Hold (Crimson Worlds V)

To Hell's Heart (Crimson Worlds VI)

The Shadow Legions(Crimson Worlds VII)

Even Legends Die (Crimson Worlds VIII)
(April 2014)

Also By Jay Allan

The Dragon's Banner

Gehenna Dawn (Portal Worlds I)

The Ten Thousand (Portal Worlds II)
(June 2014)

www.crimsonworlds.com

82515216R00183

Made in the USA
San Bernardino, CA
17 July 2018